i

VIJAY

LOUISE FURLEY

Vijay

ISBN- 978-1-7369376-8-6 (Paperback)
ISBN- 978-1-7369376-7-9 (eBook)

Cover design by Pixel Mischief Design

The characters and events portrayed in this book are fictitious. Any similarity to real persons, living or dead, is coincidental and not intended by the author.

ALSO BY LOUISE FURLEY

A Mafia Romance series

Distilled Duplicity
His Winnings
Adara
Jozadak

Satan's Brood series

Devil's Prince
Devil's Seed

Dutch Military Special Forces series

Jungle Treasure
Jancarlo

Stand alone titles

Jezábel and the Assassin

Solitar

Vijay

Halo Valley

Isle of Orainn

VIJAY

Chapter One

As each day passed, prickling uneasiness seeped deeper into Wynna Pila's bones.

With every glance back over her shoulder her pulse quickened. At the beginning of the week she had only tingles of suspicion, by the end, she was positive she was being watched and followed.

She noticed the same man show up in the grocery store and then a bookstore in a totally different town, and again when she brought her shoes in for repair. As soon as she caught him staring at her, he looked away and she didn't see him again after that.

Chalking it up to the willies from being in a different country, she forgot about it.

Chrêshdônia was a relatively obscure country hovering on the cusp of social reform. Wyn had been told that outside of the city the land was considered to be lawless, wild and raw, and hellishly dangerous.

Then, it happened again but it was a different man. The first sighting was just a flash of dark green, but it apparently imprinted in the back of her mind because her eyes were drawn right to the same swath of green at the vegetable stand.

She didn't look directly at him, just made her purchase and quickly strode home looking over her shoulder the whole way.

The next morning, when she trod up the steps to Sunday service she saw him. He was buttoning his olive green coat, standing at the corner of the building watching her.

Their eyes caught, he quickly lowered his, turned his head away in nonchalance but it was too late. She didn't see him again.

The third time it happened with a totally different man, Wyn could no longer dismiss it as coincidence or her over-active imagination.

She considered going to the police, but what would she tell them? "Uh, yes, I want to make a report of several men following me, gawking at me, stalking me...no, they have never said a word, haven't threatened me or approached me."

A snort of derision escaped her. Sure, they would usher her out the door with empty promises that they would look into it and then burst into snide laughter as soon as she was gone. Shaking her head she hurried back to her apartment.

Moving briskly down the street, Wyn rubbed her arms against the chill and thought for the hundredth time she wished she had not accepted the invitation extended to her from her aunt and uncle to visit them in the relatively unknown country of Chrêshdônia.

They had insisted before she started her first term at university that she come and spend at least six months with them.

Brought up in a severely strict and isolated girls' boarding school, Wyn had little experience with anything in life other than the tedious blocks of buildings she knew as home and school.

Her parents were lifelong missionaries and decided it would be better for her to be raised in boarding schools than traveling haphazardly across the wastelands of the world with them.

Now, for the first time in her life, Wyn was experiencing life outside of solemn grey buildings where she had seen no one other than the same girls that she had grown up with.

At first, she thought the picturesque town of Voronet was so quaint with its ancient houses strung along charming cobblestone streets. Each house was a unique design and painted a bright color.

Everywhere flowers grew so abundant and vivid it was like van Gogh and Monet had swirled around the town painting blossoms on every building, driveway, shop, school.

Yet, along with the pretty ambiance, even before she had thought she was being followed, Wyn felt a vibe of...eeriness, a pervasive foreboding hovered around her.

Feeling foolish for her fanciful thoughts, she quickly strode down the street to her apartment. The air held a shivering deep chill, the early evening grass was damp with a faint dusting of crisp frost. Her breath puffed out in vapor as she hurried, thankfully, almost home.

Home at the moment was her tiny apartment. At first, she had stayed at her aunt and uncle's mansion. But then they started strongly encouraging her to date the son of one of their best friends who happened to live next door.

The encouragement turned into exceedingly stronger coercion as Auntie Odessa continued to set her up on unexpected dates and would become so upset she threatened she would just faint away if Wyn did not cooperate. She had relentlessly begged her niece to just give Jazer Edrei a chance.

Finally arriving back at her apartment, Wyn unlocked the door and slipped inside. Letting out the tight breath she held, now that she was safely inside her cocoon, even old and tiny as it was, she relaxed.

Dropping her purse on the worn rickety table by the door, she shrugged out of her jacket and tossed it over a chair. Kicking her boots off, she padded across the thin carpet heading for the miniature kitchen. It took only minutes in the microwave to make a heavenly cup of hot cocoa.

Carrying the steaming mug infusing the air with the delicious smell of foaming chocolate, she made straight for the bathroom to indulge in a soothing bubble bath.

As she passed the answering machine she saw the flashing red light indicating messages. She hesitated, debating. Pretty sure who it was, Wyn didn't feel the fortitude it would require to listen.

"Uhh," sighing out her consternation, she pushed the button.

An accented male voice came clear, "Hey, uh, Wynnie," *oh how she hated to be called that*, he cleared his throat. "It's uh, Jazer." Then an awkward chuckle. "Of course you probably know that. Uh, anyway," he coughed and cleared his throat again. "Honey, I can't believe you ran from here, from me."

3

After an irritated breath, he continued. His cultured voice rose slightly with a hint of a plaintive whine, "Wynnie, there is nothing between Shreva and me."

A chortled snort came through intimating such a thing was absolutely ludicrous. "Really. I swear. She was only, uh, she'd hurt her knee. Her skirt was um, up, because I was, uh, helping bandage it, really, honey. Please come back and you and I-"

Click- Wyn pushed the delete button. There were seven more blinking messages. She pushed the next message.

"Wynnie, honey, you're going to be my wife, please-"

Rolling her eyes, as she deleted it with a beleaguered breath emptying her lungs. The rest of the messages would only be more of the same.

Still holding her mug, she left the offending machine and headed down the narrow hall to the bathroom, grateful she hadn't given him her cell number.

The bathroom made of tiny tiles of all shades of beige was miniscule, like most of the facilities in the ancient, practically medieval town. But, a soft smile curved her lips, it had a huge porcelain tub. She'd used the shower this morning to wash her long blonde curls, now it was tub time.

Settling in the warm water, she pushed the bubbles off her hand to reach for the chocolate. It was probably crazy to have a hot drink while in hot water, but the air outside was still so chilly and damp, and thinking of those men following her chased a shiver up her spine and goose bumps prickled over her arms.

She needed to take into account her savings. What with the strange men stalking her, and Jazer and her aunt's incessant pressure, it was clear she should cut her visit short.

Tomorrow she would make plans to go back home as soon as possible. Finishing her drink and luxurious bath, Wyn slipped on a pair of shorts over a tiny strip of panties, tugged a burgundy, light knit sweater over the silk bra then curled up on the sofa with a book.

Vijay

The sun had long set when two hours later she woke from dozing on the couch. Yawning with a long stretch, she sat up in the dark, the only illumination came through the front window.

The light from a single lamppost outside cast meagerly through the crackled mullioned glass crisscrossed with leaded strips. Gold and black shadows wove over the worn furniture and knit rug.

Wyn stretched again and flicked on a table lamp to brighten her cozy apartment. Old but thickly stuffed furniture filled the small living room.

Padding into the kitchen thinking about dinner, her recent gas bill caught her eye. It reminded her that she had been in such a hurry to get inside, she hadn't picked up her mail. She looked down at her sweater draped over satiny shorts pin-striped with burgundy and blue, and then glanced out the window. Undoubtedly it was icy cold outside.

She pulled a pair of sweatpants on over her shorts, and stepped into her hiking boots. She didn't bother to tie them, she'd only be outside for a minute.

Clomping down the steps, Wyn trod along the stone walk to the main sidewalk where the mailboxes were on posts.

The narrow street, lined with antiquated apartments and rusted European cars parked on both sides of the road, was in an older part of the city. There were few outside lights, and at late evening on a weeknight most everyone was inside.

The wind whipping her hair around sharp and biting on her face, quickly, Wyn opened the box and stuck her hand inside.

Intent on what she was doing she didn't pay any attention to the car that pulled up behind her.

The mail clutched in her hand, as she turned, a cold hard hand clamped over her mouth and another wrapped around her waist.

Before she could react she was lifted up and carried a few feet to the street where a long black car waited with a rear door open and the engine running. The car rumbled, grey exhaust poured out into the chill.

Shocked, she tore her mouth away and took a breath to scream- the hand clamped with a nasty slap back on her mouth.

Frantic, screaming against the smothering hand, Wyn kicked her feet and flailed her arms but she was shoved into the back of the black car. Her dropped mail scattered quickly in the brisk wind.

Before she could get her bearings, she was thrown back against the seat as the driver floored the engine.

As the car sped down the street, Wyn struggled to right herself in the dark. Grasping the seat in front of her, she yelled, "What is going on? Stop this car!"

A gravelly voice from the front seat snarled, "Shut the fuck up, bitch," then his fist connected with her jaw, knocking Wyn out cold.

Chapter Two

Jaw aching, Wyn's head felt like an out of control carousel, spinning madly. Blinking away some of the dissipating blackness, slowly the fuzziness cleared from her brain.

As she came to, Wyn realized she was lying on her back on a leather seat, and a man was half on top of her pushing his cold greedy hands up her sweater.

"Stop!" she screamed, slapping at him. Battling to push his rough hands away, his horrid laughter rang in her ears as he savagely grabbed at her breasts.

"I want bare skin, baby," he reached around her twisting writhing back to unhook her bra. Still screaming and fighting him, her body was sliding off the seat to the floor.

"Quit that squealing, c'mere bitch." Unsuccessful in unhooking her bra, the man cursed at her in a language she didn't understand then dug his hard fingers into her side and wrenched her back up on the seat. He rolled over on her to hold her still.

Wyn struggled to breathe, the man's torso held her down with his weight, her legs were still dangling off the seat. In her fright she squirmed, jerking her knees up, her feet bashed into the back of the seat in front of her.

"Brennan," a voice from the front of the car carried to the back, "leave off the girl. The boss said bring her untouched and in one piece. He's already gonna be pissed at the slug I had ta give her."

Apparently Brennan was deaf because he continued his molestation. Her struggles not fazing him a bit, he gripped her breasts, squeezing and wringing them like he was trying to mutilate her womanly flesh. He squeezed them so painfully she cried out at his viciousness.

"How's it feel, bitch," he sneered his whiskey breath in her face. "Beautiful women like you blow me off all the time. But ya can't now, can ya?" A snicker snorted out when he chortled, "Speaking of blowing me," he sadistically pinched and twisted a nipple, "I like the sound of that."

Biting back shrieks of pain at his brutality, Wyn shoved at his hands and chest, squirming and struggling under his weight she tried to kick him. She punched at him and pushed at his hands but it was like a fly trying to fight off a tarantula.

He released one breast to reach down and shove his hand down her sweatpants. Screaming, she twisted her head and sunk her teeth into his arm.

The man howled in pain and pulled the hand out to hit her-before he could swing at her, one of the men in the front seat reached through and socked him in the eye so hard he slammed back against the seat.

"Josef said leave off the girl. Keep your fucking hands to yourself, asshole. We'll get our shot when Boss is done with her." The man glared at Brennan then swung back around in his seat to face the front.

Brennan threw a hand over his eye and swore a blue streak.

While he was whining, Wyn let her body slither to the floor then she scrambled around him and back up on the seat shuffling to the furthest corner away from him.

His hand covering his eye, Brennan glowered threats of further violence at Wyn. Appearing average height, with nondescript brown hair and eyes, one that was turning purple, he had a pointy chin to match his pointy nose and ears. On the thin side, he was still twice as big and strong as her.

Wyn pulled her legs up and hugged her knees protectively to her chest. "Wha- what, why did you take me? Where are we going?" she stammered, bracing her shaking chin on her knees.

"Shut up bitch or I'll shut you up," was the dark response from the front seat.

The car was moving so fast Wyn couldn't see the houses they passed. Still dizzy from the earlier punch, nausea threatened. The car hurtled down unfamiliar streets to the main road and then eventually headed straight out of town.

She must have passed out again. When Wyn started to wake, she was disoriented. Her back was against a leather seat and her head bounced on a window, she was in a car. *Where-* it came back to her in a rush. Those men took her.

A hand crept up her thigh. God knows what he'd done to her while she was out. Wyn slapped his hand as hard as she could. Brennan yanked it back with a squawk.

Judging by the snickering from the front seat, the men thought that was hilarious.

She scrunched into a ball against the door. Brennan's face a twist of fury and hate, he reached for her-

"Finally," the man in the passenger seat sighed.

Brennan paused, he looked out the side window. Wyn followed his gaze. Her stomach clenched with dread.

The car crested a hill supplying a twilight view of the countryside, completely void of any trace of civilization. They were surrounded by what looked like miles upon hundreds of miles of forest.

Heading down the hill, they turned onto a dirt road that wound through a dark canopy of dense trees.

For half a mile the car bumped along the road. Wyn could see nothing in the darkness. All she could hear was the shrouded black trees like fiendish bogeymen scraping at the jostling car with jagged-branched fingers.

They slowed then rolled to a stop in front of a small, decaying stone house set in the middle of a scrappy yard of brown grass and weeds. Another car was parked in front.

Josef pulled up beside it and parked. Yellow lights shone through a few dingy windows.

Brennan clambered out of the car and scurried to the house.

Josef came to Wyn's door, pulled it open and reached in. Before she could slide over the seat and escape out Brennan's open door, he grabbed her arm and jerked her out so fast she stumbled.

He kept his grip on her arm righting her and walked her along the grassy path beaten down by many feet to the house. He growled to the third man, "Oksand, lock it up."

Wyn shot Josef a quick glance under a veil of hair, then wished she hadn't.

He looked like the kind of man that hangs around disreputable dives along the docks like a thuggish longshoreman. Josef of the gravelly voice had a thick accent, sounded something like Russian but not quite. Slavic with prominent cheekbones, light skin but weathered, wide eyes scrunched under a low forehead.

The sides of his head were shaved; a wide band of very short hair striped the top of his head like a buzzed Mohawk. His thick fingers wound around her arm felt like barbed wire. The other man who had sat up front came up behind them.

Their breaths spurts of white vapor in the freezing night, the men were bundled up in wool pea coats.

Tripping beside Josef as he wordlessly dragged her down the walk, Wyn snuck a glimpse at Oksand and shivered.

Big, heavy, bald with a big nose and eyes like blank discs. Each man was more fearsome than the last. Tough and scarred, to Wyn they looked like a scurvy foreign mob.

Brennan had left the door to the house open, Josef hauled Wyn inside.

Vijay

The stone house was cold and dirty. Full ashtrays littered the living room. In the haze of cigarette smoke, two men lounged, one on a torn up cushioned chair, the other on a broken-down couch.

Strips of faded material peeled from the old furniture. The rug smelled of mildew and urine, plain wooden tables were covered with stains and burns.

The man on the couch rose as they entered the room. He came straight to Wyn. His gaze scrolling her up and down, hesitated at her breasts, then, it slid to where her legs joined.

She forced herself to not flinch or cover herself.

A slight smirk pulled up his large furrowed face. Over six feet tall and built like a bruiser with a barrel chest, strong hips and huge muscled arms, serrated scars cut across his face and forehead. He looked at Wyn like she was dinner.

Muttering "Ahh," in admiration, he came forward, closer to her.

Wyn struggled to not shrink from him. Her stomach pinched and her skin shriveled in fear, her lids blinked rapidly, uncontrollably. What in God's name was she doing here?

Josef released her arm and stepped to the side.

Scarface reached out and grasped a curl of her hair while still scanning her body then his gaze settled on her face.

She could literally feel the color in her face drain, her legs shook like branches in a storm.

"Wynna Pila. I am Kreis Warwick." He said it like she would know who he was.

She stared blankly at him still using everything in her power to not cower. Freezing in only a sweater and sweatpants, her panicked eyes bounced around the room. She was surrounded by five big, burly rough men.

They were all staring hard at her, some smirked palming their crotches, a couple scowled. Oksand looked at her over his big nose with a completely blank stare. Her heart was sinking deeper and deeper into blind terror by the second.

Studying the lock curling like a ringlet around his calloused finger, Warwick asked, "Is the color real? It's so," he rubbed it between his thumb and finger, "light, like a child's natural fair blonde, shiny, damned pretty. I'll find out in a minute if it's natural or not."

Getting his meaning, Wyn's stomach did sick summersaults. Surely any second now her alarm will go off and she'll wake.

Letting her hair drift from his fingers, Warwick's beady brown eyes moved back to her chest before raising to her face. "Of course, you have no idea why you have been brought here. I will enlighten you."

A guileful sneer turned up his thick lips watching Wyn as her eyes darted around the room but continuing to glance back at the door.

"Don't expend your energy planning your escape, Miss Pila. Even if you, a bit of a girl could get away from us," his gaze flit around the room at the four huge men that had settled on the scattered furniture watching the pair.

He laughed. "And that ain't happening in this decade, we are surrounded by hundreds of miles of uninhabited treacherous, freezing wilderness. You would die long before you came within sight of civilization."

She barely noticed Kreis Warwick motion with his head to the other men. They got up ponderously and grumbled into another room.

He crossed his heavy arms over the barrel chest. "Now," he said, his mouth turned to a hard line, the eyes flat, "you are here because of your uncle, David Pila." The dense lips turned up a shade at the surprise on her face.

Nodding his big rocky head, his face all grainy, pitted planes and scars, the beady eyes peering at her from under thick lids narrowed harshly. The man was beyond ugly and well into hideous.

"Your uncle, as you are aware, is the people's choice for prime minister, the republic's president. If he gets elected he has the power to bring in the military to run roughshod over," he hesitated, "shall we say some unsavory businesses, costing many of us millions of dollars. He has control of the bitcoin operations in this country, additionally he will call for reforms, desiring more significant, democratic, and lawful political reforms."

Wyn's lips parted but she couldn't say anything if she wanted to. Her throat was so constricted with fear, it closed as soon as she had found herself in that car with those men and only contracted more and more minute by minute.

She felt like every breath she took was scraping up through a thin straw. Her frantic heart hammered so loud in her ears she could hardly hear him.

Kreis watched as her skin continued draining out the very last bit of color left from her already frightful day.

He carried on, "My boss wants him eliminated. Your uncle is in protective hiding, secretly secluded. He will stay secured until the elections are completed in case of assassination."

The corner of his mouth snagged up. "Of which there are many planned. Once he is elected it will be too late to eliminate him. His policies will have already snowballed into laws and action. His chosen staff will see to that."

Wyn stood frozen, only trembled and blinked at him.

"The word is, you spent a great deal of time alone with your uncle before he fled. It is presumed you know where he is stashed, or at least know people who know where he is. So, Wynna Pila, you will lead us to your uncle. Tell me who is the first person you would need to contact to initiate locating him?"

Eyes terrified and as wide as blue plates, she just stood and shook, her mouth clamped shut.

Kreis abruptly swung his huge hand out and slapped her hard- she stumbled backwards then fell to the floor.

Stunned, the bottom of her spine shooting spikes of pain, Wyn shook the dizziness from her head, her palm went to her burning face.

Kreis bent and grabbed the front of her sweater and hauled her to her feet. She swayed unsteady, blinking the shocked stars out of her eyes.

His voice devoid of any feeling or pity, Kreis said coldly, "I said, tell me who is the first contact? You fail to tell me, the hits

13

will only become more violent, Miss Pila. You are a petite, very young woman, what, if you weighed a buck five I would be surprised. You won't last long, and you won't be able to crawl away on broken arms and legs."

At her swift intake of breath, he leaned closer to her. His face became a total snarl. Mean eyes like slits, he told her, "I promise, I will do whatever it takes to get what I want. It's your choice if, or how you choose to survive it."

His gaze was as hard and cold as an iceberg. He waited, she said nothing.

"You only need to get us to the first contact. We will be able to…wrangle the next contact from that person. We will of course keep you alive until we locate him, just to ensure you've given us the correct in information. It will depend on your cooperation, the condition you are in, as we allow you to live."

Leaning back slightly, he took a deep breath and said, "Now, tell me who the person is."

Shaking so hard Wyn could hardly think. Her head ached beyond belief, her face stung, mindless with fear, she continued to stay mute, blinking at him.

Wham!

He struck her again- she flew backwards landing hard on the floor.

Bracing back on her palms, Wyn tried to keep conscious, but darkness enveloped her, pulling her under even as she felt Kreis' boots slamming into her side.

Chapter Three

Her stomach roiled and rumbled. "*Oh*," Wyn groaned as she tried to move. Her face felt swollen and aching. Cracking her eyes open, she could see little, it was dark. What she was laying on was cold and rough.

When she moved a leg to see if it was broken, it scraped on the jagged floor. Rolling on her side, Wyn flattened her palms on the ground and pushed to sit up.

The room was spinning in circles, she waited until it slowed. Putting a hand to her painfully throbbing head she looked around.

The only light came from under the heavy, dark wooden door. In the dimness she could make out that she was in a square concrete room with no windows. The floor was cold hard concrete. There was absolutely nothing in the room but her.

She looked down at her watch, her brows flew up. It indicated a different day than it should have.

Mumbling out loud, "It must have broken, no," she shook her head then winced when the conclusion that she'd been there for over six days struck her.

"*Oh my God*," she cried. Panic surged up her throat, she ripped the watch off and threw it on the floor.

Climbing weakly to her feet, she felt the cold abrasive cement under her bare feet. They had taken her shoes and socks. Her legs and side hurt probably from Kreis' kicks. She stumbled to the wooden door and tried to open it. It was locked.

The floor under her feet was wet, someone appeared to have thrown water on her, or in her at some point possibly to keep her alive. Her sweater was slightly damp. Her stomach cramped, she sure as heck hadn't eaten.

Scanning the dark room, her brain screamed louder and louder in rising terror as she searched futilely for a means of escape. The dooming realization there was no way out gripped her heart, then the door opened.

She jumped back as a man stepped in. She backed away from him, but he reached out snagged her arm and wordlessly dragged her out of the room.

Going from the dark to the sudden light blinded her. She was dragged to a door. So weak and ill, Wyn would have fallen if he loosened his grip. The man opened it and shoved her inside. It was a bathroom.

"Do your business, shower, clean up, you have 10 minutes," the man said and closed the door.

Wyn scoured the room for an escape or a weapon. The room was empty except for a few dirty towels, toilet paper, a bar of soap.

She opened a drawer, inside were several sleeves of toothbrushes in plastic, along with combs and a few other toiletries. No razors, thank goodness she did electrolysis. Although a razor could be used as a weapon.

As sick to her stomach and lightheaded as she was, positive the second she turned the water on the men would rush in, she nonetheless grabbed a toothbrush. Removing only her sweatpants, she took a two minute cold shower in her clothes, drinking in mouthfuls of water as she shampooed her hair with the bar of soap and brushed her teeth.

Dizzy and weak, she toweled dry, one hand braced on the sink to hold her steady. Her legs shook so violently, she could barely stand.

Wyn pulled on the sweatpants over her shorts and had just finished combing her hair when the door opened. She put her hand behind her back to keep the comb as a weapon. Sure, slash and bash with a comb. Right.

Vijay

The same man was there. He grabbed her arm, snatched the comb from her hand and threw it then hauled her out of the bathroom and into the main room.

Eight pairs of male eyes struck her at once. A few more men had joined the group. The room was filled with swarthy, dangerous, vile looking men. Raunchy jokes and disgusting comments abounded until Kreis Warwick separated from the vulgar group and came to her.

A fast swirling ceiling fan was quickly drying her clothes and freezing her at the same time.

His big, calloused and scarred hands set on thick hips, Kreis asked her, "You ready now to talk, bitch? You talk, you can eat."

He waited. She remained mute.

Her dizzy, likely concussed brain tumbled in circles, she was so weak from not eating, her stomach retched but she had no food in it to vomit. Her body still ached from the beating he had given her before throwing her into the cement room.

"Goddamned bitch," Kreis slapped her so hard she crashed to the floor. He bent and grabbed her arms jerked her up to her feet, dragged her over and slammed her down on a wooden chair.

Slapping her several more times until she could no longer stay seated upright, he moved away briefly then stalked back.

Shoving her to sit sideways, he grasped her arms yanking them behind her, tied her wrists together then pushed her back, smashing her arms and spine against the chair.

He leaned over, braced his hefty hands on his muscular thighs and got right in her face. Breathing whiskey and cigarettes in her face, he sputtered, "Fucking tell me, bitch what I want to know."

She could hardly see him through the disoriented, dizzy, hungry haze. Her face stung, she bit her lips to keep them from trembling, she turned her head knowing he would strike her again.

His hand already in motion, the door opened.

Everyone paused and turned to the door.

Wyn kept her eyes clamped closed.

17

A rough voice, deeper, harder, more chilling than any of the other men in the room, with a different accent uttered quietly, "What the hell is going on, Warwick?"

Whack- Kreis slapped Wyn so hard her head snapped to the side. He caught her arm to keep her from falling off the chair from the vehemence of the hit. "I'm busy, Zastrovna, I don't have time to discuss the arms deal."

"Huh." The harsh grunt came from the doorway. "You are too busy knocking restrained women around to talk deals?" Heavy boots clomped closer. "What the hell did she do?"

Kreis snorted. "It's not what she did, I want info out of her and the fucking bitch won't talk. I've starved her and beaten her; I need to up the violence I guess. As small and young as she is, I thought she would have broken by now. I had to take off for almost a week so she had a reprieve. Sort of."

Not wanting to, but she did anyway, Wyn cracked her lids to see what had come through the door.

A clenching horror coursed through her body, the blood in her veins came to a screeching stop turning her already limp limbs into gelatin. She thought she was already scared to death, but it got worse.

The most frightening man she'd ever seen in her life stood in the threshold, almost completely blocking the entire doorway.

If anyone looked like a sociopathic killer, it was that hulking huge man. Kreis Warwick was a big man but this fearsome guy towered over him and looked twice as brutal.

His expression glacially fierce, black hair combed straight back hung to just past his shoulders, the scruff on his face only added to his sinister appearance.

A tattoo was partially visible on his neck. Fierce yet brilliant blue eyes glinted out from under a low shelf, a hard ridge of raven brows, they flicked around the room at the occupants, landing lastly on Wyn.

Her heart cringed, his piercing gaze burned over her so fiercely, it was like she could feel it scalding her skin. Although bright and intense, the inscrutable eyes looked dead, empty of emotion or even a hint of compassion. A scar curved from his left forehead to his eyebrow.

His body was like that of an ancient Gallic gladiator; powerful chest, the thick slabs of layered muscles bulged at the shirt he wore under an open black, leather biker jacket. WWF sized arms flexed against the leather.

Hips so lean the black jeans held up by a belt hung low but snug down to the shit-kicker boots. If the chiseled lips weren't in a perpetual ruthless scowl, he could almost be considered handsome, albeit in a brutish, terrifying and menacing way.

Snarling, "Enough of this shit," Kreis grabbed Wyn's arm and jerked her up to her unsteady feet, her wrists still bound behind her back.

From the doorway, the behemoth's deep voice a low growl asked, "What info could the *fetita* have that could be so fucking important?"

Kreis snorted, "Little girl, Zastrovna? You see her bitchin' body? She's all fucking woman. Anyway, there's nothing you need to know about." He looked down at Wyn.

"I need to have some alone time with her. Since we were gone most of the past week, I was hoping being here alone with Oksand knocking her around and no food and very little water would bring her around to my way of thinking. But no. She's a fucking stubborn little wench. She should count her herself lucky Oks prefers his own kind, eh?"

Gripping her arm, he shook Wyn hard, scowling at her.

Seeing her fright, Kreis smirked. "I've had enough screwing around, I'm going to impale the bitch on my dick and fuck her up to her throat and push the words out that way." He grinned lasciviously at her pale face, the terrified eyes wide.

"Then, I will take the pleasure of sticking my dick in her mouth and shoving the words right back down her fucking throat. Many women have endured long hospital stints after my...shall we say...lovemaking? She will be willing to talk when I finish with her, in a few hours."

He barked a laugh and dragged her out of the room and down a hall to another room.

Shoving her inside, Kreis closed and locked the door then put his huge grizzly bear hands on her slim shoulders and pushed down until her knees bent, all the way until she was forced to kneel on the wood planked floor.

The room was empty, containing not a stick of furniture or even a rug. It had one small dirty window. Wyn tugged frantically at the binds around her hands but only managed to burn up her wrists.

Kreis plopped down on the floor in front of her. He put a hand to her chest and pushed her on her back then clutched the legs of her sweatpants and pulled them off her. Wyn screamed through her already hoarse throat.

Ignoring her hysterical cries for help, he tossed the pants aside and reached for her shorts, but she rolled and jerked her legs up and away from him.

Kreis frowned, then grinned, a nasty, stomach puking grin.

Wyn scrambled to get away, he caught her leg and yanked her back so hard her head banged on the floor.

Then Kreis crouched in front of her and gripped her upper arms. Like holding a doll, he lifted her slightly, pushing her to kneel again then he forced her to sit back on her heels.

His hands like thick strong claws, Kreis clutched her knees and shoved them apart then he got on his knees and moved between her thighs. He had her trapped so she could not move her legs at all. He gave her a little push making her fall backwards.

On her knees with her wrists tied, her back bowed as she braced her elbows on the floor behind her making her body a taut arch.

She was helpless to move at all or fight him off. Her breaths spurted in panic-stricken panting gasps, so dehydrated her eyes burned tearless, her dry throat choked with paroxysms of terror.

"Ya got anything to say yet, doll?" His lewd gaze stroked from her chest to her female core. Everything from her toes to her eyeballs was visibly shaking. His brown marbled eyes narrowed on her chest, the corner of his odious mouth turned up in a crude grin. "Let's see what you got goin' on under that sweater."

Wyn bit back a cry as he shoved his coarse hands up her sweater and roughly gripped her breasts. He smiled then frowned.

She tried to twist away, but her body was immobilized. She couldn't even hold her head up and look at him even if she wanted to. Her head draped back, the long blond curls dusting the dirty floor behind her. She could just barely see Kreis reach to his belt and pull out a knife.

Her eyes wide as screaming saucers ached with dry tears.

Grasping the bottom of her sweater, he wrenched it up, cut her bra straps then pulled it off her and tossed it aside. "That's better, huh?" With both hands he lifted her sweater to see her nude chest.

Leaning back, he gawked at her plump breasts. His eyes widened then flamed. "Hell, girl, you have crazy ass the finest tits I've ever seen! They sit up high and full like juicy tender fruit."

Ogling her, he whistled, shaking his head. "Fuck yeah, I know how I'm gonna occupy my time while waiting to track down your uncle."

Futilely, Wyn twisted and squirmed.

Kreis let go of the sweater and it slid back down. He pushed his hands up under it again to callously clench her bare breasts. Squeezing cruelly hard, his slobbering drool dripped on her as he sadistically mauled her like a man who'd just gotten out of prison after twenty years.

Her supple flesh exceeding the grasp of his big fingers, he gouged them with his ruthless kneading, then painfully pinched and twisted her nipples.

He laughed, getting off on her pain as screams caught in her sore throat and the backs of her eyes stung with dry tears.

"*Nice*," he groaned, crushing her soft globes in his huge hard hands, his erection grew pushing at his pants.

Removing his hands, he wrapped one around the side of her hip to hold her from squirming away, and spread his other hand high up on her thigh.

Wyn tried to twitch from his grasp but couldn't move an inch.

His fingers digging into her skin, his vile eyes on her face to watch her expression, over her shorts he rubbed her sex with his thumb.

Wyn threw her head back, arching her spine even more in an attempt to get away from his leeching hands. This made him laugh harder and he spread her knees as far apart as he could get them.

"Ah, I love it when a bitch fights me! It makes me fucking hotter," he snarled. Still watching her face, he maneuvered his fingers up the inside of her shorts and under her panties.

He pushed the tip of his middle finger just inside her; her shorts were too tight for him to fit his whole big hand inside. "Oh shit," he growled, his breathing heavy, his exhales loud and ragged, "you are insanely tight."

He licked his bloodthirsty lips and grinned with heinous intent at her. "It's gonna hurt like hell for you, but I'm gonna fucking love it!"

Her eyes crunched shut, her chest convulsed with terror. He tried to shove his finger deeper in her but couldn't because of her shorts.

He snarled in frustration, "Look at me bitch, see me own you. I want you to look at me with my finger inside your cunt, 'cause I'm sure as hell gonna force you to watch my cock driving in and out of you, and again when I jam it in your mouth and choke you with it."

Her chest hitched and heaved with the helpless sobs she couldn't contain.

Suddenly, they could hear a lot of banging around in the other room.

Kreis laughed. "Ah, Zastrovna must be arguing about something, he's getting knocked around for his trouble."

Removing his finger from her body, he pulled a cloth out of his pocket and tied it around her mouth. "I'll give you time to think about what you have to tell me. Trust me, when I'm done here, you will be spilling your guts so fast you will beg for me to let you talk."

With her body slung backwards forced in such a vulnerable position, she couldn't move, couldn't close her legs or put her hands up to protect herself, painful hacking sobs shook Wyn's core. Her already concave belly sucked in deeper with her cutting gasps.

Kreis splayed his hand on her chest and pushed her flat on her back while jerking her legs back out straight.

"We'll start with you on your back, then we'll turn you over and try that other luscious hole." With her arms restrained behind her back her breasts thrust up under the thin sweater.

Enjoying the view, Kreis gave them both a squeeze. "Nice, honey, real nice." He leaned over her and put one knee between her legs. She twisted sideways bringing up her knee that wasn't trapped by his body.

Ordering, "Hold fucking still, bitch," he placed his palm on the floor above her shoulder and reached for the button on her shorts. She jerked her knee up hard to kick him.

Raising his clenched fist to punch her, he thundered, "I'll teach you to fight me-"

The door crashed open causing Kreis to stop with his fist in midair. He snarled, "What the fuck do you want?"

The monster growled from the doorway, "I want *her*."

Chapter Four

Wyn couldn't see him, but his accent sounding like that of the ancient vampire monster, Dracula, thick and dark and coarsely low, chilled her to the bone. Her head spun with worse terror than already inflicted on her by Kreis.

Kreis spat, "Fuck you, Zastrovna, get the fuck out. She's mine."

Will they both use her together? Tear her in half?

Moving to the pair on the floor, Zastrovna said calmly, "Spoils of war."

Confused, Kreis said, "There is no war, what the fuck are you talking about, asshole?"

"This war." Zastrovna stomped on Kreis' fist still paused in midair- stamping it down and crushing it on the floor under the heel of his boot.

Kreis screamed like a girl and tried to jump up.

Zastrovna slugged him so hard with his huge fist he fell backwards, crashing into the wooden planks.

Then the behemoth stood over Kreis writhing on the floor and stomped on his neck again and again until it was as flat as the wooden planks. Then he turned his fierce gaze to her.

Her eyes rolling back in her head, Wyn was so terrified and sick to her stomach, it was like Attila the Hun with a Dracula voice come to life. Her screams were raw and muffled from overuse and the gag.

Without a word to her, he crouched down and scooped her up in his arms.

Carrying her in Paul Bunyan arms high and tight against his massive chest, he tromped to the other room.

Bloody and broken men lay sprawled and scattered all over the floor; they all appeared to be dead.

Through paralyzed eyes, Wyn recognized Josef's shaved Mohawk, and Oksand's big nose, the vacant disc-eyes the same even in death. Blood saturated the men and sprayed the walls, and pooled on the disgusting carpet.

A man hovering by the front door Zastrovna had left open turned and fled. At the same time, Brennan entered.

Standing a few feet inside the room, he looked around at the carnage and said, "I'm gone a few moments emptying the car and all hell breaks loose. It looks like a slaughterhouse in here. What the fuck happened?"

Still holding Wyn, Zastrovna shrugged. "Warwick said I can take the girl."

His eyes darting around the bloodbath in the room then back to Zastrovna, Brennan said, "You can't take her, she has to go to the big boss." He reached for her.

Squeaking a short hoarse cry from under the gag, Wyn burrowed her face into Zastrovna's wide shoulder to get away from Brennan.

Holding her tighter, Zastrovna turned from Brennan so he couldn't reach her and growled at Wyn, "What tis the matter, *mic scorpie*- little bitch? Have you not caused enough trouble?"

She swiveled her head slightly from his shoulder.

Zastrovna frowned at the renewed terror in her eyes.

She slid a side-glance of distress at Brennan then turned and shoved her face back into his thick shoulder.

"What? Why is she so afraid of you?" he asked Brennan. His gaze scored over the man, his lip curled at the thin, pointy-chinned male with the black eye as if intimating a child wouldn't be scared of him.

25

His voice oily, Brennan replied slyly, "Oh we had a little fun earlier in the car before Josef put the kibosh on it." He glanced down at the mangled, dead Josef lying like a pretzel in his own blood.

Back to Zastrovna, he said, "She feels real good I can tell you that. She hardly screamed when I got a little rough with her. She only cried a little at the pain, she's quite a fighter for being so slight." His thin lips pulled up in a pointy smirk.

Surprised that the behemoth held her so easily, not seeming to tire of the burden in his big arms, Wyn peeked frightened eyes over the gag at Brennan.

Brennan continued with a mild shrug, "I might have been a bit brutal in my..." he leered menacing at her, "*handling* of her..."

Then, remembering getting hit for touching her, and what she did when he tried again later, he scowled. "I owe her. She fucking bit me when I tried to get my hand down her pants."

Grinning a foul threat at her, Brennan said, "Yeah, when I'm plowing into you, girl in a minute, I'll be biting the fuck out of you, paybacks and all."

His eyes on her, his hand went to his crotch. Gripping the hard-on he was getting for thinking about it, he said to Zastrovna, "Leave her, I want my time with her. I'll take her to the boss when I'm done. Or if you want to wait and fuck her after I'm done before I take her to him," he shrugged, "whatever."

He reached out to take her from Zastrovna, snickering at Wyn's whimper as she tried to burrow away from him into the behemoth's chest.

"The fuck you say." Zastrovna set Wyn on her feet, she swayed. He positioned her against the counter for support.

He said to Brennan, "So you are such a weakling you only attack bound *femei-* women, so they cannot hurt you or fight back?" He crouched, casually wiped his bloody knuckles on one of the dead men's shirt then stood back up.

More immense and a lot taller than Brennan, he asked, "Who is your boss?"

"I doubt you've heard of him. Mr. Katakham."

"Why does he want her?"

Brennan shrugged. "Not in any of our pay-grade except Warwick to know. We're just hired muscle."

"Uh huh." Zastrovna suddenly whipped his hands out and grabbed Brennan, and with one move, broke his neck. He opened his hands and Brennan dropped to the floor with barely a rumpled thump.

Zastrovna turned to Wyn. White as snow, body shaking in horror, she swayed unsteady. He reached out and tugged the gag down.

"What do you know that Kreis Warwick wanted to beat out of you while fucking you?"

Wyn kept her trembling lips closed. His eyes scrolled down her body, from her lush breasts over the tiny waist down the thin legs and then back up.

"Tis obvious why he wanted to bang you. But what information was he going to beat out of you?"

She remained mute.

Seeing her myriad of bruises and gashes, he muttered, "Why the fuck did you not just tell him and avoid all that torture?"

Even though she struggled to understand him with his thick accent, she still didn't answer him; her eyes were focused on the floor. It was all she could do to stay standing.

He reached for her. Her hands still bound, she tried to move from him, kicking out with her bare feet. He gripped her chin, pushed a fat light-blonde curl out of her face and off her shoulder, letting it spiral down her back.

Looking into her petrified pained eyes, he said calmly, "Do not fight me. I am not going to hurt you, *fetita*, little girl, not right now. But I will if you keep fighting me."

The monster glared so fiercely at her, the blood rushed out of her head and Wyn started to crumple into a faint. Zastrovna caught her before she fell then bent and lifted her, draping her over his shoulder.

He left the building with her.

Scarcely conscious, Wyn was only vaguely aware she was slung over the behemoth's shoulder. His big hand on her ass holding her, he was carrying her like a prehistoric troglodyte off to his cave.

She heard a car pull up. Her head bouncing slightly, she slit one dizzy eye open and saw six men pile out.

One of the men asked, "Who's the *faţă*?"

Zastrovna's gruff reply rumbled against her torso. "Dunno. Warwick thought she had some valuable information. I am taking her to Mann for interrogation. You two," he apparently nodded at two of the men, "come with me. The rest of you, I left some trash inside that needs to be picked over for ID, weapons, and whatever other shit you can find. Then get rid of them, burn it down and follow us."

When he reached a car, Zastrovna opened the door and carefully slid Wyn into the passenger side then locked and closed the door.

Fighting consciousness, Wyn heard the monster climb into the driver's side and two others into the back seat.

Zastrovna turned on the engine and the car rolled, crunching over the dirt driveway back to a two-lane country road.

Wyn tried to open her eyes but they were so heavy and she was so weak.

Chapter Five

Her skin prickled, Wyn could feel a hand sliding around her arm and moving to her breast.

Blam- she heard a smash and a crack and a man howled, the hand jerked away.

"Fuck, Vij, you didn't have to hit Jack so hard, you coulda killed him," one of the men in the backseat chided.

His voice a rough growl, the monster said, "Jack is lucky. I just killed seven men who tried to stop me from taking her. No one touches her. Spread the word. I do not want her any more damaged than she is when I take her to Mann."

Other than Jack's groans, the car was silent after that.

On the edge of passing out, Wyn's head banged against the window several times as she struggled to stay conscious, but a black fog surrounded her tugging her under.

Zastrovna stopped at an intersection. He grasped Wyn's shoulders and brought her to lie down on her side on the bench seat. Her legs curled on the seat and her head fell onto his lap.

She could feel him staring at her for a second like he was going to push her off him. Then he put the car in drive and took off.

They traveled steadily, Wyn hung onto a slight string of consciousness. One time, the monster had to suddenly step on the brakes, her body jolted forward hard- he grabbed her to hold her from falling on the floor and pulled her back onto the seat.

Her hands still tied, she was now lying partially on her back. He continued driving leaving his hand on her arm, occasionally looking down at her. She could feel it every time he did that until she finally passed out.

Intermittently rising from the black cloud, she'd crack open one eye and catch him staring at her unfettered breasts jiggling from the motion of the car. A couple of times his gaze was on her legs, but she kept passing in and out not even having the strength to move.

Hours later, Wyn slowly came to and realized her head was on his thigh and his huge hand still on her arm, the gag hung around her neck. She struggled to sit up with her hands still bound and shuffled away from him to sink into the corner.

He pulled into a rest stop for a break and parked the car.

As the men in the car, and the others from the other vehicle that had caught up to them piled out to hit the restrooms and get some food, Zastrovna barked out some words in a foreign language to one of the men.

Then he grabbed Wyn's arms, turned her around and untied her ropes setting them in his lap.

She tried to move her arms but winced in agony, they hurt so badly from being tied back for so long, tears would have sprung if she had water in her.

"Take it slow *fetita*," the behemoth said, sounding like he was speaking from experience. "It will be a few minutes before you can move them more comfortably."

Not able to move her arms, it was like she was still tied. Paralyzed, keeping her eyes off him, Wyn leaned back against the seat and stared out the side window.

After a few minutes, he reached for her, she weakly, painfully hit out at him.

Surprised, he laughed harshly. "Watch out *fetita* - little girl, you are only going to hurt yourself more."

Wyn mumbled hoarsely, "I am not a little girl, I am a grown adult," she shoved further away from him.

He crudely eyeballed her up and down, then said with a cold leer, "*Yah?* You want to prove it? Take off the sweater."

Her face drained, she slowly, painfully crossed her arms over her chest. His gaze stroked from her face to her legs and back up slowly. She didn't move a muscle.

With a sneer, he grunted, "Did not think so."

He got out of the car, went around it and opened her door. The chilly air spooled in hitting her bare feet.

Seeing goose bumps spring up her legs, he removed his leather jacket, reached in and dropped it over her shoulders and ordered, "Put it on."

So weak she could hardly move, Wyn couldn't get her arms inside the jacket. He leaned inside the car and helped her get the black leather on. It was so big on her she could have fit ten of her inside it.

Pulling the gag off over her head, he tucked it in his pocket and asked, "What is wrong with you, are you ill?"

Shaking her head, she mumbled hoarsely, "Beaten, no food...days." Licking her dry lips, her eyes rolled back weakly.

"Fuck," he muttered. "Move over," he ordered. Nudging her, he helped her slide over and got in next to her with one foot out the open passenger door. Reaching a long arm under the seat, he brought out a water bottle, twisted the top off and handed it to her.

She just stared at him; her arms were useless to move.

"Fuckin' nursemaid," he mumbled and held the bottle to her lips. He put a hand behind her head cradling it, and pulled it back gently, supporting her while she drank.

"Slowly," he cautioned with gruff irritation. When he felt she'd had enough, he took the bottle, put the lid on and set it on the seat.

Then he slid his arms under her, lifted her out of the car and ignoring her croaking protests, carried her as easily as if she was a child up to the structure.

Passing the other men on their way back to the car, Jack, the man that tried to grope her, fingered his swollen nose from the punch he'd gotten and asked, "Why are you carrying her, Vij, she fucking handicapped?"

He tugged at the end of his long chin with very long narrow fingers as if he could pull thicker whiskers out of it. He had wanted to do the scruff thing that broads seemed to like, but he couldn't even get a good goatee going.

Zastrovna didn't look at him as he continued on carrying her to ladies room.

When he set her down outside the doorway, she swayed, he threw his hands out to catch her and steady her. Spotting a paper towel dispenser next to a water cooler, he dragged out a long sheaf.

"Here, lean against the wall." He helped her rest against the wall for support. Then he crouched down and wrapped her feet in the paper towels.

Standing up, he said, "Go do your thing. You run or talk to anyone or leave a note," he looked down her bare legs, obviously she had nothing to write with on her, "you do anything except piss and I will wring your neck. Got it?"

She was shaking like a leaf, hardly able to stand, she was too weak to answer him.

He set a hand on her shoulder and gave her a little push. "Go. I will be right here. You fall, call out, I will come."

Inside, Wyn staggered to the counter and braced her palms on it. She stared bleary-eyed into the mirror and gasped. "Oh good God."

The side of her face that Kreis had slapped her on was scarlet, there was a swollen bruise under one blue-green eye and a cut on her cheek. Various other bruises mottled everywhere her skin was exposed including her neck and legs.

Her hair was a dirty mussed saffron cloud around her head and down her back from Kreis' attack. She was so wan the rest of her skin was almost translucent.

Worried the monster would come in after her, she pushed from the counter and did her business. Throwing water on her face, she scrubbed soap on it and washed her hands. It was all she could do to keep standing.

When she came stumbling out, her head was spinning, and her eyes were about closed. She almost fell right into him.

He wrapped his huge arms around her to hold her up, then he bent his knees and picked her up, the paper towels fell off her feet as he carried her back to the car.

Zastrovna slid her back into the car, locked and closed her door then he climbed in behind the wheel. There was a paper bag on the seat, apparently one of the other men had left it for him. He opened it, took something out. He said, "Here," and handed her a sandwich.

She looked at it willing her hands to take it, but she couldn't lift her arms. The small act of washing her hands and face had wearied her. Her eyes flit bleakly to him

Muttering, "Ah, that fucker Warwick," he unwrapped the sandwich, then took one of her hands and put the sandwich in it, then took her other hand to hold it and helped her guide it to her mouth.

Now slightly hydrated, tears spilled, Wyn's mouth shook as she opened it to take a bite.

"Uh, listen, *fetita*, do not do that, I cannot," he turned from her, swallowed hard then turned back to her. She was chewing slowly but the tears still ran and her lips still trembled. "Ah," he took a napkin and dabbed at her eyes.

"All right, you need to stop that *rostii*, uh, shit, I mean, ahh…" he dabbed a few more times then reached into the bag, took out a sandwich for himself and a soda. Snapping the tab up, he leaned over the front of her and set it in the cup holder in her door. "You eat and your strength will return."

He gobbled his sandwich in about four bites listening to her sniffing and swallowing with difficulty.

After a few minutes, she had quarter of half a sandwich eaten. He took the rest out of her hands.

When she looked with confusion at him, he said, "You need to eat a little at first, let it settle before you eat more or you will get sick." He set the sandwich on the seat beside her so she could reach it when she was ready.

The back doors opened and the other two men piled in. The car suddenly smelled like male sweat and cigarettes. They chatted in low rumbles of a language Wyn didn't understand, but they sounded old movie Transylvania like the behemoth.

Zastrovna cranked up the car and took off with the second car trailing them.

They drove for a few hours. Her head resting against the back of the seat, Wyn dozed to the tune of rumbling male voices speaking in their language.

She woke when the car stopped but kept her eyes closed.

Then she heard the monster say in mixed languages, his and English, "Now that we are here, I want to talk about," she felt him glance at her. Grunting, "Outside," he jerked his head.

Exiting the vehicle, the three men walked over to the other car where the other four men were waiting.

The car was parked in front of a hotel. The men gathered in a huddle a few yards away, no one looked back at Wyn. If she had one chance, she decided, this was it.

Getting the handle up was hard. Pushing the door open took almost everything she had. But she'd eaten a little she must have some strength back. Leaning forward, she tumbled out of the car to her knees.

Stifling a pained cry, Wyn forced herself to her feet and started staggering towards a hedge of trees.

Only halfway there she knew she wouldn't make it. Kreis had knocked her around enough and lack of food made her too lightheaded, her knees buckled, she fell onto all fours.

The way her head was spinning and her stomach was twirling she likely had a concussion.

"Hey, Vij," Jack laughed. Said through his nose stuffed with dried blood and tufts of tissues, "Your little prisoner is making a run for it, uh, make that a crawl for it." He nodded towards Wyn fighting to get to her feet thirty yards away on the grass.

He laughed again when she fell back down on her knees until Zastrovna glowered at him, then, he meekly shut his mouth.

His expression an unreadable blank, Zastrovna trod back to his car and retrieved his jacket then headed to where Wyn struggled to get to her feet, he didn't hurry, she wasn't going far.

Jack called out, "Beat the piss out of the bitch, Vij, teach her a fucking lesson, bro."

The air on the edge of freezing was so cold the grass crunched under Zastrovna's boots as he made his way to her.

Seeing him, Wyn tried harder to stand, but her shaking legs wouldn't hold her, she only went a few feet before collapsing on the hard ground. His big shadow loomed over her. She hadn't the strength or the nerves to look up.

He crouched down beside her muttering, "Dumb *scorpie-bitch*," and dropped his jacket over her trembling body before sliding his hands under her, then he stood up with her in his arms.

Her chest hitched with gulping, dry sobs from the cold and renewed fright.

"Where were you going to go, *fetita?*" He said, "You cannot walk. Were you going to go lie down in the icy dark woods and hope to freeze to death before an animal tears you to pieces?"

Wyn wanted to fight him to make him put her down, but when she raised a hand to hit him it fell uselessly. Her body wracked with shivers. Another dry sob wheezed from her lungs at her abject helplessness.

The monster held her closer to his body to warm her. "Stop fussing, woman, you are too ill to fight, save it for when you are stronger."

The jacket was soft from wear but it still smelled of leather. Wyn felt the collar brush her jaw. The other side of her face, her cheek rubbed up and down on his sweater. Another wave of dizziness swarmed her, her head fell back as she fought the faint.

Feeling her head drape back, Zastrovna looked down at her and saw the crystal eyes rolling and realized she was passing out again. He moved his arm around her back to push her head up to rest supported on his shoulder.

Her blonde hair spread across his chest and some draped over his arm. The top of it tickled his chin.

He bumped her up higher in his arms unconsciously to inhale her scent. Beaten and starved and lying on the cold hard ground, she still had a sweet smell that lingered, he held her high and tight against his body. Her hair brushed against his face, just under his jaw.

Zastrovna carried her to the two-story building they had parked in front of. **Vatră Cămin**, In English, **Hearth Inn**, was painted in peeling black script across the front of the rural white stucco. Quaint lavender wisteria and shiny jade ivy laced the oak trim.

One of the men grasped the black iron door handle, opened and held the battle-worn oak door for them to pass through.

Zastrovna stalked through the inn and up a flight of stairs. His men were right behind him.

Wyn caught a glimpse of what looked to her like a medieval styled bar or hotel. Long wooden benches in front of long wooden tables were laden with remnants of lunch. A few heads were face down on the tables; some still clutched their beer mugs.

A woman in a white peasant blouse paused while cleaning up silver plates and baskets to watch the group go by. She wiped her hands on her long, full dark orange skirt decorated with colored embroidery, nodded to the men then went back to what she was doing.

Again, Wyn marveled that the monster carried her up a flight of stairs without faltering or even breathing heavy, proving he was indeed a monster.

He stopped outside a door and said to one of the men, "Get the door."

"*Da*, don't worry about being polite, Vij," a man chuckled. He had medium brown, short-cropped hair, looked almost as brutish as the monster, but he had mischievous green eyes that winked at Wyn and grinned at Zastrovna. Back to Wyn, he said cheerfully, "I am Alexandrescu Cosma, but you may call me Alex, little darlin'." He gave her another saucy wink.

The monster didn't smile, just pushed through. Inside he said to Alex, "I will get the *femelă* settled and meet you guys downstairs."

Alex offered cheerfully, "I can watch the *femelă* while you-"

Zastrovna dismissed Alex, shoving the door closed in his face with his boot.

Inside, the room was as rustic and threadbare as the rest of the hotel. There was a fireplace with logs in it, one lead-paned window with worn yellow curtains let in bleak light.

Two decrepit tables, several chairs, and cushioned braided pallets were on the floor for beds with pillows and blankets folded on them. An old, worn tapestry rug covered most of the floor.

He crouched beside one of the pallets and set her down on it.

"Give me the jacket. It will ensure you do not flee. I presume you are not stupid enough to try to escape again in the chill."

She didn't move. He reached for her, she cringed.

His brows already low drew down in a slight frown. He grasped the jacket's collar and lifted her arms taking the jacket from her. Then he stood back up. Something thumped outside the door. Zastrovna started towards it.

"Please, where are we?" Wyn couldn't believe how meek and shaky her voice was. It still rasped from the prolonged screaming.

Opening the door, he muttered, "Nowhere."

A duffle bag sat outside the room, he picked it up and brought it inside and set it on a chair. Unzipping it, he reached in, and brought out a gun. Stuffing the gun in the back of his pants, he reached in again and pulled out another one. He continued rifling through the bag.

She tried to make a connection with the monster, maybe he wouldn't hurt her then. Right. "Uh, wha- what's your name?"

Ignoring her, he filled some clips with bullets and shoved them in his pockets then took a length of rope out of the bag and went over to her and crouched down.

Without looking at her face, he took her wrists and tied them together in front of her then stood up and tied the end of the rope over a pipe along the wall too high for her to reach. Back at the bag he took something else out.

Staring glumly at the rope around her wrists, Wyn rasped, "How do you say beast in your language?"

He paused, a wry twitch tugged the corner of his mouth. "*Bala*," he said, then his mouth firmed. Zastrovna moved towards her, Wyn got on her knees and backed away from him.

Bending over, he set down two bottles of water and another sandwich, and a pair of men's socks on the pallet. He grabbed some extra blankets from a cupboard and dropped them around her.

Lastly, he went to the fireplace, scooped some kindling from a copper bucket, arranged it skillfully under the logs already there then took the long matches and lit the kindling. He used the poker to push the building fire around then placed the screen in front of it. The fireplace was encased in stone with a stone mantel.

Without a word to her he strode to the door and opened it.

"How- how long will you- you be gone?" She was relieved to see him leave but trepidation being left alone tied up in an inn in *nowhere*, started her nerves shaking all over again.

He didn't answer her.

The door was almost closed when he heard her say, "Goodbye *bala*."

His lip twitched as he shut and locked the door.

Chapter Six

Vijay Zastrovna moved quickly down the stairs. Heavy boots clomping on solid wood, he crossed the main room to another room, same as the first, all oak walls and floors, but in here the tables were smaller squares and some rounded, and had regular chairs around them instead of benches.

He pulled out a chair and joined the other six men already there.

"So, Vij," Jack said with a sly smirk, "you were quick. You got your nut off pretty fast with the cunt, what, were you sticking it in her before she hit the ground-"

Thwack!

Zastrovna stabbed a knife between Jack's index and middle finger and into the table.

No one else at the table even blinked except Jack whose round dark eyes were wide, glued to the blade between his fingers.

Zastrovna's big fist was still wrapped around the knife. He growled a warning, "Stop talking about the *femelă*. She does not exist to you." He yanked the knife out and stuck it back in the sheath at his hip.

He turned to the blond man to his right and spoke in his native Romanian. "Roman, I am pretty sure the man we are looking for was not amongst those I...left at the stone house. Research the ID's you found, see if any of them could be a connection."

The long wavy top of Roman Saguna's blond hair flopped when he nodded. Eyes like narrow, dark blue crayons flit from Jack's green face to Zastrovna. "On it, Vij." He got up and left the table. His boots thumped across the planked floor until they disappeared.

"Lucian, you and Miles go see if you can find Warwick's arms link." Zastrovna stretched out his long legs and crossed his ankles.

A barmaid sauntered over with a beer for him. She set it down leaning way over so he could see more of what was already exposed with the top several buttons undone on the peasant blouse.

He barely glanced at her endowments before picking up the mug and taking several huge swallows.

When he ignored her, the barmaid turned with a "Humph," and pouted away.

"Vij, not criticizing bro, but you killed our main lead." Alex's lopsided grin took the sting out of the censure.

Zastrovna sucked down some more beer then set the mug on the table. He dragged the back of his hand across his mouth clearing any foam from it.

One huge shoulder rose and lowered negligently. "The sick pig's death was a long time coming. I only wished I had the time to make it long and drawn out and fucking excruciating," he drained his beer.

Jack sat quiet and glum. He didn't understand a word of Romanian and the men usually chose to speak in it.

Vijay said to a man across the table from him, "Gage."

The mountain of a man, shaved head, gold hoop earrings in both ears, tattoos etched up and down his dark arms, his neck and his face, nodded to Vijay.

"Go sit in front of my room. No one goes in, no one comes out."

The giant man nodded his enormous head in affirmation and got up and left without a word.

Vijay turned to Alex. "*Bine*, okay, Alex, you and me and," he eyes slit sideways at Jack, the only American of the team. It was difficult to say whether Vijay hated him just for that or because he was unrelentingly obnoxious.

Sighing, Vijay hated to have the man with him but he had his orders, the freak was a nephew or son or someshit of the man that hired him and the rest of his team. He was stuck with him.

"We will go back out and hit the village, ask around to see if we can get any Intel on the man we were sent to retrieve. Let's hit it." He pushed his big body up and his men followed him out the door.

Hours later, Vijay trudged up the stairs carrying a bag, pissed because none of what they'd done today had brought them any closer to fulfilling their mission.

As busy as he was, the girl had never been far from his thoughts. The sight of entering that stone house and seeing Kreis Warwick beating the woman, *aggh*, he shook his head. He needed to stay focused on the damned mission.

Rounding the corner, he saw Gage Valenti sitting on the floor, leaning his massive back against the door. The cordons of giant muscles roped across his back and down his arms. He looked very relaxed, but Vijay knew better. Gage was as fast and as lethal as they come. He was never relaxed.

"G, any trouble?"

The big man grunted getting to his feet. He shook his shaved head, stretched his neck and rubbed it. "*Nu, mea frate*, no, my brother," he motioned his dark head to the door. "Not a sound from inside."

"Hmm," a corner of Vijay's mouth ticked. "The window is too high off the ground for her to climb out, a good thing because I do not think the sheets in this place are strong enough to tie together."

"Ah, *mea frate*, she is but a slip, a slender child, perhaps the sheets would hold her?" The most quiet and oldest of the team at 34, Gage smiled at him.

Vijay's eyes shifted towards the door. "She is slight, but she is not a child, G."

Alex trod down the hall to them. "Hey, Vij, how is she?"

A hand in his pocket, Vijay just lifted a shoulder but said nothing.

"I tell ya, *frate*, those fucking blue-green eyes," Alex whistled, "like crystal sea glass, luminous even in her…distress."

Vijay and Gage both frowned at him.

Neither intimidated him. He went on, "It is unnatural for a person to have such beautiful, unique, richly colored eyes like hers. Kreis Warwick would have wanted to fuck her just seeing those stunning eyes, the plush lips, and the light blonde hair long before he'd checked out her stacked body. Slight she is, but her curves are undeniably spectacular." He grinned broadly at both men.

"Shit, Alex, shut the fuck up." Vijay growled. "No one talks to or gets near the *femelă*. I am taking her straight to Mann."

Ignoring his threats, Alex asked, "You find out what Warwick wanted from her?"

Vijay shook his head. "*Nu*. She was as closed-mouthed with me as she was with that *gretos pula*, disgusting prick. I am sure it has something to do with our quest since we tracked the info so far to Warwick, and tis a bit of a coincidence he is trying to beat and starve some kind of important information out of her."

A brow arched over a green eye, Alex said slyly with a needling poke, "Great job with improving your English, by the way. You gonna try any of Warwick's methods to make her talk?"

"Fuck off, Alex."

It didn't break Alex's grin. "What's in the bag, sex toys?"

Vijay's eyes narrowed so far barely any blue was visible.

Alex grinned bigger.

His voice dark with warning, Vijay muttered, "You go too far, *frate*."

Alex taunted, "Hey, we haven't had a physical fight in years." He laughed. "You would kick it but I would put a hurting on you before you beat me to a pulp."

"*Basta*, enough." Vijay was stalling. He wasn't afraid of a slip of a girl, but- "Ah, see you Gage," he scowled at Alex, "And you, fool, in the AM." He unlocked the door and stepped inside.

It was almost pitch black, and cold. The fire had burned out. *Shit.* He will be bringing a curvaceous popsicle to his employer. Locking the door behind him, he could make out in the faint light from the window, her little body a lump under all the blankets he'd left her on one of the pallets.

Moving across the room to a lamp, he thought, shit, he could have at least left a light on for her and told Gage to check the fire and keep it stoked. Never having had to care for another person before, those things hadn't entered his mind until now. When he turned the lamp on, the lump stirred.

Dropping the bag on a table, Vijay went over to the fireplace, removed the screen, picked up a few logs in a bin and set them inside. Then he grabbed some more kindling from the copper bucket and lit the kindling with the matches. He placed the screen back in front of it. Hearing her move, Vijay looked over at her.

She was sitting up, rubbing her eyes, difficult with her wrists tied. The big blue-green eyes warily watched him.

He started towards her, but she shuffled on her butt to move away from him.

"I will not touch you, *fetita*, you must need to use the...uh," he glanced towards the small bathroom. He should have left the rope long enough for her to get into it.

The pink staining her cheeks indicated he was correct in her need. Moving closer, he came to stand in front of her. She backed away until her spine hit the wall.

Frowning, the brilliant blue eyes blazed from under his low ridged brow. "Get up," he ordered. Glancing down, he saw she'd drank a bottle of water and eaten less than half of the sandwich he'd left her. Her stomach must have shrunk terribly from her ordeal. Vijay hadn't even considered she might have internal injuries. Shit.

Using the wall to brace herself, Wyn struggled to climb to her feet. Vijay stuffed his hands in his pockets. He could have helped her up in two seconds and saved her the pain struggling to her feet was causing her, but she was obviously terrified of him so he stood back.

She leaned against the wall and waited.

He said implacably, "I am going to untie you. There will be towels and soap and other necessities in the *baie*."

At her confused look he said, "Bathroom." Then muttered, "I must remember my English." He stepped closer to her, reached out and grasped her tied hands.

She didn't move a muscle until the ropes were off, then she rubbed her wrists.

Vijay's eyes dropped to the red rings around them. He picked up the bag he'd brought in and handed it to her then gestured to the bathroom with his head, "Go, shower."

Instead of walking right past him, Wyn stepped back then to the side keeping a wide berth between them. Still feeling the effects of being knocked around by Kreis, it took her a long painful time to reach the bathroom.

While she was showering, Vijay stoked the fire. With nothing else to do, he went to the window, clasped his hands behind him and stared out. His lips pulled in, the window was actually low enough if she wasn't tied up she could get out it. But they were up two levels.

It was dusk, people wandered up and down the streets, in and out of bars and shops, although early spring, they were still bundled in winter coats. The water shut off. It was another few minutes before she came out.

Vijay turned when he heard the door open. She stood in the doorway as if afraid to go any further. He scanned the clothes he'd purchased for her. He'd bought a jacket, two pairs of jeans, one black, one blue, hiking boots to keep her feet warm, socks, a couple of blouses and a big shirt to sleep in.

His neck turned red remembering buying the lingerie. Not the scarlet red of the silk underwear and satin bra, but beet red. He had never bought women's clothing, much less female underwear in his life. But he had no choice.

44

They didn't know how long they'd be at their location and the woman couldn't parade around in those tiny shorts and thin sweater that clearly showed she did not have a bra on under it.

He'd seen the one she'd worn originally, it was lying cut up on Warwick's floor while he was over her hitting her and tearing off her clothes - *fuck*- Vijay spat the memory aside.

At the shop, he had to try to describe the woman's size and shape to the two giggling shop girls. He'd never been more mortified in his life. Never. Drop him in the middle of a raging war with only a knife and he'd feel more comfortable than he had at that store.

The girls chose the clothes, thank *Zue*. Besides the red lingerie he had also bought a black lace bra and panties, threw money at the hysterical girls and ran back to the inn.

Now, when he tried to look at the snug blue jeans that cupped her round little ass and the blouse that was lower cut than he would have liked, all he could do was wonder whether she was wearing the red silk, or the black lace. His pants were growing constrictive.

He coughed and turned from her and started for the door when he realized she was still standing in the doorway of the bathroom.

"What?" He scowled darkly, brows low.

The huge blue-green eyes stared bewildered at him, she stood like a statue.

His irritation thickened his accent and scoured his voice deeper, "Come on, *fetita*, what the hell is the matter with you, let us go."

She twined her fingers in front of her and asked in a small voice, "Where?"

His big hands set on his hips; he glared at her like she was dumb. "To eat. I am hungry, let's go."

She still stood as if she couldn't make her legs move.

Letting out an annoyed sigh, Vijay stomped over to her, the closer he got the whiter her face turned.

He reached out suddenly and snatched up her arm. He started to walk with her but she jerked her arm out of his grip.

"*Fetita*," he rasped, "what the hell is your problem?"

Wyn wrapped her arms protectively around her body and asked with a waver in her hoarse voice, "Are- you going to kill me now?"

Chapter Seven

His brows shot up, mouth firmed into a straight line. His gaze travelled the length of her from her light hair to the small boots and back up to settle on the quivering huge eyes.

"*Fetita*, I did not buy you clothes to take you out to murder you in them. Do not be stupid. I said we are going to dinner, that tis all. I am hungry." He eyed the uneaten sandwich. "Going by the little bit of shit you ate you must be hungry too."

Vijay was well aware many people were frightened of his appearance, he didn't give a shit. Even so, he was used to the tougher bolder women throwing themselves at him, not backing away from him in terror.

Big and heavily muscled, he'd been told that the scar over his eye only added to the menacing mystique that many women said increased his dangerous and sexy appeal.

His reputation as a bruiser, and a stone-cold killer followed him, but it did nothing to deter the brazen women. Except this one. Not that she was brazen, not even a hair. She was brave and daring but brazen she was not.

She didn't move. He snaked his hand out and grabbed one of the arms crossed over her chest and drew it down gently. Holding her loosely but still firm, his strength gently muscled her across the room to the door.

Opening it, he put his hand on her back and nudged her out. Stepping into the hallway, he held her arm again then saw that she still struggled to walk.

"Here, you hold onto me." He took her hand and tucked it under his arm. They moved slowly but made it down the thinly carpeted corridor. She pulled back when they reached the stairs.

Vijay figured she must be weak and in a lot of pain from Warwick's brutality and the lack of food.

He instructed, "Hold onto me, *fetita* and put your other hand on the railing. We will go slow. Unless you prefer I carry you?" He bent and started to slide his hands under her when she leaned away from him.

"No. I'm fine." She clutched his brawny forearm and also the railing.

It was slow moving, then her knees buckled and she started to fall, her arms flailed out with a little shriek-

Vijay threw his arm around her, catching and pulling her back against his chest. He could feel her frantic heart beating on his arm that held her secure.

"*Bine*, tis okay, you are all right, *fetita*." Her curvy bottom pressed against his thighs and her breasts propped over the arm that held her. His body had the natural reaction of having a soft woman pressed against it, his pants tightened.

Wyn turned her head to look back up the stairs.

"*Nu, fetita*, no, we are almost there, you do not need to go back to the room. Come, I will not let you fall."

She hesitated, took a deep breath then let him help her the rest of the way down the stairs. On the flat floor they moved more smoothly.

Vijay brought her to the raucous room with the benched seats and long tables. Crowded now, most of the occupants were drunk and loud and rowdy. Blowsy barmaids slipped between tables, men reached out to pinch every girl that scooted past with a giggle. Wolfish eyes instantly latched onto Wyn.

Vijay rolled his arm around her shoulder and held her close as he easily maneuvered through the raunchy room.

Then, a man stood up in front of him. "Hey," he said, leering at Wyn. Sticking his hand out to touch her, he asked, "She for sale? What's your price, bro?"

"*Nu*, not for sale. Get out of my face." Vijay tucked Wyn further under his arm and went to push past the drunk.

"Aw, c'mon mate," he slurred, reaching again for Wyn. "Share yer bitch, everyone else here does. Gimmie an hour wit her upstairs and I-"

Never slowing his step with Wyn tight to his side, Vijay slammed his fist into the man's gut. The man bent, gagged, and dropped to his knees.

When they reached the separate dining room, Alex with his rascally green eyes, and the giant Gage were standing in the doorway. As usual, Alex was grinning.

"What the hell are you grinning at, you loon?" Vijay growled, elbowing past them.

Alex's grin broadened. "We were checking to see if you were coming. We figured there might be trouble when those dogs got a sight of her. But as usual you handled it just fine on your own. Nice punch, *frate*, except you made her face turn green. I'm thinking violence is not her thing."

Reaching his arms out, Alex said, "Here, let me help," and grabbed Wyn right out from under Vijay's arm, and ignoring Vijay's glower, he ushered her into the room. Pulling a chair out he helped her sit at a large round table.

The other tables were half filled with patrons. Customers in this room were more low key. In the first room with the long renaissance-style benches and tables was where the heavy drinking rowdier people partied.

Vijay and his team needed to keep a low profile. The other men were there waiting, they all had large mugs of frothy beer in front of them. Alex settled himself next to Wyn, Jack was on her other side.

His face set in a harsh frown, Vijay glared at Jack and gave him a quick jerk of his head. Jack got up and with a grumble moved to another chair. Vijay sat in his vacated seat, disregarding Alex's stupid instigating grin.

Vijay said to Wyn, "I will introduce you to the team." He nodded with annoyance clear on his face at his flirtatious friend on the other side of her. "You know Alex," he quickly moved on at Alex's grin and wink at Wyn.

Vijay tipped his head to the barbarian appearing male with the dark skin, shaved head and gold hoops at Alex's left. "Next to Alex is Gage. Do not be afraid of his bald, black Hulk appearance. Although tough as volcanic rock inside and out, he would protect you with his life."

Gage nodded at Wyn, his face serious and unreadable.

"Next to Gage, tis Jack." Vijay had a hard time keeping the antagonism out of his voice. He glanced at the woman. She had nodded demurely at each of the men, but lowered her eyes when introduced to Jack.

Jack dragged his long narrow fingers through his shaggy brown mane and looked at her with round, dark brown eyes. His long chin rose slightly sullen and condescending. His nose still swollen from the punch Vijay had given him, Jack's thin lips thinned further with the glare he gave her.

Clearly uncomfortable with him at the table, the girl had been in and out of consciousness in the car but Vijay knew she was aware Jack had tried to grope her and Vijay had smashed his face in for it.

"Ah, next is Roman."

Roman smiled politely, the wavy blond hair long only on the top of his head flopped slightly when he briefly inclined his head to her in greeting. The sides of his head were shaved.

Vijay continued, "Then there is Miles. He is the youngest at 24." The young man at 6'2" was also the shortest of the group. He had straight light brown hair that hung over his dark brown eyes.

Miles loves women. All women, all the time. He gave Wyn a cunning smile and a wink. "Welcome, honey. Let me know any time anything I can do for you."

Vijay frowned at him and grunted. "*Yah*, moving on. Last is Lucian."

Most of the men wore pullover sweaters like Vijay's dark blue, or long-sleeved thermals.

Lucian most often wore black turtlenecks and black jeans like he had on tonight. He smoothed back a side of his sleek black hair and with a palm and smiled. "Hi sweet. You need anything, forget Miles, you ask me."

Wyn didn't know how she was to respond to any of the men so she just smiled politely at each of them.

Other than Jack and Vijay, they were polite and friendly, yet they'd kidnapped her and were, from what she could determine, hard-core mercenaries.

And, at the least, the behemoth was a cold-blooded killer. A vicious executioner. She'd seen the evidence with her own eyes. He had killed a group of vicious thugs swiftly, ruthlessly, totally without hesitation or mercy.

"So, what's your name, honey?" Alex asked her with his flirty grin.

Her response was to lower her eyes to stare silently at the table.

The men all shared a look. She was obviously trying to preserve her safety by giving them no information about her.

The barmaid came over with more beer. When she finished setting the beers down, she sashayed right back to Vijay. "Ah, my big man, I wondered what was keeping you."

She hung over his shoulders, resting her quite exposed humongous breasts like melons, on his shoulder and in his face. Flinging her arms around him, she bent to try to kiss him but he pushed her away with a grunt of a Romanian curse.

"Cut it out, Elana. I am in no mood for your shit," he groused roughly, picking up a beer. His mouth on the rim he said, "Bring the *fetita* a soda. I think everyone wants the house special."

Hearing a round of agreements, Alex leaned his head and said quietly in Wyn's ear, "The special is schnitzel with cheesy scalloped potatoes and corn, it's really good."

The barmaid finally looked at Wyn. Her wide lips, thickly layered with shiny, geranium red lipstick, curled in a sneer at Wyn. She looked her over with a sniff as if Wyn didn't add up to much.

Pawing her golden braid, the barmaid simpered, "Sure, Vij honey, a soda for the little girl. I'll be right back, handsome." She nipped his ear and took off before he could swat her away.

Through grit teeth Wyn said so only Vijay could hear, "Stop calling me 'little girl.'"

With his elbows on the table, arms up and his hands clasped together, behind his hands the corners of his mouth edged up.

Cocking his head to her, he whispered, "I do not know your name. If you recall, I gave you the opportunity to prove to me that you were a woman and not a child. And, if I recall correctly, you declined. The offer is always open. Would you prefer I call you *dragă*?"

His *d* was heavy and he slightly rolled the *r*, totally sounded to Wyn that the very Dracula himself was seated next to her. Except the behemoth's harsh face was tanned and rugged. He was insanely muscular, and seeing him kill Warwick and Brennan without hesitation or effort, he scared Wyn to death. Still, she shot him a frown.

Primly folding her hands on the table, she asked indignantly, "Are you calling me a dirty name?"

Lowering his arms so his hands were on the table, he leaned closer to her until their arms were touching. A rare crooked grin softened his hard features as he replied, "Ah, *nu, mea fetita*, no my little girl," his tone held a slight mock, "it means 'sweetheart.'"

Wyn took her arms off the table and crossed them. She said nothing.

He observed her under hooded lids with a satirical smile. "Well? What do you want me to call you? I can come up with some more names-"

"No!" Wyn snapped at him, her face flaming.

Vijay

Clearly enjoying teasing her, Vijay lifted a curl off her shoulder and watched it twine around his hand. "Tell me, *mea* little blushing *dragă,* what do you want me to call-"

"Nothing!" she snapped. Snatching the lock out of his hand she twisted away from him.

"Whoa," he teased, dipping his head closer to her so only she could hear him. "That tis a lot of fire from a sick, scrawny little girl."

She turned to him with her mouth open, sputtered, "You-you-" Obviously not knowing what to say, she sniffed, crossed her arms and turned from him again with a, "Humph."

On the other side of Wyn, Alex nudged Gage next to him with a smirk and whispered, "I've known Vij a long fucking time, and I don't ever recall seeing him...playful, teasing."

Gage snickered with a straight face. "And the pretty lady ain't liking it. Which seems to amuse him even more." The two men chuckled.

Alex said back, "Maybe it's because he hasn't spent much time with dainty little ladies like her. A lifelong warrior, he hasn't a clue what to do with her."

The barmaid came up behind Wyn with her soda. Seeing Vijay so involved with the small woman, her face a resentful mask, she lifted the soda like she was going to throw it at Wyn-

Vijay's hand shot up and grasped her wrist; he squeezed it until she yelped. It was done behind and over Wyn's head, she didn't see it.

The look on his face has frightened tough men in combat, prisons and biker gangs, and worse, he growled, "Cease," and glared at Elana until her skin whitened and her mouth pursed. He released her.

She set the glass down with a shaky hand and fled.

He turned back to the girl, but Lucian was talking to her. Vijay's lips pulled in, his face an inscrutable mask as he watched the handsome young man with neatly cut, sleek black hair, his big dark eyes glowing all over their prisoner as he regaled some foolishness to her.

Lucian was one of the best snipers Vijay had ever come across, and also, like Alex, part of his team and a good friend.

The servers brought dinner. Conversation continued even as the men shoveled the delicious food in and washed it down with more beer.

Vijay seldom spoke but he kept looking over at Wyn's plate. "You are not eating, *mici se*, you will not gain your strength back."

Setting his arm around the back of her chair, Alex leaned towards Wyn and said, "Now he called you 'small one.'" With a provoking grin at his friend, he inquired, "Are you trying to keep reminding her of how much bigger you are than her? Keep her afraid of you?"

Vijay's cross growl only increased Alex's mirth. Alex leaned over further to get in Wyn's face. Chuckling, he told her, "Don't worry, *mici se*, I will protect you from him."

An aggravated sound a deep rumble in his chest, Vijay muttered, "Fuck off Alex."

"Sure, Vij," Alex said with a chuckle and dug into his schnitzel.

When the men had eaten to their satisfaction, Vijay, Gage and Miles lit European cigarettes.

After a few minutes, Lucian stood up and came to stand near Wyn. "As much as I would like to stay and visit some more with our little prisoner," he smiled at her, "it is quite clear our leader is not going to allow us to have any more conversation with you. So, we're heading out to hit a few bars. Later, sweet." He caught up her hand and kissed the back of it ignoring the irritated grumble coming from Vijay.

Although it was past midnight, Roman and Miles both said goodnight and followed Lucian out. Jack left with them without a word to anyone.

Alex stood up and stretched. "So, Vij, you need any help with our guest? I am primed and ready to-"

"*Nu,*" Vijay said bluntly. Standing up, he pulled Wyn's chair out. "We are going to bed."

Vijay

At Alex's arched brows and Wyn's red cheeks, Vijay coughed and said, "Uh, to sleep." He added more tersely, "Tis late. Tis time for sleep." He wound his strong fingers around Wyn's arm and helped her stand up.

With Alex and Gage's snickers at his back, Vijay led Wyn out of the room, and through the other rowdy room. He glowered at every man that even looked at her.

The pair moved slowly but when they got to the stairs, Wyn stopped and looked up. She swallowed hard, took a deep breath and lifted her foot on the first step. "Oh!" the pained gasp came from putting pressure on her bruised leg.

Vijay bent and swept her up in his arms. Ignoring her squawks that she could do it on her own, he easily carried her up the stairs and to their room.

He set her down outside the door and unlocked it. Opening it, he motioned for her to go in, and closed and locked the door behind them.

Inside, Wyn stood awkwardly, twisting her fingers unsure of what the monster was going to do next.

Vijay went to the fire and stoked it then added some more logs. Without looking at her he said, "Do you want to uh, go clean up?"

Wyn hesitated, then started for the bathroom.

He said, "Wait," then went and retrieved the nightshirt he'd gotten her and gave it to her. She said nothing and went into the bathroom.

When she was done, wearing the nightshirt that went almost to her knees, and clutching her clothes, still with her boots on, she timidly opened the door and peered out.

He was standing as he had been earlier, staring out the window. He was so big he blocked most of the glass. At the door opening, he turned around and pointed at the pallet she had been on before.

All the lightness from earlier was gone. Still without looking at her, his voice gruff he said coldly, "Lay down."

Skirting him nervously, Wyn went to the pallet and sat down.

He commanded in a brusque tone, "I said lay down. Take off your shoes and lay down."

His gruff tone sounding so tough, Wyn obeyed. Removing her shoes, she laid down on the pallet on her back, her hair spread over the floor.

Vijay knelt and leaned over her. "Hold out your hands." He waited while she slowly complied then he tied her wrists together.

He didn't look at her, but Wyn stared at him while he bound her hands. He was so close his hair fell over his shoulders and almost brushed against her face.

She could feel the heat emanating from his solid body, smell his manly scent, not unpleasant, just masculine with a hint of beer and waft of cigarette smoke.

Normally it would annoy her, but, she inhaled, he smelled so male, so virile. His close bulkiness to her made her apprehensive. He was so big, if he felt like it he could crush her like an ant. Her body quivered from the daunting thought.

He looked up at her from under his low brow. "Are you cold?"

Those intense vivid eyes inches from hers, flicked from her eyes to her lips where they paused before rising back up. He was so close she could see his pupils flare. She shook her head, afraid her voice would come out wobbly.

"You sure?" He still sounded formidable but not as harsh as a moment ago. He took her hands in his large ones and felt them, pressing and rubbing her fingers. "Your hands are cold."

Tugging her hands from his, she murmured, "I'm fine.

He scrutinized her for a moment. Lying on her back gazing up at him, her wrists tied together, she bent her elbows to cover her chest. She looked so young, so vulnerable, and frail.

Vijay stood up and went to the closet, took out two more blankets, brought them over and laid them on top of her. Then he took the end of the rope and tied it over the beam as before then he went into the bathroom.

Vijay

When he came out, his long hair was wet. Wearing a t-shirt and boxers, he carried his boots in his hand. He dropped the boots and his clothes on a chair and trod over to the pallet next to Wyn.

He reached up and untied the rope from the beam, then bent and pulled the pallet and arranged it so Wyn was against the corner of the room and he was in front of her.

She would have to climb over him to get out. When he knelt on his pallet, Wyn sat up. Her skin paled as she watched him tie the rope around one of his wrists. It was bad enough to be lying beside the behemoth, and now she was bound to him.

"I said, lay down," he glared at her. Seeing the blue-green eyes teeming with unshed tears, he looked away. She positioned herself on her side facing him. Vijay settled with his back to her.

He muttered, "If you need to use the *baie*, wake me to take you." A second passed, he said, "Bathroom."

Her voice tiny and still raw, she said, "I don't understand why you are keeping me prisoner. Can you please let me go? I won't tell anyone w- what happened."

Silence.

"Please?" When he didn't respond, she sighed sadly, bunched into a ball, and set her face on her hands.

He laid there for a long time listening to her sniffle and the blankets rustling when she wiped at her eyes. He knew when she fell asleep, the sniffing stopped and she unconsciously curled up against his back for his body warmth.

At that point, he untied her wrists leaving the rope only around one hand tied to his.

She was not aware she clung to him in her sleep, or that his dick was hard as an iron club. Her tits wedged on his back, legs curved under his, her small hand draped over his waist.

Although it took him hours to fall asleep, he never moved from her or pushed her away.

Things went along more or less the same for the next few days.

Up and gone before she woke, Vijay left food and water for Wyn, he didn't tie her as Gage stayed guard outside the door. If he was in the area around noontime he would take her to the dining room with the group for lunch.

At one lunch, after seeing Wyn get angry and frustrated at Vijay's continuing to call her *fetita*, meaning little girl, Alex cajoled her into finally telling them her name.

"Come on, honey, you can't expect us to keep calling you different things. Spill it. At least tell us your first name." He hit her with one of his meg-watt smiles, all bright white teeth and sparkling green eyes.

The other men waited and watched her, Vijay stared off into space as if not listening.

Her lashes fluttering nervously, Wyn scooped her long hair up with both hands and pushed the light curls off her shoulders. For her safety, she hadn't wanted these men to know anything about her.

"Um," encouraged by Alex's smile, she gave in. "My, uh, name is Wynna. My family calls me Wyn."

"Well then, Wyn," Alex grinned, leaning over he patted her hand, "that is a really pretty name. But of course a beautiful girl like you would have a-"

"*Da, yah*, we need to head out, *frates*." Vijay stood up and nodded to Gage.

The giant got up and went to stand by Wyn.

Alex scowled at his friend. "Geez, Vij, what the hell, we were just getting to know-"

"Go upstairs," Vijay gruffly ordered Wyn, ignoring Alex's scowl and Wyn's humiliated expression at being ordered around like a child.

She got to her feet and went with Gage, and the rest of the team left to continue working their mission.

Chapter Eight

*G*age had gone around and gotten a few books for Wyn to while away the lonely time.

The men usually returned late in the evening. They all ate a late dinner together, sometimes some of the men would go out after, some would hang around the bar section of the hotel drinking.

During those times, instead of leaving her upstairs alone in the room, Vijay would keep Wyn with them while they chatted and drank.

Wyn still hardly spoke, she was so unsure of the men. She didn't know them, who they worked for, whether they were truly lawless, or not.

Alex had told her with his usual grin, "We're the men you call when the SEALs and the Special Opts fail."

A week passed, most of the men were hanging around the bar after dinner, drinking and laughing. Wyn was sitting on a chair placed between Vijay and Alex.

Vijay was relaxed in a cushioned chair sipping a beer and smoking a European cigarette. He set his bottle down to put his cigarette out when Elana the barmaid bustled in the room. Her golden blonde hair was loose, it puffed out around her head and over her shoulders.

Spotting Vijay, the very full figured woman hurried over and climbed in his lap straddling him. She wasn't exactly overweight, but her curves were huge and she loved throwing them around. Elana sought the attention of men and reveled in it.

"Vijay, you ignore me," she whined, pushing her sharp nails through his straight black hair combing her fingers down through the long locks.

Vijay grabbed her wrists throwing them off him. "Elana, I told you-" before he could say another word, most of her blouse was already unbuttoned when she'd entered the room, she was not wearing a bra. She unbuttoned the last few and pulled her blouse half way down her arms exposing her gigantic breasts.

She squirmed up Vijay's lap getting as close to him as she could, then grabbed his hands and plopped them on her naked breasts.

"Ahh," she sighed gloriously. "I've been waiting forever for you to put those big hard hands on my tits. Grind them baby, suck them," all at the same time she put her hands around his head and pulled his face into her cleavage.

A coarse groan deep in her throat, Elana told him, "You need a larger, stronger, more mature woman to satisfy your lusty needs, Vijay Zastrovna, not that skinny delicate child. She can't take a big man's rough girth like yours like I can!"

Her face flaming, Wyn jumped to her feet and hurried out of the room. Alex was right on her heels. Gage had gone to get another drink.

Alex followed Wyn to the stairs. "Wyn, honey, where're you going?"

She still had some trouble walking; it was a strain to go up the steps. Alex jogged up beside her and put his arm around her waist to help her. He asked, "What's going on?"

"Nothing, I- I, don't know what to do. Unless he goes to her room he may want to bring her to- to our room, and uh, I shouldn't be there. He needs his- his privacy. I'm not sure where I should go."

Wyn tried to move faster. The image of Vijay with his big hands fondling the barmaid's big breasts, his face in them, probably kissing them right now- it creeped her out, spurred her to go more quickly.

"Come, on," Alex said at the top of the stairs. "Come to my room. We'll do what you and Vij normally do. He ties you to him, right?" As his closest friend, Vijay told Alex what he did to secure her at night.

"Uh, yes, okay. I guess that would be the best thing to do." Wyn allowed Alex to lead her to his room.

Downstairs, Vijay put his hands on Elana's shoulders and shoved her so hard she fell off his lap and banged onto the floor. Sitting there gawking up at him, legs spread under her full orange skirt, naked breasts bouncing, she squawked, "Vijay!"

He dragged his fingers through his dark hair, and wiped his mouth on his sleeve. He could taste her perfume from having his face shoved in her tits. "Goddammit Elana, I have told you countless times before I am not interested." He wiped his mouth again scowling blackly at her.

"Now," he glanced around, his brows slashed down. Jumping to his feet, his head whipped back and forth looking around the room for Wyn. Seeing Gage approaching with a fresh drink in his hand, he barked at the giant man, "Where the fuck is the girl?"

"Huh?" Gage's shaved head swiveled, then he did a complete circle scanning the room, he shrugged, "I, uh, don't know."

Roman was sitting in a cozy chair sipping a bourbon. He informed them, "When you got all hot and nasty with that *stricata*, whore," he nodded at Elana who was still sitting on the floor at Vijay's feet, "your prisoner got all embarrassed and she took off."

"*What*?" Vijay bellowed. He swung around looking all over the area. His eyes went to the door at the front entrance, what if she'd run outside? It would be a bitch to find her, and the temperature was below freezing tonight. She had no jacket, and the fucking rural town was filled with dangerous men, *dammit*, "Which way did she go?"

Calmly, Roman answered, "Not to worry, *mea frate*, Alex is with her. I saw them head for the stair-"

Vijay was already striding to the staircase.

Taking the stairs two at a time, at the top he checked his room first. Finding it empty, he moved quickly down the hall to Alex's room. His face burned hot with rage, and he was growing angrier with every step.

When he got to the room, he didn't knock, just flung the door open, took one look inside and yelled, "What the fuck is going on?"

Alex and Wyn were over by the pallets, and Alex was tying Wyn's wrists together.

They both looked up.

Seeing Vijay's face dark with fury, blue eyes sparking wrath under his hard brow, his shoulders hunched like a gorilla and his fists clenched ready to start swinging, Alex grinned, and Wyn started shaking.

"Hey *frate*, we were just getting ready for bed." Alex's grin spread wider. He'd left the door unlocked knowing Vijay would come. They surely did not want to have to pay to have the door repaired.

Vijay's eyes about disappeared under his thunderous brow. His shoulders already huge pumped up bigger with his fury, the biceps bulged under his sweater. Through clenched teeth, his voice chilled, he ground out, "Is that right?"

"*Da*." Alex smiled as Wyn was slowly moving behind him, using him as a shield against Vijay. "Wynnie here was concerned that you and Elana would want your privacy when you brought her back to your room to…" his brows wiggled up and down.

At Vijay's thunderous expression, Alex said helpfully, "So, of course, out of the kindness of my heart, knowing you tie her to you when you sleep, I offered to do the same for her whilst you…you know, got it on with Elana down the hall."

Vijay's glare went from Alex to Wyn who was peeping out from behind Alex's broad back, and back to Alex. "The fuck you say," he took a step towards the couple. Wyn's face disappeared.

Vijay

He stomped over to them and grabbed Wyn's arm yanking her out from behind Alex. Fiercely, he ripped at the rope tied around her wrists, pulled it off and threw it at Alex.

With a threatening glare at Alex, who grinned back, Vijay wound his fingers around Wyn's arm and pulled her out of the room slamming the door behind them.

His long legs striding quickly with his boiling anger, he dragged her down the hall.

"You're- you're hurting me, please *bala,*" Wyn pried at his fingers scarcely able to keep up with him.

He stopped suddenly and swung her around. Breathing like a bull pawing the ground about to attack, the black hair flung over part of his face, he barked at her, "Do not fucking call me a beast."

Swinging around so hard, Wyn's hair flew draping over one eye. Tossing her head to cast her hair off her shoulders, she cringed from the fury radiating in the blazing blue eyes.

Her one shoulder raised, she kept the arm he held rigid while she pulled at only one of his huge fingers trying to open it but his grip was like an iron band. "You're- mad. I don't know what I did wrong, why are you so angry with me?"

He pushed her up against the wall and held both her upper arms. Her eyes popped with shock.

Guttural with rough anger, he barked, "You left my side. You know damn fucking well you are not allowed to be out of my sight. I looked up and you were gone. I find you upstairs about to fuck with Alex."

He was so angry his voice shook. His accent drew out, thickening his words, making him hard to understand.

But Wyn got what he said. Appalled, she snapped, "How dare you!"

"It was pretty clear what I saw when I went in that room. You were going to fuck. Like a *stricata,* a whore." He let go of her arms and put his hands beside her on the wall fencing her in, then leaned in until his angry chest was heaving against hers.

Now she was mad. Wyn repeated, "How dare you- you- you-*bala*!" and she slapped him, stunning herself at her suicidal audacity.

Wyn expected him to knock her flat, she waited, but he just glared at her. Her hand strummed with pain from the contact on his face, but he hadn't even blinked at the slap.

His temper smoking, the words ground out of his chiseled mouth, "I said do not call me a beast. You were clearly going to fuck with Alex."

Seeing her eyes flare with indignation, he said, "Do not slap me again. I let you have that first one so you would know how futile, and how painful it would be for you to try to fight me. I will stop you before you do it again as you will only hurt yourself, not me." He glanced down pointedly at her stinging palm.

Still holding her pained hand, Wyn gathered her pride and pique. She declared, "You have no right to call me a- a whore. Besides, if I wanted to…have uh, sex with Alex, what is that to you? It's none of your business."

The arms on either side of her stiffened, dark color filled his face as his eyes narrowed at her. "Do you want to have sex with him?"

She rolled her eyes. "Oh for the love of-" her lips pursed. "It doesn't make any difference, you don't own me, you can't tell me what to do. You can't hold me captive, against my will."

The side of his mouth rose drolly. "Apparently I can." His lip twitched at her scowl.

"It tis my business what you do. As my prisoner I am responsible for you." He moved slightly, just barely touching his chest to hers again. He could see she was so irate now she wasn't aware of their contact.

Her small elegant nose stuck up in the air, she stated, "You are not responsible for me. Even if you were, but you are not, Alex was only securing me like you would have done."

He almost smiled at her refusal to give her control to him. Then shaking his head, his hands still flat on the wall beside her, he muttered, "Whatever. You did not answer my question. I asked you if you want to have sex with Alex."

When she didn't respond, he pressed his chest more firmly against hers and demanded, "Answer me."

Slapping her hands on her hips, she replied mutinously, "I don't have to."

A dangerous light glittered in his eyes, they swept down her then back up. His voice dropped low and quiet, he said mildly but the threat was inherent in his dark tone, "You do not think so?"

Lowering her head, her lips parted in uneasiness. He appeared the epitome of a mercenary, murderous biker. Her lids fluttered low over her eyes trying to hide her fear of him.

"I am waiting, *fetita*." He looked down at the top of her head.

His big body overwhelmed her, closing her in with his presence. She glanced up at the angular cheeks, his strong jaw, the blue eyes gleaming at her from lowered lids.

Swallowing her nerves, she straightened her spine and informed him, "I don't have to tell you anything, mister. But think about it, you massacred men while kidnapping me from other murdering kidnappers. I have been, and still am being held against my will. I've been beaten and assaulted, starved and tied up, you think I would want to be…intimate with any of you?"

Frustrated with her avoiding giving him a direct answer of yes or no, his lips compressed in a frown, his eyes bored into hers. He saw that she finally became aware that his chest was lightly pressing against her breasts.

She blushed so easily it almost made him grin. She pretended she didn't notice it, but she put her forearms up to try to subtly push him away.

"Anyway," he said, ignoring her ineffective efforts to push him back, "if it wasn't to have sex with Alex why were you in his room with him?"

Her head lowered, he stared at the top of her blonde hair, she raised it to glare at him. "Alex told you, gee you're thick-headed, you were going to be with that barmaid. I wanted to be out of your way."

"I was not-"

She cut him off, face red and scrunched up, she said furiously, "You- you were groping that woman. You had your hands, your face, your mouth on her- her- naked bosom, and it was obvious you were going to- to, uh, make love with her."

Wyn's face blushed pinker. "And, I felt you would want to be alone with her. I didn't want to be in the same room if you were- were-"

Not moving, his eyes flowed from her pink lips to her pinker cheeks to her vexed eyes. "Ah, you think I am such a disgusting pig I would bring a woman back to our room and fuck her with you there? Or, maybe you thought I would insist on you joining us?"

Not responding to that, her eyes dropped mortified at what he'd said. Her voice tightened as she changed the subject, "You have not told me that I could not leave your side. I don't even know why you are keeping me prisoner. But I did not want a big mean *beast* like you mad at me, so I did what I thought you would want me to. To be secured to one of your men. Alex offered it and I thought that it would be best to go with him."

Snorting a cut laugh, Vijay said with heavy sarcasm, "Of course he did." He looked down between them. He could see her nipples hardening against his chest. She squirmed.

With a rough edge to his deep voice, he said, "This is a hideously dangerous place, that tis why I do not want you out of my sight."

Then, he leaned back and sighed out some of his angry heat. "Wynna, I was not going to fuck- uh, do anything with Elana. You saw she threw herself at me. She does it all the time."

Wyn studied his hard face. "But, why wouldn't you, I mean if it's offered, I understand men do not turn down free...uh...sex."

His eyes drifted down to her lips then back up to her eyes. The corner of his full yet harsh mouth turned up in a slight smile. "Ah, you understand wrong, *fetita*. I am not every man, and I do not have sex with every woman who throws herself at me. The *stricata* Elana disgusts me. I have to fight her off, and a few others

Vijay

just as bold, every time I come here." Now he watched her expression.

"I don't, I'm not sure I understand any of this. It's," she sighed and rubbed her head. "I am not used to this..." She squinted with slight disbelief. "Why don't you want to...you know... with Elana? She's pretty and like she said, she's a big woman and can handle, uh, you." Her cheeks brightened with fresh color as she kept on, "And of course she has, you know, an extremely large chest. All men like a-"

"*Fetita*, stop lumping me in with all men. I do not find Elana attractive even for a free quick fuck, she is," he leaned his chest into hers again, pressing against her breasts. Bending his elbows to bring his face closer to hers, big arms fencing her in, his eyes dropped to her lips and his lids lowered over his blues like they were too heavy to keep up.

Wyn put her palms on his chest. He was so buff his chest made her dainty hands look all that more small and feminine.

His gaze fell to her hands, then up to her eyes then back to her lips, he lowered his head closer to her.

"She's, uh, what?" Wyn asked, her voice still raspy from her ordeal, it ebbed out husky, breathy.

His mouth hovered over hers, his voice low and hushed, he murmured, "Who?" and moved closer- there were footsteps coming up the stairs. Vijay swallowed a curse and stepped away from Wyn.

"Come on," he muttered, "we need to go to bed. Sleep. You know."

He took her hand and brought her to their room. After completing their bathroom business they changed their clothes.

Once on their pallets, Vijay tied her wrists then tied her to him and then they laid still, each with their own thoughts.

Chapter Nine

Vijay woke before dawn. Wynna would never be aware he'd held her in the middle of the night, softly talking her through another one of her frequent nightmares about the brutality Warwick had wrought on her.

She never fully wakes from the harrowing nightmares. When she calms, he releases her and turns facing away from her and goes back to sleep. But now, as usual, Wyn was curled up against him, her arm over his waist.

He thought to turn her and pull her into his chest to keep her warm, but then, he already had wood just from her body pressed against his back. He rolled over and carefully moved away from her and watched her sleep.

At least she had stopped crying herself to sleep. He didn't know how much more of that he could have taken. He decided he could not let her go until he learned her secret. The secret that kept her in such dire peril. She would not be safe alone out in the world.

Dangerous men were after her and they would undoubtedly not stop until they captured her again. Warwick was dead, but assuredly whoever hired him would only send more thugs after her. His eyes warmed as he gazed down at her.

Wyn's round cheeks were starting to become a more healthy rosy color now that she was eating a little better. The majority of the cuts and bruises from Warwick's strikes had disappeared, a few bruises still lurked here and there but on the whole she was much improved. He'd known she was beautiful the moment he'd seen her bound to Warwick's chair even with all the bruising and swelling. But now, as she healed, the woman was cock-thumping breathtaking.

She was curled facing him, her head lay cradled on one curved hand on the pillow. The long ringlets draped over part of her body and along her back on the pallet.

Vijay reached over and gently untied the rope from her wrist. She rolled onto her back but didn't awaken.

With the rising sun and the fire, the room was actually warm; she pushed off part of her blankets in her sleep. Her chest rose and lowered with her peaceful breaths.

Vijay's gaze followed her rising chest. She was wearing the white nightshirt. His own breath hitched and his pupils magnified. Her breasts rounded against the shirt, her areoles were faintly visible through the thin shirt.

His eyes dropped to the hem of the shirt that normally went almost to her knees but now was bunched up around the tops of her thighs. Her bare legs slightly curled on the pallet had pushed the shirt up higher and the blanket lower.

Vijay blinked and quickly turned away. He rolled and got to his feet.

After a quick shower, he dressed, shot one quick glance at her still sound asleep, and slipped out the door.

He went to find Gage to guard her door and bring her food then remembered Gage had gone out late last night with Roman and Lucian on a meet and was still gone, and he needed Alex with him today. Shit.

There were places they needed to go, and his choices to keep guard over Wyn were only Miles and Jack. It sure the fuck wasn't going to be Jack. He'd be in the room and on top of her before Vijay was out of the inn. He took off to find Miles.

Not happy about leaving Miles to guard the girl, the least experienced one of the team, Vijay was brusque with his instructions to him.

"You do not leave the door. You have the maids bring food for the *femelă* and have one of them with you when you bring the food to her, otherwise, no one goes in, no one comes out. You need to piss you wait until the maid is in the room and use that bathroom. You are not to be alone in the room with the *femelă*. Is that clear?" He glared down at the shorter man.

"Geesh, *frate*, I'm not going to jump the *scorpie*, bitch, for cripes sake." Looking at Vijay through his long bangs, a short smile tugging up his mouth, Miles said, "Of course, she is one hot-oomph-"

Vijay grabbed a fistful of Miles' shirt and shoved him hard up against the wall. "Let me reiterate," his voice dropped several octaves, "you do not leave the door, you are not to be in the room with her alone. I hear differently and you and I will go talk about it out back when I return, and only one of us will be walking back in on two feet. Now, is that fucking clear?"

Under the fringe of bangs, Miles' eyebrows shot up to his hairline. His eyes went from the fist clutching his shirt to Vijay's fierce blue ire. He tried to nod but Vijay held his shirt and his fist right up against his throat, he choked, "*Da*, yeah, yeah, gotcha, all right, no prob. I hear ya, Boss."

Vijay glared at him for another few seconds before letting him go. He stepped back while Miles adjusted his shirt. He continued curtly, "You do not do anything with any women. You are on orders on a duty, when on a duty you do not involve yourself with women. They distract. Clear?"

Nodding vigorously, rubbing his throat, Miles grunted, "*Da, da*, got you."

One last glare, then Vijay turned from Miles and stalked out the door.

Vijay was heading back to the inn. It had taken him hours to meet with people who claimed to have valuable information for him. The word was spreading on the street that there was something going on in the small village. Something big, something maybe to do with the elections.

Vijay

Vijay only knew he was to find a certain person and bring him to his employer. Unfortunately, he wasn't given a name to track. Leaks and anonymous tips made their way through informants up the chain then were disseminated to Vijay.

Obviously the same info was being filtered in other directions hence Kreis Warwick.

Vijay and his men had to check out each and every lead. It was laborious, tedious and time consuming. He decided when he got back he would try again with Wynna to see if she had any connection at all to this whole thing.

He glanced at the gas meter as he parked the car and frowned. It was less than half full. Never knowing what was going to happen next, he liked to keep a full tank. Vijay decided to go talk with Wyn then come back out and go fill up the tank.

As soon as he stepped inside the hotel the hair on the back of his neck stood up. Glancing around he saw the main room at this hour was relatively deserted.

His long legs made quick work through the room of extended tables and benches, his boots tapping across the wood planks as he went right for the stairs.

Taking them two at a time, he hit the hall and hurried around the corner, his stomach plummeted.

Miles was lying on the floor to the side of Vijay's room, there was blood near his head on the floor and *fuck* the door was wide open.

He ran to Miles, looked down, saw he was breathing then he rushed into his room. As expected, it was empty. He checked the bath then rushed back out and crouched beside Miles.

The young man had a hand to the back of his head and he was moaning.

"Miles," Vijay said, and helped him sit up. "Miles, where is she- what the hell happened?"

His face twisted in pain, Miles peered up and when he saw Vijay his face paled.

Vijay grabbed his shirt collar and lightly shook him. He shouted, "Miles, what the fuck, where is she, answer me!"

71

"Uh," Miles swiped his hands down the front of his face but he couldn't hide the guilt. "Uh, the barmaid, the new one, Suzette, she- she, I'm not sure. We were just kissing a little and stuff, I mean she was letting me feel her up right there in the damned hall, and then-"

Shaking him hard, Vijay thundered, *"Where the hell is the girl?"*

Miles coughed and then spat out, "They- they took her. While me and Suzette were, uh, I got hit on the back of the head, and when I came too, the door was open, and, uh, Wynna was uh…"

"How long?" Vijay snapped, standing up.

"Not long, a few minutes. I heard them taking her down the back stairs to the back yard. I'm sorry Vij-"

Vijay ran down the stairs, tore through the hotel and bar and raced to the back door. Flinging the door open, he paused in case of an ambush.

Then he saw in the back lot, five, maybe six men were taking Wyn to a car. He could see her thin arms wailing at anything she could hit.

A man stepped out from the side of the building just as Vijay moved out the door. Expecting it, Vijay stabbed his knife in his gullet, yanked it out and ran to where Wyn was being taken.

The other men didn't see him coming until he was almost upon them.

No one wanted gunshots to bring attention, Vijay launched himself into the air at the two men holding Wyn knocking them both down.

Vijay kicked one of the men in the head knocking him out cold and stomped on his head sideways instantly killing him. Before the other could get up, Vijay stuck his knife in his chest, had to leave it there as he turned a third man.

Dodging a hard swing, Vijay slammed his fist into the man's stomach. With a hack, the man bent over and Vijay grabbed his head and broke his neck.

A fourth man roared and leapt at Vijay- the two men hit the ground and rolled with fists flying. Vijay quickly got the advantage. Scrambling on top of the man, he pounded his fist punch after punch until the man no longer had a face and wasn't moving, wasn't breathing.

Jumping to his feet, Vijay ran to the fifth man trying to escape in the car. He got the door open and one foot in when Vijay grabbed him with both hands and hauled him out. Bashing his fist in his stomach then his nose then both eyes, Vijay held onto his shirt as he slumped to the ground.

Behind and to the side of him, Vijay saw movement. It was Wyn hurrying over.

"Stay back," he warned her, but the stubborn woman kept coming. Vijay had to turn his attention to the man he held. He picked him up and slammed him against the hood of the car.

Fisting his hand in his shirt to hold him steady, Vijay said, "All right you fuck," and slapped the man to keep him conscious. "You want to die fast, you tell me why they want the girl. You want to die slow, you do not tell me until you cannot take it anymore, and then you tell me anyway while you beg me to kill you to put you out of your agony. You understand?"

Blood pouring out of his nose, the man was sniffing and slobbering. His mouth opened and closed like a stupefied fish.

"You got one second, fucker before I start killing you slow. Tell me right now and I will make your death quick and painless."

"Mr. uh, Zastrovna?" Wyn's soft frightened voice was near to his side.

He barked at her, "Get the fuck back, Wynna." He didn't spare her a glance. When she hesitated, he yelled harshly, "*Now!*"

When she moved away a few steps, he turned back to the man. The guy's bloody face was swelling and sweat slid off in bullets.

Vijay raised his fist over him- the man sputtered, "Okay, okay, I'll tell you, you make it painless. You promise?"

"*Da.* Now talk." Vijay kept his fist raised.

The man spat out a hunk of blood and teeth, sniffed hard then said, "She's the president elect's niece, Wynna Pila." The man didn't notice Vijay's body go rigid.

"We were hired to get her, bring her to Gerald **Katakham**. **Katakham** wants his competition squashed, for good. He will do what it takes to get that done. The niece will know how to find Pila and lead us to him. Then we take him out." He shot a look at Wyn.

She stood several feet away with her hands over her mouth, shocked at Vijay's brutality, sickened eyes peering over her fingers. She was too far away to hear the man's mutters.

"More will come for her, there's already some on the road on the way here now as backup." Spitting out more blood, he inhaled then coughed and wheezed.

He chuckled with rueful mirth, "Some good that back-up is. No one counted on you getting in the way, Zastrovna. They'd of sent bigger guns if they knew. How the hell did you get involved in this shit anyway?"

When Vijay didn't answer, the man watched him with hopeful dread. "So, you uh, said you'd do it quick and painless? You keep your word?"

Vijay barely glanced at him. He muttered absently, "*Da*," and crashed his fist into his face. One punch, Vijay let him go and he slid into a pile on the ground. He lifted his boot over the man's head-

Screaming, "No! Don't!" Wyn ran forward and clutched at Vijay's massive arm.

He tried to shake her off. "Let go, Wynna, he knows the score. One less to come after you."

Knowing he could shrug her off like a flea on a stallion, she still clung to him, begging, "Please, not in cold blood. Vijay Zastrovna, what if it was you?"

He looked down at her. His eyes blank and hard, he grasped her hands and pulled them off his arm. "We do not have time for this. Go get in my car. Now."

His voice and demeanor so cold Wyn shivered. She looked down at the unconscious man. "Please-"

"Go."

She glanced up at him.

Vijay

His eyes inscrutable discs, his face was so hard he looked like he could be the chiseled part of a granite mountain.

Wyn turned and ran.

She wasn't halfway around the hotel when he was right behind her. He caught her arm, and holding it so tight it hurt, he pulled her with him to hustle her faster.

They were a few feet from the car when they could see vehicles winding down the hill coming towards the hotel.

"Move it!" Vijay pulled her to the car, opened it, ordered, "Get in and slide over, hurry."

She did as he said, and he climbed in beside her, and had the car moving before the door was closed.

Smashing the accelerator to the floor, he held it there. The car fishtailed out of the lot and peeled rubber in the opposite direction of the oncoming cars.

Thrown back against the seat, Wyn sat stunned.

"Put your seatbelt on," he told her. She froze, he shouted, "Now, dammit!"

She quickly grabbed it and snapped it on. She noticed he didn't bother with his.

The car raced so fast the countryside was a blur. It jostled and bumped hard over holes and rocks on the old tar and gravel road.

Wyn saw Vijay's eyes hopping to the rearview mirror. His knuckles gripped the steering wheel like he was strangling it.

Wyn dared to ask, "What's going on? Why do those men want me?"

His eyes knifing the road, he didn't respond.

Vijay drove like a bat out of hell for miles until he felt he could slow down. His gaze continued to hop from the mirrors to the road to the mirrors to the road.

Beside him, Wyn twisted her fingers in her lap. Seeing they had slowed a bit, she asked again, "What is going on?"

Vijay forked his fingers over his scalp, the long hair was tied back in a ponytail revealing more of the tattoo on his neck, it ran up to his strong rigid jaw.

Gripping the wheel again with both hands, he took a breath and said, "You, Wynna *Pila*, you are the person I was sent to…get. You are my fucking mission."

Chapter Ten

He didn't look at her, keeping his eyes trained between the rocky road and the mirrors.

Wyn turned and stared at him. "Your mission? Me? How can I possibly be a- a mission?"

She didn't think he was going to answer, then Vijay said, "The same as Kreis Warwick. My employer wants your uncle too and I am to get out of you, like Warwick, the contacts to your uncle, or get directly to him. I was not given your name, just a small bit of info that the person I sought was a relative of David Pila's."

He shot a side glance at her, his lip twisted wryly. "I assumed I was looking for a man. More the fool me."

Her lashes fluttered while she tried to take in what he was saying. Trepidation threading her voice, she asked him, "You are trying to find my uncle, to kill him, or what?"

His tone void of emotion he said evenly, "The rest of my orders will be relayed when I get my info from you, and bring you in." He closed his mouth without another word and continued his hopping scan from all the mirrors to the road.

She waited for more, but he said nothing.

After a few minutes of silence she said in a quiet voice, "I see. Will you be beating me and raping me too? Will you be locking me in a cement room and starving me?"

He didn't answer or look at her. He had no expression, but his jaw was working and a vein beat at his temple, he kept his eyes on the road.

To Wyn, he had turned back into the cold-blooded stranger who had taken her from Warwick. Apparently she'd been snatched from the frying pan and tossed into the fire. Sucking in a breath, she said, "If, say if I helped you, would you then let me go?"

She watched emotions flicker over his hard face, he was going to lie to her. Then, he stated brusquely, "*Nu.* I get the info to get the balls rolling, then I take you to my employer."

"Mr. Zastrovna?" She waited, he said nothing. "I didn't ask for this, I did nothing wrong."

She fell silent, and waited. Still he said nothing. "Please," she implored him, "what are you going to do to me?"

Compassionless eyes narrowed to slits turned to her. His face implacable steel, not answering her question, he said, "I have already been too soft on you," and turned back to look at the mirror.

She stared for a long time at him with big wide eyes in disbelief and desertion. Tears stung at the back of her eyes, she blinked fast to keep them at bay and bit her quivering lip to still it.

Suddenly they heard loud bangs, zinging thumps into the sides of the car- gunfire!

"Get down!" Vijay put his hand on her head and shoved her down to the seat. He floored the car again and lowered his head as bullets winged the metal and flew past them.

Several cars were bearing down from behind, the bullets came from the front one. That car hurtled up fast, started to pull up alongside them.

Wyn poked her head up and shrieked, "They're right here!"

Shoving her head back down, Vijay slammed his foot practically through the floorboard. The car was gaining on them, the bullets mostly slamming into the trunk and sparking off the fenders. They wanted her alive, they were trying to take out the tires.

Vijay

The thugs' car inched and inched until it was right beside them. A man had the window down, he yelled, "Give us the girl, Zastrovna, and you can split! We don't need to kill you!"

Vijay didn't spare him a glance, his attention tense on the road in front of them.

The man shouted, "If you're scared to stop, then just slow down, push her the fuck out and take off-" As he said that, Vijay wrenched the wheel and their vehicle turned almost on two wheels as he spun off to another road, squealing, smoke and the acrid smell of burning rubber following them. The thugs' car going too fast sped right past the turnoff.

The other two cars back a distance managed to follow them off the road and stayed behind them.

Wyn gasped frantically, "Mr. Zastrovna, stop and let me out. They want me. If you're with me they will probably kill you. Just let me out and you can keep going-"

Hunched over the wheel, his fingers clenching the wheel he kept his boot planted hard on the gas, dirt spewed from the spinning speeding tires.

Jolting in her seat from the rough ride, Wyn screamed, "Stop the car!"

As they passed a grove of trees, Vijay jerked the wheel and the car plunged into the woods, both of them slammed to one side then to the other. The ground so rough and rocky, they rocked and bounced inside as he tried to maintain control of the vehicle.

Wyn sat up and put both hands on the dashboard to hold herself still. "Please, save yourself, there is no point in both of us dying, let me out!"

He drove with his chin almost on the wheel trying to watch the front of the car. He suddenly yanked the wheel again and they were now on a dirt road.

His shoulders relaxed a fraction, they were hidden in the belly of the forest. The ground was too hard to leave tire marks.

Beside him, Wyn gripped her fingers and held them over her heaving chest.

He still did not utter a word, just kept driving. It was quiet, deep in the woods, just the squeaking sound of the car as it rolled over rocks and jutted in holes.

Vijay drove for over an hour before the car gave out. It coughed and made some odd sounds before it ran out of gas and came to a complete stop.

Yanking the door handle up, he barked at her, "Get out," and he slid out.

He trod around to the back of the car and opened the trunk.

When she cautiously came around, he was throwing a backpack with rolled blankets attached over his back, and grabbed a shotgun, slinging it over his shoulder on a strap to hang down beside the backpack. He shoved other things in his pockets then closed the trunk.

Lastly, he pulled his wallet out, hooked a chain to his front belt loop and the wallet then stuffed it in his back pocket.

Hovering nervous and awkward, Wyn watched him. Her arms wrapped around her body, she shivered uncontrollably.

Guns, knives, the chained wallet, his long hair tied back, he looked even more the deadly biker she had perceived him to be. He reached for her, she sank back from him. Scowling, he snatched her arm and said, "Go."

They hiked through the woods for an hour until Vijay found the clear fast stream he was looking for. He stopped and filled two canteens then handed one to Wyn.

Still without saying a word to her, he snagged her arm again as if she was going to run and they kept marching. The air was chilly but because they kept moving they were warm enough.

Following the stream, he headed for the mountains. The sun was setting; it was so quiet it was clear no one was following them.

When he came to a pile of large rocks, Vijay slipped the pack off and set it on the ground. He untied blankets from the pack and laid them out.

It was almost completely pitch black. Vijay had a flashlight but he used it sparingly. He said without looking at her, "Lay down on the blanket."

Vijay

It was so dark, Wyn could not see more than a few feet in front of her. Knowing she had no choice, if she didn't do as he ordered he would make her.

She trod to one of the blankets and knelt down. When he came near with the shotgun in his hands, she rolled into a ball and clasped her knees.

Dropping down on his knees beside her, he took her wrists, tied them together and tied them to his belt. He tossed a blanket over her then pulled one over himself.

Wyn's teeth were chattering. She had a jacket on but the air was near freezing. She put her face under her blanket but it wasn't enough. Her body wracked with shivers, her teeth clattered.

Vijay moved closer to her, put his arm around her and pulled her against his body. He tucked her under the inside of his jacket and drew her in tight.

She felt his chin set lightly on top of her head. Hearing him breathe, he didn't sound any more relaxed than she did. But at least now she was warmer.

A hand shook her shoulder. Wyn peeled open one eye. The dawn was on the verge of breaking.

His voice rough, "Come on, we've got to go," Vijay handed her a power bar then he rolled up his blanket. As soon as she got to her feet, he took hers and tied them to the backpack and slung it over his shoulders.

He started walking assuming she was with him. It took him a few seconds to realize she was not.

He turned back with a glower, "What is wrong, *femelă,* we need to keep going. We have a long way ahead of us."

Wyn sat on a boulder staring at him.

The harsh hardening of his face, the scar over his eye white against his tanned skin, the brilliant eyes glowering under the low shelf of brow would be enough to frighten a seasoned soldier, it made Wyn quake. But she didn't move.

Even when he stomped back and stood in front of her looking like a crazed grizzly about to tear her in half commanding, "Get. Up."

"You can threaten me all you want, beat me, kill me, starve me, but I will not take you to my uncle or tell you or anyone else how to find him. I know full well that horrible man, Kreis Warwick would have…eventually killed me after long torture." She sucked in a deep breath.

"I was petrified beyond belief of him, but I did not tell him. I am just as frightened of you. I will not tell you either. So, murder me now, or let me go." She put her hands behind her, set her palms on the boulder and leaned back.

His brow quirked, the corner of his lip ticked in. Arms crossed over a chest that rivaled the boulder she sat on. Peering down at her under hooded lids, he said, "Oh yeah?"

His tough, frightening expression brought a fearful lump to her throat, but Wyn didn't move.

Then he stalked over to her, grabbed her arm and hauled her off the boulder. "You have *nu* say in the matter." He started to pull her but she dug her toes in the hard earth. He swung around on her so fast she turned her head expecting a blow.

Instead, he swore then told her, "You will come with me. I can carry you over my shoulder. I have carried heavier packs than you for days on end up and down steep mountains, but eventually all your blood will be pushing into your head, and believe me, that is an agonizing way to travel. So, you walk, or I carry you. Which will it be?"

His intense gaze stroked in one movement down her body then up to meet her eyes. His were like flints of ice.

Wyn faltered, she could see in his set expression he meant what he said. With a "Humph," she muttered, "*bala*," under her breath then stalked past him and kept going.

Behind her, he shook his head then caught up in three strides. He snagged her arm and turned her to a different direction. "This way."

Knowing she wasn't used to the heavy hiking and with no food, Vijay held onto her just in case she fell, or ran. He could easily catch her but she could get injured in the meantime.

After a couple of hours, seeing her dragging her feet and her head drooping, he said, "We will stop here. I will get us something to eat. Sit there and do not move." He pointed to a downed tree.

When she wearily sat on the tree, he said, "You run and a bear or wolf pack will probably get to you before I do." He narrowed an eye at her and said, "Then again, they might go easier on you than me."

His brow arched at her weary glare but she did as he said.

Before he left, he gathered dry wood and using matches in the pack made a fire. "Stay here," he ordered her again, took both their canteens and disappeared into the brush.

Sitting alone, Wyn's head spun like the exorcist every time she heard a noise. Things were rummaging around in the bushes.

A bird flew out and loosened a leaf, Wyn almost jumped out of her skin when it fluttered down landing at her feet. She was so furious at Vijay, taking her to some awful man so she can be further tortured.

The forest was a terrifying place with him, she thought about how it would be without him.

Her brows drew down. They planned to kill her Uncle David and she would never be a part of that. She would die first. She needed to get away from Vijay. He was only going to brutalize her to get the information he wanted, he was no different from Warwick.

She started looking around for an opening in the woods, a trail to follow, he will probably be a long time, she could be far away before he came back.

At least traveling alone it would be less embarrassing than having to go a short distance from him to pee in the bushes every time she had to relieve herself. Thank heavens for the disposable toilet paper he carried in the backpack.

When he had to go, he barely stepped off the trail and didn't wait for her to avert her head when he opened his pants. Modesty was not his strong suit. He was used to hanging around with a bunch of other alpha high-octane males like him. Plus, she had to share his toothbrush- ick.

Her stomach rumbled. "Shut up," Wyn admonished it. She needed to get away before he returned- his chuckle behind her almost shot her out of her skin.

"Talking to yourself? Did you miss me so much?"

Wyn jumped up scowling. "You-" she stopped. He carried several birds in his hands. "How did you-"

He held up a slingshot. "Ever since I was four. I never miss." Unhooking his sheath, he pulled out his knife. Her eyes wide, Wyn backed away from him.

He said drily, "Sweetheart, if I wanted to kill you, I would have already done it with my bare hands without making a bloody mess."

Wyn's face turned white. His lips pulled in at her fear, he put the birds on the ground and started to cut off their heads.

"Oh!" Gagging, Wyn spun around to face away from him as he cut off the feet and skinned the feathers. He picked up some branches, carved the shoots off them and one by one stuck the birds on them.

Ignoring Wyn's quailed cry at the grotesque chopping and stabbing, he put them over the fire.

She looked away, trying to focus on something other than the butchered birds. He handed her a canteen. She took it warily from him. Unscrewing the top, she commented, "I thought it was dangerous to drink water in the wild, it could be contaminated."

Putting his canteen to his mouth he drank, and drank, and drank, his Adam's apple hopping with each swallow. Finally satiated, he wiped his mouth with the back of his hand and twisted the lid on.

He told her, "I have been all around this area. I know what tis good and what tis bad." Leaves and twigs crunching under his boots, he traipsed over to the fire and turned the roasting birds on their spickets.

Vijay

Wyn came to stand beside him enjoying the warmth of the crackling fire. The air from it felt like soft heat oozing over her chilled skin. "Won't the smoke show them where we are?"

Vijay shook his head and gingerly took off one of the cooked birds. "We are around the side now and much of the smoke will billow into that cave opening over there and be scarcely noticeable, at least at a distance when it fans out. Here. You will have to use your fingers."

"Um, thanks." Wyn tentatively accepted the bird. She hated to see the lovely thing dead, but her stomach had no feelings and it was hungry. She sat on the tree and ate.

Vijay loped a few feet away and flopped down on a big rock as if he wanted to put space between them so they couldn't talk.

They ate in silence. By the time they were done the sun had set. Like last night, Vijay laid out the blankets. He stood looking at her with the rope in his hands.

Her eyes went to the rope then flicked around the camp. It was dark; she could quickly hide in the forest. She took a couple of steps back.

"Wynna," he warned with narrowed eyes, "do not fuck around. I will only catch you, and make you regret you tried."

Her gaze flit to an opening, and she ran for it.

He tossed the rope down and went after her.

Chapter Eleven

Wyn had never run so fast in her life but she could hear him coming after her. She ran faster, then she was grabbed around the waist and swung up in the air with the momentum-

Her scream panicked and angry, "Let me go!" Kicking wildly in the air, she tried to twist and hit at him, but he wound both arms over hers still holding her in the air with her back against his chest. He spread his legs so couldn't kick him.

"Let me go you monster!" she shrieked, trying to throw herself from his grasp.

Vijay had been a soldier, was a black belt in a variety of martial arts, even Krav Maga used by the Israeli defense forces special units, and he still fought and trained. He boxed, his arms were thick bolts of solid steel, his legs as strong as tree trunks.

There was no doubt of him subduing her; the question was how long she would futilely fight him.

Wyn's chest pumped with her frustrated cries and struggles. Her screams lessened as her strained vocal cords burned raw, she still refused to give in.

Vijay tucked his mouth down next to her ear and said softly, "Stop, Wynna, stop, shh." As he spoke quietly and calmly, he nestled his face against her hair.

Eventually she tired. Setting her on her feet, he loosened his grip and turned her around.

Holding her arm, he brushed hair damp with her tears off her face. Murmuring, "*Mici dragă,*" the pads of his long fingers drew down from her cheek to her jaw in a gentle caress. His voice deep with accent, he whispered, "Calm down."

Her skin flushed. Panting for breath, she turned her head from his caress and lowered it to hide her tears of frustration.

Mumbling at the ground, she said, "Kill me now, *bala*, save us both more trouble, I will not tell you where he is." Fresh hopeless tears tumbled over cheeks reddened like ripe apples.

Murmuring, "Wynna," he cupped her chin raising her face, forcing her to meet his gaze. "I was hired to do a job. My opinion about it has no bearing. Stop fighting me. You will not win and you are only injuring yourself and sapping your energy." His hands so big and weathered, he gently wiped at her tears with his thumbs.

She looked up, her eyes flickered around his hard face, all harsh planes, tough jaw, brow a low hard ridge. His straight black hair was tied back in a ponytail; it hadn't come loose even with his struggles with her.

When she raised her eyes, Wyn saw his piercing blues were focused on her mouth before rising to connect with her own blue-green orbs. Her attention flitted to the scar over his brow, then, to his lips. They were nicely shaped for a man, but they were normally compressed in an impassive scowl.

"You are a cold-blooded, heartless monster, an evil *bala*," she whispered.

"*Da*, that tis true, *mici Wynna*," his voice so low it was quieter than the brisk wind that stirred their hair.

His head lowered until his face was inches from hers, he said, "And I told you to stop calling me a beast." His lips came upon hers, covering her words. The strong hands slid to embrace her jaw, holding her while he fused their mouths.

Wyn's gasp was smothered by his kiss. Her hands automatically went to press against his chest, but she didn't push him away. Feeling heat suffuse her body, it rose from her female core to spread through her chest and up further into her head, taking away all thought except, *the monster is kissing me, and he has the softest lips...*

When her hands twisted in his sweater, crushing it in her fists, a moan growled from his strapping chest to rumble against her knuckles. His fingers gripped, holding her face tighter, merging their lips harder together.

Vijay moved a hand to splay over her back to pull her body against his, and forced her mouth open wider to take in his tongue.

Heady with a startling hot flush of desire, Wyn let him explore her mouth.

He licked her lips, inside and out, drew his tongue over her smooth teeth before chasing her tongue to taste her. Laying siege on Wyn, Vijay pulled her taut against his broad chest, the enormity of his iron hard body enveloping her, his masculine scent making her senses spin.

His hand left her chin to cradle her head, the other dropped low on her hips pulling her closer. His erection like a thick steel rod throbbed at her abdomen- she broke from him.

"St- stop- stop-" her lips parted with heaving breaths. Heat burned her core and her cheeks, her eyes muddled with confusion and desire. Pushing at his chest was like trying to move a brick wall.

Struggling to tune down her body's reaction to him, to collect herself, Wyn gulped, swallowed, looked up at him.

He was a reflection of her with streaks of deep red staining his rugged cheeks. The blue eyes deepened to cobalt, clouded with seething passion. He blinked like he was trying to climb back from an abyss that was sucking him down.

"Ah," Vijay groaned, dragged his sleeve across his eyes then gripped her upper arms.

His voice deep and hoarse, he started, "Wynna, I," his Adam's apple bobbed, the red drained leaving his skin pale beneath the burnished tan of his skin. "That should never have happened. It will not again." The cloud of scorching passion left his eyes and was replaced with his normal frigid, merciless, abject blankness.

Vijay

An angry line compressed between his lowered brows, his jaw clenched, Vijay brought her back through the woods to their camp.

Dragging her over to the blankets he'd set out, he pushed her down so roughly she fell back on her butt, palms smacking the ground behind her.

A grimace constricted his face, he went to hold his hand out to her, but then his face shut down, he dropped his hand.

Looking up at him through a veil of light hair, Wyn said with sarcasm, "I see you have no interest in rape tonight, so is this where you commence to beating me?"

Towering over her like an enraged bear, looking every bit as terrifying as the day she watched him stomp on Warwick's neck until he was dead, his voice hushed and dangerous, Vijay warned, "You need to not talk."

Her head tilted up at him defiantly, she sniffed. "Don't worry, there is absolutely nothing I have to say to you except kindly keep your hands, and mouth, to yourself."

Vijay's lids lowered over fierce eyes, he started towards her, then stopped. He turned abruptly, stormed over, swiped the rope off the ground then stomped back and crouched beside her. Without a word, he snatched up her wrists and tied them, then fastened the other end to his belt.

Choking back tears that swarmed, with a short shake in her voice Wyn rebuked him, "You are a monster that uses brute force on people to make them do what you want."

He suddenly gripped her chin and moved his face so close to hers the heat of his breath misted her skin. "Because I can, *fetita*, remember that."

His anger ground through his words, "You try to run again and I will be forced to tie your hands behind your back." Flopping down hard on his side facing away from her, he pulled his blanket over himself.

Angry, mortified and afraid, Wyn rolled over on her side to face away from him. Tugging her blanket up, she worked hard choking back the tears, she'd be damned if she'd let him see her

89

cry again. No wonder he called her 'little girl' all the time. So frustrated at her situation, and the fear and confusion engulfing her, she stuffed her face under the blanket so he couldn't hear her sniffing back tears.

Shivers wracking her body jolted Wyn awake. Although he had left the fire going and gotten up at some point in the night to add more wood, it wasn't enough to chase away the frosty night air.

She almost bit her tongue trying to keep her teeth from chattering and waking him. She did not want to aggravate him anymore tonight.

He heard her anyway and moved his burly body to spoon her. Dropping his arm over her, he pulled her against his torso and tucked her under his jacket.

Wyn struggled to get out of his arms, grousing angrily, "I don't need your heat."

His arms tightened, she pulled away harder. "Zastrovna, I do not want you touching me. I do not need your warmth. Let go of me."

His arm still curved over her, he slid his hand under her waist making it impossible for her to move even an inch from him.

Conceding she was fighting a losing battle, Wyn sighed and stopped struggling. His body heat warmed her quickly making her drowsy. As she drifted off to sleep, she snuggled into him.

Vijay lowered his head so his chin was against her hair, he would smell her natural fragrance as he slept.

The next day they hiked for hours not saying a word to each other.

Early afternoon, he asked, "Do you need to stop for a break?"

She didn't answer him. He looked down at the top of her head, but she kept moving.

Twenty minutes passed and he asked her again. She still did not respond so they kept going.

Thirty more minutes went by, she was barely lifting her feet and moved slower and slower until she stumbled and fell to her knees.

He dropped down beside her. His voice steeped in irritation, he chided, "I asked you, Wynna, if you wanted to stop. Now you are beyond weary and will need time to recoup. Why the hell did you not answer me?"

She turned her head from him.

Cursing, "Goddammit woman," he clasped her jaw turning her to face him. "Fucking answer me when I ask you a question!"

She tried to pull from his grip but couldn't. Her chin rebellious, she said imperially but with aching exhaustion, "You told me not to talk."

"What the fuck, Wynna-" he released her jaw. "Women," he grunted like they were a mystery to him. "When you want them to shut up they do not. When you need them to give you vital information they clam up with a temper tantrum."

"Oh!" She swung her head up to him, brows slashed in indignation. "How chauvinist, sexist, you caveman-" she broke off at the lopsided grin he gave her.

"There now," he said smugly, "I knew your *femelă,* your femaleness would not allow you to keep quiet for long."

She sputtered, "You- you, oh!" Then she just plopped down on her back and fumed.

He took off his pack and the shotgun and settled down next to her.

After they had rested, Vijay got them hiking again.

They didn't stop until early evening. Turning a deaf ear to her protests, he tied her hand to a tree limb and started off to procure dinner.

"Zastrovna, please, you leave me trapped like this, what if an animal comes!"

"I will be back *fetita* quickly and I will not go far." He disappeared into the dense trees.

He caught a rabbit, skinned it and was cutting it up before he brought it back to the camp figuring Wyn would not eat it no matter how hungry she was if she knew what it was.

Leaving her bound to the tree, he prepared the rabbit on a stick and placed it over the fire he'd built.

When it was cooked, he placed the roasted meat on flat leaves and brought some to her. He handed it to her but she didn't take it.

"*Aie*," he sighed, "you are an exasperating woman, Wynna Pila. Take it."

Shaking her head, she demanded, "Untie me."

He set the meat down next to her then went and got some for himself and sat leaning against another tree with his back turned partially to her.

His grumbles loud enough for her to hear, "This is why I do not engage in relationships. Fucking women have only one job, spread their legs. We males should not have to put up with the rest of the shit." His lip edged up at the piqued gasp from the other tree.

"You don't have relationships, *bala*, because no sane woman would have you!"

Finished already with his rabbit, Vijay licked his fingers with a small grin. He could hear her chewing even though she had refused to take the meat unless he untied her.

He'd keep his peace though, because the stubborn little witch, *diavolită,* would certainly stop eating if he made any comment about it. But he did taunt, "Do you need me to come over there and show you what I will do if you do not stop calling me a beast?"

Nothing but silence came from the other tree. He smirked, "I thought not."

After cleaning up and completing their toiletries, they settled down to sleep before the sun had set.

Vijay thought their location was a good place to stop for the night. He started to fall into a light sleep right away. He didn't know how long he was drowsing when he turned to his side to pull her against him like he had been doing to keep her warm- his eyes flew open- she was not there.

He sat up pushing his long hair back, his head twisting all around looking for her. The rope, still tied to his belt but not her, lay on the blanket. *Maybe she had to go to relieve herself,* he shook his head, she knew she was to wake him, he would not allow her to go into the woods alone.

He jumped to his feet with a string of curses, "*Fuck*!" Still a hint of sun was out, she couldn't be hard to track, and she wasn't. He found her footprints and squashed grass trail right away.

Trotting after her, slow burn roiled up his body, he could feel his neck heat and bristle with anger at her stupidity leaving his safety to run away into the treacherous fucking woods. He'd paddle the shit out of her ass when he got his hands on her.

Fuming, he stalked down the trail until he could hear the rushing of water. They were at a particularly dangerous run of the stream where it was more of a racing river.

A scream peeled through the trees- and then a splash and another muffled scream-

Vijay ran through the woods as fast as he could.

When he reached the river he saw she had fallen in, her arms flailed as she thrashed in the white water.

"*Shit-*" he raced back into the woods heading for a trail that led down river. He hit an incline and stepping sideways to keep from falling, he climbed down as fast as he could.

Chapter Twelve

When he got to the river, Vijay scanned it rapidly looking for her, praying that she hadn't already been pushed past by the rapids- no- there she was heading towards his location-

He kicked off his boots and socks, rolled his jeans up and jogged down the bank and into the river.

As she got closer, he could see her arms were no longer flailing and she wasn't screaming. He moved out further, just as she was forced past him- he reached out and grabbed her jacket and her hair, and jerked her out of the water and up.

Lifting her limp body over his shoulder, he plodded through the rough water to the bank. Striding up the side of the hard-packed dirt bank, when he reached the grass, he slid one hand under her head, the other her thighs and he gently laid her down.

Her eyes were closed. He knelt over her, calling, "Wynna, Wynna, wake up," he lightly slapped the side of her face. She was breathing but unconscious.

Leaning over her, he pushed her wet hair aside then stroked her face, coaxing, "Come on honey, open your eyes."

Her lids levered up halfway then flew open seeing him hovering over her. "What..." her cold sodden clothes reminded her what happened. The horror of the white water hurtling her like a leaf in a hurricane, dragging her under, suffocating her, she knew she couldn't fight it, the world was going dark as her body shut down.

Vijay

Just as she went out, she had felt Vijay's great huge hands grab her and with Herculean strength whip her up and out of the raging river.

Wyn had passed out not knowing they were out of the water, still thinking she was dying in the rapids, the panic slammed at her like a baseball bat. Her eyes all wild terror she opened her mouth to scream-

He rolled a hand under her head and lowered his face to hers. Embracing her in a careful hug, he told her, "You are all right, Wynna, you are safe, baby." He spoke quietly, gently, but in his mind he was picturing her over his knee and her ass meeting his hand for being so foolhardy to run from him.

Then a coughing fit attacked Wyn, she couldn't stop, couldn't draw a breath. Vijay grabbed her shoulders, pulled her up to sit, folded her over his shoulder and patted her back like a baby until the fit eased.

Her breaths dragged out of her, hitching and scraping. Holding her and patting her gently, Vijay spoke soothing unfamiliar words in her ear.

Wyn's head was on his shoulder, her limp arms draped over his arms, her body pressed against his.

When her breathing calmed, Vijay set her back to sit. He put on his socks and boots then stood up, took her hand and pulled her to her feet. Without a word he marched her back up the hill and back to their camp.

Her body was shaking violently from the cold; he brought her to the fire.

Wyn pushed her soaking curls off her face and her shoulders letting the bulk flow down her back. She raised her eyes to his and saw his furious, unwavering stare was on her chest. She looked down and caught her breath. Her freezing nipples were pushing through her wet shirt that had turned see-through from the water. She crossed her arms over her chest.

Barely containing his rage, Vijay shifted his glare from her chest up to her eyes.

95

Drops of water clinging to her lashes, she pulled her lips in to keep them from shivering.

He barked at her, "Take off your clothes."

Her brows flew up. "What?"

"Take them off. You will get hypothermia." The words hammered out hard as nails, his fury at what she'd done still raged, blackening his face and scourging his tone.

She didn't move, he snapped, "Do it now!"

"I- I can't, I don't having anything to p- put on," her words broke off in spasms of shivering.

"Goddamn women, stupid brainless creatures." Muttering a flow of unintelligible curses, he stalked to his blanket. He grabbed up his leather jacket and handed it to her. "Take everything off, your shoes, socks, *everything*." His glare fired at her like fierce blue bullets.

She took the jacket, then waited.

Impatience dragging his brows down, he growled crossly, "What the hell is the problem now?" His gaze dropped to her wet pants clinging like a second skin then back up to her chest. Staring at her chest, he said, "Take them off or I will do it."

Blinking the river out of her eyes, Wyn stammered, "T- turn around," the words fell out around her chattering teeth. Rivulets of water dripped down her face.

He finally moved his gaze to her eyes. His lips twisted. Vulgar crudity clinging to his words, he said, "If I had any desire for you, *fetita*, I would have already fucked you, with or without your consent, would I have not?"

But the bulging erection clearly outlined in his jeans belied his statement. He took a step towards her, she backed away, droplets of water slipped off her hair plopping into a puddle under her.

Growing angrily, he snarled, "Take them off or I will rip them off."

She clutched his jacket to her chest. "Please, Zastrovna."

He glared at her, his furious mouth rigid as a dagger. "Take everything off, put the jacket on and then hand them to me. If you

96

even think about running again I will tan your hide so bad you will not sit for a week. Got me?"

He waited until she nodded, then crossing his arms, he turned his back as broad and hard as an iron wall to her.

Unsure how much time he was giving her, Wyn peeled her clothes off as quickly as she could, set them in a pile on the grass, swung his jacket on then picked up the pile of clothes. Her voice weary and shaking with chill, she said, "I'm ready."

He turned around. Looked from her still wet face down his leather jacket then down to her knees, and further to her bare feet. Satisfied, he trod over to her, took the wet clothes, and grasped her arm and started to move her, then the jacket opened, fair bare skin flashed.

Swearing, "*Niaba,* Wynna, what the fuck-" he grabbed one side of the jacket pulling it over the other. "Zip it up for *Zue's* sake." He waited fuming, eyes averted, while she fumbled with the zipper finally getting it up.

When she was done, he ordered, "Sit down."

Still shivering, Wyn was afraid of what he was going to do, but she obeyed knowing she had no choice. His patience appeared totally gone.

Once she was sitting, he left to pick up the rope and came back to her. He crouched behind her and took one of her hands pulling it behind her back then he did the other and tied her wrists together.

Her eyes wide and fearful, she cried, "Please, Zastrovna, please, you can't leave me like this. I am too- too vulnerable." She begged, "Please, don't do this, I don't want-"

He snarled, "I do not give a fuck what you want. You should have thought of that before you ran. You would have died out there you stupid bitch."

Finished binding her, Vijay slid his hands under Wyn's arms and knees, picked her up and carried her to a tree near the fire. Setting her down, he moved her so she was leaning against it then retrieved a blanket and placed it around her.

"You're nothing but a big cruel bully," she sniffed, tossing her head to get her wet hair off her face.

"Oh *yah*, my beautiful drowned kitten?" Looming over her, his hands on his hips, he glared at her looking dark and angry like a ferocious warring Mongol.

Leaning over, he put his palms on his thighs and got in her face. "Well, this *avan brută,* cruel bully saved your fucking ass. Again." His long hair swung over his face, he shoved it back with seething ire. Standing up he started to turn from her.

Sniffing loudly, hurt clear in her voice, she said, "You didn't do it for me, you did it for your stupid job."

Vijay paused, his shoulders stiffened. Then he stalked from her, took her clothes and spread them over rocks to dry.

The red silk bra and panties in his hands, the tips of his ears burned. Not that he was going to see her in them, he sighed. The black lace ones were nice, but he had preferred the red over them.

He laid the bits of silk on the rock then strode across their camp and right into the woods without telling her what he was doing.

Wynna watched him until he disappeared. Hoping he was going to catch dinner, and not leaving her to die alone, she pulled her knees up and leaned back against the tree.

She stared at the place where he slipped into the woods, only looking away briefly to scan for anything coming towards her thinking she was dinner.

As usual, he wasn't gone long. Wyn wondered how that man found and caught a wild animal so quickly, and without a shot fired. She remembered he'd told her he had lived in the wild in different countries for long periods of time while in the military.

He didn't go near her or speak to her. He'd already skinned and cut up whatever he caught and did like before, stuck the meat on branches and perched them over the fire.

His face even grimmer, more ominous behind the few days' growth of heavy whiskers, he never looked at her, even when he brought her some meat.

Vijay

Crouched in front of her, his body still vibrated with fury, the heat resonated off him. Wyn could feel his rage like he had cloaked his body around her and choked her with it.

She didn't dare look at him, he had killed men with his bare hands in one move. If he chose to unleash his wrath on her...she shivered, she only hoped it would be quick and painless.

Seeing her shiver, he asked gruffly, "Are you cold?"

Wyn shook her head.

He untied her so she could eat with her fingers. Not sitting down, Vijay moved away from her to go lean against a tree and stare off into the woods while he ate.

It was hard for Wyn to eat. Her stomach pitched from her death-ride in the torrential river. She remembered his hands grabbing her and wrenching her out of the water and throwing her over his shoulder.

Before she had passed out, she remembered feeling so safe even though she was hanging over his burly shoulder like he was a caveman stalking back to his cave with his hunted prey. His strength and bravery and warmth had comforted her. As he pointed out, he had rescued her, again.

Whether for his gain or not, nevertheless he had put his life at risk to save her. He had killed a group of men all at once to take her from Kreis Warwick when he hadn't known who she was yet. She contemplated why he had done that.

At the time he didn't know she was the person he sought. It couldn't have been because he wanted her for her body, he would have assaulted her by now if that was the case. She was clearly helpless against his rugged brawn.

Wyn's lips bunched remembering he had just told her he had no interest in her. But he had an erection. Maybe he was just very sexually sensitive around any woman.

She wondered why he had kissed her earlier. To punish her for calling him a beast? To show her he could do anything he wanted to her- show her he was the boss? What an ass! And *he* complained that *women* were confusing!

Suddenly his boots were in front of her. She looked up.

He held his hand out without looking at her. She took it and he pulled her to her feet.

He led her to a hedge of brush and let her do her personal thing and use canteen water and his toothbrush to brush her teeth. He didn't have to warn her, she wasn't about to run again. Especially with no clothes and no shoes.

When she was done, he brought her to her blanket and this time helped her sit down more gently. But he still moved behind her and tied her hands behind her back then wrapped the rope several times around his waist before tying it in a knot.

He had put her blanket closest to the fire and his in front of hers. For her to run, she'd have to either walk through the flames or over him.

Still silent, he dropped down next to her with a grunted exhale like he was tired and still pissed as hell. He faced her, but he didn't pull her in against him like he usually did.

Relieved, she let out a held breath. She had expected him to give her a beating for attempting to escape and putting him through having to risk his life pulling her from the river. But he never touched her.

Wyn felt the lack of his big hard body wrapped around her. She had gotten used to it and now felt bereft of his warmth, and, just the feel of him pressed against her back, his arm curved over her holding her tight, protectively to his chest.

She had even been aware of the trouble he had taken to keep his hard-on from touching her. She peeked at him. Then jumped, startled. He was staring at her. The brilliant eyes piercing the dark bored into her.

He closed his eyes.

It seemed forever before Wyn heard his deep steady breathing and knew he was asleep. Only then was she able to relax herself and fall asleep.

Hours later, Wyn woke, groggy, then- *Oh no*. He was on his back lying half towards her and she was lying with half her back against him in a partial spoon. His arm was crossed over her shoulder and down her front, his palm on her breast over the leather jacket. His other hand was on her bare thigh, only inches from her naked womanhood.

She tried to move from him, but he held her tight. She squirmed trying to get out from under his hands but he gripped her tighter.

In her ear, his deep voice gruff, an accented mumble thick with sleep, he growled, "Lie still, *dragă*." His hand firmed over her breast, the other moved up her thigh.

Oh dear, she shuffled her body to get his hands off her. "Please, I...I have to..." he didn't budge.

Arching her back to push at his heavy weight, Wyn realized he was still asleep. She spoke loudly, "Zastrovna! Wake up!"

He jolted awake. His gun materialized in the hand that had been on her thigh, his body rigid ready for fight, he looked around.

"What? What Wynna, what tis wrong?"

"I have to pee."

He froze, realizing how he was holding her. "*Shit!*" Spitting a string of Romanian curses, he snatched his hands off her and jumped to his feet then grasped her arms to help her up. Walking her to the bushes, he untied her.

When she was done, yawning heavily, Vijay led her back to the blankets and tied her hands behind her. They diligently did not make eye contact.

She hadn't really needed to go to the bathroom, she just wanted to get him to take his hands off her and she didn't want to make a big deal out of his unconscious groping. Her face was already flaming with her embarrassment of how he had been touching her so intimately.

They settled back down. He deliberately faced away from her.

Another couple of hours passed, it was almost morning. Wyn was awakened again by Vijay. This time he lay partially on top of her and was voraciously kissing her. His thick fingers held the back of her head like iron nails keeping her completely immobile.

Growls vibrated deep in his chest, she could tell again he was sound asleep, he was dreaming. He was not just kissing her, he was devouring her like a wild savage, like he was crazy ravenous to taste every inch of her, inside and out, before consuming her completely.

His strength and intensity frightened Wyn, but, his savagery ignited a hot flush down between her legs. The more fiercely he kissed her, the more fiery the rush of heat up her body.

Wyn couldn't fight him with her hands restrained behind her back, but she squirmed and bucked. Tearing her face away for a brief second she called out, "Stop! Zastrovna! Stop! Wake up!"

His mouth burning hers up, his hand floundered over the front of her torso before landing on the zipper of the jacket. Catching it, he pulled the zipper down almost all the way open.

Pushing the lapel apart and off her shoulder, he found her bare breast. Caressing it, he moaned against her mouth then he kneaded it more vehemently and drew his leg over one of hers.

Struggling under him like crazy, Wyn finally tore her head away again and screamed.

He stopped for a second, his eyes still closed, then he sealed his mouth back over hers, kissing her, thrusting his tongue into and around the inside of her mouth. Sucking her tongue, he mumbled with a sleeping slur, "Ah, Wynna *dragă*." At least he wasn't dreaming of Elana.

His hard hand gripped her breast, cupping it, he brought his mouth down over it with his wet heat. Cuddling her soft flesh, he kissed and sucked, nipped and squeezed it. His leg moved forcing her legs to spread apart and started moving his hips to position between them, his other hand was working on his belt.

She was seconds from being raped. An untried virgin, in his wild frenzied sleep he would tear her apart! Wyn screamed at the top of her lungs.

He froze again, lifted his head, struggled to open his eyes. He stared blearily at her, then his eyes popped open in astonishment, he squawked, "What the hell are you doing?"

Trapped under the weight of his body and his hand clutching her bare breast, she blustered, *"You* are on *me,* get off of me you big oaf!" With her hands bound, she was helpless to push him.

Like coming out of a dense fog, blinking and shaking his head, he looked down and saw his hand on her breast, reddened and wet from his mouth. But he didn't let it go.

Palming it, her fair flesh mounded through the long fingers in his big hand. His gaze filtered down her naked skin exposed from the open jacket, not stopping until he reached the spot the last of the still zipped jacket managed to cover.

Watching him pour over almost every scintilla of her body, Wyn held her breath, it didn't appear he was going to stop what he'd started, and she was defenseless to make him.

The way his eyes stroked her bare legs was so arresting, it felt like he'd physically skimmed her skin with his rough hands. His gaze moved back to her covered sex. Wavering as if he was considering unzipping the jacket the rest of the way and seeing the tender bits that lay hidden underneath.

His pupils dilated with the awareness he was lying between her legs. It appeared as if he was contemplating how little it would take to be inside her. He only needed to finish unbuckling his belt, unbutton, pull the zipper down, she had no barriers in his way.

With a slow, animalistic blink, his gaze unhurriedly moved back up to the breast he still held.

"Zastrovna," Wyn yelled, "let go of me! Get off of me!"

His eyes flicked to hers then down at the plush globe still held tightly in his hand. Irresistibly drawn like a bear to honey, he bent and licked her nipple, then closed his mouth over it and sucked it.

Wyn could feel his full, rock-hard erection straining against her thigh; he was positioning it to her sex. Her head arched back, she swallowed the moan the heat striking her core induced.

But, she was afraid, right now he was so rough, savage and huge, he'd hurt her. She gasped, "Zastrovna, please."

He pulled his mouth away, leaned back and stared with glassy eyes at her creamy nudity. Still gripping her breast, he looked at it. His lips pulled in, he licked them, then clamped his mouth closed like it was all he could do to keep from continuing to suckle her plump flesh.

Her chest rose and fell rapidly in her struggle to fight him off her, and fighting to subdue the searing flash of desire burning between her legs.

He suddenly leaned over her, kissed her hard, then moved to the side and pulled the jacket closed over her. Grasping her shoulders, he lifted her up to sit and untied her wrists. Stuffing the rope in his pocket, he got up and stalked off.

Wyn sat trembling for a minute, not sure what to do. When he didn't come right back, she got up and dressed in her dry clothes.

He still didn't return.

She sat on a rock by the diminishing fire and waited.

As time went on and he still hadn't returned, Wyn started to panic. Dawn was coming but it was still pitch black and she couldn't see a thing.

Thinking, "Maybe I should go look for him," she considered trying to follow him but didn't even know what direction he had gone in.

More time passed and now she thought he must have left her and wasn't coming back. Beside herself with fear, she heard a noise. Her heart slamming in her chest, she stood up and looked around for a weapon.

The rustling noise was getting closer, she couldn't see even a limb that looked strong enough to swing. Her hand pressed in fright at her throat she stared frantically into the dark…then she could see Vijay coming through the brush.

Her arms strung around her body, Wyn doubled over with a wrenching sob.

Vijay rushed to her. "Wynna, what tis wrong? Do not be afraid of me, I am sorry for what I did. I was asleep, I thought I was dreaming, *mici dragă.*" He reached out and gently brushed her hair back off her face.

Tears poured down her cheeks, Wyn covered them with her hands.

Vijay

Not knowing what to do, for the first time in his life Vijay stood helpless. He pulled her into his arms, she sobbed against his chest. Holding her tight while she wept, his tone soothing, he whispered unintelligible Romanian words against her ear while stroking her hair.

After some time, Wyn got a grip on her fright, and relief, and drew back from him, wiping her eyes.

Still holding her and stroking her hair, he waited for her to calm down. Then said quietly, "What tis going on, Wynna? Why are you crying? Did I hurt you?"

Trying to compose herself, she choked then swallowed. "I- I thought you left me. I was so scared," she wailed and the tears started again.

Chapter Thirteen

$\mathcal{V}$ijay's rough exhale lightened some of the tenseness in his shoulders. "Oh, *mea Zue*, my God, Wynna." Setting both hands on her shoulders, he pulled her back to his chest again, one hand cradling her head the other wrapped around her holding her close.

"Honey, I am a callous assassin, and an animal who assaults defenseless women in their sleep, but I am not so bad that I would leave you alone in the forest. Why do you think I was so mad at you for running? I was scared out of my mind you were going to die."

He drew her back and wiped at the tears with his fingers then stepped from her.

She looked down at his hard-on clearly bulging against his jeans and blushed.

He said wryly, "That is not helping, honey."

She blushed deeper as the hard ridge in his pants grew even bigger as she stared at it. He awkwardly cleared his throat, and she quickly shifted her mortified eyes away.

With red creeping up his neck, Vijay said, "There is a fresh stream, I, uh, washed up some." He had gotten rid of his boner so he could keep his mind on getting them out of there.

Picturing her all pearly nude when he had woken up, his hand and mouth on her chubby breast, knowing she had not a stich of clothes on under *his* jacket, it hadn't take long.

Vijay

But holding her again now kicked his rod right back into action. And her staring at it, shit, made it want to come all that more to attention.

It was crazy erotic, and with an odd possessive feeling picturing her naked in his jacket, their scents mingling, like she was enveloped in him, from under, around and on top. He had almost not been able to pull back, to stop himself from stripping off his clothes and lying naked with her, settling between her slender legs- ah.

It had taken every ounce of strength he'd had to take his hands from her insane body, his mouth from those pouty lips, and get off her, and walk away.

Dragging a hand across his mouth, he took a deep breath, let it out, said, "Let me break down the camp and I will take you there."

"Okay," she sniffed, embarrassed at her crying. First she'd run away from him and now she despaired of being left alone. Of him leaving her there. "Here," she started to take his jacket off to give it back to him.

His eyes jackknifed to her breasts pushing at the blouse while she tried to shrug out of the jacket. Thinking about the red silk bra now on her, his face darkened. He held his hand up and said, "*Nu*, you better keep it on for now. Tis still a...little chilly."

He stroked his fingers over the red rash on her face. "Ah, baby, my beard roughed up your perfect skin, I am so sorry."

His hand slid around the back of her head to hold her, then he softly kissed the redness he had caused. Quickly releasing her, as he turned from her, he growled, "We need to go."

After a stop at the small stream, they continued their journey through the forest.

They were in a less dense area and were walking in an open expanse treading on mostly soft grass. The sun was full and bright warming the chilly air.

"Look!" Wynna said with glee pointing at two deer yards away. Their heads came up at her voice and in a blink they were gone into the woods. She crowed in delight, "Weren't they just beautiful?"

"Uh, *yah*, sure." Thinking what a tasty dinner they would have made, Vijay moved his attention from the deer to Wynna.

Her bright curls bounced down her back, her steps were made with more ease. Even with their harsh conditions of little food and sleeping outside, her cheeks were rosy, her lips a cheerful bow. Ripe health gleamed in those beautiful eyes that looked at everything with curiosity and joy.

Walking side-by-side, Vijay asked, "Wynna, how did Warwick capture you?" Seeing a streak of distress cross her face he wished he'd not said anything to bring back that terrifying day.

But she answered right away. "For days I had noticed I was being followed. It was early evening, but almost dark, I was in my apartment when I remembered I hadn't gotten my mail that day. So when I went out to get it, I didn't really pay attention to this big black car slinking slowly down the street.

"I mean, I noticed it peripherally, but didn't pay it any mind. When my back was to the street, men leaped out and grabbed me, and," she shrugged, trying to dispel the horror of not knowing what was going to happen to her and fighting off those wretched men.

Seeing her shudder, Vijay said softly, "*Bine*, okay, never mind, let us not go back and revisit it. I do not want you to have more nightmares."

Her head tipped up at him. "Nightmares? You say that like I've been having them."

He looked down at her pretty face tilted up at him. The sun lighting her hair to the color of creamy butter, and showing the clear milky complexion to perfection. Resisting the urge to touch her skin or run his fingers through the blonde curls, he nodded. "*Da*, at the hotel you had them almost nightly."

Her brows knit together. "I don't remember waking up with them…"

He shrugged one big shoulder. "I held you and talked to you until they went away, so you never actually woke in the midst of them. I did not want them to become indelible in your mind by waking while still in the depths of the terror."

"Oh." Her eyes slid at an angle up, peering at him through her lashes. "I didn't know. Um, thank you," she said with a small shy smile.

"*Yah.*" He cleared his throat then said roughly, "I needed my sleep and you were disrupting it," he started walking faster.

Her smile deepened when she saw his neck tint red with embarrassment.

Picking up her steps, Wyn asked him, "Zastrovna, what do you do? I mean, as a living. Who is the man you are working for, taking me to..." her voice trailed off as she remembered his mission.

Vijay was every bit the cold brute she'd called him, but he still cringed inside at the fear in her voice. His mouth ticked up at her trying to sound brave and unworried, he glanced at her.

Her chin was boldly up in the air but the skin around her eyes and mouth had tightened with her effort to remain calm.

He told her, "Ah, I am basically a mercenary. I get hired to do things like this, acquire people and take them to others that want them for whatever reason. My team and I do extractions, that is rescuing captured people, that others, businesses, governments want rescued but on the DL." He glanced at her again, seeing her brows dip down as she listened.

"Uh, that means on the down-low. They, such as the government do not want their country's names involved so they hire people like us to do it. If we get caught, they look the other way, claim no knowledge. That tis why when that man, the one you asked me to not kill," he paused, "you said what if it had been me?"

She nodded recalling the men grabbing her and running with her off to the car. She had known Vijay had killed all those men the day he took her from Warwick, but she hadn't seen him do it. But the time at the car, she had stood frozen, watching him literally decimate a group of men as ruthless and violent as he.

Vijay went on, "When we, I mean men like my team and me, when we do a mission, we know the consequences. We go into other countries and into prisons, gangs, wars; we know we can be killed. But to be captured like that man who was not directly attacking us, he was leaving in the car," his shoulders rolled.

"Ah, that was more like in cold blood. You made me aware of it...and I stopped." He glanced at her. "Do not get me wrong, I put a bad hurting on him, but he will live."

They walked in silence for a bit. Wyn spoke, "So, when you take people to people, like me to the man who hired you to capture me, you don't know what these people are going to do. You just bring us, drop us off, and go on your merry way counting your cash not knowing if that person will be tortured...killed...sold into sexual slavery, whatever. Right?"

His skin darkened and his pace slowed. He replied, "Tis not my business, Wynna, to know why the person is wanted, my job is to bring them their person and that tis it."

They walked a mile in silence before she spoke again.

"Do you know what your, uh, the man that hired you to bring me to him will do with me when he is done with me?"

No good, or peace, ever came out of talking to women, and this is why Vijay didn't bother speaking with them, just took what he wanted and saved conversation to have with men.

"Zastrovna?"

He sighed and shook his head. "*Nu.*"

"So, he might kill me, cut me up in little pieces, maybe skin me while I'm still alive, pretty much anything, right?"

Muttering, "Wynna," he scowled, increasing his pace.

But she slowed and made sure she stayed a few feet behind him the rest of the day.

They ate a silent lunch of some type of pheasant and continued on, without speaking another word, until it started to grow dark.

The sun crept down the horizon and they stopped for the night. As before, Vijay made a fire, left and hunted down their dinner.

110

After they ate, he set her blanket down beside the fire. He held his hand out. "Give me the jacket."

Wyn was freezing but she took it off and handed it to him.

He pointed to the blanket and said, "Lay down there."

He was back to his normal gruff self, barely looking at her. Her legs rubbery with apprehension, Wyn got down and curled on her side watching him.

He bent over her, she cringed from him. His brows pulled down in a frown, he laid the jacket over her then added her blanket. Apparently both aware she was not going to try to run from him again, he didn't tie her up, he trod to the other side of the fire and lay down on his own blanket.

Surprised, and disappointed, Wyn supposed he didn't want anything to do with her. She closed her eyes and tried to sleep. But, she was so cold. And afraid without him near that an animal would come and snatch her.

The sounds of nocturnal preying rustled all around them every night. Her teeth chattered, she sniffed back anxious tears.

Suddenly hearing his voice, she held her breath, then cautiously opened her eyes. He was crouched beside her, his brawny forearms on his knees, his large hands clasped together.

Softly, he said, "What tis the matter, *mici dragă*? Why are you crying?"

Huddled under his jacket, she sniffed, "I'm not c- crying, I'm just c-cold and scared."

He was quiet for a moment. Then, with a hint of mirth in his voice, he teased, "You miss me, *fetita*?"

She scowled at him and huddled into a tighter ball, but she couldn't still her chattering teeth.

"*Mici* Wynna," his voice deepened with uncertainty. "I am afraid to sleep next to you. I obviously do not know what I am capable of doing in my sleep. I do not want to hurt you. If I...uh, assaulted you and you could not wake me up, I would easily overpower you, you could not stop me. I would not be able to control myself, or my strength while asleep. I can protect you from the dangers of the forest and from other men, but I cannot protect you from me."

Sniffing back her tears, she said through chattering teeth, "It-it's okay, I'll be all- all right."

Ah," he sighed. "*Mici copula,* it would be foolish for me to take you from the ravaging river just to let you freeze to death or be taken by an animal." He stood up.

Her eyes followed him as he walked back to his blankets. He leaned over, scooped them up and returned to her. "Move over," he ordered.

Confused, Wyn shuffled over on her blanket.

He dropped down beside her with a huff of air. "Put the jacket on and zip it up."

Still unsure, she did as he said.

He took the rope he had tied her up with last night, slid it in his belt loops and wrapped it a few times around his pants then knotted it. It would make it a bit more difficult, but not impossible, for him to get his *pula* out of he was asleep.

"We are both fully clothed this time, Wynna, I hope tis enough. Come here, turn around." He lifted his arm.

Wyn hesitated, then did as he said. When she settled, he moved close to her, spooning her then dropped his arm over her, pulling her in to him for his body heat.

She was like a rigid statue, then he felt her shudder, but he didn't think it had anything to do with her chilliness, more likely nerves. He nestled his chin over the top of her hair and inhaled before he could stop himself.

He was already getting hard with her in his arms and pressed against him, the scent of her was going to really fuck with him. But then she sighed and her body relaxed against his.

In her ear, he murmured gruffly, "You feel warm and safe now, *mici dragă?*"

In answer, she snuggled more closely to him. "Yes. Thank you, Zastrovna."

Inwardly he groaned, that little innocent snuggle into his groin was going to cost him a few hours of sleep. "Can you stop with the Zastrovna," he groused. "My name is Vijay. How would you like it if I called you Pila?"

She giggled; it made her body jiggle against him. He bit back a groan.

Wyn said, "You call me lots of things, *Vijay*, most of the time I have no idea if you're being nice or rude."

He snorted, "I am never rude."

Her laugh bounced her butt into his groin. "Yeah, right."

Wincing at her tight little ass pressing harder into his pelvis, he grumbled, "Go to sleep."

Chapter Fourteen

Neither woke again through the night.

The next day as Vijay smothered the fire and they broke camp, he said, "Only a little further and we will be near a tiny village and I can contact my men to come and get us." His cell hadn't worked in the forest and when he surged into the river to grab her it had gotten soaked.

Wyn stopped rolling up the blankets and looked at him.

They both stood for a minute regarding one another. Their time in the forest was uncomfortable, nerve-racking, and yet intimate. It would be soon when he would hand her off to his employer.

He broke eye contact and finished what he was doing.

On the move again, Wyn lagged behind Vijay. He had to keep reminding himself to keep to her pace, but sometimes he got ahead of her then would wait until she caught up.

The trail curved, Wyn couldn't see where he was. She started to jog to catch up when suddenly, one of the men that had been with Kreis Warwick popped up right in front of her.

Laughing at her shock, he said, "Ah my little woman, when I came back to the house everyone was dead. Good thing I left when I saw that maniac, biker-looking bruiser come in, huh?"

Wyn stepped to the side to go around him, but he moved and blocked her.

"So, gorgeous, I figured the bruiser took you. How the hell did you get away from that big fucker? We've been trying to track you for days. I finally chose the right trail, eh? I had prayed it was you. And here we are, just you and me."

He swiped out a hand to grab her; she dodged it and started to run.

Not even three steps and he snatched her hair and yanked her back.

Wyn screamed-

"Yeah bitch, go ahead, you'll only bring the others then they'll want their turn, but me first." Throwing his arm around her waist, he picked her up and about slammed her on the ground, knocking the wind out of her.

He immediately grabbed at her clothes trying to tear them off her body.

Getting her wind back, Wyn sucked in a breath and screamed again, punching at him.

He hauled his hand back and slapped her. "Knock it off bitch," he snarled, "all you got to do is lay there and open your legs." He grasped her blouse and jerked it hard- all the buttons popped open.

Wyn frantically felt on the ground for a rock to brain him with- Yes! Finding one, she brought it up and bashed him in the head- but it only glanced off him making him mad.

"Fucking bitch," he snarled and viciously smacked her again.

Stunned, her head fell back. Fighting the blackness sucking her under, Wyn refused to pass out.

He was crushing her with his weight. She held her breath, he reeked of booze and cigarettes and male sweat. With a shriek, she raked her nails across his face.

He howled, slapped her again then rolled his body over her arm and held the other above her head and tore at her pants.

One second he was there tugging her pants down and the next he was gone.

Hearing the man screaming, Wyn braced her palms behind her and pushed to sit up. Shaking like a leaf, she looked on in horror as Vijay had his big long fingers around the front of the man's face and was squeezing it, crushing it, smothering his mouth and nose.

Forced to his knees from the pressure of Vijay's strength, the man hit at his huge arms but Vijay ignored the punches like they were moths striking at him.

Wyn screamed, "Vijay! Don't kill him! Stop!" She climbed shakily to her feet and ran over and tried to get between the men to stop him.

Vijay's dark face twisted in a psychotic grimace, raging eyes mere creases, his strong legs braced on the ground, his bicep was a huge pumped rock as he kept squeezing the man's head and closing his air passages.

He gave Wyn a shove out of the way, she fell on her butt still shouting for him to stop- but he continued until the man dropped to the ground, dead. His face a mangled, bloody, squashed mess.

Wiping his hands on his jeans, panting in his rage, big chest heaving, Vijay stomped over to her. He leaned over, grabbed her arm, hauled her to her feet and stalked off with Wyn stumbling alongside him.

"You- you killed him! You didn't have to-"

He stopped so suddenly he had to hold her from tripping. Pulling her around to face him, he gripped her arms.

His face a furious snarl, the blue eyes now blank, enigmatic, he said, "I let the last one live. I made sure he would not be up and around for a few months but I let him live because you begged for his life. That one," he jerked his head behind them, "was nothing but a rabid dog and needed to be put down."

"But-" her words were cut off as Vijay gripped her hard and lifted her up on her toes.

In her face, he snarled, "He hit you, Wynna. He would have viciously raped you, then passed you to the other men before killing you without mercy. I would have destroyed him just for striking you."

Shaking her, he told her, "You do not fucking ever get between me and another man again. Ever. Or between any fighting men. You could have been seriously injured or killed."

Adrenalin coursing through his veins, unable to control his agitated strength, he realized he was being rough with her.

"Goddammit, Wynna," he released her, then brushed his fingertips over the red imprints on her face from the man's attack. "This place is too wild and dangerous for you, I need to get you the fuck out of here."

She tried to look defiant but the tears still gleamed. "What do you care if I die? Oh, right, you won't get paid when you hand me off to some strange man who wants to use me." She started to stalk past him when he shot his hand out to stop her.

Holding her arm, he looked at her angry frightened face, muttered, "Wynna, listen, I-"

She twisted and pushed at him, almost hysterically, trying to get out of his grasp. "Let me go. Let's just keep going, we don't want to keep your employer or your wallet waiting."

"Wynna, stop," he ordered, clutching her jaw, holding her taut.

Her big eyes glistened like the tumultuous sea with unshed tears.

His gaze slid down to her open shirt. Her breasts mounded over the top of the silky red bra. He felt his face redden as he raised his eyes back up to her.

She struck out trying to get out of his grip.

Holding her chin, he rolled his other hand around her back and jerked her against him then lowered his mouth over hers in a fiercely ravaging kiss. He pushed at her lips with his, trying to force them open.

She pounded her fists against his chest then, she stopped resisting, her lips parted to accept him.

His tongue slid over her lips, felt the smoothness of her teeth then searched for her tongue. Finding it, their mouths mated.

His body growing rigid with male hardness, Vijay splayed his hand across her back, holding her so hard against his body, he could feel her budded nipples pressing through the red silk and through his shirt, into his chest.

Vijay moved his mouth, her breath panted against his skin. He kissed her jaw, prowled over her neck where he kissed then sucked her delicate skin.

Hearing her moan rasp low in her throat, his body fired like it was a plug stuck in a live outlet. He kissed and bit lusty trails down to her breast leaving red marks along the way.

Cupping the silk, Vijay kissed then sucked her soft breast, gently at first. His desire intensified, building more and more like a belt unbuckling hole by hole.

Holding that breast with a clenching grip, he moved to the other globe, sucking so hard with predatory hunger Wyn moaned first with pain then with pleasure, her held fell back. Her knees would have buckled if he wasn't holding her up.

Vijay's heady gaze burned with white heat seeing her heavy lidded eyes aglow with passion. Sunlight glistened on the dampness of her lips from his lathing. He pulled the red silk down to suckle her nipple.

"Vijay," her groaned whisper was like a struck match to his groin. He pulled from her, scanning the area for a place to lay her down and-

"Shit," he swore, what the hell was he thinking? They were out in the open with murderous thugs looking for them. He froze.

Misreading his thoughts, Wyn pushed from his hold. Her face abruptly turned livid with gall. The tempest of passion clouding her eyes was now buffeted with hurt fury.

Standing from him with her hands raised in front of her defensively, umbrage cutting the edges off her words, she blurted, "You- you," she let out a scathing breath.

Bemused, he just stood with his hand scraping through his hair.

"What's the plan, Vijay, get in a little sex before you turn me over? Then changed your mind, decided you don't want me? I'm not the kind you like, one of your giant-breasted, tough whores?"

Pain lancing her eyes, she swung her head away so he couldn't see her tears.

Vexed at her words, confused at her sudden change from soft and moaning in his arms to spitting rage, squinting at her Vijay growled, "What the fuck are you talking about?"

"Nothing. Who cares. Let's go, hurry and get me to your man," she strode away from him.

Rolling his eyes, Vijay cursed, "Women!" Who the hell can ever figure the feminine brain out? She was right. She was not like the women he normally tumbled. She was soft and sweet and dainty and, she stirred heavy feelings in him that the coarse women never had.

"Wynna," he called, jogging after her.

Catching her arm, he stopped her. Voice weighty with sarcasm, he said, "You need to button up honey, before one of us rapists that cannot control ourselves sees your wares." He looked pointedly at her chest.

She followed his gaze. Her cheeks blushed bright pink. Her shirt was completely undone, her bra showed, exposing most of her breasts still blotched with red from his mouth.

They both stared at the still damp mounds. Her nipples puckered as she recalled the feeling of his lips and tongue on her flesh. And, he itched to put them and his hands back on her.

Snapping out of her revelry, Wyn hastily did up the buttons and started quickly walking away.

"Wynna, wait." He grabbed her arm.

She wrenched out of his grasp and kept going. "Don't touch me!"

Muttering again, "Women," rolling his eyes, Vijay traipsed after her.

They hiked for an hour when Vijay said, "There, see the tower?" He pointed in the distance to an electrical power tower. "Tis the village."

She said nothing and headed towards the tower.

It took them thirty minutes to reach the town, and Vijay quickly led them to a pub.

The town was small and rural and ancient, the pub was a hole in the wall.

He led her inside and sat her at a table then went to the bar.

The bartender came right over.

It was midday so there was only one other patron, and he was face down on the bar.

The building was dimly lit, all rustic wood, floors, tables, chairs. In a far corner there was a billiards table, a dartboard off to the left of it and beyond that tiny restrooms. Paddle fans listing around in the ceiling stirred the dust.

While Vijay was at the bar, Wyn went to the restroom. She couldn't wait to hit the flushing toilet, running water and real toilet paper. Luxuries she had taken for granted before.

The bartender greeted him, "Hey, Vij my man, been a while, what's doin'?" The man in his mid-forties, long hair tied back like Vijay's but much thinner and lighter in color. He had a neat beard and sparking brown eyes. A small black apron was tied over his jeans, his sleeves rolled up to his elbows. He spoke Vijay's native language.

"Fredirik, good to see you."

The men fist-bumped.

Vijay said, "Bro, I need to use the phone, and can you get us a couple of sandwiches? Maybe that thick roasted turkey and cheese with lettuce and tomato, heavy on the mayo, some chips and sodas?"

While greeting the bartender and asking for the order, Vijay's eyes never left where Wyn had disappeared into the restroom.

Fredirik had watched Wyn cross the room. "Nice, Vij, stacked, with an ass that I would-"

Vijay's warning growled from deep in his chest. "*Basta*, enough." Still watching the bathroom, he said, "Get me a beer while we are waiting, *bine*- okay?"

Fredirik chuckled. "Ah, who is she then, Vij? Looks ladylike, certainly not one of the bawdy types you normally entertain. You are being abnormally protective, a little sister perhaps?"

Vijay turned his slit eyes to the bartender and coldly remarked, "Just get us the food and bring me a beer, *bine*?"

The bartender laughed. "*Da, bine, bine,*" he replied and left to place the order.

Done with his phone call, Vijay got his beer, and sat at a table and waited for Wyn to return.

When she did, he could see she had washed the grime, and his saliva, from her face and neck and hands. He was betting from her tits, too. Somehow that bothered him. That she had deliberately wiped all traces of him off of her.

The hair around her face curled in damp tendrils. His gaze slid to the bar where Fredirik was eyeing her like she was candy he wanted to lick. Vijay cleared his throat, loud.

The bartender turned his attention to Vijay. Seeing the eyes in narrowed warning, Fredirik winked and grinned at Vijay then hustled off to get their food.

Vijay called after him, "Bring us water too."

He stood up when Wyn reached the table and pulled out a chair. She sat without looking at him and mumbled a small thank you.

Fredirik brought their sandwiches and sodas and set them down. He smiled widely at Wyn. "Good afternoon, Miss, I hope you enjoy your meal." He picked her hand up and kissed the back of it. He said in his language, "You are a very beautiful woman, what is your name?"

Wyn's brows inverted. "I'm sorry, I don't understand?"

Glaring at Fredirik's hand holding Wyn's, Vijay said, "Never mind." In Romanian he warned, "Get lost, bro, before I have to hurt you."

Fredirik laughed at Vijay's threat but he set her hand back down on the table and bowed. He said in English, "I am sorry you do not understand our language my beauty, because I-"

A guttural warning, "Fredirik," Vijay pushed his chair back.

Fredirik smirked, said to him in Romanian, "*Bine, bine*, bro. Never seen you all fucked up over a broad before. It's hilarious."

He held his hands up as Vijay started to rise. "*Bine*, I'm outta here." Fredirik winked at Wyn and walked away chuckling.

Vijay ate his sandwich in six huge bites, slurped down his soda and asked for another beer. Sitting back in his chair, he crossed an ankle over a knee. Crunching on a handful of chips, he watched her nibble at half of a half of sandwich and said, "Listen, Wynna-"

Shaking her head and chewing, not looking at him, she spoke over him, "There is nothing to talk about. Just take me and drop me off and move on. I know you won't look back." Wyn swallowed hard over the lump in her throat. Reaching for her soda, she drank some to force the food down then pushed her plate towards him. She sat back with a sigh, her soda in her hand.

He immediately chomped down the rest of her food. Licking a finger, he leaned back against his chair again and said, "Wynna, we need to talk-"

"No. Don't talk to me. Please." She kept her eyes averted so he couldn't see the pain in them.

He reached across the table to take her hand. "Wynna listen to me-" there was commotion at the door.

Sighing, he rose to his feet and tossed some money on the table. His men had arrived.

Chapter Fifteen

Alex went straight to Wyn and pulled her out of her chair into a big bear hug.

"*Fericită eşti tine a zări,*" he greeted her cheerfully, laughing at Vijay's scowl. He grinned over her head at his friend. "Ah, don't be jealous *mea frate*, I am happy to see you too!"

Under his breath Vijay grumbled in Romanian, "You will not be if you do not take your hands off her."

"*Frate.*" Gage bumped Vijay's fist. "Good to see you both are well." As serious as always, he bowed slightly to Wyn still in Alex's embrace, the low lights beaming off the top of his shaved, brown head and glinting off the gold hoop earrings.

The amber bar lights made the enigmatic tattoos on the side of his face and neck appear darker, more disturbing, and the ones on his lumberjack arms with the flexing of his massive muscles moved sinuously as if they were speaking some ancient, secret language.

Lucian was there as well. He grasped hands with Vijay and clapped him on the back. "Glad you are safe, *mea frate*."

"*Multumesc,* thank you, " Vijay replied with rare warmth then muttered quickly in Romanian, "just shake her hand, she tis tired, she does not need hugs."

"*Da,* sure, *frate.*" Lucian grinned, went over and pried Wyn from Alex's arms and squeezed the hell out of her. He stroked his hands up and down her back sending snickering smug grins at the black looks Vijay lanced at him.

Groaning, "Ah, *mea Zue*." Rubbing his head, Vijay looked to the heavens, muttered, "If these are my friends who are my enemies?"

"Aw quit whining big guy." Alex's smirking grin pricked Vijay's already rising temper. In Romanian, he said, "So that's the way it is, *frate*, you finally admitting you've laid claim on her?"

"Shut up, Alex."

The grin only grew wider. "Does she know? I noticed she is not looking at you, actually she is quite obviously not looking at you, and when you get near her she subtly scuttles a few inches away. What happened out there? You make a pass and she shut you down?"

Vijay's voice a bare growling grumble, he warned, "Alex, you had better shut the fuck up before my fist finds its way through your teeth to your feet."

Alex opened his mouth for another taunting retort when Vijay's eyes narrowed into needle slits so that only a bit of blinding blue light lanced at him.

Slapping Vijay on the back, Alex grinned. "*Bine*, you can spill later when she's not around. Let's go. Car's out front. We traced your GPS and brought it back."

"Thanks," Vijay grunted. He moved over and wound his fingers around Wyn's arm, pulling her from Lucian's embrace and walked with her to the door. He waved a salute to Fredirik, then they all went outside.

Gage and Lucian piled in the back of the car. Vijay held the passenger door open and said to Wyn, "Get in and slide over, that big ugly brute behind you will have to sit up front with us, there is not room enough in the back for those three goliaths."

In Romanian, "Speak for yourself, asshole," Alex joked, climbing in next to Wyn sandwiching her between him and Vijay in the driver's seat.

"Whatever." Vijay grumbled in their language, "Just keep your hands to yourself."

Vijay

"Whoa, sounds like our big team leader has a little crush." Alex's grin sly, he peeked at Vijay while setting his hand on Wyn's thigh. "Let's see that little green monster, Vij," he teased, squeezing her leg.

"Let us see me pull this fucking car over, *frate*, and kick your ass and leave you here, you can hike back." Vijay white-knuckled the wheel, his jaw clenched and working.

"*Bine, bine*, lighten up." Alex chuckled, gave Wyn's thigh another squeeze before moving his hand.

Not understanding what they were saying, Wyn sniffed. "I am not a toy, please stop playing with me."

"Oo," Lucian crowed from the back, "baby chick has claws. You go girl, tell them both to go fuck themselves."

Alex and Lucian kept a running conversation on the way back to the inn.

Gage was normally a quiet man, and Vijay and Wyn were both silent, deep in their own contemplative thoughts.

At the inn, Vijay pulled in front of it and put the shift in park but didn't shut off the engine. The other three men shuffled out.

When Wyn started to slide to the passenger door, Alex leaned in and said, "Sorry, sweetie, you're not coming with us."

Dropping his voice, he said with a kind smile, "He's all bark, no bite, Wynna, but only with you. Don't be afraid of the big shit."

He gently closed the door on her confused eyes that flit from him to Vijay and back to Alex, wide with a silent plea of '*Please don't leave me alone with him-*' he wiggled his fingers at her with a smile and a reassuring, saucy green wink.

Vijay rolled down his window as Alex came to his side. They spoke in Romanian so Wyn had no idea what they were talking about.

Alex patted the car door then stepped back. "*Bine, mea frate*, take care of our girl. We'll see you at the appointed meet."

In English, he said to Wyn, "See ya, gorgeous," and winked at her again.

125

Her weak smile steeped with uncertainty, Wyn gave him a little wave. The other men watched while Vijay pulled back out of the lot.

Wyn stared at them until they drove down the drive to the main road. Her fingers clutched, she twisted and pulled at them, her apprehension as clear as the fear on her face.

"*Dragă,*" Vijay set his large hand over hers to still her fidgeting. "Stop. There is no need for nerves."

She huffed, "Sure, easy for you to say. You're not getting tossed mercilessly from the skillet to the fire."

"I have been trying to tell you, Wynna, I am not taking you to my employer."

Her golden brows arched, she swung her head at him. "What? What are you…going to do with me then?" Her voice filled with dread.

He must have dropped his men off so they wouldn't be a part of her murder. How could he kiss her so passionately, save her life over and over and now…ruthlessly dispose of her?

He pulled over to the side of the road and stopped the car. Turning in his seat to face her, seeing her apprehension straining her face, he sighed.

"Wynna, come on, stop with that shit, I am not going to kill you." His face pulled in an offended scowl. "After all we have been through, you still think that way?" Irritated that she still feared him, didn't trust him, he said evenly. "I am taking you home."

Her body stilled, she studied his harsh face for deceit. He looked unwavering back at her. Confused, she said, "I don't…understand."

He set his hand on her shoulder. Fingering her hair, he said quietly, "Wynna, the moment I saw you at Warwick's place, hurt, frightened, abused, already my heart, my stone cold heart, twisted, witnessing your pain.

"Then you looked at me with those blue eyes ribboned with shimmering strips of green, I," he sighed. "I wanted you for myself. Even so, even if you were ugly as sin or even a man, I still would have had to get you out of there. Those vicious *avan porc, pulatas*, cruel pigs, fucking sick pricks," his fists clenched. His deep breath expanding his broad chest, he let it out in a shudder.

She said quietly, "But you kill too, Vijay."

His eyes dropped. Then raised to her. "*Da*, I do, but tis defensive, Wynna, and I may threaten torture to get compliance or answers, but I do not just go and do it just for fun."

He took a hard breath. "And I sure as hell do not hit or sexually abuse women." His brow quirked wryly. "I mean except beautiful defenseless ones while they sleep."

Bewilderment rippled across her soft face. "But, what were you planning on...doing with me once you rescued me from Warwick?" Her eyes tilted up at him.

His intense steady gaze at her was blistering, but his expression remained inscrutable. Scrubbing his fingers down the front of his face, he shook his head slightly. Shrugged. "I had no fucking idea."

Remembering how he felt seeing her in such wretched distress that day, and fiercely wanting to destroy, break into tiny pieces those men that had harmed her, which he actually did.

Although he would have preferred Warwick die slowly, and in that bastard's case, he would have committed torture without a blink, and with as much agony as he could have forced him to suffer.

But, he had to hurry and stop Warwick before he inflicted more damage to Wyn. And he knew he needed to get her out of there before others came.

Flashes of recalled terror flickered over Wyn's face. She moved imperceptibly from him on the seat.

"I just knew I had to get you out, protect you while your injured body healed...then," he let out a breath and another shrug. "I could not think beyond that. To be honest, if they had not come after you, forcing us to run, I do not know what I...would have been capable of, regarding you."

His lips pulled in, he was not a nice guy. Deep down he feared he would have kept her. Whether or not she acquiesced.

When he realized she had some sort of valuable information, he used that as an excuse to keep her, telling himself it was part of his job to take her to Mann, his employer for him to...interrogate. Except, he knew in the back of his mind right from the start he would never hand her over to another male. For any reason.

Then, before he could formalize a plan, all hell had broken loose and he'd had to get her out of there. His gaze swept her lovely fresh face, down that rocking body, up to her pure beautiful eyes.

So sweet and kind, if only he could hold her and some of that sweet purity would soak into him. Make him a human being again. That's why it bugged him so much when she called him a beast, because he was.

His mouth compressed, no, it wasn't likely he would have let her go. He'd been addicted to her the second their eyes collided in that shitty little cabin. He didn't know how, or for how long he would have kept her, or what he would have done to her.

It was clear he wouldn't have been able to keep her near him without eventually having sex with her, and how forceful he would have gotten if over time she didn't yield? Well, he damn well wasn't going to think about those questions now.

He had to look away from those big guileless eyes; he didn't want her to see the darkness inside him. "Um, so," he continued, "when I realized who you were, the person I was sent to get, ah," he dragged both hands through his long hair.

"*Yah*, I kept telling myself I was taking you to my employer, but, the truth is," he brushed her cheek with his thumb then slid his hand around her neck. "I never had any intentions of doing that. I would never, not for all the money in the world turn you over to him. Or any other man for that matter."

Wyn's lips parted, doubt clouded her eyes. Her dismayed gaze scanned his eyes. She discerned sincerity, but the intense blue orbs were narrowed under their low-ridged brow. "Vijay, I still don't understand what you're saying."

Stuffing the guilt, and fear of her rejection, he smiled at her, pulled her head close, so close their noses almost touched. "I am saying, Wynna *dragă*, I want you. Not just for a night, or two, or ten, I want us to be together."

He tipped his head and touched her lips with his, lightly, then he tilted further to kiss her harder. His tongue thrust through her lips, sweeping the inside of her mouth before meshing with her tongue.

Still, he held back to ensure her response was willing, that she was as into him as he was to her. She accepted his kiss, but tentative, only touching mouths, she kept her body apart, away from his.

He drew back, studying her for her reaction. His hand still webbed the back of her neck, his thumb brushed her jaw. "Wynna? Tell me what you want. Do you, do you think you could…want me too?" If she were any other woman, he wouldn't need to ask, but if she was any other woman he wouldn't be asking.

Her eyes flickered all around his face, to his mouth, his brooding eyes, the scar, his strong jaw. She saw his gaze following hers, watching her studying him in return. "Vijay, I…" she trailed off.

His lids lowered in dread, he didn't know how he was going to let her go if she didn't want him. But he would. It would kill him, but he would. "Tis…all right, *mea dragă,* I know I am the beast you have called me." His snort deprecating. "Tis who I am, what I have become. A crude, hard-hearted mercenary with many deaths under my hands. And you are…"

He stroked his thumb up and down her jaw. "You are sweet, and precious, and pure. Deep down I knew inside you would never want an unconscionable brute like me. You are too…nice." His hand dropped, he sat back with a heavy exhale.

"Vijay," she grabbed his shirt with her fists and pulled him back to her. "I have to be honest, I don't know what I want. I've been through a…life-changing ordeal that you were a big part of."

Nodding, his lips pulled in. He glanced down at her hands clutching his shirt then up to her still bewildered eyes. "I cannot tell you how sorry I am that all that happened to you. I can understand you not wanting to see big ugly me as a reminder of-"

Unbuckling her belt, Wyn climbed to her knees and shuffled over to him and planted her mouth on his. Her hands slid up his enormous chest and up around his neck.

Surprised, stiff for a second, Vijay set his hands on her waist and let her kiss him. Then he drew back, his brows raised in reservation. Was she just giving him a goodbye kiss?

Wyn put both hands on the sides of his face, feeling the hard rugged planes under her soft fingers, she kissed him again. So close, their body warmth wove like a downy basket between them.

She said, "I don't know what I want, Vijay, but I do know I like kissing you, and touching you, sleeping beside you, and when I thought you'd left me in the woods, yes, I was scared of the wild, but, I was also afraid I'd never see you again."

Her lips brushed his. "When you didn't lie down next to me that night, I felt so...abandoned. You make me feel safe, Vijay."

His gaze flit around her face. "I am glad of that, Wynna, but I want more than that. I want...your heart." *Because you have taken mine.*

It figures the one time in his life a woman snuck in under his guard and stole through his senses. Made herself at home, built a nice little nest right inside his heart, it has to be a woman the extreme opposite of him in breadth as well as grace.

She was way too good for him, unattainable. He'd felt he'd made her dirty when he had put his tainted hands on her pure skin that night he'd woken to find he was assaulting her in his sleep.

He watched her, waiting with his heart splintering by the second. None of his dark feelings and thoughts mattered, he wanted her with his every breath and there wasn't a thing he could do to change it.

She smiled. "Can we just start with just, uh, getting to know one another? I need to make sure what I feel for you is more than just as...my rescuer...my hero..."

The muscles of his stomach loosened one by one as hope seeped in. He returned her smile. "You did say you liked kissing me, and touching me, I can live with taking it slow for as long as it takes for you to know for sure."

Vijay

His smile curved to a leer. "You said you liked touching me, that goes both ways, *dragă*,"

His hands on her waist, Vijay lowered his head to meld their lips. The kiss turned torrid quickly. His mouth crushing hers, his hands clinching the soft sides of her waist, he was already hard, his arousal started when he had first turned and faced her, and only grew harder by the second.

In his ratcheting urgency, his tongue pushed practically down her throat, he skimmed his hands up her sides, over her ribs, to cover her breasts. Their moans mingling, he kneaded her supple flesh, he knew too roughly, but his tongue in her throat, her breasts in his hands, his head was about to burst off.

Never moving his lips from hers, he unbuttoned her blouse and pushed the halves to the side then looked down at her.

"*Mea Zue*, Wynna, you are so beautiful, you have the tits of an angel. I cannot wait to see you naked." Cupping his hands under both breasts, pushing them up and together, he put his face in her cleavage, inhaled sharply then kissed them.

Her breathy sigh lightly whisked his hair. His lips and tongue in a frenzy on her flesh, he sucked hard, too hard. Realizing he was losing it, Vijay drew back.

His chest heaving with heavy, fast breaths, he moved his hands to cradle her face. "Ah, *mea dragă*, I am sorry, I lose my head with you. Tis not the time or place. We need to go."

She blinked bleary-eyed, delirious passion at him. Her tongue rolled around moistening her lips, she chewed on the lower one, staring at his mouth like she wanted to chew on it too.

"Do not look at me like that baby, or we will never leave this place." He smoothed her hair off her face then reluctantly, awkwardly buttoned her blouse with his big fingers. "Not used to dressing women, I am not very good at it. I am usually doing the opposite. But I like anything that lets me touch you." He smiled at her.

"Thank you, Vijay. But, can you not mention other women when you have your hands all over my breasts?"

131

"Ahh," his body tingled at her words. "Thanks for the picture. You talk like that and you will see what it *really* feels like." Two fingertips slid under her chin, he lifted it for a light kiss.

"Wynna, with you in my life, there are no other women. Ever again. I have waited my whole life for you." He shoved the gear in drive and pulled back onto the highway.

Settling back in her seat, Wynna looked out the window. "Do you want my address for the GPS or do you have a map?"

"*Nu*. You are not going back to your apartment."

Brows up, she cocked her head at him.

He had a hard, strong profile. He looked just as menacing from the side as the front. But Wynna didn't fear him like she had. At least not at the moment. "What do you mean? You said you would take me home?"

He leaned back comfortably with one broad hand on the wheel. "You were taken from your apartment. They know where you live and you sure as hell cannot be there alone."

"Are you planning to stay with me?"

His lip quirked. "*Zue*, if I could, I sure as hell would. But I cannot, not right now. I am taking you to your aunt and uncle's where you first stayed."

Her mouth pursed out, brows lowered, chin tightened with a stubborn tilt. "I don't want to go there. I left because…well I left and got my own place and that's where I want to go."

"You are not going there, Wynna. You can either go to your aunt's or I will take you to the airport."

Fists clenching in her lap, she said, "You can't tell me where I can or cannot go. What about with you?" Not that she would go stay with him but she was curious to his answer.

He turned to glance at her. His heart flipped over. Would he ever tire of looking at those glowing eyes and pretty lips? He didn't look lower; it would only stir his blood again.

"If I had to, to protect you I would keep you with me. But right now I am living with the other guys. When we are on a mission we stay at a place but tis like a lodge, only a few rooms, a living room and we all sleep in the other room."

"Together?"

The frown he sent her made her giggle. "Of course not. We all have our own beds, tis like a dorm. But it makes it more convenient to our mission and we are seldom there. You see why the guys went girl crazy when we were at the inn?"

He patted her knee. "But, Wynna, if I absolutely had to, trust me, I would squeeze you in my bed, but you would likely be pretty uncomfortable with the other guys snoring away all around you."

He laughed at the twist of her lips. "I am not around much, I have to be in the field, so I could not stay with you at your apartment. And even if I could, I do not want you there period. Tis not safe. Neither will I put you unprotected in a hotel by yourself."

"Nonetheless, Vijay, I don't want to go back to the mansion. I want to go to my own place."

"Why do you not want to go back there?"

She didn't answer right away.

He shot her a questioning glance. "Wynna?" His brow furrowed. "Are you afraid of something? Did someone hurt you?"

The more he asked, the more he could see her face closing, and the lower and harsher his voice became. "Did someone touch you improperly?"

"No, no, I'm not afraid to go there. I just don't want to." Her lips pursed out again, she crossed her arms over her chest.

Looking back over at her, he chuckled. "You look so cute when you pout. Makes me want to nibble the shit out of your lips."

A giggle slipped out. "Vijay," she tried to sound admonishing but couldn't make it.

"If there is nothing to be afraid of, then I am taking you there."

Her sigh was loud and annoyed. "You do and I will just go back to my apartment when you leave."

"*Nu* you will not."

"Really Vijay, stop the big bad guy stuff. You can't force me to-"

"I will take care of your apartment so that you will be unable to reside there."

Her eyes squinted at him, mouth firmed. "What does that mean?"

His shoulder bumped up. "I will make it so that you cannot live there. Do not ask me how, what I will do, because I am not going to tell, I will just do it. I am a hired mercenary, Wynna, I can do a lot of things I am not proud of, but will do if I find it necessary. And it is imperative that you not stay there."

He glanced at her mutinous expression. "Got it?"

She didn't answer him.

He tried a different tract. "I know you have too kind of a heart, *dragă*, you would not want another person to suffer because of you."

Her head snapped to him. "What? You would hurt people at the apartments?"

He looked quickly at her then back to the road. "I will do whatever is necessary to keep you safe. Do not doubt me."

Wyn's skin quivered. She knew this man was dangerous, lethal, she'd seen him kill firsthand. Seven men at once for heaven's sake. What was she getting herself into being with him? Maybe she should let him drop her at her aunt's then just cut ties.

Her gaze shifted over at him.

Those brilliant, chilling blue eyes, long black hair tied back, hard face, granite body. And those lips, she sighed, what lips they were. They were soft but tough, and could they rush shivers down her body and send heat gushing between her legs. She faintly shook her head. No. She wanted to be with this man, deadly dangerous or not.

He said, "If there are things you want from your place, you give me a list and I will get them after I take you to your aunt's. You will not go near that place, even with me."

"I'll have to tell the landlord to let you in. I don't have my keys."

"Do not bother. I will get in."

Her eyes flashed at him, "You're going to break into my-"

"Let it go, baby, we will talk about everything when we get to your aunt's."

"Fine," she sighed sullenly, "take me there."

He did.

Vijay drove up the long winding driveway to the luxurious mansion.

Hedged by perfectly manicured round shrubs and abundant leafy trees in the summer, the three-story stone building framed with white trim sat majestically exuding wealth.

It didn't bother Vijay, his own family had wealth and he made insane money doing what he did for a living. But he'd have to start considering something else if he was going to stay involved with Wynna.

With the jobs he did now, he would be gone for months at a time and no sane man leaves a drop dead gorgeous woman alone for any length of time.

Besides, he glanced at her. He wants to be with her. His plans are to buy them a house and have her in his bed every night. He has no intentions of letting her be away from his side.

At least once this crap is resolved.

Chapter Sixteen

As he shut off the engine, the huge double white doors in front of the mansion opened and a woman in a black maid's uniform appeared.

Wyn had called ahead to tell them she was all right and that she was coming back to stay with them. She had been missing for a few weeks.

Her relatives had been preparing to call the police. They had thought at first she had gone touring the countryside, then perhaps was visiting with friends. Not that they knew of any, she hadn't been in the country for that long. But when Wyn hadn't returned her aunt's calls they became concerned.

Vijay observed Wyn's clenched jaw, and she was strangling her fingers like she did when anxious. He felt bad. She did not want to be here, he would have to pry why out of her. But for now it was the safest place he could think of for her to stay.

He got out of the car and went around to her side and opened the door. Her face was ashen, she didn't move. He reached in and took her hand. "Come on, honey, it will be okay."

She looked up at him. "But you've brought me here and you're leaving me. I won't see you again." She looked at him like she didn't believe he would come back.

Her aunt had made it clear that she would not allow what she understood to be a ruffian stay at the mansion. As far as she was concerned, the little Wyn had told her on the phone, she decided

Vijay

Vijay was a lawless soldier paid to come to this country and was up to no good.

Vijay had already told Wyn he had to go meet with his men and continue his mission, and others they were working on. He'd let her know when he could be back to see her.

Pulling her gently out of the car, he cupped her chin, leaned over and kissed her. "Wynna, I will be back. You are not getting rid of me that easily." He kissed her again.

"Now, come on, I am going in with you." He grinned at her pout. "I will not dump you and run baby. I have to see that you will be all right here. And," he leaned over and licked around her ear smiling at her shivers.

He watched her nipples pebble under the blouse. "I would love to make love to you, tonight. Believe me, I could get in and out of this house and no one would know," he smiled at her blush. "But you are not ready yet baby," he ran the tip of his finger with affection down her nose.

His voice low rough velvet, he murmured, "I dream of a night, soon, of holding you in my arms in our own privacy. Inside on a warm bed with pillows where I can strip you very slowly, then even more slowly make love to you. Or," he chuckled, "actually, the way I feel about you, I am already on the edge of exploding. Our first time will likely be fast, too fast, so the second time, well, maybe not until the third will be more slowly."

"Vijay." Peeking up through her lashes at him, her smile shy, voice soft, she said, "I miss you already." She ran her palms up his chest and around his neck pulling him down and kissed him.

They clung to each other kissing until a polite cough sounded from the house.

Breaking apart, Wyn peered around his wall of shoulders to see her aunt and uncle had joined the maid on the broad portico.

Her cheeks pink and lips red and plumped from his kisses, Wyn took his hand and brought him up the yard to the house.

Vijay regarded her relatives through wary eyes.

The pair stood stolidly waiting for Wyn to reach them.

His gaze narrowed. If it had been his niece that had been kidnapped, possibly tortured and assaulted, he would be hugging her until she screamed.

Taking in her uncle's perfectly tailored, designer, three piece suit and her aunt's equally right off the runway dress, her $500 coif and those heels with the red soles, he looked down at his own clothes.

He had taken his pullover sweater off in the car, the air was considerably warmer now that they were out of the forest. He was wearing a black t-shirt, black jeans, and his biker boots. The long chain was still hooked to the front of his belt and his wallet in his back pocket.

The short sleeves not only exposed his enormous muscles and brawny forearms, they also revealed his arms covered with tats, including the one that swarmed up the side of his neck. "I think I should have changed first," he muttered ruefully.

Wyn stroked her fingers down his thick long arms. "You are perfect the way you are."

"*Da, yah*, whatever, let us proceed." He set his hand on her lower back and the couple trod the rest of the way to the wide steps and up to where Wyn's family waited.

Her uncle, fiftyish, stepped forward and grasped Wyn's arms. Holding her for a moment, he checked her out then pulled her into his arms. "Wyn, so glad you are safe and back home with us." His grey hair was sort of a poufy cloud around his head. With a small grey moustache he was fairly tall at 6 feet. His wife stood almost as tall as him in her heels. He released Wyn.

Wyn moved to her aunt.

Odessa Eastwood warmly hugged her niece then set her in front of her. She brushed a long yellow curl off Wyn's shoulder. "You gave us quite a fright, dear niece. We told you that you should stay with us, safe here under our protection. Under Jazer's protection. Speaking of, are you going to introduce your…friend?"

Her hair still dark with only a few streaks of grey was tied back in a loose bun. Twisting a loose tendril near her ear, Odessa's dark eyes over wide cheekbones swept Vijay from the top of his black ponytail to the scar over his eye to the tattoo on his neck. Her gaze traveled over the massive shoulders and chest, to the bulked arms also covered with tattoos.

"Oh, of course. Aunt Odessa. This Vijay Zastrovna. Vijay, this is my aunt, Odessa Eastwood."

Vijay could see Odessa's lip curling into a snobbish sneer of disgust more and more the longer she looked at him. She kept her arms firmly at her sides, she was not going to shake his hand. Not that he was offering it.

Her gaze roved over his jeans, along the big chain hanging in a loop down the front of his jeans to the back, down to the heavy boots and back up to his tapered blue eyes that glowed blindingly under the low ridge of his brow.

Nose wrinkling in distaste, she looked around him to the front yard. One brow arched. "No motorcycle, young man?"

A slight bow to his head, only one side of Vijay's mouth turned up. He deliberately let his gaze roam down her figure and back up, mirroring her condemnation of him.

The side of his mouth tilted up further at the pink that flared across Odessa's wide cheeks at his impertinent perusal. His blatant rudeness in not replying to her question further darkened the pink. Odessa snapped her eyes from his.

Wyn's uncle stepped to Vijay and held out his hand. "Good day, I am Sheffield Eastwood, Wyn's uncle. I want to thank you for bringing her to us."

Vijay shook his hand. "Vijay Zastrovna. Pleased to meet you."

Sheffield's moustache twitched. "Ah, I hear a strong accent." Without inquiring about Vijay's origins, he held his arm out for them to go into the house.

The women entered first. Vijay and Sheffield walked in together.

Sheffield ushered them across a wide round vestibule. Their shoes tapped along the luminescent Caribbean green and **Carrara white marble** that stretched in a vast diameter.

A double wide staircase split the room, leading up to the other levels, with a sparkling, dynasty chandelier dangling over the center.

To the left of the staircase, he escorted them down a long corridor with doors on both sides that eventually led to a salon.

The room was painted in pale yellow and white with a stone fireplace, a big bright window, and bookshelves crammed albeit strictly neatly with books.

The group settled on cushioned chairs in yellow and green flowered print.

"You were telling us where you are from, Mr. Zastrovna," Sheffield nodded to him.

The maid scurried in with a tray of tea and pastries. Placing the tray on the coffee table, she poured four teacups then set the teapot down on the tray.

"*Da*. I am from a village outside of Romania. *Multumesc*," he thanked the maid as she handed him a cup of tea and ignored her coy glance down his body pausing at the fly of his jeans. He held a hand up in refusal when she gestured to the cream and sugar.

"Oh," Sheffield said politely, smiling neatly to Vijay. "My only knowledge of Romania is that from the old Transylvania movies, you know, Count Dracula and all. Oh, and of course there're the gypsies." He chose a pastry and set it on a small plate. Pouring cream into his tea, he primly stirred then gave it a tentative sip.

When Vijay started to comment, Sheffield smiled and glanced at Wyn then back to Vijay. "I don't believe Wyn knows Romanian? I've heard it's somewhat like Latin mixed with Russian?"

Vijay's smile was cold. His voice colder, he responded, "Somewhat. My village was so secluded we bastardized the language. We string words together improperly. However, we do understand each other and that is what counts." His smile warmed as he turned to Wyn. "And Wynna will be learning it."

She smiled up at him, missing the look her relatives shared.

"Oh?" Odessa's nose crinkled. "We understood you were just providing her with a ride here and that you would be...moving on?" She ignored the teacup set aside for her.

Seeing Vijay's brows draw down in a glower, Wyn stood up in front of him. "No. Vijay and I are...together."

"What!" Odessa slapped her hands on her thighs. Her mouth dropped, dark eyes narrowed. She glared at Wyn. "You can't be serious, what about-"

"Darling!" a male voice intruded from the doorway.

Wyn cringed and glanced at Vijay.

His face impassive, he eyed the young man on the threshold who was hurrying towards Wyn.

When he snatched Wyn's arm, hauled her into his arms and hugged her, Vijay also got up.

Hoping to avoid a scene, Wyn pushed from the man.

"Wynnie, my princess, I was so worried!" He carried his hardy physique well on his tall frame. Handsome with chestnut hair and dark eyes, he appeared wealthy, aristocratic, and like Sheffield, he was also attired in an expensive suit.

"Uh, Vijay, this is-"

"Wynnie's fiancé, hi." Thrusting his hand out, he announced, "Jazer Edrei, nice to meet you."

His expression unreadable, Vijay's skin darkened. He looked at the proffered hand, up to the man's face then to Wyn. Ignoring Edrei, he grasped Wyn's arm and growled, "If you will excuse us, Wynna and I need to talk."

Before anyone could object, Vijay whisked Wyn out of the room and out to the hall. His head jerked back and forth as he sought a place to go. He stalked to a door and shoved it open and pulled her inside then closed the door.

His hands on his hips, fingers gripping his hipbones, eyes blazing, he said tersely, "What the hell is going on, Wynna?"

She stood awkwardly, her face pale. He looked as fiercely dangerous as he had the day they'd met.

"Uh," she swallowed several times thinking of what to say. They were in the den. Paneled walls, a thick carpet covered the floor, and dark wood furniture with a blue sofa and comfortable matching chairs filled the room.

"Knock it the fuck off, Wynna," he snapped. Grabbing her arm, he brought her to the sofa and made her sit then plunked down next to her. "Spit it out. Who the fuck is that guy and what is he to you?"

"Vijay," she set her hand on his leg, "he's why I didn't want to come back here."

Pins and needles prickled up Vijay's back, alarmed at what he had just heard. "You never mentioned a fiancé." Of course he realized he'd not asked if she was involved with anyone. He hadn't cared, she was with him. "You let me kiss you while you were fucking engaged?" He said tersely, "Talk. Now."

Sucking in a deep breath, Wyn said, "Okay, please calm down." She went to move her hand but he set his over it holding it on his thigh.

Another long inhale and she explained, "Jazer is a neighbor. When I came here, my aunt pushed me to date him. I mean really pushed. She kept setting it up so I would find myself alone with him. She begged and cajoled and pleaded for me to date him. Finally I went out with him.

"Then, one day, I walked in on him and my cousin, Shreva Vanguard. They weren't quite- ah, involved, but they looked like they were in the process of about to be and had seemed to have suddenly, guiltily broken apart when I came in. Actually, Jazer was on his knees and pushing her dress up."

Wyn tried to pull her hand away again but Vijay kept it still. She looked at him. His face inscrutable, eyes tapered to slits never left her face.

Wyn went on, "So, not only was I really not that interested in him, I suspected Jazer was bedding Shreva on the side so I tried to break off our budding relationship. But, uh, his countermove was to propose to me."

Vijay's raven brows drew down so low his eyes were almost indiscernible. "Go on."

She cleared her throat. "Yes, so, he had roses, champagne, got down on one knee, the whole nine yards. The worst part, he did it in front of both of our families and his friends at a party. Not wanting to humiliate him, I said I would think about it. Worst thing I could have done.

"Now everyone thinks we are engaged. When I tried to convince people we are not, they chose to not believe me because he keeps saying differently. He has his hands on me all the time, kissing me, um…"

Vijay's color turned black, his eyes disappeared. He squeezed her hand so hard she cried out.

He let up slightly, but he looked like thunder.

She hurried on, "So, hence, the moving out to my own apartment. But, he still would not give up. He pursued me relentlessly. I was preparing to set up a time when I could give him his ring back and tell him he needed to tell everyone we were not engaged, or I would."

"Why the hell did you not do it right away?"

Wyn frowned at him. "I didn't want him at my apartment where I'd be alone with him, and," she sighed, "my aunt is so hard to- to discuss things with. She makes up her mind and that's it. I," she took another deep breath. "I'm weak. I kept hoping the longer I stayed away they might forget about it."

"Why did you not go home, return to the states?"

"My uncle had talked me into letting him keep my money where it would be safe. He has my credit cards, passport and my visa, and I have only enough cash to pay rent and food. Every time I've asked him for my stuff back he stalls me. Even without my work visa I was going to try to look for work the next day…then I was…taken."

"I will talk to him-"

Swiftly, she said, "No! He is wealthy and well known here. He would have the police all over you in a New York minute."

"Wynna," he squeezed her hand gently this time. "I am not afraid of your uncle, the police, not even your scary aunt." That brought a tiny smile to her face. He smiled back then he looked down at their hands.

He lifted hers and asked, "Where is the ring?" If she'd been wearing a ring, he would still have rescued her from Warwick but he would never have touched another man's woman. Then again, this was Wynna and he likely would have ignored the ring and still sought to seduce her.

"I never wore it. It's in a box at my apartment." She smiled with a hint of coquetry. "Should I add it to my list of things for you to get?"

He shook his head, a wry twist pulled in his mouth. He scrubbed his fingers over his scruff. "*Nu*, I will remember it." He reached around and pulled out his wallet and opened it. "Here," he took out almost all of the bills, mostly $100's and a credit card and put them in her hands.

"No, Vijay, I can't-"

He closed her hands over the money. "*Da* you will, I am not leaving you here without funds." His gaze strolled over her. "In fact, I do not want to leave you here at all. I had not wanted to put you up in a hotel, I felt it was too dangerous, you would have no protection. But now," his mouth pressed in a line, "I will take you to a hotel where-"

"No, I will be fine here. I promise. I can handle things, I am an adult."

"Barely."

"Whatever." She rolled her eyes. "I can take care of myself."

"Sure you can," he said drily as pictures filled his mind of her, after being beaten, lying on the floor with her hands tied behind her back and Warwick taking her shorts off, then onto the men grabbing her at the hotel, and again with that bastard in the woods attacking her.

Even the aborted run and fall into the river. Vijay shook his head to dispel the images. He looked at her. He could tell she knew what he was thinking.

Setting his hand on her shoulder, he said, "Wynna-"

"No, Vijay. I will be fine. You were right, this is the safest place for me. Those men chasing after me won't be able to get past the security guard and alarm systems. I will be here waiting for you."

Their eyes connected. He cupped her face with one hand and pulled her in, kissed her deeply, longingly.

When they parted, he slipped the cell from his pocket Alex had provided a new one for him. "Take mine. I will get yours and bring you your stuff day after tomorrow." Unlocking it, he told her the password and showed her his contacts.

"Call me any second you are fearful, unsure or uncomfortable. I will come. I want you to call me tonight at ten. Dial Alex, I will be with him." He handed her the phone.

Hearing loud voices coming down the hall, they stood up. His mouth near hers, Vijay whispered, "If he so much as tries to kiss you, touch you, I will remove his lips, one at a time. Then his fingers."

"Vijay!" Wyn exclaimed with an appalled giggle. "Stop that."

He gave her a light kiss. "I mean it. You know me well enough that I mean what I say. And I truly mean this, Wynna, *mea dragă*, I love you." He kissed her gently again then opened the door before she could respond to his statement.

"Young man! How dare you appropriate my niece!" Odessa's entire outraged face was scarlet.

His arm around Wynna, Vijay shouldered past her aunt, uncle, glared menacingly at the fiancé fuck. They all walked all the way back to the front door where they stopped and the rest of the family caught up.

"Listen here, mate," Jazer stepped in front of Vijay and got in his face. Jazer was a big, tall man. Vijay was bigger, taller, and he had muscles on top of muscles. "You will keep your hands off of my fiancé, you will not-"

"She is not your fiancé, you shit."

"Language, gentlemen, please, there are ladies present!" Sheffield moved to them but was smart enough not to get between the two sparring men. Both young men ignored him.

His scowl as black as night, Vijay threatened, "You will not touch her. I will be back in two days. I hear you came near her and," his thick ridged brow covered most of his piercing eyes, "I will make you regret it."

"Uh," Jazer hemmed and backed a fraction from him. His voice went up an octave, "Is that a threat?"

Vijay leaned his face in so close he could smell the man's expensive French cologne, it made his nose itch. The words grit through his clenched teeth, "You bet."

"Mr. Zastrovna, please, this is not how we act in this home. Please conduct yourself accordingly," Odessa admonished him with her haughty air. But she did regard him with a hint of unnerving fear. An angry Vijay Zastrovna was not a pretty sight.

"Walk me to my car," he said to Wynna then turned and strode out the door.

"Wyn," Odessa said, "don't go-"

"Wynnie!" Jazer shouted.

Wyn ran after Vijay.

He stopped at his car and leaned against it pulling her into his arms. "*Dragă,*" his sigh beleaguered, "I so fucking hate to leave you here."

"It's only for a while, right?" She smiled at him, stroking her hands up to twine around his neck.

He muttered an irritated, "*Yah.*"

Their mouths joined in a deep, heart palpitating kiss.

Vijay pulled back. His breaths came fast and harsh, his ebony eyes heavy-lidded. He rebuked her, "You should have told me about that shit fiancé of yours, I never would have brought you here."

She pressed her palms on his chest, drawing her fingers over the taut muscles. Her head lowered, she peered up through her lashes. "I figured I could deal with it. I had hoped you wouldn't have to know about it. I didn't know he'd be here tonight," she sighed, "but I should have. Once I called and told my aunt I was returning to their home, there was no way she wouldn't have called and told him."

Vijay curled a finger under her chin raising it. "You will never keep secrets from me again. You understand?"

Her hands skimmed over his pecs and his shoulders to twine around his neck. "Works both ways. You must always tell me the truth, and not keep secrets from me."

His mouth curved up. "I promise, *mea dragă.*" He kissed the tip of her nose, then her lips.

Hearing the disgruntled group up on the porch watching them grow louder, he said reluctantly, "*Bine*, I have to go. Call me if you need me, baby, or for any reason even to just say hi. Regardless, remember to call me tonight at ten. Okay?"

She nodded.

He kissed her one more time then got in his car. A quick nod to her family, another warning glare to Jazer, and a tender look to Wyn, and Vijay took off.

Behind her, Odessa scolded, "Really, Wyn, that man, he looks like the leader of one of those dreadful American motorcycle gangs one sees on TV, the Outlaws or Hell's Angels, or something like that."

"Yes, really, Wynnie," Jazer chastised huffily. "I allowed you stay at your own place and this is what you do? Dirty yourself with a gangster foreigner?"

Sheffield piped in, "Wynna Pila, you are an engaged woman, it is scandalous that you are out of the front yard making out with that heathen!"

"That's it, Wynnie, we will start planning our wedding immediately," Jazer insisted arrogantly, stomping back and forth for emphasis with his hands clasped behind him. Then he stopped in front of Wyn and grasped her hand.

"Yes, yes," Odessa agreed, nodding vehemently. "That will put things back in order. You two will marry as soon as we can get it arranged, and that- that- gangster, he will be turned away if he comes back here."

"Stop! Stop it all of you!" Wyn yanked her hand from Jazer's and said hotly, "I, we, Jazer, you and I are not engaged."

Protesting, "But darling," Jazer tried to grab her hand again, "you have been traumatized, you will come to your senses. He has forced himself on you. Don't worry darling," he stroked her hair then set his hand on her shoulder. "I will protect you from him. Once we are married-"

"No!" she practically screamed.

"Really, Wyn, please remember yourself," Odessa said calmly, "your upbringing, you are not a fishwife. It's that man's fault. His influence on you, he is a hoodlum, he-"

"*Basta*! Enough!" Inside Wyn smiled a little, she felt some satisfaction using one of the words she'd heard Vijay say. Then with a dark frown, she turned to Jazer. "Jazer, we are not getting married, I never agreed to it. We discussed this. You must tell your family."

She turned to her aunt and uncle, "Jazer and I are not getting married. That's it. Final." She stalked away from them to the house.

Wyn managed to avoid Jazer for the next few days. She claimed a stomach flu so she could stay in her room and not have to listen to her aunt and uncle go on and on about the wedding.

Although she declared it again and again, that there would be no wedding, they all ignored her and proceeded with plans.

Chapter Seventeen

The morning of the second day, she received a letter in the mail. Taking it to the privacy of her room, she opened and read it.

'Miss Pila, your uncle David Pila requests you to come to him. He does not feel you are safe. You are to go to a party Saturday night at Winston Amber's estate. An invitation will be there for you. Get close to Mr. Martine Cartiér, he will be a link to your uncle.'

The letter was unsigned.

Wyn folded the letter and put it in her pocket. She showered and changed into one of her aunt's loaned pants and blouse. The slacks were so long she had to roll the hems several times. Then she went and stood by the window to wait for Vijay. He had promised he would be back today.

As the third day passed, her stomach started aching, maybe he wasn't coming back. Maybe now that he was away from her, he realized he only cared for Wyn because he'd felt sorry for her, felt responsible for her because he'd rescued her.

Or it had only been a physical attraction and now he'd had sex with one or more of those other women and was sated and doesn't crave her anymore. Her head drooped miserably, she looked over at her bed. His phone was there.

They had talked the first night at ten as he had said, but when she tried the next night Alex's phone was not in a satellite area. The call didn't even go to voicemail. She tried texting but that didn't go through either.

Should she call him again? No, if he didn't want her she wouldn't push herself at him, if he didn't-

Her head popped up, was that a car?

She pushed the curtain aside, her heart started banging so hard she though it would jump right out of her chest!

Wyn ran down the stairs and to the door before anyone else knew he was there. The mansion was filled with servants, her aunt, uncle, cousin Shreva, Shreva's parents and her little brother.

Throwing the door open with absolutely no decorum, Wyn flew out the door and down the steps.

By the time she reached the driveway, he had parked the car and was getting out. Suddenly unsure, Wyn came to a slow stop. He stood beside the car, their eyes connected and they stared at each other.

He raised his arms and said, "Wynna, *dragă.*"

Wyn ran to him, leapt up into his arms and threw her legs around his waist. He wrapped his big arms around her, and their lips latched.

After a long, heady kiss, Vijay drew back. Supporting her with one arm under her butt, he caressed her face. "I have missed you terribly *mea fetita.*" He set her on her feet keeping his arm around her waist.

Wyn laid her head on his shoulder and gazed up at him. "I thought you might not come," she said when he bowed his head to kiss her.

"Always baby, always." He gave her another hungry kiss. "Here, wait," he let go of her to go to his trunk. He opened it and took out several suitcases.

"Oh Vijay, my things! Thank you!"

Closing the trunk, he groaned, "Shit, there goes the neighborhood." Tucking one case under an arm, and picking up the other two, Vijay nodded at Odessa and Sheffield standing in the doorway watching them.

Wyn led him into the house.

Odessa looked down her nose at him. "Mr. Zastrovna, we thought we'd seen the last of you."

"*Da*, well, there you go." He followed Wyn who moved quickly through the vestibule heading to the stairs.

"Wyn! You are not taking that young man to your room! It is unseemly!" Odessa hurried after them.

Her hand on the bannister, Wyn turned to face her aunt.

"Auntie Odessa, please. I am an adult. He is bringing my things."

"Tell him to leave them. Jazer can fetch them for you later," Odessa insisted, crossing her arms over her green and white dress with puffy sleeves and a full skirt.

Hearing the man's name made Vijay's ears burn. "Show me to your room, Wynna."

"Mr. Zastrovna," her voice growing strident, Odessa turned to her husband for support.

But Sheffield stood there saying nothing. He remembered what Vijay had looked like in his T-shirt: over 6'5 of sculpted muscles, carved chest, enormous shoulders with cords of muscles strung across them, the only thing narrow on him were his sinewy hips. Nope, Sheffield was not getting his ass handed to him by the mercenary gangster.

The hulk carried three big suitcases like they were straw baskets. There were no male servants in attendance today either that Sheffield could sic on him, not that it would matter, Wyn had told them much of what had happened to her, not the gritty details, but enough.

Slaughtering seven armed thugs at once, without firing a shot. Yeah, so, at the moment anyway, Vijay Zastrovna would be doing just as he pleased.

Upstairs, Wyn brought Vijay to her room.

151

He followed her inside and set the bags on her bed. He looked around. "This is nice, Wynna, this room alone is twice as big as your apartment."

Pale rose walls, wallpapered with faint green stripes and darker roses, creamy curtains matched the bed cover and shams and rug. Honey light furniture, desk, dresser, armoire, everything was light and elegant and feminine, just like Wyn.

She replied, "Vijay, I would rather live in a hovel than where people push me around and try to make me do things I don't want to."

He studied her for a minute.

Vibrant rosy cheeks that matched the walls, creamy skin that matched the pillow shams, startling eyes a blend of ribbons of blue and green. Long curly blonde hair, and a rocking body.

He felt like he had his cake and his ice cream and the cherry on top and so much more with this woman. He snapped his fingers as he remembered something. "Oh *yah*." He went to one of the suitcases and unsnapped the tabs opening it, and took out the small jewelry box. "Here."

Wyn glared at it like it was a wasp.

"You need to give it to him, baby. I am more than thrilled to do it myself, but it would be cruel." He handed it to her.

Holding it gingerly as if it might bite her, she reluctantly agreed, "Okay, yes, you're right." She moved to the dresser and set it down.

He wanted it done now. Right now. Frowning, he pulled on his lips. "When? When are you going to give it to him?"

She swung around to him, her lips parted. "I...I'm not sure. He's coming for dinner. You're staying right? You said you would."

He took big steps to her and slid his arms around her, hugging her close to his body. "*Da*, baby. I do not have a lot of time. I have to meet a man in Monaco who can give me a lead to your-" he broke off. "Uh, sorry, Wynna. My job is still to find your uncle. I am just not going to do it through you."

She snuggled into his embrace. Rubbing her face on his thermal, she slipped her hands around his waist. "Thank you, Vijay."

"*Da*, I do not want anything to come between us, baby." He palmed her round bottom, squeezing each globe then pressed her hips against his growing arousal.

"The election is in a month. I hope we can be together before then, but with my having other jobs I am still doing, I am travelling all over and it would be too dangerous to have you with me. I will not do anything that might endanger your life."

Wyn stood on her tiptoes to mesh their mouths. She opened to the slight pressure of his lips to let his tongue in to mate, bind the heat of their mouths.

He squeezed her lush tush then moved his hands up under her blouse to cup her breasts. As he molded her plush flesh in his big hard hands, her sigh of delight breathy in his mouth made his dick throb.

Wyn lowered her mouth to graze her teeth over his nipple protruding from the cream-colored thermal.

"*Mea Zue*, Wynna," he groaned. Kneading her breasts, he thumbed her nipples over her bra then gently pinched them.

A purr of desire rippled in her throat. Vijay moved his mouth to where the sound was on her throat and sucked it. The sound deepened.

His mouth on her neck, one hand clutching her breast, he moved the other stroking it down to between her legs. When he drew his fingers lightly up her thigh then palmed her mound, she gasped, her knees shook.

He clamped his mouth on hers, bent and scooped her up in his arms and carried her to the bed.

Their mouths clashing potent and inebriating, Vijay started to lay her on the bed when there was a knock at the door. He cursed a rasped, "*Fuck-*"

"Wyn? I've been sent to get you guys and bring you to dinner." A female voice sifted through the door.

Vijay spat a dozen Romanian words thankfully Wyn didn't understand and set her on her feet.

"Okay," Wyn called out, "we'll be right there."

"*Mea Zue, dragă,*" Vijay groaned, stroking a finger down Wyn's face. "As soon as I can, I am going to get us our own place together. As soon as I can ensure your safety."

On tiptoes, Wyn kissed him then she remembered the letter. "I got this letter." Retrieving it from her pocket, she showed it to him.

His forehead wrinkled pushing a line between his eyes that tapered from the letter to her. "You are not thinking of-"

She nodded. "Of course I am. He is my uncle. I need to warn him that he is in danger."

"Wynna, the man knows he is in danger, tis why he is in hiding. Someone wants to draw you out so you can lead them to him. You are not going." He folded the letter and stuffed it in his pants pocket.

She crossed her arms, frowning her irritation at his response. "Of course I am going. I need to go. I'm a big girl, Vijay, no one is going to hurt me at a party where there's tons of people." She stroked her hand down his arm.

"*Nu,* I will not allow it. You will not go." He folded his heavy arms over his chest. "I mean it, Wynna."

She trod to the door and put her hand on the knob. "You can't tell me what to do. I can borrow an appropriate dress from Shreva and-" his hand slammed on the door over her head keeping the door closed.

Wyn turned the knob and tried to open the door, but it was like it had been super-glued shut. She turned to face him. "Vijay, stop it, you can't stop me."

"Then I am going with you."

"You can't, you already said you had to question someone in Monaco. You won't even be in the country. Now, step back, we need to go to dinner."

"Goddammit Wynna," he growled, "I refuse to allow you to put yourself back in danger."

"Wyn?" The woman's voice came through the door. "Are you all right, cuz?"

Wyn glared at Vijay, he glared back. Then he dropped his hand. She opened the door.

He wasn't giving up, "Wynna, I will send someone to be with you, I think Gage might be free-"

She stood on her toes, quickly kissed him on the mouth then strode out the door. "I will be fine. Don't worry."

Waiting just outside of the room, a young woman with golden blonde hair and hazel eyes was waiting.

Vijay could see the slight resemblance between the cousins. But Wyn's hair was lighter and brighter. Her eyes glowed blue-green whereas the other woman's were paler and it looked like she wore color enhanced contacts.

She was taller than Wyn, heavier, she had curves too but hers were fuller, her limbs thicker than Wyn's lissome legs and slender arms. She sure didn't have Wyn's graceful neck.

Wyn's complexion was roses and cream, this woman's makeup was so heavy it was hard to see her natural complexion.

Vijay knew he was being biased, but he loved Wynna and he would forever be blind to any other woman. And, he recognized the fleck in Wyn's cousin's eye.

The way she brazenly checked him out head to toe going back and staring at his crotch. The sly curve of her lip, the bold invitation in her eyes.

"Vijay, this is my cousin, Shreva."

Shreva's chest moved up and out. Tilting her head at him, she twirled a lock of hair and set a hand on her full hip. "Well, I've heard a lot about you. It all looks true."

She scanned his muscled body again, lingering on the scar over his eye, then his lips, stroked over his buffed chest and back down to his fly.

Then she raised her eyes to his, lowered her lids and licked her lips. "*Very* nice to meet you," she purred, holding her hand out.

Vijay's eyes turned icy blue. He said a brief, "*Da*, pleasure," and he turned his attention to Wyn, ignoring Shreva's gesture for him to shake, or she more likely expected him to kiss her limp hand.

Not put off but challenged by his rudeness, Shreva cooed, "Oh, my, they told me about that accent. Heavens above, Mr. Zastrovna, you sound just like Count Dracula stepped out of the TV. I must say, it's pretty hot. Good thing you don't look like the count."

She studied him carefully with a wicked smile. "No, more like Drake the Conqueror from the 15th Century. Let me escort you into dinner." She slipped her hand in under his arm and pulled him down the hall.

"Oh my," she crowed, pushing his sleeve up. He'd worn a cream colored thermal with dark brown Dockers and his thick boots.

"Those tats sent Auntie Odessa around the bend I'll tell ya. Called you everything from biker-gangster to brigand to Viking warlord if you can imagine!"

Laughing, she set her fingers on his arm and said, "But, shit, hon," she bit her tongue and rubbed his tattoos. "Those biceps, yikes, they're bigger than my damned thighs." Her sigh sounded more like a drool. "Wyn, how did a little scarecrow like you capture a real man like this?"

Vijay had to go with her or he would appear rude. Oh wait, he didn't care. He pushed her hand off his arm and turned to Wyn following behind them.

"Baby, c'mere," he reached for her tucking her hand in his arm. "I apologize for my rudeness, Miss Shreva," he said not sounding sorry, "but Wynna and I have so little time together I need to touch her all I can, while I can."

Dinner was an uncomfortable affair. Odessa, Sheffield, and Shreva's parents Meredith and Thomas Vanguard, never looked directly at Vijay as he fielded questions about his 'business.'

Meredith was a pasty carbon copy of her daughter except she was skinny, and nervous, both women used the same golden blonde hair color. Meredith and Odessa were sisters. Odessa was actually more Wyn's cousin not aunt. She was related to Wyn's uncle.

Pompous Thomas Vanguard had a big round pillow belly and was never without a drink in his hand that kept his cheeks and big round nose red.

Etched clearly on the Vanguards' and the Eastwoods' stiff aristocratic faces was their imperial disdain for what they considered a lowborn, insolent outlaw.

Fear and apprehension bubbled in their flitting anxious eyes that never landed for long on the man sitting so formidable and confident with his powerful body and sinister face.

None of them wanted to connect with those enigmatic eyes barely visible under hooded lids peering in narrow disinterest at them.

Except Shreva and her brother, who stared blatantly at Vijay.

Shreva with a cunning, sinful, with 'come hither' in her wanton eyes, and her younger brother, Donovan, twittering with excited curiosity.

To the 17 year-old, the heavily muscled dangerous looking man who was also most likely heavily armed, Vijay was all Don could aspire to be. It was like one of his warrior heroes had leaped right out of his Xbox with huge ax swinging.

Vijay disregarded all of them except to occasionally wink in conspiracy to the young Donovan. His attention was fully on Wyn and hers never left him.

Vijay was the one that called a halt to the awkward evening. His cell buzzed. He slid it out, glanced at it. It was from Alex, said to come ASAP. He stood up. "I apologize, I must leave. Urgent business."

He nodded to Odessa and Sheffield. "Thank you for a…fine dinner." To Mr. and Mrs. Vanguard, "Pleasure to meet you. You too, Don." Ignoring Shreva, he said to Wyn, "*Dragă,* please walk me to my car."

He waited for Wyn to leave the table and they headed to the door.

Behind them, Shreva swooned. "Ah, did you hear that sexed up accent? What he called her, it sounded, so," she fanned her face with one hand, "carnally romantic."

"Shreva!" her father scolded her, "act like the lady we wish you were."

Donovan snickered.

Jumping up with a scowl, Shreva made a face at her family and dashed out the door to follow Wyn and Vijay.

Outside, Vijay started again, "Wynna, I forbid you to go to that party. I mean it. You will not leave this house until I return to fetch you."

Wyn started to argue, then she said, "Wait, I forgot to give you your phone back, I'll be right back." She pivoted and headed quickly back to the house.

"*Nu*, wait," he called to her, he'd bought a new phone, a burner. He could wait to get his other one back. He actually liked her having something of his with her. But she was already gone.

No sooner did she disappear into the house than Shreva slipped out and hurried over to him.

He was leaning against his car in the dark. She came boldly up to him unbuttoning her blouse as she approached.

His arms crossed, he shook his head with a forewarning, unfriendly smile. "Knock it off, Shreva. I have less than zero interest in you. Take a hike."

She kept coming, slipping her blouse off her shoulders to reveal large breasts, they would have been floppy but they were held up by a pushup bra that barely covered her areoles. Inches from him, she pulled down the sheer cups of the bra exposing all of her flesh.

Vijay didn't move, kept his arms crossed in front of him. "Shreva," he sighed, "I love Wynna. I have no interest in you or any other woman. Especially such a wanton slut. For *Zue's* sake, cover up, your parents could come out any minute."

"Aw, come on, big boy, you and me, she won't care," she inched closer.

"Wynna and I are together. We will be getting married." His big hands on his hips, he jerked his head in disgust at her body. "You have no shame."

Her face a veneer of sexual ooze, Shreva purred, "Yeah, so Wynna and Jazer were also to be married. Who cares?" Closer, she pushed her bared breasts against his chest.

He put his hands on her shoulders started to shove her. "Fine, you fucked Jazer, but sweetheart, I would croak before I would stick my wick in your nasty well."

As he pushed, she grabbed hold of his shirt. "You're right Mr. Big and Hunky, I did fuck Jazer, and he sucked at sex. But you, I can see how big you are down there, you are huge and I'm betting you know how to use it," she held on as he pried her fingers off his shirt.

"Oh my God!" Wyn's pained gasp came from several yards away. She cried, "Vijay, you, I believed in you!" then turned and fled.

"*Fuck.*" Vijay struggled to unlatch Shreva's fingers.

He shouted, "Wynna! Come back! Tis not as it looks-" he bit it off. That's the same thing that fucker fiancé said to her.

He saw her run around the mansion and disappear into the dark. He roughly yanked Shreva's hands off not caring if he hurt her or not, and shoved her, then ran after Wyn.

Calling, "Wynna!" he skated the back of the mansion and saw there was no sign of her.

Groves of trees and trimmed hedges surrounded the entire area. She could be anywhere. The sight of the hurt and betrayal in her face caused an agonized stab of pain right into his gut.

"Wynna!" he called, running back and forth. His phone buzzed again, he knew it was Alex. He had to go.

He yelled, "Wynna, I love you, do not trust what you think you saw! I will be back."

Louise Furley

When she heard his car drive away Wyn came out. Her face streaked with tears, her heart split into two and fell shattered into tiny broken fragments to the ground.

Chapter Eighteen

Wyn put his phone in her drawer and shut it off along with hers. He had called every hour on the hour for three days. Alex, Gage, Lucian and Roman had also called. She had clicked the 'answer' button when Alex had phoned.

"Wyn, honey, listen, Vijay would be there on your doorstep if he wasn't needed urgently, lives depend on it. He's unfortunately in Monaco. Wyn, he loves you. I've never seen the big galute like this. He has stars in his eyes, you make him smile."

Alex took a quick breath before hurrying on, "He's never cared about a woman before you, Wyn, never. Please, whatever you think transpired, trust him. He is not some other man like...well he told me about your...asshole fiancé, he is not like him. He was set up by your cousin. Wyn, please, honey, are you there? Wyn?"

Alex called again as did the others but she put the phones away. Her heart felt like it had died. Bled out then shriveled until it turned to ash tasting bitter in her mouth.

She wandered to the window, as much as she hated him, she missed him terribly. She gazed out looking up at the stars. The same ones Vijay could see if he- she shook her head and dashed at the tears that spilled, not going there.

"Miss Wyn."

She didn't turn at the maid's voice but she heard her quiet footsteps on the carpet.

"If I may, Miss Wyn." In a timid small voice the maid asked, "May I speak?"

A soulful shudder shook Wyn from her head down her torso to her feet. Her head dropped forward, then fell back as she looked up at the ceiling to blink back her tears.

With a deep sigh, gathering herself, she clasped her hands together in front of her stomach and turned with a tight smile. "Of course, Alisha."

In her black uniform with white collar and white apron, the maid stepped forward slowly. But nerves struck her and she couldn't speak.

Wyn smiled kindly, said softly, "It's okay, Alisha, whatever you have to say. It will stay between you and me. Now, what is it?"

The maid raised her chin, scrubbed a few fingertips over her pale lips, her dark hair was pinned back so tightly in a bun her eyes looked cat-like. "Yes, Miss, it's…it's that young man of yours."

Wyn's lids shuttered, her smile vanished to a sad bow. Not wanting to hear that Vijay came on to the maid too, like he had been with Shreva, shaking her head she said forlornly, firmly, "Alisha, I don't want to-"

"But you must, Miss." Alisha took a brave step forward, then moved in front of Wyn to block her from leaving.

"Get out of my way, I need to go." Wyn tried to nudge past her.

"Miss Wyn, I was outside the other night. When he was leaving. I was in the shadows, actually," her face flushed with red,

"I was with my…" she glanced at the door. "Please don't tell the missus, I would be fired, but," she moved closer to Wyn as it appeared Wyn was going to flee the room.

"Please hear me out. Your cousin, Shreva, came at him undoing her blouse the hussy." Alisha's voice hardened, "She was all over him. He kept telling her he had eyes for no one but you. That you and he were to be married. He told her that while she, excuse my language Miss, had fucked Jazer, he would not stick

162

his wick in her, uh, he say…pond, or words to that effect. He was literally tearing her hands off him and pushing her away when you came out."

Wyn's mouth dropped, her heart fluttered, was it true? Could she believe the maid? Her brow knit in suspicion, she asked "Alisha, did Vijay or Shreva put you up to this?"

"Heavens no, Miss! Never. I'm telling you what I saw and heard. I saw how the two of you glowed in each other's company, you and your young man. I couldn't let that tramp-"

"Alisha! Where are you?"

The maid whitened at Odessa's strident call. "I'm sorry, I have to go," without another word she ran out the door.

Wyn could hear her rushing footsteps hurrying down the carpeted stairs. She stood motionless, did Alisha speak the truth? Or had Shreva most likely paid her off to lie?

There was no way to know. Wyn decided to go to bed early. The party was tomorrow and she wanted to be fresh and alert to meet with her connection.

She firmly, or tried to, put Vijay out of her mind.

Wyn had planned to go to the party unescorted, but she had no car and her aunt called the limo and cab companies instructing they were not to come to the mansion. Which, as Odessa planned, put her in the position of having to allow Jazer to take her.

Unfortunately. He blathered nonstop about how he loved her and he and Shreva didn't do anything, and that big man who had brought her home was nothing but trouble and we need to set the date for the wedding…blah, blah…would she prefer summer or fall?

He preferred the summer as it would be sooner and on and on. Every time she tried to tell him there was no engagement, no wedding, no us- he talked right over her.

The estate where the party was being held took up a block.

Jazer had the car valeted and walked her up the steps and inside the brilliant, gaudy, building.

Lights glowed everywhere outside and in. There was a crowd of people mingling in several different rooms but most of the dancing was in the main ballroom.

Gleaming ivory floors and lavender walls. Lamps along the walls cast golden glows, whereas a gluttony of chandeliers dripped showers of sparkling diamonds over the room.

It was so beautiful and romantic, if she weren't on a mission, if she was there in Vijay's arms- a shake of her head at her annoying thoughts she snagged a glass of champagne off a server's tray as he passed by.

She refused to allow herself to dwell on Vijay. What they had was done. Over. If she thought about him she would be a slobbering mess of tears crumpled in a miserable little ball sledged in a corner somewhere.

As soon as Jazer started speaking to some pretty young thing, Wyn ditched him, slipping quickly from the big ballroom to one of the others.

Dropping her coat with the hatcheck, she entered the room.

All eyes turned to her.

Hesitating just inside the doorway that arched to the ceiling, Wyn's gaze travelled the room. She wasn't sure who she was to look for or if they would come to her.

The walls in this room were honey with different antique lamps on the wall, the candles in them flickered soft glowing light over the room.

"Wynna."

Her heart stopped. She struggled to keep her breathing slow and calm. She didn't need to turn around; he came from behind to stand in front of her.

Her chest pounded and her legs turned to rubber, he was crazy gorgeous in his tux. Every female in the room was staring at him.

His shoulders stretched the fit of the tux, the pants held up by suspenders hung slightly low on his lean hips. His long black hair was slicked back and tied. Even in the suit he looked like he'd just walked off the gladiator field after a win. The blue eyes veritably glittered at her.

She moved to step past him, with slight movement he blocked her. "Wynna, we need to talk."

Her hurt eyes flashed her pain at him. "No, we don't. You talked plenty with Shreva. I need to go."

"Wynna, do not you throw away what we have for shit your cousin pulled. I had nothing to do with it. You know I have the pick of any woman I want, why would I keep with you if I desired other women?"

At her frown, he said, "I do not mean you are less a beauty or less desirable than them, you know I find you breathtaking. I mean I want you, only you. Since the heartbeat I laid eyes on you the rest of the world ceased to exist. If it were not a matter of life and death I would not have left your side. Your whore of a cousin was all over me, with her back to you, you could not see me shoving her away."

Wyn stood still, her gaze traveling his strong, earnest face. Her lips pressed, it had stung like a knife to her heart when she'd seen him and Shreva doing...whatever they were doing. How could she believe him over her own eyes?

Sliding a finger down her arm, his voice growled deep, hushed, "I love you, *dragă*. You said you would give us a chance."

Her skin quivered at his touch. She firmed her resolve. "I said that until you...did what you did."

His eyes widened then narrowed. He said in a harsh whisper, "What the fuck are you wearing?" His gaze swept her, anger and heat entwined, his eyes flared and his teeth clenched. Leaning close to her ear he grated, "Your tits are hanging out all over for every fucking man to see."

The dress' diamond shaped bodice was cut quite low. Spaghetti straps went from the edge of the bodice to around the back of her neck. It clung to every inch of her curvy figure from her breasts to her thighs, then it wavered out in several feminine layers.

The steep heels made her slender legs look miles long. The sapphire blue brought out the blue highlights in her eyes, and was a dark foil for her light hair. The blonde locks were pinned partially up, the rest of it was a long brilliant curl down between her breast and her arm.

She whispered back fiercely, "What do you care? And don't you dare use that language with me!"

At that moment several men came over and surrounded her, throwing out outrageous compliments and offers to dance.

Feeling Vijay burning up beside her, his scowls were not enough to frighten the men away, Wyn smiled at them all and engaged in teasing flirtatious conversation. She took one man's offer to dance and he swept her away.

She held her breath worried Vijay would cause a scene or hurt one of the men. Peering below her lashes, she saw him get a drink and go to a wall and lean a hip against it. A hand tucked in his pocket, he sipped his drink. In seconds a flock of women surrounded him.

Wyn tried to convince her heart that she wasn't jealous. Her nose in the air, she sniffed. She didn't care what he did.

After many dances, while being twirled in a man's arms, she searched the room for him but didn't see him. She struggled to squash the disappointed sinking of her heart.

He must have gone. She thought he would have tried harder to win her back. He could have at least asked her for a dance. Oh well, it must have been a fleeting physical thing on his part and he probably found a lovely, or in his case, several lovelies to take home and salve his ego.

Swung into another man's arms, Wyn swallowed her pain and smiled weakly up at the man.

Tall, his coifed dark hair tinged grey at the temples, his wide mouth turned up in appreciation of her beauty. Dark eyes dilated into almost entirely black pupils.

He crooned, "I must say, you are one of the, no, make that *the* most striking woman here, I'd wager to say anywhere." His hand at her lower back was warm, he clutched her other hand a little too tightly and held her a little too close for her comfort. She tried to put a bit more space between them.

"Um, well, thank you." Self-deprecating, she said softly, "Of course I can hardly compete with the gorgeous women here."

"Ahh, modest and beautiful, what a treat."

The music ended abruptly as the band went on a break.

He frowned, annoyed. "Well, that is disappointing. By the time they start back up one of your other admirers will try to snatch you from me." He regally held out his hand. "Let me introduce myself, I want you to remember me."

He waited until she carefully set her dainty hand in his larger palm. He had sturdy masculine hands, but nowhere as big and rough and manly as- Wyn closed her eyes. She must stop doing that. She smiled up at him.

"My name is Martine Cartiér. Tell me whom I have the pleasure of dancing with tonight?" He grinned perfectly straight white teeth at her.

Her eyeballs about fell out of her head. "Uh, oh." This was the very man she was to talk with regarding her uncle! "I- my name is Wynna Pila."

Now it was his turn to look surprised, then his brows lowered. "You are David Pila's niece?"

She nodded. "Yes. I received a letter telling me to come to this party to speak with you about-"

"Shh," he warned and leaned in close. "Not here. Come." He took her hand and drew her across the floor, much to the other men's chagrin that planned on asking her for the next dance. He brought her to a set of French glass doors that opened to a balcony.

"Here," he said and led her across the slate floor to the railing. The balcony overlooked the panorama of city lights.

Maneuvering her so her back was against the railing, he moved in so close Wyn put a hand to her chest as a tiny block.

"Um, Mr. Cartiér…"

"*Chérie*," he cooed, "please call me Martine." He rested a palm on the railing beside her waist. His fingers grasped a lock of her long curl. Twining it around his finger, he stroked his finger with the hair around it down the side of her face. He dipped his head to hers.

"Uh, please, Mr. Cartiér, can we discuss my- my uncle?" The closer his face came, the further her spine arched back over the railing.

"Martine, dear, Martine," he said, his lips just brushing her neck.

"Mr. M- Martine, please." Wyn put her hand on his chin and pushed him back. "You said we could talk about my uncle. Can you take me to him?"

His eyes all huge black pupils dropped to her chest where they stayed for a moment, glowing, burning. She could almost feel the heat of them touching her flesh. Then he raised them to her face, his phone buzzed. He fished it from his pocket, glanced at it then slipped it back in his pocket.

The heat in the dark eyes cooled to cold coals. "Unfortunately, I must leave, little Wynna Pila. I had hoped you and I tonight could," he glanced at his watch, his mouth tightened, "but there is no time. Give me your address, quickly." He took his phone back out.

"But-" Wyn felt an attack of nerves.

"Quickly dear, quickly. Think of your uncle's safety."

"Okay, it's 1200 Amaryllis Ave. But-"

He tapped it in and dropped the phone back in his pocket then reached out and set his hand on the front base of her neck, his palm rested on the swell of her bosom. At Wyn's sharp inhale, he bent and plastered his lips on hers, slicking his tongue across her mouth and down her throat.

She put both hands up to his chest and pushed. A smile stretched his mouth as he leaned back but kept his hand on her chest. "Apologies, *ma chérie*. We Frenchmen," he sighed, the edge of his mouth furled from the smile to an unrepentant sexy grin.

"We are just too- ah, too romantic, yes? I could not resist your amazing beauty. Forgive me, I will not take such liberties again." He kissed the tips of his fingers and flickered them in the air.

"*Enfin*, I will send a car for you tomorrow morning. Be ready at 8 my flower, I most certainly will be."

Wyn tried to turn away from him but he held her with his hand splayed on her chest. And, contrary to what he'd just proclaimed, he leaned in quickly and kissed her again before dropping his hands, and then abruptly turned and left the balcony.

Crossing her hands, Wyn pressed them over her chest. Her heart was hammering away. She wiped her mouth with the back of her hand and felt like gagging and spitting out the taste of him.

"Here. This should help." Vijay was right beside her. He held out a glass of scotch.

Her cheeks flaming with embarrassment, she looked down at the glass then up at him.

Black hair, intense blue eyes gleamed in the faint outside lights, the man was achingly handsome, big and powerful in the fine tux. The other night he could have been a fighter from her cousin Donovan's Xbox, tonight, he looked like he stepped off the pages of a fairy tale, the Warrior Knight.

"Go on," Vijay insisted, pushing it into her hands. "Alcohol is a good bacteria killer. Swirl it around and spit in that flowerpot. I will look away." His eyes lowered from hooded lids giving the image of an enraged bull ready to slaughter the matador. He was seething with fury.

When she didn't move, he snarled, "Tis either that or I go get him and rip out his tongue, all of his teeth and his fucking lips before I tear his hands from his fucking arms like I really want to do." He turned away. Wyn did as he said.

She took a big gulp, spun it around in her mouth then spat it out at the pot, then coughed. Her eyes and tongue and mouth burned.

When he turned back around, she could see her own hurt reflected in his eyes. "Vijay, he can help me."

"I know baby, he told you he can take you to your uncle. I heard the whole thing. Saw the whole thing. The only reason I did not remove his head and toss it over the balcony was because I was afraid it would sever, no pun intended, our relationship for good."

He stood in front of her, his hands clasped benignly behind his back. His enigmatic eyes glimmered at her from under the low lids. His temper was clamped back beneath a steel-willed lid.

She handed him his glass. He took it and set in on a table.

Off to the far corner away from the main bell of the balcony, they stood motionless staring at each other. Around them surged voices of people coming and going, murmuring and laughing. Lips smacked as lovers kissed, chairs scraped tile as people sat at patio tables. The band had started up again in the other room.

"Wynna," he tried to keep his hands to himself, he lost the fight. He touched her face, his thumb gently brushing her cheek.

"I did not come on to, or do anything with your cousin. I swear to *Zue,* uh, God. Shreva either always wants what you have, or she just wants to make you miserable by hitting on your men."

Her head tipped up enjoying his touch. She murmured, "It could be she just wanted to have sex with a couple of good looking men."

He dropped his hand to her shoulder. "Uh, can we not lump that ex-never was-fiancé of yours in with me?"

Reminding him, "You just referred to him and you as my men." The weight of his hand on her shoulder a feeling of security, a small smile curved her lips.

"*Da*, I did. Let us not do it again. This is all about you and me, just you and me." His hand massaged her shoulder before sliding up to her nape where his fingers laced behind her neck, and he traced his thumb along her jaw.

"Wynna, please, I want you. Only you. I never touched or even had a speck of desire to touch that slut of your cousin. Even if I was not crazy about you I would not have given her the time of day. She tis grasping and greedy and her promiscuity clings to her like soiled filth. And I am insanely crazy about you. Please believe me."

170

Wyn gazed up at the big warrior's face crushed with emotion. So rare, it was heart-wrenching and beautiful at the same time. He was clearly an old-fashioned sexist man.

Just because women liked sex with various partners did not make them bad. Vijay had a lot to learn about chauvinism. Then again, he called Shreva's card. She had sex sometimes just to deliberately cause conflict, hurt and anger.

Even so, deep down, Wyn knew he had no interest in any other women. He had bare-handed killed men for her, dragged her across the wilderness to keep her from evil clutches. He pulled her from certain death in that raging river, fed her and kept her warm and safe, and even tied himself up because he desired her so much he feared what he'd do in his sleep. And here he is tonight.

If it was only physical, he would have as he'd said before, assaulted her in the forest, dropped her at his employer and forgotten about her. Sure, he wanted to access her uncle, but as he'd said, he had made zero moves in trying to obtain any information from her.

She put her hand up to stroke his hard face, ran her fingertips over his rough but soft lips, remembering them on her body, her cheeks heated turning crimson.

A smile tugged up the side of his mouth. "What is it, baby, are you remembering my mouth on your-"

"Hush!" She held her fingers on his lips. "People will hear you!"

His hands circled her waist, he moved to her. "*Dragă*, we will find that ex-ass of yours, dump him and I will take you home. Then, I promise I will not bend over right now and put my mouth on your fucking exposed tits that you let all the world see, and suck them until they are red and swollen, and you are wet and moaning my name out loud-"

"Oh my God, Vijay! Shut up!" Mortified, the only way she knew to shut him up was to clamp her mouth over his. It worked.

Immediately, he angled his head, pushed her lips open to receive the thrust of his hungry tongue. He kept his hands on her waist although they both knew it was all he could do to not slide them up and enjoy her womanly attributes.

When they pulled apart gasping for breath, Wyn nodded. "Okay. Take me home, but we can't, you know…"

His lips greedily captured hers again. Against her mouth, he mumbled, "Uh huh, I know, but soon."

They walked back through the ballrooms, this time his hand possessively circling her waist, and his fierce black scowl keeping every man from venturing to approach Wyn.

When she retrieved her coat and they were out front waiting for the valet to bring Vijay's car, Jazer came hurrying out the door and to them.

Chapter Nineteen

"Wynnie, for Pete's sake, what the hell are you doing?" Jazer glared at Vijay who kept his hand on her waist. "I brought you. You're mine. I will be the one bringing you home. I'm your fiancé remember? You can't leave with this- this- hoodlum!"

His hand tightened, Vijay frowned at Wyn. "*Dragă,* have you not yet given him his ring back?"

Her eyes lowered as the pink stained her cheeks. "No. There has not been the opportunity." She turned to Jazer, Vijay made it difficult because he kept his grip hard on her waist. "Um, Jazer, I've tried to talk with you about-"

Jazer held up a hand. "Not here. Not the time nor place. We will discuss this at home. I mean your home." He glared at Vijay. "For now, I will be the gentleman, and assume he will be a gentleman and allow him to see you home. But, let me warn you," he held a finger to her face. "You will not fuck him. You do and I will tell your uncle-"

"That you banged her cousin Shreva while you were supposedly engaged to Wynna?" Vijay interjected smoothly with sarcasm, moving Wyn out of Jazer's reach.

His lips a hard compressed line, Jazer's face turned dark. He narrowed furious, and guilty eyes at Vijay. "I did no such thing. If you slander me like that again I will sue you and take every penny," his gaze raked Vijay up and down with disdainful scorn, "that you don't even likely have."

The smirk on Vijay's face did nothing to calm Jazer's anger. He started sputtering when he saw the valet pull up in the car Vijay had rented for the night. A white Bentley.

His arm never leaving her, Vijay ushered Wyn to the door the valet opened, handed him some bills, and gave him a look as he tried to take Wyn's hand to help her into the car.

Blanching with a whip of fear, the valet dropped his hand then awkwardly strode briskly away.

Vijay helped her in, closed the door and shook his head at Jazer as he went to Wyn's door to get her to open the window. The look, the same as he'd given the valet, could wither a redwood, made Jazer stop in his tracks.

Vijay pulled the Bentley out and took off down the street. He had considered hiring a driver, but they were so seldom alone he cherished what little time they had to themselves. There was no way he wasn't going to be driving her home tonight. He took Wyn's hand and held it all the way home.

In the driveway he parked in front of the mansion then turned to face her. The moonlight streamed across her face making her skin golden and her eyes sheen like blue-green crystals.

He lifted her hand and kissed each individual knuckle. Her head lay back against the seat as she watched him under low dreamy lids.

His voice deep and husky, he asked, "Baby, are we good?" He appeared calm as a brick, but he held his breath, the vein at his temple hammered.

Her lashes swept down then up framing her pretty eyes. She smiled dreamily at him. "Did you know your friends, all of them, called me to tell me to trust and believe you? Alex practically stalked me."

He looked slightly embarrassed. "*Nu*. I had no idea. Tis none of their business. When I see those sons of bitches-"

"I missed you so much, Vijay," she said softly, the yearning in her eyes palpated over his hard face. "So much my body ached with the longing of feeling you with me, touching me, me touching you. I missed your body snuggled with mine as we slept, your voice…"

Vijay grabbed her up in his arms, hugged her, choked back tears he didn't know he was even capable of. When he composed himself, he drew back and combed her hair from her face. "I love you, Wynna. I would never do anything to hurt you."

She nodded her head wearily. "I know, Vijay, my cousin is a viper always ready to pounce. I believed without a doubt she and Jazer had been together, or were going to, whatever. I saw them. I don't care now and I didn't care then. But you," she caressed his face with her palm. He turned his head to lean into her caress. "I-I, I didn't believe it, but our, relationship is so new, so fragile, that I lost faith in us."

"Never again, Wynna *dragă*, never doubt me. Tomorrow-"

"Oh!" She sat up remembering. "I'm meeting with Mr. Cartiér in the morning."

The line between his eyes deepened. "Wynna, the man only wants to fuck you."

"Vijay! What a disgusting crass thing to say. He is going to take me to my uncle. He said so. He's sending a car in the morning."

Vijay's head fell back on the seat, he dropped his arm over his closed eyes. "Wynna, come on, I saw him look at you, molest you, fucking kiss you. If not for my concern that you would hate me, I would have taken him out right then. I should have. I will-"

"You will do no such thing! He is a virtuous-"

"Motherfucker who only wants in your pants, baby. Trust me, men know men. You are not going and that is it."

Now she dropped her head back in disbelief. "Oh for the love of- we have gone over this before."

She turned to face him again. "I repeat for the millionth time, I am an adult. I make my own decisions, my own choices. As you see, nothing dire happened at the party as you prophesied. And nothing will happen tomorrow. Now," she opened her door. "I'm tired, I'm going in. You have a lengthy drive back to where you are staying."

"At least let me come with you tomorrow, Wynna." Vijay climbed out and strode around the car to get to her.

He held the door until she got out then closed it. Taking her hand, he walked with her up the stone path to the house. The dark night a shroud of silence around them except for the rustling of budding leaves in the slight breeze.

"Vijay, I don't know…"

"Please. If he is all innocence, he will accept it. What time?"

When she hesitated, Vijay said quietly, "If you think tis so I can learn where your uncle is, you can meet alone with him in private in a separate room. I will not intrude. But I want him to know that I am nearby."

Chewing on the inside of her mouth, Wyn considered what he said. Admittedly, she had felt uncomfortable with Cartiér. He had touched her inappropriately and kissed her without permission, twice, and without being in a relationship with her.

To take such liberties, he would undoubtedly have no qualms with doing more. She should have slapped him, and would have if she hadn't craved so badly to get to her uncle. "I didn't think that you were being deceptive."

"Thank you." He walked her to the door. "Wynna, do not do anything without me. I still believe he only wants to fu- uh, have sex with you or use you against your uncle. You could be walking straight into a dangerous trap."

Wyn yawned and sighed. "Maybe. But, Vijay, he is my uncle and I love him. I would do whatever I had to, to save someone I love. Wouldn't you?"

Nodding reluctantly, he agreed, "*Da*, but I am a trained soldier. You are not. But let me tell you, you get yourself in trouble with him and I will release my wrath on your behind. I worried enough about tonight, and then had to suffer through other men dancing with you, and that asshole molesting you.

"You even got in a car with that bastard Edrei when you know he is not after your best interests. Your best body parts maybe," his lip pilled. "I- well, just saying, if something happens to you, you will be punished for not heeding my warning." He stared down at her appalled face.

"What? Don't be ridiculous, you would certainly not- not use corporal punishment on me?" She stamped her foot. "I am not a child. You do not own me! I will not be treated as a-a slave that is to be disciplined!"

His head tilted back as he calmly regarded her anger. "I need some way to impress upon you, *fetita*, that you are in danger here and you need to be alert to it and avoid it, and not run headlong and go to some strange man's, some single man's house, alone, over some silliness he could have told you at the party."

As she sputtered angrily, he sighed and cut her off, "But, baby, as hot as your little round ass is, I would only get one good spank in before I had my hands on your beautiful female parts and my fingers up your-"

"Vijay!" she squawked, her face filling with color.

He gripped her upper arms, pulling her in and kissed her fiercely, and long. So long, his shaft was hard as an iron club pressing against her. Their breaths in tandem shot out fast and shallow like asthmatics fighting for air.

When he felt her nipples pressing into his shirt, he stopped the kiss. Bending back from her, his eyes fell to the low cut dress.

His fingers tightened around her arms. "*Dragă*, promise me you will not ever wear shit like that again unless you are on my arm. I find for the first time in my life I am a jealous, possessive dick."

He trailed the pads of his fingers across the mounds of her breasts. Remembering Cartiér's fucking hand on her chest started Vijay's blood boiling again.

Feeling her breasts swelling to his touch, wanting, desiring more, Wyn whispered, "It isn't my dress, I borrowed it from Shreva." The pressure of her body when she leaned into him forced his palm harder over her breast.

His fingers slid into the top and side of her bodice to cup what he could of her plump globe. His other hand clutched her bottom pulling her hard against his erection.

He murmured against her lips, "Every time I look at that dress I want to peel it off you. Slowly. Kissing every place it exposes as I strip it down your body." His mouth fell onto hers again, his hand on her ass holding her close, the other scooping deeper seeking more of her tempting flesh.

He ground his erection against her, his breaths heavy and fast-

The porch lights suddenly popped on.

"Ahh, goddammit, Wynna." He pulled his hand from her dress, dropped his head to stare down at her bosom, and brought both hands to clench around the curve of her waist.

"I need to go inside," Wyn said with a dazed and lusty but happy smile.

He nodded, the ponytail flopped on his back. Dark color suffused his face. "Uh huh. Inside is where I want to be." He sucked in a heavy breath and put his hands on the sides of her face,

"Baby, I want you. I am sure as hell not going to deny I want to be inside you. Are you, ready to, I mean, I will wait forever for you," his words caught in his throat. He didn't want to push her.

The tantalizing smile that spread across her face, limp eyes beguiling, ignited Vijay to curl his long fingers on her face with both hands, and die to kiss her and lay her down- anywhere, and do what was promised in her eyes. Make her his.

She put a finger to his lips. "I want you, too."

He pulled her finger in with his lips and licked it then sucked it deep inside his mouth, where his tongue rolled around it, lapping and sucking. Her head fell back, an erogenous groan churned.

Wyn could feel the same churning tugging between her legs. She looked up at him under sultry lids. Her word heavy with a rasping whisper, she told him, "I'm ready for you, Vijay. For you to make me, fully, your woman."

"*Zue*, Wynna, *dragă*," he groaned in relief and surging arousal. Crushing her against him, his mouth charged over hers-

The door swung open.

"My God almighty, Wyn Pila! What disgraceful whorish behavior on the front steps for all the country to see!" Odessa's

178

aghast expression almost brought giggles to Wyn, but she bit them back.

Wyn was thinking it was a good thing she wasn't there a moment ago when Vijay had his hand down the front of her dress! Or a few minutes later when they would have likely been even more entangled with each other.

She could see Vijay's voracious eyes on her breasts even now. If the door hadn't opened she would probably be bare to the waist.

"You come inside immediately, Miss, right now. And you," Odessa's dark eyes glared, flashing her haughty ire at Vijay. "You base, immoral thug, how dare you sully her reputation! Taking advantage of an engaged woman." Her gaze dropped to the bulge in his pants, her mouth parted, her pupils flashed, but she didn't look away.

Vijay wasn't embarrassed and did nothing to hide his hard-on. "*Da*, whatever. Can you take a hike for a moment so we can say goodnight?" His voice calm, low, and disrespectful, it bugged the shit out of him the way they treated Wyn. The way they forced that fucker Edrei on her. The sooner he could get her out of there the better.

Vivid red splotches scorched her wide cheeks as Odessa opened her mouth to retort, then she saw Vijay's chilling eyes. Spikes of blue ice sliced at her from under his hostile crocodile lids, and her mouth snapped shut.

"Trust me, Mrs. Eastwood, you do not want to watch me say goodnight to your niece. I will not care about your modest sensibilities." One dark brow rose indicating she needed to let them say goodnight in private.

"And," he said, "Wynna is *not* engaged to that fuck-" Wyn gasped, "Vijay!" He finished, "Jerk, Edrei."

"Oh!" Odessa spouted. "Your language is appalling, and you know nothing of what is between Wyn and her fiancé. My niece is just a bit confused right now. Of course who could blame her, getting snatched off the street right in front of her apartment, and then spending days and nights alone in the woods with the unscrupulous likes of you," she sniffed.

"Of course you took advantage of a very sheltered, young naïve woman, and apparently, for now, you have spellbound her with your- your-"

Her haughty eyes raking him from head to dress boot, she spat, "Muscle-bound bad boy behavior. But," a hand on her hip, the other pointing her finger at him, she decreed, "Let me tell you, young man, she will get her wits back and then you will be history!"

Ignoring Odessa, Vijay cupped Wyn's face and covered her mouth with his, turning Wyn slightly so her aunt could only see the wall of Vijay's broad back.

Sputtering, searching for scathing invectives but failing to find any, Odessa's words splatted out with a high-pitched peeve, "Well, fine then, you have one minute and then I will be forced to have Mr. Eastwood call the police and have you forcefully removed from the estate!" She turned and slammed the door behind her.

Now Wyn did giggle.

Vijay smiled in delight down at her laugher. "You disrespectful little minx, c'mere," he took her face and kissed her a slow deliberate goodnight.

He pulled his head back slightly to gaze down at her. "When we return tomorrow, you are going to give that dirtbag ex of yours his ring back. If you do not, I will take it and shove it down his throat." He waited.

She nodded, her lips curved up dreamy. "Sure, and then we can discuss this bossiness of yours."

His grin belied his words, "*Da,* sure," and he kissed her again, long and hearty.

After too short of a time, he released her. "*Bine, mea dragă,* I will be here tomorrow to escort you. Do not leave without me." He kissed her briefly then waited until she went inside before going to his car.

Vijay

Driving down the long driveway, Vijay smiled to himself. He had a throbbing hard-on that could drill through a manhole cover. But he felt good. He got her back, and she said she was ready. All he had to do was get this whole uncle business behind them so they had no distractions.

He had declared himself, now all he needed to do, wanted, was to make Wynna his.

Chapter Twenty

*T*he next day the doorbell rang at 7 a.m.

The maid answered it then went to call Wyn. Wyn was finishing breakfast. "Miss," the maid said, "there is a car here for you."

Dabbing at her mouth with a linen napkin, Wyn dropped it and stood up. "What? He is not due until 8."

The maid shrugged. What could she say, the car was there and the driver was standing in the foyer waiting.

"Oh dear." Flustered, Wyn told her, "Please tell him I will be right there." She hurried from the room. She was up earlier than the rest of the house so thankfully she didn't run into anyone who would be asking questions about where she was going and whose car was that out front.

She dashed upstairs to brush her teeth and hair and grab her phone. Tucking the phone in her front pocket, she wore black slacks and a yellow blouse a few shades darker than her hair, and had a frilly collar and tiny pearl buttons.

Down the stairs she found the man in a black uniform waiting impatiently for her by the door.

"Sir," she addressed him as she entered the vestibule. "I understood from Mr. Cartiér that you would be here at 8?"

He nodded sharply. "Mr. Cartiér had something come up. A meeting in the later morning. He said to apologize, but he didn't have your phone number to call you. Are you ready or would you prefer to cancel?"

Wyn tapped her fingers on her mouth. "Uh, yes, yes I'm ready, but I am waiting for someone. But he won't be here until 8."

The man ducked his head. "Oh, I am sorry then. We will have to cancel and reschedule for another day. Mr. Cartiér will be out of the country for a month, perhaps then-"

"No- no, I can come now. I need to make a quick call." She pulled out her phone and dialed Vijay.

The call didn't go through. In this foreign country, and way out in this rural area where she was, there were many empty cell areas.

"Just a minute, please." She darted off to grab Alisha. "Alisha, you know Mr. Zastrovna?"

A blush shifted up the maid's face, she nodded. "How could anyone miss him?" She skewed a slight glimmer of envy at Wyn, "I'm glad you made up, Miss. The way he looks at you," she rolled her eyes with a swooning sigh, "you are so lucky, he is obviously head over heels for you."

Wyn smiled. "Anyway, he was supposed to go with me today to a meeting. But the car to take me came an hour early and the driver can't wait. Can you please tell Mr. Zastrovna that I will be just fine and will call him later? He is apparently on his way here and out of the zone of the cell towers."

Alisha bowed. "Of course I can, Miss Wyn. I will wait for him."

"Thank you, Alisha, I appreciate it." Wyn gave her a brief hug and ran off to where the driver waited.

The driver rolled up the privacy window between them so Wyn sat in the back seat of the shiny black limousine, watching the countryside pass by.

Although in a small foreign country, the land didn't look all that much different than her native America. She wondered how her parents were. She hadn't called them since her return. They didn't know about the kidnapping or any of the business about her uncle, her father's brother. And she wasn't about to tell them. They would hop a plane and come across the world and give her a royal chewing out.

She chuckled, eventually she would either go home or they would come to her and they would learn she'd thrown over the wealthy, aristocratic neighbor her aunt and uncle desired her to marry, for her rescuer.

Wait till they got a load of him. Vijay looked like a fighting warrior that just climbed off a motorcycle. Physically intimidating with his muscles upon muscles and scarred but still harshly masculine, handsome face. His inscrutable penetrating blue eyes would unsettle them immediately. Not to mention his tats.

Dad had always eschewed that men that had tattoos were destined for or had come from, prison.

Alex had told Wyn that some of the tats they had gotten were to make their infiltration of certain mobs, gangs, prisons, whatever they needed to get into, blend more smoothly.

"Sinister recognizes sinister, and accepts sinister," Gage had added.

Wyn's parents would take one look at their petite dainty daughter and the highly dangerous, vicious looking, huge barbarian next to her and they would freak out.

She would need to find a discreet way of describing what he did for a living. What parent wanted their daughter dating a fearless, fearsome, bloodletting, mercenary?

And, she'd definitely have to keep the fact to herself that she'd seen him kill men with his bare hands, even though it was to save her. It was hard enough for Wyn to reconcile her feelings about it. She abhorred violence.

But, she sighed, just thinking about him, his manly chest, enormous arms and shoulders, those lean sinewy hips, and what would be behind those snug jeans he wore, brought a rush of heat to her female core. Her skin flamed suddenly.

Fanning her flushing face, she needed to get a grip on her lustful thoughts before she reached Mr. Cartiér's!

Vijay

But her mind drifted back to that time in the woods when her hands were restrained behind her back, and she wore only Vijay's jacket. She had woken to find him over her, with his hand fiercely gripping her bare breast, his savage assault on her mouth and then her breast.

She knew if she hadn't woken him, he would have had the jacket completely unzipped and spread open, his legs were already between hers, he had unbuckled his belt and the hard, thick length of him was pressing- she was grateful, and regretful when he'd woken- oh!

But he had been the ultimate gentleman and stopped his assault. He had even expressed guilt over his attack on her. Fanning herself harder, she redirected her thoughts to wondering what help Mr. Cartiér could give her.

After an hour or so, the limo pulled up in front of a wrought iron gate. It opened automatically and let the limo in then closed behind it. The car traveled up the winding drive until it reached a semi-circle in front of the estate. There were several other limousines in the driveway.

The mansion was white stone and stucco, three stories with the front top to bottom windows. Wings stretched off to either side of the main building. The double-decker, twelve-car garage sat detached across the drive.

Turning off the engine, the driver got out and went to open Wyn's door.

He held his hand to help her out. She gracefully exited the car allowing the driver to assist her then he led her up to the house. He opened the door and ushered her right in.

A burly man with jagged scars like someone had gouged him with a claw-hammer across half his face approached them. His beefy eyes slid insolently down Wyn's body and back up.

So blatant and crude was his gaze, Wyn felt like he was picturing what positions he would put her in once he got her naked. She shivered, wishing she'd brought a jacket. Or bulletproof armor.

The man spoke with a thick guttural accent, "Mr. Cartiér sends his apologies. His meeting was moved up and he is currently in the middle of it. I have orders to take you to the drawing room where you can wait until he is done." He spoke to her but his eyes never left her chest like he had x-ray vision and was lasering through her clothes.

"Uh, oh, that's, well I guess it can't be helped." Wyn crossed her arms over her breasts. Seeing him blink then lick his thick lips, she said, "Uh, thank you, Mr. um…"

"Huh?" His beefy eyes rolled up to hers then back to her breasts. "Name's Micah. Come." He started across the foyer.

Wyn turned to thank the driver but he was gone. An uncomfortable feeling was tiptoeing up her spine. She bit back a grin. Vijay would tell her that it was her instincts advising her there was something wrong and to leave.

The grin purged to a frown. Maybe she should, no, she shook her head. She was just being fanciful. Everything was fine. She needed to be as brave as her uncle was.

Micah strode so quickly it was hard for Wyn to take in her surroundings, and she was sure she would never find her way back to the front without assistance. She only caught an image of a lot of black, tans and gold on her way through the opulent mansion.

He brought her to the drawing room and gestured for her to enter.

It had pale blue walls, and ritzy white furniture on the plush ivory carpet. The entire back wall was all huge windows. Beyond the glass looked like a wall of green; early spring grass studded with budding trees and manicured topiaries.

Pointing to a cushiony white sofa, Micah mumbled, "Take a load off." His voice dense and heavy like his body, he said, "Help yourself." He gestured to a station constructed of glass and gold where there was a coffee urn, sodas and bottles of water in an ice bucket. Wine and liquor bottles lined the counter.

Plates of mini-sandwiches and pastries, glasses, coffee cups and anything else needed for comfort was laid out. Four, white wrought-iron stools flanked the bar.

Micah abruptly turned and stalked to the door. He turned and announced, "Mr. Cartiér will be with you when he can." He closed the door behind him.

"Well!" Wyn said out loud. "You would think such an opulent place would have professional well-dressed staff instead of that ogre-ish, squint-eyed brute." She was feeling more and more uneasy.

She waited a few moments then went to the door and turned the knob. But, as she had feared, it was locked. Why would you lock a guest in? She hurried to the floor to ceiling windows. They were latched with locks as well.

The glass looked three layers thick; she could literally see the layers. It was doubtful one of the fancy barstools if thrown at it would get through.

Pondering, "Now what?" she had no choice but to wait for Mr. Cartiér. Then she remembered her phone. She would call Vijay.

She took the phone out, her stomach fell when she saw she had no bars. There was no service here. Or at least in this room. Stuffing the phone in her pocket, she got up and paced then wandered over to look out the window.

Near the glass she could just barely hear car engines. They sounded like they were heading away from the estate. Maybe it was the people at his meeting leaving.

On one hand she was glad they were going if it hurried Cartiér up, on the other hand, she was starting to worry she was alone in the mansion with just Cartiér and a bunch of thugs.

She hadn't wanted to think about it at the time, but even the driver, under the neat uniform, his shoes were scruffy, his beard untrimmed, he never made eye-contact with her. She groaned aloud, "Oh my God, what have I gotten myself into?"

Just as she was deciding what to throw at the window, the door opened. She jumped up. Mr. Cartiér came in.

He was dressed as debonair as he had been at the party. Wearing a tailored suit, his Cambridge wingtips gleamed from professional polishing. Wyn was sure she would see her face in them if she looked. His hair was combed back and looked sprayed to keep in place, the moustache was neatly trimmed.

Apology in his foreign voice, "My dear," he came forward with his hands out. "I am so sorry, what a terrible mix-up. First the meeting was later, then it was earlier, then it came much earlier! I am so sorry for the trouble I've caused you."

When he reached her, he took both her hands. "That is no way to treat an honored guest, right?" His welcoming smile was made of big bright teeth that did not carry through the rest of his face.

Wyn hadn't noticed it last night, but now she saw his eyes were...blank...and rapacious, like a piranha's. Vijay had lethal, predatory eyes, but his were without guile. Cartiér's were...slimy.

Goose bumps prickled all the way up her arms. She tugged at her hands. More alarms went off when he didn't release her. She yanked hard and they slipped out.

"Mr. Cartiér," she said, taking a few steps away from him. "My uncle, you said you could take me to him."

"Yes, yes, of course, but first," he went to the bar and picked up a bottle of wine. After deftly removing the cork with a slight pop, he plucked two wine glasses off the counter and brought them to the sofa where he set them down on the glass table in front of it.

A resin sailfish was half in and out of the top of the glass like it was leaping out of the water. Incredibly huge, the light blue, yellow-striped marlin had to be over five feet long, at least 70 lbs. Its spiked bill looked to Wyn like a sword stabbing into the sky.

"Please Miss Pila," Cartiér said as he sat and patted the cushion next to him on the sofa. "Have a seat. Let me pour you a glass of wine, it's the least I can do for making you wait so long."

Wyn swayed from one foot to the other. "Well, uh, really, if you could just tell me about my uncle?"

He actually pouted. "Please, Miss Pila, Wyn, if I may, you must let me show my sincere apologies for being so inhospitable to you. Just one drink, a sip perhaps. My feelings, alas, I would be so hurt if you rejected my olive branch."

188

"No, really, Mr. Cartiér, it's way too early for alcohol. If you could please just tell me what you know."

His lip stuck out, he cocked his head in a winsome pose, he protested, "Now, now, *ma petit chérie*, I refuse to tell you or take you to your uncle if you will not accept my apology. And, please, it's Martine."

Her eyes narrowed at him with suspicion. "Are you sure you know where he is? I have others I can contact. I hadn't wanted to bother them, you said you would help, I thought that would be better."

She drew an anxious breath. "But, uh, I think maybe I should leave and we can reschedule." She glanced at the door. She was pretty sure he had locked it behind him.

His hand went to his heart in affront. "Miss Pila, Wyn, you-you wound me," he sat up straight, tightened his tie. "I would never lie, I don't believe in subterfuge. If you refuse to be a little bit sociable with me, well," he sighed, "you must see, I am surrounded by oxen men. It's not often an elegant, beautiful young woman graces my home. But, if you must leave…how about just one little sip with me to honor our friendship?"

Wyn was starting to think the only way she was going to leave that room was if he let her. She decided she needed to appease him, get him at ease. Maybe a small drink and then she could ask for a tour of the house. Yes, then she could make her way to the door and out. She'd walk home if she had to.

"Um, well, okay, if you insist." She moved slowly towards the couch.

His hokey smile went from ear to ear. Wyn swore she could hear his wolfish undertone, 'come into my den, little lamb.'

He busied himself pouring the wine as she perched a few feet from him on the sofa.

He said with a cheerful smile, "Ah, that's better, Wyn," and handed her a glass. Toasting, "To our friendship," he held his glass up and waited for her to clink glasses with him.

She did then set the glass down.

He frowned. "*Chérie*, it's bad luck to toast and then not sip. You continue to wound me."

He looked anything but wounded. He actually looked cross. The pupils expanded like before, taking over the already dark eyes. His mouth hardened and lines deepened in the folds around them. Again she felt his piranha-like blank eyes on her as they circled her, the big razor teeth chopping.

"Uh, okay, just a little. I mean it's really too early in the day for me to be drinking." She reached for her glass.

He assured her, "Oh, it's all right," his mustache rose over those sharp teeth. "Some people have mimosas for breakfast and that's champagne. It's just wine. We're good. Drink up, little flower."

He observed every move she made. Her fingers encircling the glass, she lifted it to her lips. He even seemed to be peering over the rim of the glass as she tipped it to her mouth to see if she actually drank some of the liquid.

He was watching her way too carefully. She was starting to suspect he had doused her glass with a drug. Wyn allowed some of the wine to go into her mouth, but as she started to lower the glass she let it pour back into the glass. She set it down on the table next to the huge rapier fish.

Trying to appear calm and poised, she asked politely, "Did you catch that, um, fish there? It must have been quite a fight!"

An actual amused chuckle rolled out of him. "Of course not, aren't you precious. It came with the table. Go on, have some more wine, you don't want it to go to waste do you?"

Cartiér sat back and crossed his legs. Elegantly sipping his wine, his lids lowered over his eyes as he regarded at her. His gaze on her face slowly made its descent.

Mumbling a nonsensical, "Uh huh," Wyn made as if to reach for her glass but didn't. "So, then, my uncle, you were telling me about where he is?"

"Huh." An inelegant snort jolted out. "Honey," he moved closer to her, the veneer of amiability gone, "if you don't drink up and play nice with me, I won't tell you anything." His tone turned coldly empty. The piranha eyes seemed to feed on her, as if she were already floundering wounded in the deep water.

Lurching gracefully to her feet, Wyn wiped her damp hands on the black slacks. "I think it would be so nice to see the rest of this lovely estate." Smiling prettily at him, she asked, "Can you give me a tour?"

The blankness in his eyes turned to a bestial glare, he lowered them to the glass in his hands. Leaning over, he carefully set it on the table. Ordering, "Sit down," the command scraped out coarse from deep in his chest.

Wyn edged towards the door. "I really think it's time I left, Mr. Cartiér. We can set something up later."

Rising leisurely, he nonchalantly shrugged out of his suit coat. Setting it neatly over the back of a chair, he stuck his finger in the knot of his tie loosening it, all the while he moved unhurried towards her.

Wyn struggled to hold her ground. She wasn't going to bend to his intimidation. "Mr. Cartiér, I said I think it would be best I leave."

"Honey, the only way you're leaving here, is after I've gotten my information out of you. I want the names of the people that can get in contact with your uncle. After that, I plan to devour your delicious body, then I promised my men they could have a go at you."

His lip lifted in a curled sneer as his lascivious eyes ate up and down her body. "Then, after that," he shrugged, his grin sheer malevolence, "we will see."

He looked at his shirtsleeves as he coolly folded them up his forearms. "I must warn you though, *ma chérie*, I have what some people have called…depraved tastes. Hopefully you will last longer than your predecessors." His sadistic gaze rolled up to her pale face.

Wyn recognized the same soulless, venomous look Kreis Warwick had displayed to her.

Without a word, she turned and ran to the door. Grabbing the knob she twisted and turned and yanked and pushed, it was locked. She pounded her fists on it.

"You keep doing that and you will only bring my men, and they may be too impatient to wait their turns. And I'm not ready for that yet."

She swung around in horror at his voice right behind her. She feinted right and then ran to the left as he reached out to grab her.

Drawling, "Ah, my little pet, you are a fun one," his lewd grin sharpened his mouth into points at the corners. He spun to go after her, he still didn't hurry, the room wasn't that big and there was really nowhere for her to go.

She darted around a chair and he shoved it over, snatched out a hand and snagged her blouse. He pulled her screaming and kicking into his arms. Holding her with his arms wrapped over hers, he lowered his head and bit her on the neck.

Wyn's scream was piercing, she kicked and twisted harder.

He lifted her off her feet to make it harder for her- she kicked him in the knee- he yelped and threw her to the ground.

"You little bitch, that's the way you want to play?" He dropped to the floor as she scrambled to roll away. Grabbing her shoulders, he pushed them hard, slamming her back on the carpet.

Anger in his dark eyes, he threatened, "I'll show you how to play, my pet." He clutched a handful of her blouse and pulled her up to latch his mouth over hers, she twisted her head.

Furious at Wyn for battling him, he shook her so hard her eyes wobbled, then he roughly shoved her down on her back. Climbing over her, he straddled her and ungently forced her shoulders to lay flat on the floor.

Face a furious mask, huffing with exertion, he said, "The harder you fight, honey, the more violent I will be. It's up to you. I'm going to take you now, we can do the question and answers later." Holding her shoulders immobile, he lowered his mouth to her lips and raised his leg to push between hers.

Wyn shoved her knee up as hard as she could, kneeing him smack in the groin.

He bellowed and doubled over, then rolled off her to curl up on his side. Clutching his bruised testicles, he gasped and gagged and cursed.

Wyn jumped up and ran to the glass doors. She picked up a heavy looking bowl and hurled it at the glass. As she expected, it bounced right off and tumbled to the floor.

She ran frantically around the room, searching for something bigger, heavier, when she heard his growl behind her. Wyn ducked out of his grasp at the last second and ran blindly.

Cartiér roared, "All right, I've had enough!"

Panting hard, his face slightly green from the kick she had given him, he glowered fearsomely at her. "You will not destroy my possessions. For everything you throw I will punch you in the chest. Now, come here, stop making me chase you. You can't get out of this room."

He stalked towards her.

Chapter Twenty-One

Running across the front of the window, Wyn grabbed up anything she could get her hands on and hurled them at the glass, and at him.

Cartiér ducked and bent over. His face becoming darker, his eyes blacker, mouth grimmer as he chased after her.

She finally reached the bar and picked up one of the stools. Lifting it as high as she could Wyn threw it with both hands at the window- it made a terrible cracking, banging sound but didn't break it.

Cartiér bellowed in rage as he raced at her between the couch and the window.

With a yelp, fleeing him, Wyn jumped up over the back of the couch and fell forward on top of the cushions.

"Bitch," he snarled. Following her, he lifted his leg over the back of the couch to step on a cushion.

Wyn rolled off the couch and ran around it. As he lifted his other leg to land on the cushions, she was back behind the couch, behind him- and she shoved him as hard as she could.

He was off balance with only the toe of one foot on the soft cushion and the other in mid-air. His arms flailing like windmills- he shouted as he fell, unable to avoid crashing onto the sailfish in the glass table.

Wyn screamed as the razorbill stabbed, slicing through him like the sword that it was.

Impaled by the fish, Cartiér's body landed hard with the momentum. Crashing onto the table, it shattered it into pieces, the fish broke in half. Cartiér slammed onto the broken glass with the sword stuck all the way through him and out the other side.

Not sure if he was dead or alive, Wyn hurried back to the windows still searching for something to break them. Surely his men would come looking for him with all that noise, shortly they'd be knocking the door down.

Then a huge bang at the door made her swing around in terror. They were coming for her now!

Her head darted back and forth, there was just nowhere to hide, and nothing to use as a weapon.

She ran to see if she could pull the bill out of Cartiér and out of the fish and use that like a knife, but she tripped over the broken table in her haste and fell screaming on top of the man.

Sprawling over him, Wyn saw his head was turned at an awkward angle and his dead eyes stared blindly at her.

The door crashed open- she couldn't help it, Wyn shrieked in fright, and rolled into a ball to protect what little she could of herself.

"Wynna!"

Her mind screaming she didn't hear Vijay calling her.

When his hands wrapped around her arms to help her up, she fought him screaming.

Unmindful of the broken glass she laid on, he shoved his hands under her and picked her up. Still in a ball in his arms she shrieked and punched out until his calm voice finally reached her.

"Wynna, baby, *mea dragă,* hush now, you are safe my little warrior," the last was a chuckle.

He took in Cartiér impaled on the sailfish's bill atop the broken table, dead as a doornail, and Wyn was undoubtedly the culprit who got him there. Holding her high and tight against his chest, he perused the dead man.

Finally realizing it was Vijay who held her, Wyn threw her arms around his neck and shrieked, "Vijay!" then sobbed against his shoulder.

"*Bine*, baby, shh," he held her while she calmed. He said teasing, "I told you not to leave without me. Now you see the consequences, poor Mr. Cartiér lays dead by your hand."

She pushed herself up to look at him, wiping at her tears. "It was an accident, I didn't mean to kill him. I mean I didn't at first, but then..."

"When he threatened to rape and kill you then you decided it was okay. You need to tell me how you did it, *dragă*, I cannot wait to tell the guys. After they die of laughter they will be so proud of you. Like me." He kissed her nose.

"Oh, Vijay," she wailed. "I killed him! I killed a person, oh God."

"Calm down, if you had not dispensed of him I would have when I got in here. Either way he would be dead, and it was his fault. You," he kissed her nose again, "are the bravest, smartest most ingenious woman, make that person, I have ever met." He glanced down at the dead man.

He commented blithely, "You got lucky. The bill missed a rib and went right through his heart. It might not have killed him otherwise, and he would have been *really* angry then." He chuckled again, something so rare for him, but that was feeling more and more normal the longer he was with Wynna.

"Vijay, it was an accident," she sighed and laid her head on his shoulder. "Can you please take me out of here?"

"You bet. But I owe you a punishment." Stepping over the glass, he headed for the broken door.

Her head popped up. "What? Punishment? What punishment, for what?"

He carried her over the threshold and down the hall. "I told you he was no good. I told you he only wanted to fuck you, or use you for information. I warned you. I told you not to leave without me. I was wary and got there a half hour early but you were already gone."

When he had been told the driver had come an hour early for her, his already suspicious paranoia ignited and uneasiness took hold, tightening his stomach and squeezing the air from his lungs.

Vijay

Good thing he had previously researched Cartiér and had his address.

Very matter-of-factly, Vijay informed her, "There is only going to be one man you fuck from now on, and listen to, *and* obey, and I am going to make sure you remember that. Come on, let us find a place for your punishment. The mansion is empty, at least for now."

"Wait." She looked at him to see if he was kidding. It was hard to tell. He didn't look angry, he looked...like he was on a mission to...she didn't know.

He wasn't looking at her, his gaze revolved around as if checking for danger, searching for somewhere to go? But then he glanced down at her, and she saw raw lust flare at her like white heat.

But under that heat stirred a mixed trace of anger, fear, and a wickedness that titillated and frightened her at the same time. "Uh, Vijay, are you okay? You're not mad at me are you?"

He shifted his eyes from her to hide the searing hunger in them and strode down the hall looking left and right at the doors, and glancing out the windows to ensure the driveway remained empty.

Along the way, he stepped over a man lying face down on the floor, his neck at a funny angle.

As he strode through the foyer, he passed several more men lying motionless; some still had guns in their hands.

"Vijay! My God, what did you do?" Her hands tightened around his neck.

He shrugged. "They said they preferred I did not go look for you, and I preferred that I did."

He turned the corner and saw they'd entered the kitchen.

An oval table took up the center of the room. In front of the table was an emerald green tiled island. Bordering all around the kitchen, green tiles went halfway up from the counters to the modern cupboards with glass fronts.

He set her on her feet and instructed, "Hold still, one sec."

Leaving her wobbling on her unsteady feet, Vijay went to the sink and quickly washed the blood off his hands.

Wiping his hands on a paper towel, he tossed it into the sink and ran water over to displace his DNA or prints and used another paper to pull out a chair.

He picked her up, then he sat down and brought her to straddle him. Demanding, "Kiss me my brave warrioress," he cradled her face with his hands as they kissed.

Wyn gripped handfuls of his shirt then put her palms on his chest to feel the play of his amazing muscles.

Vijay's hand strode up her neck to splay around the back of her head the other went to her waist. Their tongues tasting and twining, he suddenly lifted her, flipped her over and laid her on her stomach across his legs.

"Vijay! she cried out. "What are you doing?"

"I said you had punishment coming. This is as good a place as any. There is no one here to bother us, anymore anyway. Hold still." He grabbed her bottom with both hands and squeezed both rounded globes.

"Yep," he nodded, "they are ripe for spanking." He lifted one of her feet and took her shoe and sock off then did the same to the other one.

She squirmed, protesting, "No, stop it, right now, we're in someone's kitchen for heaven's sake, you can't be serious!"

"Ah, but I am," and he gave her a wallop, not hard, but hard enough to make her yelp.

She tried to put her hand back to block him but he caught it and spanked her again. Again, not hard enough to sting, but enough to shock her.

"I order you to stop this right now, dammit Vijay!" Wyn squirmed.

"Okay." He helped her stumble to her feet.

Rubbing her butt, she glowered at him. "You can't do that to me!"

"You are right, *mea dragă,* tis not working. I cannot get a good smack through those slacks." He grasped her waist pulling her in between his legs.

Holding her from fleeing with his knees, he quickly plucked at the button on her slacks and pulled the zipper down before she could stop him.

"No, wait, Vijay," some fear edged into her voice, worried now that he really meant to paddle her.

He held her legs at the knees, forcing them together keeping her off balance and unable to have any leverage to get away.

She fell forward with her hands on his thighs with a grunt, "This is insane! You can't spank me like I'm a child- what are you doing!"

He loosened his legs long enough for her to awkwardly stand back up then he gripped her slacks and drew them straight down her legs to her ankles.

She shrieked, "Oh my god! Vijay!"

He grasped her waist and again laid her belly down over his thighs. Her legs thrashing, she squawked her protests.

He caught her legs, pulled her pants off and dropped them. "This is much better, eh?" He set his hand on the wisp of her sheer panties.

She froze. "Vijay…"

Kneading her rounded flesh, a groan rumbled out of him. "Every part of you, Wynna, is perfect, like sweet peaches."

She stopped struggling, until he pulled her panties down just enough to slap his palm on her bare skin.

"Ow!" Her hips bucked over his thighs with her cry. Again, he'd slapped her just hard enough between the edge of pain and pleasure. She squirmed and thrashed her legs so hard he had to let go of her panties to hold her still. The underwear snapped back up over her cheeks.

Holding her with his arm over her back, he nudged her thighs apart with his hand and slipped his strong fingers under her panties to stroke the divide between her cheeks.

Her thighs tightened. Shocked, she tried to press them back together. "No-"

"Hush, *mea dragă.*" He forced her legs apart and held them as he drew his fingers back down between her spread cheeks. He set his thumb just at the entrance of her bottom, pressed gently while moving his fingers up the other side to caress her female core.

There was silence in the room. She lay across his lap without moving. He stroked her tender lips, softly fingered her bud, rubbing it while still pressing his thumb against her tush's opening.

A grating groan seethed from her slightly parted, taut lips, his hand grew wet.

He murmured, "There, baby, that is it." When he pushed just the tip of his finger inside her, her body twitched, a sound rolled out of her so erotic, Vijay almost came in his jeans.

He put his hands under her arms, lifted her and stood up with her legs wrapped around his waist. She clinched his face, holding it, her lips fell on his, dizzily seeking with rough desire the lust flaming inside his mouth.

He carried her to the counter and set her down. Their mouths bound, he undid each button on her blouse. When they were all open, he leaned back and pulled the sides of her blouse apart.

Lowering his head, his mouth went to her ripe full pulp. Cupping her breasts, he sucked the lush flesh that swelled over the bra. Her body undulated against him.

"*Zue*, baby," he growled and kissed back up her neck then slid one big hand under her butt lifting her, with the other he snagged her panties and pulled them off.

Shyness took her over. Wyn dropped her head and put her hands over her nude femininity and crossed her ankles.

"*Nu, mea dragă,* do not hide your beauty from me. I have dreamed too long to see you like this. Let me see." He lifted her chin and kissed her.

Then with their lips locked, he took her wrists and moved her hands up over her head and back slightly to hold onto the cupboard. "Do not let go, sweetheart."

Still kissing her, Vijay nudged her legs apart and moved his hips between them so she couldn't close them. He set his fingers over her woman's mound and smiled at her moan of pleasure. Her legs loosened slightly. He lightly rubbed her clit, running a broad finger up and down her slit until he felt her wetness.

He stepped back and pulled her so she was closer to the edge of the counter and drank her in.

Her hands raised over her head arched her back, eyes half-closed, hair a disheveled yellow cloud around her head. Her blouse open exposing her luscious breasts in the red silk bra, her thighs spread revealing her femininity all pink and tender. Hell, she looked like a model on a sexy Playboy shoot.

"*Mea Zue*, baby, I have died and gone to heaven. I want so damned badly to take you right now."

"Hmmm," slid out of her parted lips as if she couldn't form words, her eyes cloudy slits.

"Watch me touch you, baby." He caressed her breasts that were pushed out from arching her back.

She lowered her head in a daze and stared at his big tanned hands dark on her fair skin, molding her sumptuous flesh with his fingers. He squeezed a bit hard, then gentle, then harder while dipping his head to kiss them. Red marks rose everywhere his heated sucking left.

He could see the goose bumps pill on her arms, her nipples hardened through the silk. It was hot watching her watching his hands and mouth on her.

Her head rolled back with her hushed cry, "Oh God, Vijay, oh God."

His answering, "*Da*," just as hushed, he skimmed his big hands down her sides, then he crouched to kneel in front of her.

"Vijay?" she whispered, bereft when he removed his hands from her body.

"Hush baby. Do not move, stay just like you are, I just want a small taste." He put his mouth on her core and licked her pebbling bud.

"Oh!" Her head lolled back, a moan rippled up her arched body making her shiver, her fingers dug into the wooden cupboard.

His smile brushed her slit before he thrust his tongue inside her. Her hips jolted, he put his palms on her thighs to hold her still. He licked then sucked on her bud, moved a hand to her ribs to push her until she lay on her back.

Writhing on the counter to the motions of his mouth, breathy gasps slipped out, "Vijay…uhh…Vijay," his name oozed in a succulent moan.

"Baby," he murmured, his voice a buzz against her clit giving her another jolt.

"Ah," she groaned. "What- ah…"

"I do not have any condoms with me, but I want to make you come. *Bine*?"

Her pulsing groan was her answer. She really could no longer hear him, the blood rushed to her head, her core felt like it was on fire. Her hands lay on the countertop beside her head as if she hadn't the energy to move them, her legs spread open to him.

He smiled. That was enough for him for right now. Pleasuring her. They would complete their love making when they were in the right place.

He licked her tender flesh, rubbed her clit with his thumbs using them to shift her folds open. Pushing her thighs wider apart, he slowly inserted a thick finger inside her.

A gushed gasp choked out of her throat, Wyn's hips bucked to the shock of his finger forcing it in further.

He froze. "Wynna."

"Hmmm? Don't stop,"

"*Mea Zue*, are you a virgin?"

Her hips undulated against his finger, her body writhed under his grip. "Doesn't matter," she mumbled, "please don't stop, Vijay, my body is…burning…"

"Wynna, for *qruttes stead*, why didn't you tell me? I cannot, this is not right." He reeled, struggling for the words to say. He stood up, leaned over and set his palms next to her shoulders and again, almost exploded in his jeans.

Wyn's breathtaking face, mesmeric and rapturous scrunched with pained pleasure. Her eyelids fluttered exposing brief blurry mists of impassioned blues and greens. Her tongue stroked her parted lips just like he had licked her. Arching her back seeking his touch, her breasts thrust up in his face.

"Vijay, don't leave me," her words exhaled on a threaded moan. She moved her hands to clutch the edge of the counter.

"Dammit Wynna." *Zue*, she was so gorgeous, so hot, his hands and mouth were wet with her silk. His erection throbbed like it was going to burst from his pants.

He pushed the sides of her blouse apart to nibble and suck on her nipples over the thin silky bra. Her body shook and shuddered and rolled, her head flopped back and forth with the thrill and agony of it.

"*Please Vijay*," she begged, her knees drew up then dropped back down to hang off the counter.

He watched her, his own arousal off the charts. Her eyes were closed, brows knit hard, still licking her lips. His one hand clenched a breast; he moved the other back to her core.

When he slid his finger up her slit, her urgent moan almost undid him. He pushed his finger inside her, slowly, until he reached her virgin's blockage.

Thank *Zue* he hadn't had a condom, not knowing she was a virgin, in the raw primal state he was in he might have shoved right into her before preparing her and, damn, would have hurt her badly.

"Do it Vijay, do it now, so I will be," she took a deep gulping breath, "ready for you later." Sucking in another deep breath, she whispered, "So when we can finish, with you inside me, it won't hurt then."

His head dropped. In all his experience with women he had never been with a virgin. He didn't know what to do. A wave of satisfaction roiled up him. He would be her first. *Her only.* He smiled, he'd assumed she had been with that asshole fiancé, but she hadn't. It was saved for him to teach her. And boy did he have a lot to teach her.

No wonder she was so shy and skittish when he'd stroked the lining of her bottom, pushed his thumb against the rosebud opening. If he'd known she was a virgin he would have gone a helluva lot slower. The spanking, he had been thinking sex games, she must have been terrified he was going to beat her.

"Vijay?" her voice trembled with need.

He didn't deserve this- this gift. The harsh and bawdy were designed for his big, rough, herculean body, not this precious, dainty, sweet little pure thing.

Looking down at her glazed eyes, he devoured her with a needy hunger, damn; he'd never wanted anything, anyone, more in his entire life than this woman. She made his blood boil like no other had.

Zue, he wanted her so badly…and God knows he didn't deserve her, but he couldn't bear to hurt her. He just couldn't look at her delicate innocence and gentleness and deliberately harm her.

"Ahh, my sweetheart, it will hurt. I cannot, we need to wait until-"

Her voice shaky, she acknowledged, "I know. I know it'll hurt, Vijay. I trust you. If you do it now, then it won't hurt when you…are…inside, me,"

Entrusted with a woman's initiation into the world of men and women, "Uhh," he growled. He was built rough and tough, not soft and gentle. She was asking him to- break her.

He hadn't even known her the day he rescued her from Warwick, and even then it was a like a knife in his stomach seeing her hurt. Seeing Warwick slap her, he tried to get to the man and take him apart for it, but he'd had to fight through seven men to get to them giving Warwick more time to harm her.

And now she expected *him* to be the one to deliberately cause her pain. He rolled his thumb around her bud feeling it harden, hearing her sigh, her thighs quiver. He looked at her.

Her eyes were closed. She looked like an angel about to be…deflowered…sort of. He would sure be looking forward to the next lesson.

"Do it…" squirming on the counter, her body trembled, voice a hush of needy pleading.

Stroking her clit, he inserted his finger, slowly, his other hand went to her breast, he pinched her nipple and kneaded the flesh as her shiver made her body shudder in his hands. He moved his finger in and out, stroked her clit, caressed her breast, he moved according to the thrust of her hips and the rhythm of her moans.

Faster, deeper, faster, her thighs were clenching and unclenching his hand. Vijay watched her face, it was such a beautiful goddamned thing, his dick was about to burst with want.

He felt humbled to have this honor. Deflowering his beloved. He will never forget this day, her gift to him. He bent, nudged her nipple out of the silk bra and sucked on the tasty morsel.

When he felt her on the edge, about to peak, he went faster, moved to seal his mouth over hers and then pushed through-breaking her hymen and kept going.

A piercing scream, she bolted up, forking forward with the pain, her anguished cry against his lips.

His big hand splayed against her back holding her, he manipulated his fingers over her clit, inside stroking her hot spot until through the pain she crested and hurled into strident release.

Her head fell back and Wyn gasped, hitched his name over and over as her body flung spasm after spasm against this hand.

He felt her silk bathe his palm as her sheath compressed, squeezing his finger. As the spasms lessened to tremors, her chest panting like she'd been running, Vijay gently helped her lay back down. He pulled his finger out with a bit of worry.

She was really small, smaller than he'd thought. And being a virgin, damn, he was a big guy, he was afraid this day wouldn't be the only painful time for her. His fingers so big and thick he had only been able to fit one inside her.

Mea Zue, he needed to really think about this. He loved her too much to inflict more fucking pain on her. She really needed a smaller man. He shook his head, *goddammit*.

Her chest hitched and heaved with her rapid breaths panting, trembling out. His one hand still on her core, Vijay wrapped his other hand around the side of her waist then bent over her and kissed her.

He waited until her breathing slowed, then he stroked her slit, and brushed her bud lightly until her hips started twitching again. Her arms wound around his neck. Easing his finger back inside her, not as far as before, he skillfully wrung her into a second rushing orgasm.

This time her scream was less pain, more pleasure. Vijay put his hands on her thighs, licked then kissed her clit then stood back bending over her and kissed her mouth.

He could feel her smiling on his lips. He leaned back. Her eyes were partially open gleaming with flushing passion, her lips a sultry bow. She raised a hand to stroke his face.

"Vijay, thank you, it was…amazing. I can't wait for the rest. For you."

"Uh, *da*, yeah, we need to talk about that. But first, let's get you dressed before someone decides to come and check on this place." He snagged some paper towels and held them to her core and patted gently. When he removed them they had blood on them as did his hand.

Worried, she exclaimed, "Vijay, what is that?"

He smiled, stuffed the papers in his jean's pocket so as to not leave her DNA floating around. After washing his hands, bowing his head, he kissed her gently. "*Nu* worries, just proof of your virginity, which you honored me with, *mea dragă*."

He had this odd feeling of being in an ancient time where the older husband was in charge of teaching his young bride the delights of man and woman. He wasn't but ten or so years older than her, but he had lived several lifetimes already.

Vijay

His heart bounded with possessiveness, and the urgency to protect. He helped her sit up and went to gather her pants, panties, socks while she fixed her bra and buttoned her blouse.

While she was busy, Vijay made a call. He spoke in his language.

When she was dressed, she stood but her legs wobbled.

"Stay here one sec, baby, I need to make sure your prints are not left anywhere." He hurried back to the room she'd been kept in and washed the wine glasses and the items strewn about that he assumed she'd thrown to break the windows."

After checking to make sure everything she could have come in contact with he rushed back to her. She was leaning against the counter. "Baby," he grinned tenderly at her.

Smiling shyly up at him, Wyn asked, "Vijay, when do you think we can, you know," slightly dizzy she teetered to the side.

"Here." Seeing her unsteady he grabbed her waist and jerked her up so her legs could wind around his hips.

He grinned more broadly at her. "I can carry you in my arms, but I like this so much better. It will be even better when you are naked." Then he frowned. He carried her out of the estate and to the car.

"Vijay," her brows beetled with her sudden concern. "What about all those...men? Mr. Cartiér? Shouldn't we call the police? I'm sure they would understand-"

"*Nu* authorities. My people are coming to take care of it." He didn't share that the place would be burned to the ground to destroy any lingering trace that Wynna and he had been there.

Wyn glanced at the gates that were now hanging awry. "Vijay, did you-"

They reached his car and she noticed the front end was damaged. "Oh my goodness, Vijay! You drove your car through the gate?"

"They were not cooperating with opening it, Wynna. Tis just a rented vehicle, I can get another." Carefully, he settled her into the front passenger seat then climbed in behind the wheel and they were off.

Vijay was silent as he drove them back to the mansion. He could feel her confused eyes light on him every few minutes.

She asked quietly, "Are you mad at me?"

Shaking his head, he reached out, took her hand and held it. "*Nu.*"

"Do you, um, not like me anymore because I am, was, a virgin? Did you not like the way I looked? The way I acted? What you did to me? Because," her cheeks pinked, "I really liked it and can't wait until we can do everything."

The skin around his eyes tightened. Parking the car in front of the Eastwood's mansion, he shut it off and turned to her. "Wynna, I am," he looked down at their clasped hands.

"What, Vijay, please talk to me." Her head cocked, she tried to see into his eyes.

When he raised them, the brilliance of his blue eyes so filled with love, stroked over her from the blonde curls to her dainty hands. "Wynna, I am a big man, uh, all over."

She smiled. "Yes, and handsome too."

His mouth quirked at the compliment. He was usually told his face was too hard and scary to be good-looking. Of course he had never cared before what anyone thought.

"The thing is," he squeezed her hand, "you are really, petite, all over. What I am afraid of tis that I will be too big for you and I would hurt you, rip you apart, and it would be impossible for us to- to-"

"Are you kidding?" She laughed. Teasing him, she said, "Vijay, really, you need to take the time to learn about women and not just rut away like a wild animal."

At his scowl, she said, "Anyway, have you ever heard about women having babies?"

He nodded, rolling his eyes sarcastically, then frowned. "Of course. But not you," he squeezed her hand harder. "I could never bear to see you go through that agony- never." With a shiver, his voice roughened in the resolute statement.

Vijay

Now she rolled her eyes. "Vijay, come on, women are designed to, uh, expand. Our bodies are made to adapt to babies and to men whose egos are as big as their manhood."

Blinking at her, he got her teasing. "*Da*, but-"

"Vijay, I am going to have children. Are you saying you want me to have them with another man?" She cocked a brow at him.

Forehead knit, he spurted angrily, "*Nu*, you will not be with any other man. But Wynna, the pain of childbirth-"

"Is forgotten the second you hold your newborn in your arms." Her voice soft and sweet, she leaned over and rested her head on his shoulder and wound her arms around his arm. "I want children, Vijay, your children. You'll see, we'll make love, I trust you to take care of me, you will know how to do it without hurting me."

She rode up on her knees, wrapped her arms around his neck and kissed him. He was still in deep thought and absently kissed her back.

He had not grown up in a normal household. The term 'mother' had really no meaning to him. His parents were soldiers and jungles, danger, fighting, grisly deaths.

He had never entertained the thought of children, a wife, family. The people he hung with were like him, rough, tough, heartless, ruthless. They were not the kinds to have families like that. His warrior brothers were his family.

But, he had to admit, the thought of tiny Wynnas dancing around his feet made him feel all warm and squishy inside. And wanting. Brand new feelings he'd never experienced before assailed him. He had a lot of thoughts to chew on later.

She let go of him, then slid across the seat and opened the door and hopped out before he got a word out.

Calling, "Wynna, wait," he threw his door open and went after her.

Unfortunately, there were several people on the lawn heading into the house. Odessa was having a ladies luncheon. They all turned to gawk at the couple.

Vijay linked their fingers and walked her to the door.

209

There, in front of everyone, he cupped her chin and gave her a chaste kiss. "I will call you later, *mea dragă*. I beg you, please, do not leave this place without me. Do not make me have to be frantic with worry every time I bring you home. Well, here to this place. Our real home is where we will live together."

That made her beam. "I promise."

They kissed again chastely then he watched her go inside. Not giving the gawkers an iota of attention, he strode across the lawn to his car with his hands casually stuffed in his jean's pockets.

Without a look back, he drove off.

Chapter Twenty-Two

Wyn didn't see Vijay for several days. He left messages that came through at odd times because he was constantly in and out of satellite distances.

After dinner one night, Jazer Edrei came over to see her. Odessa was all aglow.

Exclaiming, "*Finally*," she beamed from the petite Wyn to the much taller, Jazer. "We can make plans for the wedding!"

Wyn had given up trying to tell her aunt that she was not going to marry Jazer. The elder woman just ignored her and talked about Wyn and Jazer as if they were already together.

"Come," Odessa said cheerfully to Jazer, her pendulum skirt swinging around below her knees, "let's get you a drink, young man."

Her aunt pushed the couple into the salon and told one of the maids to fix Jazer whatever he wanted. She said to Wyn, "Isn't he handsome with that deep chestnut hair and those rich chocolate eyes? I can already picture your offspring; with your extremely opposite coloring they will look beautiful and unique!"

"Really, Auntie Odessa, we are not-"

Cutting her off, "Dear," Odessa set a firm hand on her niece's shoulder quieting her, "you should have a drink with your fiancé. It will make you more excited making your plans." She said to the maid, "Sasha, please bring Miss Wyn, oh, how about a martini?

Yes," she smiled slyly at her niece. A nice powerful martini should lighten her up enough for Jazer to press his suit.

Wyn groaned, everyone was trying to get her drunk to make her malleable. "No, Aunt Odessa, really, I don't want a-"

"Hush dear, you never know what's good for you. Right, Jazer?" the older woman smoothed her hair back into its neat chignon.

His hand tucked imperturbably in the pocket of his black slacks, Jazer accepted his drink from the maid and looked at Odessa over the rim of the glass with a conspiratorial nod. His dark blue suit coat rode up over the wrist of the hand in his pocket, a glinting gold Rolex watch boasted below his shirt sleeve.

Wyn hovered near the door, she didn't like the way things were being pushed at her. She announced, "I'll be right back," and headed out the door.

"Wyn! Come back here!" Odessa commanded.

When Wyn kept going, Odessa glared at Jazer, accusing, "This is your fault for messing around with that tramp, Shreva. If you blew this…"

"Not to worry, Odessa, calm down." Jazer calmly sipped his Armagnac. He told her with sublime arrogance, "I'll bring her around."

Her face snarled in an annoyed recrimination. "I don't know, you couldn't keep your hands off that hussy and keep your tool in your pants. Then heaping more injury on, you let Wyn get away to her own apartment. Now she has that- that- biker thug sniffing after her." She crossed her angular arms over her equally angular chest. She looked like an anvil in a flowered dress.

Jazer sighed into his drink. "Where is Sasha? I need another."

The maid came in with Wyn's martini.

Jazer ordered her, "Get me another, Sasha, make it a double," he slapped the maid on the ass as she left the room. He saw her back stiffen in offense but didn't care.

Servants put up with everything because cushy jobs in this backwoods indigent corner of the world were hard to come by. And if they went and complained to the authorities? He shrugged, who was to be believed, the maid or the blueblood? The cops wouldn't give her the time of day.

They wouldn't complain to Sheffield either because he took plenty of his own tastes of the help. Part of the rules were that all comely young women working at this estate, or Jazer's, had to be on birth control.

"Huh." With an ugly snort, Odessa sneered, "That's part of your problem. You like to play too much. Drink too much, gamble too much. Normally I would be telling you to keep it in your pants. But," she sighed with irritation, "now, it might be your only strategic defense."

Her face hard, she told him, "Go after her, Jazer. Once you get...into her as it were," she grimaced at the picture, "that hoodlum will wash his hands of her, damaged goods and all that. You might even mange to get her pregnant and it'll be a done deal then."

Jazer took his drink from Sasha without a thanks and swigged a healthy slug. Licking his lips, he said smoothly, "Are you suggesting I force your precious niece?" His eyes glowed as if he eagerly agreed with the suggestion.

With Odessa on the sidelines cheering, Wyn would have no recourse, no one to complain to if Jazer took her against her will. The girl was basically trapped in the mansion. She had no funds, Sheffield held her ID, passport, she wasn't going anywhere.

Again, the police would side with the Eastwoods. Wyn was nothing but an alien visitor with few, if any, rights.

Thoughts of silk tied around Wyn's delicate wrists and ankles as she lay splayed on her back like a naked starfish in his bed danced through his head. Or, he could just shove her over a table and take her from behind; she couldn't put up much of a fight that way.

"No," Odessa said, bursting his fantasy bubble. "Not with that outlaw hood hanging around her. She cries rape to him and I can see him burning this entire town to the ground. Try seduction first, you fool. Get her drunk, but," she sighed. "If you have to force it then do what you have to. We will find some way to suppress the thug, money of course always paves the way for- oh, darling, there you are," she broke off as Wyn returned.

"Sweetheart," Jazer said, sweeping over to her with the martini in his hand, "you look stressed. Here, this will help ease your tension. Have a seat," he handed her the drink and led her to the couch and almost pushed her to sit.

"Let me massage that slender little neck of yours," he offered, sitting down next to her, one leg bent under him so he could face her. "Turn to your back for me, my sweet."

"No, really, Jazer." Wyn set her drink on the coffee table and turned to face him.

He grasped her shoulders and tried to force her to turn back around.

But she protested, "Jazer, stop it. I don't want a massage, I don't want a drink, Aunt-" She glanced around for Odessa but her aunt had discreetly left the room closing the door behind her. Wyn pushed to get to her feet.

"Come on, Wyn, just let me explain." Jazer grabbed her harder and forced her back on the couch.

Wyn twisted to loosen his grasp. "Jazer," Wyn said firmly. Getting up and moving quickly to the door, she decried, "Enough of this. I said I don't want to."

He raced after her, grabbed her and threw her against the wall.

Wyn's back and head slammed hard, knocking the wind out of her. Stunned, she shook the stars from her head as he gripped her arm and dragged her back to the couch.

"Don't piss me off, Wyn," he warned crossly and shoved her down on the couch. "You've played hard to get long enough. I should have taken you while I had the chance, before you caught on that occasionally Shreva and I get it on. So what, it's nothing to do with our relationship."

Wyn moved to spring back off the couch but Jazer grabbed her arms and flung her down. Pushing her on her back, he quickly climbed to straddle her before she could get back up.

Vijay

His hand clamped across her throat, Jazer held her still and jammed his mouth over hers. When she fought him, he grasped her wrists pinning them down. The harder she fought him the harder he kissed her.

Finally, he took a breath, panting harshly, his eyes swept her face. Her lips were red, she was breathing hard, and she was furious.

"Let go of me, Jazer, now!" She jerked her arms to loosen his grip, struggled to sit up.

Lust and covetousness emanated from the hard chocolate eyes. His smile cocky and lewd, he advised her, "Honey, our families bless and want our union, and there's no doubt I want a honeypot like you. You will learn to accept me. With our good looks we will make stunning children. So, come on, let's make this totally official, we can consummate our engagement right now." Forcing his legs between hers, he shoved her back down.

"No! Jazer stop!" Still fighting to sit up, Wyn punched at him. He snagged her wrists painfully, bending them backwards, hurting her to make her comply.

Crying out, she threatened, "I'll scream, Jazer!"

"Go ahead, no one will come. Odessa gave me her blessing. You will only embarrass yourself letting everyone know we are in here making love. Now," he pushed her down with his chest and forced her hands over her head, twisting and pinching her wrists.

Not caring if he hurt her, his mouth came down hard on hers, he pushed at her lips but she refused to open her mouth.

He ground so fiercely at her, she could feel her teeth pushing through her skin. Tears of pain and fright pooled, but she still fiercely fought with all she had, she would not give into him.

Jazer swore like a sailor, "Dammit Wyn," he slapped her and tried again to force her mouth open to take him, but she clamped her lips together.

Infuriated, he hit her again and again. His breath heaving, he hissed, "Open to me, goddammit, you can't refuse me!" But she turned her head from him.

He put her hands into one of his to hold then gripped her jaw so hard his fingers dug into the bones trying to force her to open to him, but her teeth were clenched tight.

Grunting with the effort of trying to pry her mouth open, Jazer cursed, "You try this shit when we're married and you will fucking regret it, Wyn. Women have no rights here, males have full rights to beat them to keep them in line. You need to get that through your head and submit to me."

Her lip was bleeding from his strikes. Giving up trying to kiss her, he reached for her blouse. Clutching the collar, he prepared to wrench it completely open and just strip her.

Once he christened her with his body, even if he had to use force, Wyn would give in, maybe with shame, so what. He'd say it was consensual, and she would marry him without further argument.

Wyn slammed her knee up right into his groin. It had been her only defense with Cartiér, and it worked again now.

Jazer's hacked inhale was sharp and without sound as he folded in half.

Wyn rolled out from under him and ran for the door. She sped up the stairs, down the hall, into her room. Slamming the door, she locked it and threw her back against it, chest heaving with panic.

She put her hand to her lip and looked at it, her stomach clenched, her fingers were bloody. Exhaling a slow shuddering breath, she trod over and peered in the dresser mirror and blanched.

Her lip was swollen and split, there was a cut under her eye, and there was at least one bruise purpling on her jaw. Her stomach went queasy at the fingerprints bruising on her neck.

Her wrists ached, she looked at them. Jazer's roughness had gouged raw rings and bruises on her wrists. Her nerved stomach felt like it was shriveling.

She couldn't stay here, she wasn't safe. If Vijay saw her he would- her blood froze. What if he did something that would get him arrested? Her mind spun, what should she do? He had begged her not to leave the mansion, but what else could she do?

Vijay

Jazer started knocking on the door. First he was cajoling, "Come on Wynnie, you know you want me, open the door, sweetie."

She put her hand over her stomach that was flip-flopping. When she didn't unlock the door, his voice and knock hardened, he shook the doorknob.

"Wyn Pila, you unlock this goddamned door right this minute. You are going to be my wife, you will obey me."

When she didn't obey his order, he pounded on the wood so hard the door shook, he shouted, "You open this door right now, Wyn, or by God when I get my hands on you, you will pay!"

Wyn couldn't believe her uncle would allow Jazer to yell like that and pound on her door. The longer it was, the louder and more violent the threats and the pounding.

Her phone rang. Hurrying, she tripped over to it and picked it up off the bed. It was Vijay. Thrill warred with fear. If she didn't answer he would know something was wrong. Taking a deep breath, she blew it out slowly, and slid the bar to answer it. Her voice came out weak and shaky, "H-hello?"

"What tis wrong?" he barked through the phone.

""Uh, what do you mean, I mean nothing is w- wrong, I miss you," she could feel tiny beads of sweat pop all along her hairline.

"I can hear it in your voice. What the fuck is going on, Wynna?" His voice grew louder, harsher, his accent thickened.

She tried but couldn't speak.

He waited, impatiently, then snapped, "Are you in danger?" Silence. "Answer me, Wynna," he demanded.

She moved to the window wondering if she was up too high to climb out. Looking out and down, on the second floor there was no way she could consider jumping. Every few minutes Jazer banged on the door.

"Goddammit Wynna, what the fuck is that noise?"

"It's- it's," she yelped at a sharp bang.

"Wynna!" While talking to her, Vijay dialed #2 and said in their language, "Gage, Wynna is in trouble at her house. You are closest, go get her. If anyone gets in your way, burn them." Back

217

to her, he yelled, "Wynna, talk to me, is that fucking Edrei at your door? Are you hurt?"

She tried to sound calm but her voice squeaked, "I'm really not hurt too, uh, much, I mean I'm fine…he- he wants me to open the door."

His violent growl burned through the wires, "Motherfucker. Do not open it. Shove a chair under the handle honey." He waited. "Do it now Wynna," his voice commanding.

Setting the phone on the bed she ran and picked up a chair from the desk and stuffed it under the handle.

Grabbing up the phone, "Okay," she said with a short, scared rush of air.

"Baby, I am not in the country, I cannot get to you but I am sending someone to you."

She tried to stifle it, but the sob she struggled to choke back came through. She could literally hear him scraping his fingers through his hair.

He directed in a low fierce voice, "Get your passport, and pack a bag. Gage will be there as soon as possible. He's the closest to where you are." He waited again. Anxiety crept into his voice, "*Mea dragă*, talk to me, *please*."

She pushed the words through her closed throat, "I- I'm…all right, Vijay, I promise. I can't get my- my passport, my uncle has it."

His alarmed exhale pulsed through the phone. He needed to stay calm and not make her more frightened. "*Bine*, baby. Pack up and stay in your room until you see Gage. He'll come to your door to get you, all right? You remember him, he's big, Black, and very mean looking, but he will not harm you. Do not leave your room until he is at your bedroom door. *Bine*?"

"Okay." Then, "Oh!" she squealed at the renewed pounding and cursing.

The sound carried through the phone, Vijay's voice tightened, "All right, honey. Get packed, stay away from the fucking door, if it sounds like he tis coming through, run to the bathroom and lock the door. I am going through a tunnel if I lose you I-" the phone disconnected.

Wyn slid off her weak knees to sit on the bed. Her panicked heart beat like a jackhammer. Then she roused herself to get up and pack a suitcase.

Jazer continued cursing and pounding relentlessly, it went on and on. Wyn glanced at the clock on the dresser. He had been banging on her door for thirty minutes.

Afraid he would take the door down, Wyn stood beside it, her suitcase at her feet. If he was able to smash the door in, then he could get the bathroom door open too.

"This is it, goddammit, Wyn, I'm fucking coming in and you're going to be sorry! You'll be goddamned lucky if you heal by the time our wedding comes around, because, believe me, Miss, you are marrying me!" He threw himself at the door so hard it buckled.

Wyn screamed and jumped back.

Then she heard a muffled shout, a howl, a bunch of thumping sounds then it was quiet. Her legs shaking, she stood with her hand over her mouth. Had he gotten a weapon? What if-

"Wynna," a heavy accented, low gruff voice came through the door. "Tis me, Gage. Open the door."

Tears sprung in relief. But, she whispered, "Is it really you, Gage?" She heard his deep chuckle.

"*Da*, honey, open the door, tis safe."

She unlatched the door. When she opened it, the wood was only hanging by a partial hinge. She threw herself into the mountain of dark skinned man with the gleaming shaved head.

He had twice the tats that Vijay had, even some on his face, and wore gold hooped earrings. He could have stepped right off a pirate ship.

If Odessa thought Vijay was a scary looking hoodlum gangster, she'll poop when she sees Gage.

He wrapped his huge powerful arms around her, patting her back. "Tis *bine*, uh, okay, *fetita*, that fucker will not bother you again."

219

She peered around his brick-house of shoulders and saw Jazer crumpled up against the wall down the hall.

"Let's go." He reached into the room, grabbed her bag, tucked her under his arm and ushered her down the hall and to the stairs.

When they reached the bottom, a male servant stood there with a shotgun aimed at them, his hands shaking so badly the barrel bobbed up and down. Sheffield and Odessa hovered behind him.

One of the maids, Alisha stood off to the side, her worried eyes on Wyn.

Sheffield announced, "You are not going anywhere with that-that criminal, Wyn. You march yourself back up those stairs and apologize to Jazer and beg for his forgiveness. And you," he gestured imperiously at Gage.

Odessa stood omnipotent beside her husband, nodding smugly at Wyn.

Sheffield told Gage, "You best be on your way or Johnston here has orders to shoot you."

A big, shit-eating grin split Gage's normally austere face. "*Da*? Oh yeah? That true Johnston?" He narrowed his eyes at the terrified servant.

"Uh, uh, uh," Johnston stuttered like a train chugging down the track.

"Enough of this bullshit." Sheffield barked, "Shoot him, Johnston, now! We will tell the police it was in self-defense! Shoot him!"

Wyn pushed to stand in front of Gage, her hands up, she yelled, "No!"

"*Fetita*." Gage literally picked Wyn up and set her down behind him. He waited with one brow raised at Johnston. "We need to get going, Johnston, so if you're going to shoot you need to-" in a flash, he leapt the few feet and snatched the gun from the servant's frozen hands.

Gage took it, smashed it over his knee and threw the broken weapon at Sheffield's horrified feet.

Vijay

Behind Sheffield, Wyn saw Alisha's grin and thumbs up. Johnston even gave her a weak, relieved half-grin.

"*Bine*, let's go," Gage urged Wyn to move forward.

"Wait," Wyn said. "I need my passport. My uncle has it."

Gage didn't want Sheffield or Odessa out of his sight. He jutted his chin at Sheffield and ordered him, "Tell the maid where it tis. Tell her quick and true or I will tie that shotgun around your scrawny neck in a bow."

Sheffield blinked then Gage stomped a foot at him. Sheffield blurted to Alisha, "M- my den, top drawer, key is under the- the lamp."

Alisha raced off. She returned in only a moment with the passport. Wyn took it gratefully with a smile at the maid.

Gage picked up her suitcase and tromped over, took Wyn's arm and walked her out of the house.

Outside, he led her down the yard to his truck. He opened the passenger door, set her bag in the back, lifted her in then hopped in the driver's side and the truck was already moving before he got the door closed.

He glanced over at Wyn. Seeing her chin trembling, he asked, "You okay, honey?"

She smiled at him. "I am now. Thank you, Gage. I don't know what would have happened if you hadn't come." She dashed at an errant tear.

He shot another quick glance at her then shook his head. "There tis going to be hell to pay when Vij sees your face. You sure you are all right? I can take you to the hospital."

"No, Gage, really." Her body slumped wearily. "I just want to get away from here as fast as possible."

He winked at her. "*Nu* prob. We are heading for the airport." He swung the wheel, the truck turned onto the main road and he aimed towards the expressway.

"Where are we going?" Wyn didn't care, anywhere but here was fine with her. She laid her head back against the seat.

Gage looked at her again, the outside lights sliding over her pale face as they drove by. He shook his head again, if he'd seen the injuries to her face before he'd gotten to the fucker trying to knock her door down, he would be leaving a corpse behind at that mansion instead of a critically injured body.

As he watched her tired eyes drift closed, he murmured, "Monaco."

Chapter Twenty-Three

Gage parked the truck and ushered Wyn inside the airport.

They went to the desk where there was a ticket there in her name.

He took her as far as he could, she'd have to go through Customs and he wasn't going to Monaco. He had work to do here.

"*Bine*, honey, this is as far as I can go. You have a safe flight. Vij will have a car pick you up. He is at a meeting in the town and will meet you at the hotel," *and have an attack when he sees her face.*

Her lip was swollen and split. It looked like she'd been kissed brutally and hit. There was a cut under her eye with several bruises blotting along her jaw.

He glanced down at those delicate little wrists covered with red rings and bruises and cringed. She had fingerprints on her neck, and he'd seen her favor her side, she might even have cracked ribs.

"Thank you, Gage, I so appreciate it. You saved me from-"

"Tis okay, honey, I am just glad I got there in time. You have a safe trip. I will see you in a few days."

He bent over so he was closer to her and said seriously, "Do not talk to anyone, even the person next to you on the flight. When you arrive, a driver will be holding a sign that says," he smiled embarrassed, "*dragă*. Ignore anyone else that has a sign even if it says your name or Vij's or anything except what I told you."

At her nod, he stood up straight and said, "Vij got you first class but still, stay away from everyone until you get boarded and after. The driver will take you straight to the hotel then right to your room. *Bine*?"

"Okay. Thanks again, Gage." She stood high on tiptoes, hugged him hard and kissed his hard cheek. She didn't see the red blush tinge the tips of his ears.

As he watched her walk away he pulled out his cell and dialed Vijay's number.

The flight was uneventful, thank goodness. She had tried to sleep but the horrid business with Jazer kept playing in her mind. What could she have done different? What if Vijay hadn't called and sent Gage?

Her brows tugged down angrily, her aunt and uncle were all for Jazer assaulting her, raping her. They had prodded and encouraged him, had deliberately left her alone with him. Even let him smash down her door!

Then, the terror she'd felt when her uncle forced that poor butler to threaten them with a gun. Aside from Vijay, Gage had to be the bravest, quickest and most skilled warrior in the world!

When she came out of Customs she saw the sign. Her cheeks turned pink and she couldn't help but smile.

A man dressed in black held the sign with *DRAGA* written in big bold letters. His eyes were already on her before she had even spotted him.

Short dark hair and eyes, built big like the rest of Vijay's team, he also looked around the same age as them, late twenties, early thirties. He went straight to her. "Miss Wynna Pila?"

Nodding, she replied, "Yes."

He bowed slightly, politely, and introduced himself. "I am Connor Cope, please come with me."

"Oh, wait," she said and started to turn from him. "I need to get my suitcase, I'll be right back."

"*Nu*, I have orders not to leave your side." He looked up and saw the sign for baggage claim. He lightly took her arm and led her in that direction.

Once there, he told her to point out her bag. When it rolled around the carousal, Wyn pointed at it, "That's mine," she said.

He easily swung it off the circling carousel with no effort just like Gage had.

Wyn had barely been able to pull it off the bed. She had boots and a jacket, heaven knows what else weighed so much. It was an old suitcase and heavy all by itself.

Connor took her to his car parked right out front.

Ushering her to the back passenger side, he said, "Mr. Zastrovna was going to have me drive a limo, but then he said he thought you would be more comfortable, feel safer in the back of this smaller car not too far from me." He smiled kindly at her.

She returned his smile. "Yes, Vijay is such a sweet thoughtful man." She caught the crooked grin he tried to hide.

Thoughtful and certainly not sweet were never words used before to describe Vijay Zastrovna. Connor could see why Vijay was so taken with the sweet petite beauty. He had understood there had been some trouble at her home.

Observing her injuries, his forehead creased, his neck heated with fierce ire. Who could hurt such a pretty little defenseless thing? His head shook slightly, there was sure to be payback hell for some shithead. Zastrovna will make him wish he'd never been born.

Then again, he knew Gage Valenti had retrieved her. Her abuser would be lucky if he still lived, and walked without a limp. For the rest of his life.

Connor drove through the fascinating seaside city. Homes and businesses wrapped around the harbors and jumbled colorfully up the hills.

The hotel wasn't too far from the airport. He parked in front. Retrieving her bag, Connor helped her out.

He already had the key card to her room so they didn't hesitate in the lavish lobby of the posh hotel. He brought her straight to the elevator then down the grey and rose carpeted hall.

When they reached the room, Connor opened the door and held it for her.

Wyn's mouth dropped. The suite was insanely ornate and lush. As she tried to take it in, Connor had put her suitcase on a case rack in another room and came back.

"Here," he said, handing her the key card. "I will leave you now. You are to please order from room service anything you desire. There is a fridge in the kitchenette with bottled water, soda, liquor, snacks. You are to avail yourself of whatever you desire. Mr. Zastrovna said, well, his instructions were to tell you to not leave this room for any reason until he arrives."

He looked a little abashed at repeating Vijay's strict directorial orders, but Wyn smiled.

"Yes, bossy, that sounds like him. Don't worry, Connor, there is no reason for me to leave this heavenly chamber."

Although sweet and fragile, Connor grinned inside, this gorgeous young woman was not afraid of the big bad Vijay Zastrovna who made even the most violent men in the world shudder.

Connor could see she stands right up to Zastrovna, and even finds him affectionately amusing. Pigs must be flying somewhere. He dipped his head to her and said, "Well then, I will take off."

He trod to the door. Turning as he opened it, he said kindly, "Take care, Miss Wyn, and take care of Mr. Zastrovna. It's nice to finally see someone is here to care for him. He deserves it." And he was gone.

Nodding, Wyn murmured under her breath, "He sure does."

A suite, or more like an apartment, she looked around the living room section. The area was warm and elegant in colors of muted blues and lavenders with plush furniture, soft lighting, and every amenity one could desire.

The bathroom was bigger than her entire apartment, all white and gold marble, the tub as big as her couch.

She wandered into the bedroom.

"Whoa," she spouted in awe. The bed was *huge*. But then so was Vijay. Her cheeks flamed picturing him lying on it wearing nothing but a beguiling grin on his coarse face, and his piercing eyes pulsing blue desire at her.

Further into the room, she saw a separate suite. Her brows rose, maybe he didn't plan on her sharing his bed with her?

A bit dismayed, Wyn pressed her hand against her side. It stung so badly she could barely draw a breath with each step. The other bruises ached terribly around her body; her head was clanging like a hammer against a cymbal inside.

She wandered slowly back out and went to the large picture window. Outside, there was a balcony with a round glass table and chairs. Perfect for early morning breakfast or late night cocktails. Hmm. She was getting ahead of herself.

Vijay might not even being staying here. She sighed, God, she sure hoped he was.

A light knock at the door disturbed her musings. With painful steps she trod over and went to open it, but then she could hear Vijay's voice in her ear, "*See who it is first.*" It might be a maid. Surely it would be safe to open the door to a maid?

She peeped out. It was a young man in a uniform. He looked like a bellhop or something. Must be okay then. She opened the door.

The young man bowed. "Madam. Manuel at your service. I will show you the suite." He sort of pushed past her. She stepped aside.

He strode through the suite showing her everything she had already just looked at.

Back in the living room, he bowed again formally then smiled broadly at her. "I am your attendant. Anything you need, call the front desk and ask for me." He smiled again and moved imperceptibly closer to her.

His tone lowered to a husky lilt as he purred, "That is anything at all, Miss, any time day..." he moved closer, "or night," his voice dropped to a seductive burr.

Her brows arched at his unexpected forwardness. Wyn said quickly, "Oh, well, thank you, no that is fine. Thank you." She tried to urge him to the door but he resisted.

He didn't hide his admiring perusal of her body, going from her face to her chest to her legs stopping where they joined then back to her chest.

"Listen," his voice lowered even deeper inflecting a sultry tone. A sly smile lifting in his dark face, he offered, "There are a lot of things I can do for you, Miss, help you with. It looks like you could use someone to run to for comfort. Did your sugar daddy get too rough with you?" Indicting the bruises on her face and arms.

He nestled closer, lifted a curl off her chest letting his knuckles brush the top swell of her breast. "He probably doesn't treat you right. I can do for you what he can't, honey, I don't need Viagra like he undoubtedly does," he leaned in to inhale the scent of her hair.

Wyn ordered firmly, "Manuel, let go of me, you need to leave." She tried to step away from him but he wrapped the lock of hair around his wrist.

"Come on honey," he cooed, I can give you-"

"I will give her anything she needs. Get your fucking hands off her."

Both Manuel and Wyn's eyes shot to the door.

An infuriated Vijay was standing just inside.

Seeing Vijay towering in his biker jacket, black jeans, shit-kickers, tattoo crawling up the side of his neck, long black hair, the scar seething white over his dark scowling face, Manuel blinked rapidly.

His Adam's apple bounced with his hard, suddenly dry swallow. "Uh, yeah, yeah, listen, I didn't mean anything, she, uh," Manuel dropped her hair and moved to the side, away from her.

"You are no longer our attendant. I will request another from the concierge. Get out."

"But sir, I, I am assigned to you-"

Vijay took a step towards him. "*Pula*, I would thrill to break your arms, take you apart piece by piece. But alas, she," he nodded to Wyn, "would just bitch at me all night long about killing yet another man for her. So," his smile grim at Manuel's loss of color.

"I will not say it again you *va yebat pula,* cock-sucking fuckhead. If I see you so much as look at her, I will endure her bitching. You get me?"

Gulping hard, Manuel gurgled, "Uh," and skipped sideways past Vijay's reach and scooted out the door.

Without a word to Wyn, Vijay stalked over and snatched up the phone. He dialed one number.

"*Da*, this is Mr. Christopher Owen in suite 1600. Number one, I want the attendant, Manuel whatever-the-fuck-his-last-name-is, suspended for the time we are here. Number two, I want a new attendant, and third I want the physician to come to my room immediately."

He listened then said a cryptic, "*Mulțumesc,* ah, thank you," and hung up the phone.

He turned to face Wyn and rebuked her harshly, "You never should have answered the door, Wynna. Do not answer it again unless tis me or one of my team. I do not care if tis a maid or the fucking Queen of England."

She stood with worry etched on her face now that things had started on such a bad foot.

He moved to her, frowning at the hint of distress in her eyes.

A hoarse, "Wynna," tumbled from his lips as he dropped to his knees and wrapped his arms around her.

She rested her head on the top of his and put her hands around his neck. Vijay nuzzled his face into her chest. They stayed like that, relishing the feel of each other.

Then he leaned back and looked at her. The blue in his eyes darkened until there was very little bright color in them. He stroked a finger down her cheek.

"Baby, he is a dead man." He lightly brushed above her swollen split lips. "He kissed you, hit you, what else?"

When she went to shake her head, he tenderly held her chin. "If he raped you, Wynna, I will have him suffer the same before he dies. After I chop his balls off I will have men-"

"No, Vijay. He was a- a little rough. I got away before he did uh, too much. Gage, um," she swallowed blinking hard, her eyes watered.

"I know, *mea dragă*, he called me." His big hands went to embrace her waist. As soon as his thumbs touched her ribs, she winced and arched inward.

"What?" He lowered his hands to her hips. "Your ribs? Did he fucking break your damned bones?"

There was a knock at the door. Vijay got to his feet, bent over and put his hand behind her neck under her hair, kissed the top of her head, then went to the door.

He looked through the peephole before opening the door. "Thank you, Igor, for coming so quickly."

"Of course, of course, Vijay, now what is the prob-" The chubby white-haired man in a suit pushed his rounded glasses up his round nose when he saw Wyn.

"I see. My dear," he clucked going to her. Lightly grasping her arm, he brought her to the couch. "Lie down here, dear."

She glanced at Vijay who nodded. When she nervously sat down, the man pulled a chair over and sat down on it.

A kind smile, bright blue eyes regarded her from behind the round lenses. "I am Dr. Igor Swann. This big lug," he gestured to Vijay who grunted, "and I have known each other a long time. What is your name, honey?"

Wyn's gaze went to Vijay, when he nodded again, she said, "Wynna," and allowed the kindly doctor to put his hands on her shoulders and gently move her to lie back.

"Very nice to meet you, Miss Wynna. Now, just relax, I am going to examine you. Tell me does it hurt anywhere particularly badly?"

"You will not believe this, Igor," Vijay chuckled causing the doctor to eye him with surprise. "She threw herself in front of Gage to protect him- from a man who had a shotgun aimed at them!" He said it proudly but with a hitch in his throat at her foolhardiness.

Swann's brows arched with interest, taking in the petite young woman, "Really? A tiny thing like you protecting that giant of a gorilla?"

"Well, he was in danger because of me," Wyn said, embarrassed at the attention.

"Huh. Anyway little soldier," the doctor smiled, "tell me where it feels the worse."

Vijay came to stand beside him.

Swann looked up at him with a frown. "Vij, you may go in the other room until I'm done. How can I work with you scowling over me, watching every move I make?"

Vijay shook his head and crossed his arms. "Not on your life. Get on with it. And watch your hands."

The doctor rolled his eyes. "See? I can't work with your restrictions and glowering at my every move."

Vijay grunted but didn't move.

The doctor sighed with good will. "All right then. Where does it hurt the most?" he asked Wyn again.

She pushed her long curls off to the side and put her hand to just below her breasts.

"Might be broken or cracked ribs, Igor," Vijay offered.

One brow arched over Swann's raised eye at Vijay. "So, you're a doctor now. Please let me make the diagnosis." He turned back to Wyn.

Swann said, "Just relax, honey," and he grasped the hem of her blouse. Lifting it he set it above her pink bra exposing the swells of her breasts then set his palm on her belly.

Vijay's growl came deep in his heavy chest like the warning of a wild animal.

"That's it." Swann declared. "You go in another room or I will stop right now and you can get another doctor that you don't know at all to do this." He waited, his hand still on Wyn's stomach.

Vijay hesitated; his eyes went from Swann's hand setting over a huge bruise to the pain clenched on Wyn's face. He scowled, snapped, "Fuck, fine."

He growled a warning before he moved, "You watch your hands." He touched the top of Wyn's head briefly, then went to wait in the kitchen area which was still in sight of the couch but he couldn't see over it to observe Swann's examination.

Taking a beer out of the small fridge, Vijay leaned his hip against the counter to see what he could.

Swann chattered softly to Wyn as he examined her ribs, and the bruises and cuts on her face and wrists.

She kept her mouth compressed through most of it, keeping in the gasps of pain, but he pressed a little hard on her ribs where there was a big bruise and she cried out.

"Stay there," Swann commanded knowing Vijay was starting to come back over to them. He grinned at Vijay's curse.

A few minutes later, completing his examination, he put antibiotic and bandages on her open cuts and said, "Bring a glass of water, Vij, we're done."

A cupboard squeaked opened, the water ran and seconds later Vijay was standing beside Swann with a glass in his hands.

"Okay, here ya go honey." The doctor went to help her to sit up, her blouse still pushed up exposing her bra and a bandage that wrapped around her ribs.

"I got it," Vijay handed the glass to the doctor and knelt beside Wyn. He tugged her blouse down, put an arm around her back and cringed at the flinch of pain that tightened her mouth and the corners of her eyes.

"*Bine, mea dragă,* I have you." He turned to take the pill and the water from Swann and asked, "Well? How is she?"

Swann chuckled. "I never knew you had a child, Vij, you're acting like her father."

Handing the glass and pill to Wyn, the scowl Vijay glared at the doctor did nothing to change the teasing grin.

"She is fine, Vij. The ribs seem slightly cracked. We can order an X-ray but the treatment will be the same if they are broken. The cuts and bruises will disappear as you know in a few days." He peered one eye up at Vijay and demanded, "You want to tell me what happened? Who did this to her, and where the hell were you when someone-"

"Listen Igor-"

"Thank you, doctor," Wyn cut in with a shaky smile. "I am responsible for me." Setting the glass on the table she shifted to the edge of the couch to get up. "I appreciate your help. What do I owe you?"

The corner of Swann's mouth twitched at Vijay's irritated grunt. "Don't worry, honey, it's already taken care of. Your boyfriend and I barter services." He said to Vijay, "Call me if she has any reactions or excessive pain, or the headaches persist, or difficulties-"

"I will," Wyn cut in again with a firmer voice. "Thank you again, Doctor Swann. Let me walk you out." She struggled to her feet pushing Vijay away as he tried to help her.

She didn't see the doctor's teasing wink at him. The three of them walked to the door, Wyn bent slightly sideways with her hand on her ribcage.

"*Mulţumesc,* Igor, I will be in touch. You know I appreciate it." Vijay saw his friend out. Then he turned to Wyn catching the wince in her pressed lips.

"*Dragă,*" he murmured. Bending, he slid his hands under her and lifted her up in his arms.

"Vijay, please, I am not an invalid," she protested.

"I feel like bad enough shit I was not there to protect you, Wynna, let me take care of you now." He stalked through the living room.

She said stiffly, "Vijay, I am the one responsible for my own safety. I thought being from a good family Jazer would be a gentleman. I won't make that mistake again."

He nodded. "You are too inexperienced and sheltered to have learned that rattlesnakes come in all sizes and colors. Your aunt and uncle are fucking assholes to let him attack you like that. Why the hell would they do that to you, their own niece?"

She slipped her arm around his neck and nestled her head against his thick shoulder. "They are an old aristocratic family, as is Jazer's, but their money and stock are in separate corporations. If they merge the families they would get over 50% of the voter's block."

Her tone had a bitter edge, "I think that's why they invited me here in the first place and pushed me so hard to date him. Not knowing this, when they invited me, my father had insisted I take time off from school and get to know my relatives out here.

"My dad wasn't aware of the political tension surrounding my Uncle David. No one expected me to get on so well with him, or for him to suddenly go into hiding. Uncle David told me he would get word to me, tell me where he was."

He held her tighter, muttered, "All the wretched shit that has happened to you." Remembering Warwick and all the other torments she'd suffered, he said, "are all thanks to your relatives bringing you here. Great family you got there."

Smiling at him, Wyn kissed his jaw. "But if they hadn't, I would never have met you." She snuggled against him seeing the brief shadow of his smile.

His voice gruff with emotions he never knew he had, he said, "When your ribs are healed, I will give you self-defense lessons."

"I want a gun."

His arms tightened more as he carried her into the bedroom. "*Nu.* Women with weapons only get them taken away and then used on them."

She snorted. "What a sexist thing to say! Women are just as capable as men with guns. I will buy one."

His eyes rolled to the ceiling. "I will try to stop you, but if you do, I will teach you how to use it. We will practice shooting at the target range. Now," he strode to the big bed and set her down then stood staring at her.

"Um, Vijay, are we going to have…separate rooms?"

His face a blank, he asked, "Do you want to?"

"I- well, I saw there's a separate bedroom. I thought maybe you didn't want to- to sleep with me." Her head tilted, lips pushed out, she watched him, his expression still a total blank.

He growled, "Baby," now heat flickered in his eyes. "I do not ever want to sleep apart from you again. The other room is if *you* desire to sleep separately. I wanted you to know you have a choice."

Her gaze drifted down the front of his jeans then her cheeks brightened with color, he had a very obvious hard-on.

"Oh," she gasped. Her eyes travelled up to his face then like a magnet drew back down to the bulge in his jeans. Shyly she said, "I want to sleep with you too." Her lashes lowered on the round cheeks that grew ever redder.

She shifted back on the bed in invitation, pulling her legs up to curl beside her to make room for him.

He sat on the edge of the bed. "Not now, sweetheart, you are injured. I cannot even kiss you," he said sadly with a frown at her split swollen lips.

Wyn moved to kneel on the mattress near him and sat back on her heels. She put her hands on his chest. "We don't need to kiss," her lids lowered not quite covering the desire in her eyes. She grazed her fingertips over his nipples watching in wonderment to see if they hardened like hers do.

Vijay sat still, his eyes closed, feeling her hands on him. A shiver raced through his body when she scraped over his nipple. His thick erection throbbed with her every stroke. He peered at her from under heavy hooded lids.

"I would not feel right making love to you without kissing you, Wynna, and your beautiful lips are not your only injury. I am too big, too strong; in your condition I will only hurt you more."

He looked at her midsection then to her injured wrists. Her hands still played across his iron-hard pecs, she stroked them down and over his granite abdomen.

Watching her stroke her palms back up he saw her wince again. "*Basta.* Enough, I cannot stand to see your pain." Vijay gathered her hands gingerly and drew them off his body. He caught her stifling a yawn right through her consternation of him moving her hands.

With a gentle growl, he told her, "The pain pill has kicked in. You are going to rest now. Lie down, let me tuck you in."

Wyn struggled to push her heavy lids up, shaking her head with a sleepy frown. "No, we can still make love…"

"*Nu*. I will hurt you. *Basta*, get under the covers." He let go of her hands to put his hand on her back to help her lie down, her face crinkling with pain as he moved her. He picked up each foot and slipped off her shoes.

Disputing his refusal, "But- but," sitting back up, she covered another yawn, "I can do things to you, like you did to me." She reached over and curled her hand over his erection.

Not expecting it, Vijay jumped, coming close to losing it. "*Nu*, stop." He lifted her hand again. "I said *nu*. I will not have you further injured and that tis it. Now,"

She smiled sleepily. "You are so bossy." Yawning, she mumbled, "I want to see you naked, Vijay. Take off your clothes and lie with me."

His head shaking, if he took his pants off he would be in her in a flash. He was so on the edge he wouldn't have the willpower to stop. His heart warmed and his boner swelled at her offer to take care of him, but he wanted the whole deal with her. At least the first time, then they can do other things. His giving her pleasure at Cartiér's was different.

Maybe it was sexist of him, but he felt it was okay to pleasure a woman without doing anything else, but to sit here while she gave him a hand-job, it wouldn't be a blowjob with that injured mouth.

Shit, he shuddered picturing her small mouth on his cock looking up at him with those blue-green eyes, surrounded by a veil of blonde hair, damn, his shaft was pulsing like a fucking generator about to explode.

But just a hand-job before they had really made love, *nu*, he shook his head, he'd feel weird. They would wait until they could do it right.

He clutched her shoulders helping and forcing her to lie down. "I cannot take any more of this talk, baby, and you are almost asleep."

When her head hit the pillow she reached for his dick again. A white heat blasted up from his groin to his head, he moved out of her reach, and before her hand fell down she was asleep.

Vijay sat watching her. His heart squeezed, he was in deep. The ruthless mercenary soldier had lost the heart he never knew he had to a woman. A delicate, sweet, feisty woman. Who would have ever thought it? Certainly not him.

He brushed a wisp of hair off her face, leaned over and kissed her on the forehead then covered her and slipped from the room.

Chapter Twenty-Four

Vijay was gone a lot the next few days. He had leads to chase down on another job his team was working on. If he hadn't already agreed to do it, he would have declined and stayed with Wynna.

He had Roman sit guard outside the hotel room. He didn't trust that although he'd used aliases, that someone hadn't tracked them. He also didn't trust that fucking suite attendant Manuel. He would have broken something on him so he couldn't get to Wynna, but he couldn't do it in front of her.

He made sure he was at dinner with her every night. They ate out on the balcony with candlelight, talking about their hopes and dreams.

"What do you want, Wynna, if you could have anything?" he asked one night feeding her a piece of cake by hand so she'd lick his fingers. Damn he liked that a lot. Her eyes soft and sultry turning wicked as she sucked on his thick fingers.

"Mmmm." She swallowed and licked her lips. "I want eventually to have a home and family, children, but first, I've always wanted to live on a boat and travel the world, for, like a year. I could do my studies by computer."

Feeding him a spoonful of chocolate ice cream, she sighed. "But that certainly isn't likely to happen, is it?" She smiled languidly watching his mouth as he savored the ice cream.

"What about you, Vijay, what do you want?"

"I want you, Wynna, only you. If children come, great, if not, I would be the most happy and satisfied man in the world if I have you."

Her lips curled up tenderly, her eyes warmed. "That's so sweet, Vijay. Simple. But what about employment?" The smile turned pursed. "It, well, it sounds like what you do might not only be dangerous, but, um, unlawful?"

His big shoulders rose in a half shrug. "Tis better I do not go into great detail some aspects of what I do." He brushed an errant curl off her round cheek.

"Anyway, I am capable of doing many kinds of…work. Actually, my team and I have been discussing working with the Feds, using our skills more…uh, differently. I work because I want to, I do not need to. My family is wealthy, I am wealthy, the only thing I desire is you."

He noticed her lids flutter and knew she was tiring. "*Bine, fetita*, time for bed."

She had two days of pain pills left. She took her pills every night with dinner and they knocked her right out almost as soon as they had finished eating.

When he saw her grow sleepy, he carried her to bed and later would come in and settle next to her. She would roll over in her sleep and cuddle against him.

To survive, Vijay beat off in the shower, more than once, before coming to bed. He seldom took his eyes off her when he was at the hotel, so happy and content that she was finally with him. Due to work, he was gone every morning before the sun rose.

In the morning, Vijay had met with an informant.

The informant advised that no one knew where Wyn's uncle was hiding.

Vijay brooded on the ride back to the hotel. Until this shit with her uncle was done, she was in danger. He no longer cared about the job he was hired to do. He wanted to find her uncle to keep them both under protective custody until the elections were over.

When he pulled into the underground hotel garage, out of the corner of his eye he caught a figure standing behind a car suddenly duck down.

Parking the car, Vijay acted like he hadn't seen the person and ambled to the elevator a few yards from where he had ducked down.

The elevator door pinged open and Vijay got on. He rode it to the first floor, got off then ran down the stairwell back into the garage.

He raced to the car but the man had hopped in and almost ran Vijay over as he floored it out of the garage.

By time Vijay got to his car and went after him he would be long gone.

Hitting the stairwell, he wasn't trusting there wasn't anyone waiting on every floor to jump him or follow him. As he took the stairs two at a time, he pulled out his phone.

Alex answered on the second ring. "*Da*, Vij?"

"We have been made. Someone was here lurking in the garage. He tried to run me over when I went for him. We need to move. Call the others."

Vijay clicked his phone off and clipped it on his belt. He ran up the rest of the six flights and strode down the hall without even breathing heavy. He watched his back making sure no one followed him to the room.

Roman was sitting guard and got up when he reached him. "Hey, Vij, all quiet on the-"

"We have to move, we have been made. Get me another car."

Roman didn't even say anything, just took off to do as Vijay ordered.

Vijay opened the hotel door and was surprised to see Wyn sitting out on the balcony with a cup of tea. He paused, watching her light hair sail around her head in the dancing breeze.

She took a dainty sip then set the cup down and looked out over the town. She didn't hear him come in until the door closed behind him.

She twisted around at the sound, and grinned when she saw it was him. She jumped up and ran to him leaping into his arms. "You're back!" she shouted redundantly but happy. Her legs wound around his hips.

"Wynna," he scolded as his arm supported her luscious butt, "you are still recovering."

"Oh posh, I am perfectly fine. Look." She gave him a big smile. There was very little trace left of the cut on her lip or the one under her eye. The bruises had faded. She clasped her hands behind his head and pulled him in to kiss her.

He resisted, worried he would hurt her, but as her little lips pushed at his to open, he gave in with a longing sigh.

Their mouths making up for lost time, his head spinning with flushing desire, Vijay started carrying her to the bedroom. Then he stopped abruptly and drew his mouth from hers.

Shit- that pout and those passion filled eyes- it was all he could do not to set her down right there and take her on the carpet.

Nu, not now. "We have to change hotels, Wynna, right now."

"But-"

"Tis no longer safe here. I will get your suitcase and help you pack your stuff." He set her on her feet and left to retrieve her case.

Returning with it, he set it on the suitcase stand and popped the latches.

Wyn said, "You go take care of your own stuff, I can pack. I am not an invalid." When he hesitated she waved her hands at him, "Shoo."

They packed and were out of the hotel in twenty minutes.

Roman was around back with a different car and waited while Vijay put the cases in the trunk then helped Wyn into the backseat.

The two men sat in the front seats to discuss what their next plan was.

In the back, Wyn fumed at being treated like a child. She had no say so in any of their discussion, and it all had to do with her. But Vijay was already on edge. He shut her down every time she said anything, his face a permanent scowl. He couldn't believe they had been tracked. They needed better precautions.

"It was likely with her looks and that light saffron hair, combined with you being such a big, tattooed ox that they asked around and easily found you," Roman offered.

"*Da.* I know. We will take her in the back way next time. I need to change, cut my hair-"

"No!" Wyn gasped. Her face flushed when Roman looked at her in the rear view mirror and Vijay turned with a frown.

She said abashed, "Please don't, I like it long. It's sexy."

Vijay stared at her, took in the pink cheeks, twinkling eyes. He said nothing, just turned back around in his seat.

Then he grumbled at Roman in a low voice, "Not a word to the others, or I will fuck you up." He only left his locks long because he was lazy in getting them cut and his hair seemed to grow fast and was always in his face, so it was easier to let it stay long and tie it back.

It also made it easier for him to blend into gangs. He didn't care one way or the other if he cut it.

Roman laughed out loud at the threat. "*Da*, sure, good luck with that, pretty boy!" He moved just as Vijay's fist connected with his shoulder breaking some of the force of it.

They stopped at a chain department store. Roman went inside.

"Why are we here?" Wyn asked, looking around at the shopping plaza.

His eyes never stopping surveillance of their surroundings Vijay muttered, "We need to disguise ourselves a little. Apparently we are too noticeable. Beauty and the beast you know."

Vijay!" She scolded him, "Don't you dare talk like that! You know how handsome you are."

He just grunted, his eyes shifting everywhere searching for someone watching them.

"I will show you later how attractive I find you, in any way you want," her impish voice was filled with sultry promise.

From the back seat she watched the red creep up his neck to the tips of his ears. She smothered her giggle at his obvious physical reaction to her sexual offer. Leaning forward, she drew her fingers through his length of hair.

"Uh, oh *yah*?" His ears turned darker. "I wĬll hold you to that, *mea dragă.*" He allowed himself a short smile, his attention never leaving the area.

Roman returned with a bag and three coffees. He drove them to a deserted area and Vijay opened the bag. "Here, put his on," he said to Wyn handing her a wig and glasses, and a cup of coffee.

She obliged, pulling on the wig that was straight black hair past her shoulders with sleek black bangs. She slipped on the glasses.

He said over his shoulder as he put on his own wig of short brown hair, "You need to wear your highest heels when you are outside, Wynna, so we will not stand out so much me towering over your dainty little body."

"Hmm. Okay. What about in the bedroom? I can wear them there too if necessary…you know, so we're closer in height…"

Roman spat out his coffee while Vijay choked on his own tongue. Both picturing her naked except for a pair of stilettos, neither man said anything, but Vijay elbowed Roman hard in the side.

Roman's 'oomph' from the hit ended in a snicker.

Wyn sat back quietly with a smug smile on her face and watched out the window as Roman put the car in gear and they took off.

Chapter Twenty-Five

$\mathcal{R}$oman pulled into the parking garage of the new hotel and parked.

As Vijay exited the car muttering under his breath, "I am going to fucking hold her to that," he cringed at Roman's bark of laughter behind him. He hadn't realized he'd said it so loud.

He stepped back to open Wyn's door and help her out. His eyes popped, mouth dropped open.

Beside him, Roman croaked, "*Holy shit*," and got another elbow to the side.

Wyn slid her legs out taking Vijay's hand as he helped her. She had put makeup on while in the back, discreetly changed her clothes, and put on the heels.

As she stepped out, both men gaped at her. She peered up through the long, sleek black bangs. Her lips were deep red and she'd used liner to make her eyes less child-like round to a sultrier cat's eye.

The blouse she'd changed into without either man noticing, was so low cut she looked in danger of tumbling right out of it. She'd changed her jeans into a tiny flirty skirt.

"*Shit,*" Roman gurgled again, stepping away from Vijay's fist. He crowed, "Wyn baby," you changed from sweet honey-sexy to vavoom dangerous sexy. You look like a villainous secret agent spy from like James Bond or something. You're a gorgeous woman already, now you look like your own evil twin. Hot and fucking danger- *ow*-" his breath crunched out from the hit in the gut.

Vijay punched him without taking his eyes off Wynna.

"Baby, you look," his gaze swept her head to sexy toe, "different. I like you better as yourself, but the disguise is kind of cool. Except Roman went way overboard with the clothes. We are trying to attract less attention."

He nodded to the low cleavage and short skirt. "Dressed like that, I will still have to fight the guys off you," his voice cracked as she slid the glasses on.

"Whoa," Roman took a long side-step from Vijay's reach. "It gets better. Now the sexy, librarian-secret-agent. Every guy dreams of fucking a hot yet demure, prissy librarian," he slid further away from Vijay's reach.

"*Bine, basta*," Vijay snarled at Roman's blatant ogling. "Enough, go meet the guys, I will talk to them by cell later."

When Roman's eyes stayed glued to Wyn, Vijay barked, "*Now!*"

Roman laughed at him. "*Da*, sure thing, Vij, but it's like having to get used to her all over again. We all worked hard to not check her out all the time to appease your newfound possessiveness- remarkable in itself, none of us knew ya had it in you for a *femelă*." He ducked Vijay's swing with a laugh.

"Now we have to start over. *Bine*, I'm going," he laughed as Vijay took a step towards him. He tossed him two room cards.

"Room 808." He grinned at Wyn. "Bye sweetness, or should I say bye Miss Sinful, see ya later," he grinned at Wyn then slid back into the car.

His head out the window, Roman said, "We'll pick up another couple of clean cars in case the last one had bugs. I'll be thinking of you in those…heels…Wyn girl, later kids." He roared with hilarity at Vijay's threatening scowl as he drove out of the garage.

Vijay picked up their suitcases and they walked to the elevator.

Wyn tripped slightly. Vijay moved close to her, "Hey, be careful, I got my hands full, honey, I cannot catch you."

She giggled. "I don't wear these very often, I'm not used to such high heels." Every time she stumbled slightly, her breasts jiggled over the cleavage and the skirt flipped and fluttered around her thighs showing peeks of her panties.

Wyn giggled harder as Vijay's face turned redder.

It felt like he was watching an accidental burlesque show. Unable to take his eyes off her, he taunted, "Oh *yah*, *fetita*, you laughing at me?"

He said with a smiling threat, "Paybacks are a bitch. We will see how you like your punishment when we are enjoying dinner out of the hotel room for a change." He smirked when she cocked a confused look at him.

"Oo," she grinned wickedly, "another punishment? I can't wait!" Giggling at him, she said, "Going out to dinner doesn't sound like punishment."

Her ankles wobbled, she stretched her hands out to keep her balance while bending over slightly picking her way carefully over the stoned walkway.

"Except for a brief glimpse that night in the woods, I have not seen those tits totally unfettered yet sweetheart, and I am looking forward to dessert." Carrying their bags he stuck out an elbow and told her, "Hold onto my arm."

Little giggles spurting from Wyn, she clutched his arm. Asking with interest, "What exactly do you mean by punishment this time?"

His heated gaze glued to her breasts looking like they were trying to jump out of the top of her blouse, he muttered, "You will see baby, you will see." He hurried them up to their room.

Once inside, he set the cases on the stands.

"Go ahead and unpack, I have to make a couple of phone calls and then we can go to dinner." His eyes went to the scarlet lips. It was clear that he wanted very badly to kiss her but he would be covered in red and she would have to redo her makeup taking up more time.

So ingénue, she was unaware how enticingly she peered up at him from under the long sleek bangs.

"Do not change, sweetheart," he ordered with a smack on her butt.

"Hey!" she yelped at the hit. Her eyes narrowed under the black fringe. "You like spanking me. I can see your eyes brighten then get darker and your lids lower. But I'm wondering," she stood with a finger to her chin and slid her gaze towards his own chiseled behind in his snug jeans. "If you like to be the reciprocator as well."

His neck flushed, obviously not finding the suggestion appealing. He started to scowl, then he smirked again. "*Da*, sure, baby, if you can hold me down you can spank me, or punish me." He grinned in satisfaction at her frown. Then he saw her lips roll up in a sneaky smile.

Now he frowned. "What? What are you thinking?"

She shrugged innocently. "Oh nothing, it's just," she casually studied her nails. "A person has to sleep sometime, and we have plenty of rope." Her mouth broadened in a mischievous smile as his eyes widened then narrowed.

"But then again, maybe I have other ways of restraining you and paying you back." She turned and sashayed towards the bathroom.

Vijay swallowed down his suddenly dry throat. Then he called out, "Sure baby, works both ways."

First he pictured her lying on her back naked, legs spread wide with those heels on, wrists bound above her head.

Then he remembered they were talking about spanking. In his mind, he flipped her over on her belly, her arms and legs still tied but her little round behind was propped up waiting for his mouth and his palms.

"*Shit,*" he cursed as a shiver struck his body and he hardened more than was comfortable in his pants. Rubbing his hands together that itched to fondle the little beauty, he went to see if there was a beer in the fridge to suck down while he made his calls.

They each did their own thing for thirty minutes or so. Vijay changed into an Oxford styled shirt, and black slacks that hung low on his lean hips, and black dress boots.

He came out of the second bedroom hooking his phone back on his belt. Wyn was out on the balcony.

Stepping onto the balcony, he stood behind her and wrapped his arms around her, hugging her to his chest. "I do not want us to ever be apart again," his voice came out a throaty rumble.

He pulled her in tight so the ridge of his erection was pressed against her bottom and his nose tucked in her hair. He thought he had everything under control until she wriggled against him.

Coughing to clear his suddenly thick throat, his voice a deepening husk, he asked, "Uh, you ready for dinner, honey?"

"I'm ready," she purred. "Are you?"

"*Mea Zue*, Wynna, I have created a monster. One tiny bit of playtime at Cartiér's and you have become a bewitching siren."

Wyn wriggled her bottom again, enticingly rubbing his shaft that was already hard as a club indicating he was definitely ready.

She said, "Oh? I've become a siren, huh? It's your fault. You're the one that stoked my dormant virginal fires. But if you want me to be demur, I can go back to being a chaste, do not touch me girl."

"Ah, no way, baby. I hope you have become an insatiable vixen, because as soon as we are able to start, I sure as hell plan on going all night long." He hugged her tight, pulling her hips into the curve of his so his shaft was pressed so tight she could feel the hardness of it as it continued to swell into her soft body.

Against her ear, he said regretfully, "I made reservations." Sounding like the last thing he wanted to do was leave the room, he said, "We need to go. I would say let's skip dinner but we have not eaten all day and there is no food here, and they tell me there is a problem in the kitchen tonight so we cannot order in."

Wyn arched her back against his chest and lifted her hands up and behind to stroke his face. "I can feel you a lot more through those pants, they're lighter than your jeans. What about ordering a pizza delivered?" she suggested hopefully. Shifting her butt harder against him, she rubbed her bottom against the fabric of his pants.

"*Bine,* my little tease, they do not have a lot of that in this area of town."

Her hands were strung around the back of his neck, her head tilted back, she kissed under his jaw causing her spine to arch against him. In the stilettoes she was taller than normal.

He took the opportunity to stroke his big hands up her belly and over her breasts. Cupping them, he kneaded her full softness, dropped his head and nuzzled his face in her neck with a smoldering growl.

"Like I said, once we start, baby, we are not stopping, not all night." He had the height advantage so he could peer down her cleavage.

Gripping her breasts, he tucked his fingers in the bodice and started to pull the blouse down with one hand while he bent and slid his other hand on her bare thigh and up her skirt- when she suddenly moved out of his arms.

"You do that and we won't leave," she scolded. Fixing her blouse and straightening her skirt, she left the balcony and headed to the door, she said merrily, "Let's go. The sooner we leave the sooner we get back."

"Do not forget your glasses," he reminded Wyn, following slightly dazed behind her, grabbing his wallet off the table as he neared the exit.

Catching up to her when she reached the door, he slipped his arm around her stroking his hand up her side to grasp her breast again.

Squawking, "Vijay!" she twisted from his hold. "Behave! We are about to be in public."

He said with a squeeze of her plump globe, "*Fetita*, you know I cannot keep my hands off you."

As she opened the door, Vijay slid his hand down to grab her tush and said, "Hey, Wynna wait, leave your panties here, and the bra too. You are with me so tis okay."

Shaking her head at him, she chided, "You are naughty. I most certainly will not go out in public without my underwear on. Men!" Sliding the glasses on, she swished out the door.

Muttering, *"Da,* we are a wicked bunch," leering at her ass, as the door closed behind them, he swatted the firm round sashaying butt.

Her squeal echoed down the hall. He grinned while she chastised him as they walked to the elevator. He had hoped they would be the only ones on it so he could feel her up some more, but there were several other people already there.

He pulled her to the rear and wrangled her so her butt was pressed against his still rock-hard erection. She tried to pull away and whispered for him to release her, but he just held her and leered down her blouse.

When she caught him doing that she sighed and leaned her head against his shoulder letting him look all he wanted.

Vijay didn't move when the door slid open with a ding. He was content where he was with her cuddled in his arms and was enjoying the view.

She shrugged at his arms, saying, "Vijay." When he ignored her prodding, pushing at him, she said louder, "Vijay, we need to get off."

Lifting the black hair, he kissed her neck. "We will get off baby, later." He laughed when after a second she got his innuendo and blushed.

Taking her hand, he led her out of the elevator with the other people who were shooting glares at them. The rest of the occupants were going down to the parking garage.

The men gave Vijay a knowing man's smirk, the women shook their heads at the young couple's less than virtuous behavior on the ride down.

The pair paid no attention to them, they saw no one but each other. Holding hands they strolled down the city street for several blocks.

Vijay smiled at Wyn's oo's and ah's at the ancient coastal town she was seeing for the first time.

Vijay

Vijay brought her to a restaurant that catered to the balmy outdoors. He'd been in town a couple of weeks and had taken the time to scope out where he'd like to take her to when she arrived in Monaco.

He had planned on bringing her out to Monaco just not quite so soon. He wanted his business to be completed so she wasn't dropped into the middle of it. But, after that asshole's assault, Vijay had no choice but to get her the hell out of that house.

The restaurant was perfect. Outdoorsy and romantic, it was designed more like a tropical island than the rocky coast.

The roof was open letting in the fresh evening breeze. Tables scattered throughout the middle, and thickly cushioned booths lined a low wall. The dining area was like a partially enclosed, leafy patio.

Slender palm trees and huge blossoms of vivid flowers filled the entire area making it seem like they were on a paradise island.

A girl dressed in a flowery sarong and a gardenia in her hair led them to their reserved booth.

Vijay had Wyn slide in and he sat next to her.

When their server approached with menus, Vijay ordered a bottle of wine. He held Wyn's hand again setting it on the table and turned to face her. Silently he studied her face for a minute then his mouth curved in a crooked smile.

"What?" she asked, studying him just as intently.

"It does not matter what you do to change your looks, Wynna, you are the most beautiful creature I have ever seen."

"Creature? I'm an animal now instead of the little *fetita* girl you call me?" She teased squeezing his hand.

His smile broadened. "*Nu*, I am the beast, you are the mythical mystical siren." He lifted her hand to kiss it.

"Vijay, stop that." Her lips firmed. "You are not a beast. I only called you that because I was so terrified of you, and you were mean and cold to me. You are beautiful too."

He barked a laugh. "Men are not beautiful, Wynna." His expression turned serious. "I was mean and cold to you, Wynna, because I had to protect you, and at the same time keep myself

251

from throwing you down and taking you. Are you still frightened of me, *mea dragă?*" He kissed each knuckle one by one, looking deep into her eyes, marveling at the streams of blues and greens that rippled in them behind the plain-lensed glasses.

Her mouth tipped up happy, then a little serious. "I trust you with my life."

The backs of his eyes stung, his head lowered until his forehead was on the hand he held. Getting a grip on his unfamiliar, new emotions, he raised his head connecting their gazes. He said with a quiet promise, "I would give my life for you, *mea dragă.*"

He reached in and pulled a small long box from his shirt pocket. "Here, this is for you," he held it out to her.

She just looked at it without moving. Her eyes went from the box to him to the box. "What is it?"

His smile tender, he opened it and took out a bracelet. The string of colorful gems sparkled in the candlelight. Setting the box on the table, he said, "Hold out your wrist."

She still didn't move. "I don't understand."

Chuckling, he took her hand. Holding it up, he clasped the bracelet around her wrist.

"There is nothing to understand, *mea dragă.* I wanted to give you something that you can look at every day and see that I love you. Until I can get you a ring. There is not a suitable shop in this tiny village, we are on the lesser shopping side of Monaco. So the ring will have to wait."

He watched her hold her wrist out and move her arm to look at the slim, iridescent glittering bracelet.

"I…it's beautiful, Vijay, I don't know what to say," she kept admiring it.

"Say thank you my wonderful Vijay," he smiled.

"Thank you, my wonderful Vi-" her mouth still open, he closed his over it, holding her hostage in a lingering adoring kiss.

The server brought the wine. Opening the bottle, he poured a bit for Vijay to taste.

Never taking his eyes from Wyn's, Vijay nodded and pronounced, "Perfect."

"Yes sir, it is an excellent vintage," the server agreed in heavily accented English. He poured their glasses then set the bottle in the bucket and covered it with a cloth napkin.

The corner of Vijay's mouth lifted, his eyes on hers, "*Da*, the wine is perfect too."

Wyn giggled. "That is so cliché, Vijay. But thank you." She slanted face up, he took that as an offer to kiss. They did. Deeply.

Until the server cleared his throat.

Reluctantly Vijay moved his head back. Keeping his hand behind her neck, he tore his eyes away from hers and tried not to glare at the server.

"Uh," the man's voice had a slight shake at the pique on Vijay's dangerous face. "Are, uh, you ready to order?" Holding his pen and pad, he clasped his hands behind his back.

Nodding sharply, "*Da*," Vijay ordered for them both. Lobster pasta for her and a blood-red steak for him.

Trying not to wipe his sweating brow, the server gratefully took their order and quickly left them. Even with his short wig of hair, Vijay still looked like he should be on a motorcycle raiding and terrorizing towns, or cutting a swath through a jungle with a machete and an AK 47 strapped across his back.

Vijay cut a piece of juicy steak and fed it to her, she fed him a chunk of buttery lobster.

Watching her chew so gracefully, Vijay asked, "What were you studying at the college?"

"Advertising marketing."

His dark brows low crescents over the brilliant eyes, he regarded at her with interest. "Really? That sounds quite interesting." He buttered a warm roll and bit half of it. "Tell me about it. What do you like to do?"

Wyn laughed at him. "You take such big bites." She bit the end of an asparagus spear.

The roll rounding inside his cheek, chewing heartily, he said, "I keep telling you, sweetheart, I am a big guy, I do things in a big way. I cannot nibble daintily at a big hunk of steak like you with your pretty teeth."

Watching her eat, Vijay thought about her little pink tongue and what he'd like to teach her to do with it. He ran his right hand down her arm and under the table to her thigh.

Chapter Twenty-Six

When he moved his hand up her leg, her lips paused in mid-chew. "Um, Vijay…"

He stabbed a chunk of baked potato smothered with butter and sour cream and sprinkled with green chives and shoveled it in his mouth. After a few chews, he murmured nonchalantly, "Hmmm? You were telling me about marketing advertising."

Her eyes shifted to him and down to his hand that disappeared under the table and onto her leg. "Uh, okay. I like to do jingles, and coming up with ideas for ads then talking people into wanting them, you know, making a pitch."

"I do not see you having a problem selling anything to anybody. Tell me what your actually studies are like. Describe what you do."

"I," her cheeks brightened as he squeezed her thigh then moved his hand up. "Listen, we're in public, stop- oh!"

His hand continued up between her legs until the side of it was pressed against her panties. She squeezed her thighs together to keep him from touching her so intimately in public!

"Vijay," she whispered, her skin colored in embarrassment.

"*Da*?" he said innocently, and moved his hand pushing her thighs apart then wiggled his fingers against her panties.

Her head lowered, she whispered louder, "Stop, what are you doing?" She reached down to push his hand away but he was too strong and she worried about drawing attention to them.

Now caressing her lady parts over the panties with his fingertips, he grinned and kept eating. "I told you paybacks were a bitch, honey. Open your legs for me, Wynna, sit back and enjoy it. Talk to me, I want to hear about what you want to do in advertising marketing. I do not know anything about it. Tell me why you want to do it. *Zue*, I love being ambidextrous."

"No!" she gasped as he maneuvered his fingers to the side of her panties to touch her bare skin. Her ass wriggled on the seat trying to move away, but he had her boxed in against the corner of the booth and the wall, there was no stopping him.

Without moving his hand, he poured them both more wine. "Come on, *mea dragă*, drink, it will loosen you up." Setting the bottle in the bucket, he lifted his glass, tipped it in a salute to her with an evil grin. The grin grew bigger seeing her flushed face.

She looked angry, he took a sip, but he could see the desire darkening her gorgeous orbs. Under the table, he stroked her nether lips. The frissons of her natural silk inside her body wet his hand. Her temples dampened, she was definitely feeling the heat he was building between her legs.

"Everyone tries to get me drunk to- to-"

"To what, *dragă?*" One fingertip slipped between her lower lips to press her bud.

Groaning, "Uhh," her eyes closed, her bottom squirming on the seat pushed her sex against his hand, "acquiesce," she uttered almost incoherently.

His lips near her ear, he whispered, "You never have to do anything you do not want to with me, baby." His finger slicked across her clit. "Maybe I should stop," he nibbled on her lobe.

"Hmm?" Wyn mumbled absently. She stopped pretending to eat. Her lashes sweeping her cheeks, she struggled to not move her hips to force him to rub her harder.

Her lips parted, her tongue slicked around them, then they closed and she swallowed. Taking a heavy breath, she parted them again and her tongue did another circle.

His eyes on her tongue, Vijay put his wine glass to his mouth. Setting his teeth on the rim, he peered at her from under low lids.

His finger moved in a circle around her tender core as he watched her tongue circle her lips.

He was teasing her, but he was turning himself on like crazy too. His pants were so uncomfortably tight, he had to discreetly adjust them as he swelled.

But it was so worth it. He had planned earlier to do this to her when he'd seen her in that cleavage baring blouse and tiny skirt. The skirt made her accessibility too much to resist.

He'd told her paybacks would be a bitch, but he was also concerned at her relatively virginal state and wanted to make sure she was a hundred percent ready for him.

Keeping her turned on until they were back at the hotel would have her so primed, he hoped she would be ready for him to jump her bones the second they entered their suite. Because *Zue*, God knows, he felt he'd been waiting a lifetime for her.

Feeling his hand getting wetter, he slowly inserted a finger inside her, smiling at her choked gasp. She was mortified, but she was turned on too, her thighs opened wider.

The wetter his hand became, the further inside he pushed his finger. A groan escaped him at the silky feel of her. His dick was so hard he didn't know how he was going to walk out of the restaurant.

Bending his head, he lightly sucked at those pouty lips and tangled with her tongue but she was so dazed with heady sensation she was hardly responding. Just left her lips parted while he licked and nibbled on each one, occasionally diving in to suck on her tongue.

He wondered if he should bring her to orgasm in the restaurant. It would be something that would fuel his dreams forever. He'd have to cover her mouth with his to smother any scream-

"Would you care for coffee or perhaps some dessert?" The server's voice startled both of them out of their cozy, steamy little world.

Vijay awkwardly removed his hand before the waiter could see what he was doing. He wanted to tease, not embarrass, Wynna.

He looked at her. Her eyes fluttered to his mouth then up to his heated gaze. She chewed her bottom lip. Her cheeks glowed with color and heat.

"Uh, *da*, I mean, yes, bring us an aperitif." They didn't need coffee to keep their bodies hot. He needed time to cool down or he'd embarrass himself more than her when he walked out with iron wood.

"You want dessert, baby?" He slipped his arm around her shoulders.

She shook her head and laid her hand on his thigh. "No, thank you." As the waiter and Vijay discussed what drink to order, she tip-toed her fingertips up his thigh to settle on his erection.

Her smile innocent and sweet, she felt him twitch and his voice rose. His hand tightened so hard on the wine glass she feared he would snap the stem. His arm around her shoulder became almost painfully tight.

She reached low and dragged her fingers up his throbbing testicles, Vijay thought he would skyrocket through the roof. He covered a coarse exhale with a quick sip of wine as she started at the head of his cock and drew her fingers slowly all the way down his shaft. Vijay couldn't stop his head from dropping back.

"Sir?" the waiter inquired.

"Uhh, *da*," Vijay muttered. Blinking hard, he gulped, straightened his head. "I was uh, trying to remember some, uh, liquor I had a long time ago…never mind," he couldn't look the waiter in the eye.

He now could tell what it felt like to be tied up and not be able to use his hands to stop from being molested. The corner of his mouth hitched up. The little minx had managed to do it and without using shackles. Talk about paybacks! *Mea Zue*, she was always surprising him. Life was going to be a joy with her.

They decided on an after dinner drink.

"Thank you, sir."

As the waiter wrote down the order, Wyn squeezed and rubbed his aching phallus, giggling silently at Vijay's strained face. Every time the waiter started to leave, Wyn asked him a question about different liquors, and fondled Vijay more fervently.

Beside her, she could feel Vijay holding his breath as he grew ever larger and harder under her hand.

When the waiter finally left she quickly took her hand away and folded her fingers together resting her hands primly on the table.

Vijay expelled a long breath.

He brushed her hair away from her ear and leaned towards her. Drawing his tongue down the rim of her ear he nipped her lobe. Feeling her shiver, he licked behind ear and whispered, "You are going to pay for that, *mea* sweet."

Another half fearful, half-delicious shiver, Wyn's head sloped back, her eyes closed.

His eyes were on her slim neck enticing him to suck and leave his mark on her right then and there. *Fuck*- he would never make it back to the hotel before he jumped her.

The waiter returned fairly quickly. He was jumpy, the big guy with the menacing face appeared upset, or angry, or who the hell knows, his face was red, his lips compressed, and he kept whispering in his woman's ear.

The server hoped it wasn't threats. He slipped a surreptitious glance at the woman. *Oh, duh, now he got it.* He felt his own cheeks flood with color at the blue-green eyes that were glazed with passion.

Coughing to clear his suddenly dry throat, he mumbled, "Uh, I'll be back with your check, sir," he slapped their drinks down and took off.

"Sip your drink slowly, baby, you have had wine and tis a strong drink." Vijay cuddled Wyn against him and picked up his own glass. They had consumed less than half the bottle of wine, Vijay didn't want them to over imbibe and ruin the evening.

They chatted quietly. Unused to the stronger liquor, Wyn only drank a portion of her drink.

The server brought the check. He rushed out an awkward, "Thank you, have a nice evening, uh, hope to see you again," and fled.

Vijay set cash on it. "You ready baby?"

She nodded. He slid out of the booth and waited for her.

He suggested, "How about we stroll along the coast on the way back, work off our dinner, get some fresh air."

Taking the long way back, they sauntered along the waterfront hand-in-hand. Enjoying the night lights rippling colors across the water Vijay paused every so often to kiss her.

He appeared relaxed and fully wrapped up in her, but a part of his brain scanned constantly for anyone watching them. They'd had so little romantic time together he wanted to stretch it out.

He probably shouldn't have brought her out in public, but she was in a disguise with the sleek black hair and librarian glasses. A soft grin curved his mouth; she was so hot she'd melt the books.

Back at the hotel, Vijay entered through a side door. If anyone was watching for them they couldn't hide in the open hallway and he could see anyone present or coming towards them. He brought Wyn to the staff elevator.

Other than a maid on the elevator, they encountered no one else as they traipsed down the hall to their room.

Vijay keyed the door and opened it. "I will go in first, you stay right here by the door." He didn't ask her, he told her.

Pulling out his gun, he saw her eyes widen fearfully. He cursed himself and moved the gun out of her sight until he checked out the living room and the kitchen then went down the hall to the bedrooms and bath.

When he returned tucking the gun in the back of his pants, he saw her standing tensely in the middle of the living room.

"Goddammit Wynna, I told you to stay at the fucking door," he cursed a blue streak in Romanian.

"Don't you yell at me or talk to me that way." Wyn plopped her small hands on her hips and turned her defiant chin up at him.

A grin tugged at his mouth. Damn she was even hotter angry. He didn't tell her that, she would likely take offense to it. It was so cute the way she was all petite and feminine facing off to him several times bigger and stronger than her. She'd call him sexist again.

Trying to keep the stern look on his face and in his voice, he said, "Wynna, tis not right of you to put yourself in danger and make it impossible for me to protect you if someone was here waiting. You could be grabbed and used as a threat to get control of me. I need you to follow my orders when it comes to your safety."

She crossed her arms and tapped her foot, hummed, "Hmmm." Tipping her head, she regarded him coolly, or at least she tried to gaze coolly at him when in fact her body pricked with pins and needles craving to touch him, and be touched by those strong hands.

"All right," she conceded, "in the realm of our safety I will follow your orders. But you better not try to boss me around otherwise."

"Oh *yah*?" He started walking towards her, his face hard, eyes blue ice.

She dropped her arms and started to back away from him. "Vijay-"

He kept coming at her with a menacing swagger. Eyes glittering from under the primitive hard ridge of his brow, he looked every bit as dangerous as his reputation.

She kept moving until her back hit the wall. Unsure of his intent, seeking an escape, she looked from him to the door, to the hallway.

But he reached her in a few long strides and put his hands beside her shoulders with his palms flat on the wall fencing her in.

"Vijay...you're...scaring me." She braced her hands on the wall next to her hips as if to prepare to push off quickly and run.

Fear, and burgeoning desire conflicted through the haze in her colorful eyes peeping up at him through blonde lashes so long they flittered against the glasses.

Chapter Twenty-Seven

"Am I?" Bending his elbows, he leaned into her. His chest brushing over hers, he looked down and smirked with cocksure smugness at her nipples pebbling through the blouse.

She followed his simmering gaze. Seeing what he was pointedly staring at she blushed. Her palms flattened against the wall, she held her breath. "Maybe…maybe you should back up a little…"

He murmured, "Why?" and took off her glasses. Tossing them aside, he removed her wig next letting it drop to the floor then bent his head near to her.

"Because," her breathy whisper blew softly against his mouth as it continued to descend towards her.

"Because what?" His lips were almost but not quite on hers.

"Huh?" She raised her head, bringing their mouths closer together.

"Mmmm," a soft growl as his tongue came out and just barely licked her top lip urging her to part them. "I do not remember," he murmured.

"Remember what?" Her mouth opened to his and he came hard at her. Vijay slanted his head, fastening their mouths then thrust his tongue inside like a marauder pillaging a village.

And like the village, she surrendered. Melting, her groan was a rough breath flowing over coarse sand in her taut throat.

The sound inflamed Vijay. He moved his hands behind her, lifted her skirt and shoved his hands down inside her panties to grip her ass.

His hands splayed over the small but plump globes, squeezing them. Shifting his fingers to just inside the separation of her cheeks he squeezed harder, forcing her body to press hard against his erection. Her palms moved up to his chest, she scrunched his shirt in her fists, their mouths ground together.

His kisses hungrier and more demanding, he pulled his hands from her panties and reached between them and unbuttoned her blouse. Spreading the sides apart, he grasped her breasts and moaned against her mouth, "*Mea dragă,* I want you so badly I cannot fucking stand it."

Wyn put her hands on his washboard stomach and felt the ridged contours. She skimmed her palms, flexing her fingers all over them. His responding hard-on pushed against her belly.

Vijay lowered a hand, stroking down her curves to her thigh then he pushed her skirt up and cupped her mound. *Damn, if he could only keep her in a skirt all the time, he could do this whenever he wanted.*

He felt her slightly nervously try to move from his hand, but she was backed up against the wall, she wasn't going anywhere.

"You are hot and wet already, baby, I can feel you right through your panties. We are not in public anymore, now I can take them off."

She gasped as he grabbed her panties and impatiently ripped them off her and threw them to the floor. "I will buy you more," he murmured with his mouth pressing hers.

In her surprise and shock at his barbaric tearing off her clothes, Wyn's mouth clamped closed.

Licking her lips, he whispered against them, "Kiss me, baby," and her lips instinctively parted.

Their mouths bonded in a torrid kiss, his hand palming her sex, he stroked her until she pulled her head from his to take a shuddering breath. His lips went to her neck and sealed on her flesh sucking and licking her skin like she was a melting creamsicle. Her hips started rocking with the movements of his hand.

He pushed at her thighs demanding, "Open baby, open for me." She slightly parted her thighs and he ran his finger up her slit and thought he'd buckle at the enchanting sound she made.

Nudging her thighs further apart, he slid his finger just inside her and almost burst at the thrumming shiver, the baying groan deep in her chest.

His hand was instantly wet. He dropped to his knees and shoved her skirt up. She started to protest, then he pressed his mouth against her core and she cried out with another body-shaking shiver instead.

Pushing her legs even wider, he licked her slit and tongued her bud while moving his finger deeper inside her.

"Oh, God, Vijay, *please*," a low keen sifted up her throat.

Opening his mouth wide, biting lightly all over her entire sex, he said, "Please what, Wynna?" He chuckled at her inaudible response.

He put his hand on the back of her hip to hold her stable. Licking her and sucking on her clit, he moved his finger feeling her sweet softness inside, then he carefully wedged a second finger inside her.

A rumble from her and a stiffness in her hips made him slow his fingers down until she expanded to take him. Again, he felt that concern at the size of him and the size of her.

Nevertheless, he kept kissing and sucking and licking, biting her hard nub, and moving his fingers faster as her hips started moving rhythmically at his hands. Until he heard her breathing so fast she was almost squeaking with every inhale, her legs started shaking.

On his knees, "Go baby, let go, I have you," he encouraged, stroking and licking circles on her tender flesh. He kept his fingers thrashing in and out until her body went rigid, her breathing stopped- then, bending forward, she cried out, "*Vijay!*"

Continuing maneuvering his fingers pulsating on and inside Wyn, he moved his other hand to brace her on her ribs, letting her fall over to his shoulders.

Her vagina clenched his fingers with jagged contractions, her chest heaved like a roller coaster until she dropped limp with a harsh cry over his shoulders.

When the spasms lessened to tremors, Vijay pulled his fingers out and held her while she collapsed on him. He stood up, lifting her in his arms and looked down at her.

"*Mea Zue*, you are so fucking incredible my precious Wynna. You were made for loving. I do not know why I was blessed with you, but I am eternally grateful." He kissed her while carrying her down the hall to the bedroom.

Setting her on her feet, their lips meshed and he pushed the blouse off her shoulders.

The lights from the harbor streaming through the open window were sufficient to add gold and creamy illumination in the semi-dark room.

Devouring each other with their ravenous mouths, he let the blouse fall to floor and reached behind her to unclasp her bra. Pulling it from her arms, it joined the blouse. Then he stood back and beheld her wearing just the little skirt and heels.

"*Mea Zue, dragul meu eşti minunat.*" His chest constricted with desire so sharp it hurt. "Ah, riveting, *mea dragă,* you are riveting." Never looking away from her, he removed the gun from the back of his pants and set it on the nightstand. Then set another one and several knives beside it.

Moving back to her, he raised his hands and enveloped her breasts with them, wrapping his long hard fingers over each chubby globe.

Holding them, Vijay felt their weight, their feminine softness, enjoying the exquisite differences between their bodies. She felt so damned good.

As his body became more and more aroused, he ground her plush flesh with his hard fingers, feeling the full globes yield in his rough hands. He had to force himself to lighten his grip before he hurt her with his lusting strength.

But she didn't seem to mind. Wyn's glazed eyes focused on his big hands caressing her.

He rubbed his thumbs over her nipples and felt a shocking buzz in his groin watching her watching his strong hands sensually massaging her plump breasts. He thrilled at the raw thrum he could hear steeping in her chest and spreading as goose bumps popped on her skin.

"Like they say, baby, juicy ripe fruit blooming firm on a tree just waiting for me to pluck and taste and devour." With that, he lowered his head and sucked the very centers of her suppleness, drawing an areole into his mouth.

Cupping her breasts, Vijay could feel her pliant pillows swelling in his hands and mouth. He licked at each of her nipples, caught them with his teeth and sucked until they puckered with her roiling moans.

She pushed his wig off then dragged her hands through his hair. Twisting her fingers in his long locks she pulled, hard, while urgently pushing her breasts into his palms, his mouth.

Wyn wrenched so hard at his hair, she pulled his head back, but he didn't let her nipple out of his mouth. But it did amp up the volts, raising his excitement to bursting level. His laugh a sensuous growl, her aggressiveness made him burn white hot with need for her.

Vijay dropped his hands to reach behind her and struggled with the clasp on her skirt.

Tugging her fingers from his hair, Wyn moved them to the buttons on his shirt. Letting her nipple slide out of his mouth, he paused his efforts to undo her skirt to watch her slender fingers fumble his buttons open.

Since his every waking moment was picturing him stripping her clothes off her, this was a picture he'd slept with many nights, watching her undressing him.

All the buttons undone, she shyly reached up to push the shirt off his shoulders. The tips of her nipples brushed against the hair on his chest while she struggled to get his shirt off, but due to his height and the breadth of his shoulders she could only get it partially off his shoulders.

His arms slightly trapped by the shirt, his voice low and seductive, he murmured, "Touch me baby, touch me with just those prima tits."

He stood still with his arms behind his back, huge biceps bulging, while Wyn arched her back and achingly slowly, started with her nipples pushing through the hair until they reached his skin, then she pressed her breasts slowly until they were wedged against the granite wall of his chest.

"Ah, Wynna, fuck," he groaned, his head dropped back. "That tis it, honey, now rub 'em all over, press them hard, let me feel them."

He kept his hands back. She put hers on his hips to balance and did as he said until he couldn't take any more. He shrugged out of his shirt and tugged at his belt releasing the buckle.

"You have such huge arms, Vijay, with tons of big muscles." She wove her hands over his biceps tracing a dragon tattoo. "I like this one going up your neck, tell me what it means. It freaked Aunt Odessa out. She swore that with your heavy accent, scars and tattoos you were with the Russian mob or something equally as horrifying."

Remembering her aunt's intense fear of Vijay, Wyn giggled and wound her hands around his neck keeping their naked torsos pressed together.

"Later," he muttered, reaching behind her again to fumble with her skirt. Frustrated, he gripped the sides and went to tear it off her when she said, "Wait, don't rip it, I'm already out a pair of panties," she giggled and stepped back from him.

His arms at his side he watched her with her hands behind her back working at the skirt. Her eyes on him, her bare breasts pushed out for him to slather over.

When she got the clasp undone, and pushed the zipper down, he stopped her. "Let me, please. Tis all I ever think about." First he clutched her breasts again, filling his hands and squeezing before sliding his palms down her sides to the skirt. Tucking his fingers in the waist, he slowly pushed the skirt until it pooled on the floor.

"Oh yeah," he growled. Finally, the way he'd wanted her. She wore not a stitch of clothing except the fucking stilettoes.

"Heaven baby, died and gone to heaven." He just stared, from the blonde locks that curled around her dainty shoulders, to those creamy breasts down to her apex, where her legs joined.

He absently rubbed his cock over his pants. "You are slender and voluptuous at the same time. Curvy and willowy, you kill me." Before she could blink he slid his hands under her, lifting her he set her on the bed.

Her legs curled to the side, she sat up and went to remove her shoes.

"Wait," he held a hand up. "I want you to lie flat on your back, with those heels on and your legs spread."

A rosy tint rolled over her cheeks, her lids lowered. Suddenly self-conscious, Wyn laid an arm across her chest.

Vijay tucked his thumbs in his loosened belt. "You can do it, *mea dragă*, please do it for me."

Her head lowered, her hair veiling part of her face, she looked through the light strands at him.

His gaze seared so hot it seemed to laser right through the dimness of the room and scorch her skin.

Shyly, she did as he asked. Uncurling her legs she moved them in front of her, then gracefully unfurled her body to lie on her back. Her eyes on him, she slowly opened her legs. As she spread them his eyes lit, glowing like burning coals.

"Put your hands up by your head, baby."

Like she was sliding on silk, she leisurely slid her hands up, palms facing out, her slender arms slightly bent. She lay splayed like she was waiting for him to crawl over her, to between her parted thighs, and thrust right into her.

Steam hissed from his lips as he said, "*Da*, that tis it, *bine*, do not move baby." Vijay tugged at his belt, releasing it completely then tore at the button on his slacks, his eyes never leaving her.

Vijay

"Vijay," her voice a purl of desire wrapped like a sensual ribbon around his body, "hurry."

Cursing a few foreign words, he uttered, "Shit, Wynna." His gaze hard on her, he bent and unzipped his dress boots then stood and kicked them off. He pushed the zipper down then shoved his pants and briefs down removing them and his socks all at the same time.

His shaft sprung iron hard. He gripped the thickness of it in his fist while reaching for the condom on the dresser.

Roman must have snuck back while they were out and left a box of condoms there. Vijay saw them when he'd checked the place out for intruders. He had removed one then stuffed the box in the dresser so Wyn wouldn't see it and be embarrassed knowing Roman knew they were going to have sex.

He tore the package open, took the rubber out and tossed the wrapper on the dresser. His hand stroking his cock he moved towards her with the condom in his hand, and looked down at her.

Pearly skin, arms up in feminine surrender, hair a golden pool around her beautiful face, breasts just waiting for the clutch of his hands and mouth, and, his gaze moved down.

Her heels still on, her shapely legs spread wide for him. Just for him. *Mea Zue*.

Chapter Twenty-Eight

Vijay put a knee on the bed then climbed on, moving to lie to the side of her.

In her shyness, Wyn started to close her legs. He dropped his leg between hers so she couldn't.

His voice soft, he said, "I am sorry, baby, this first time is not going to last long. I have waited too long for you."

Her lips curved up. "I don't care Vijay, as long as you…are inside of me and make me yours."

A fist clenched his heart. "I love you, Wynna." His mouth landed on hers, his hand found her breast, the kiss deep and vital and fervent, he fondled her breast feeling her arch into his hand.

Her palms skimmed up his hard block of chest to scrape up and around the back of his neck, then back down to rake over his nipples and down his taut stomach.

She hesitated, then wrapped her small hand around his manhood, swollen and pounding with the need to be inside her.

"Vijay," she whispered, winding the fingers of her other hand around him until she was feeling the length of his solid flesh with both hands.

"You…are…big." Her eyes wide as she felt him, stroked him. "I can't imagine, I mean I know what I said about babies, but I can't imagine you fitting inside…" One hand holding his shaft, she dipped the other with curious exploration to cup his tight testicles, laughing when he jumped and they contracted in her hand.

He choked out a breath, "Uh, *da*, wait." He grasped her wrists, lifting her hands off him. "You have to wait until later to touch me, I am about to go off like a damned rocket. Let us make you ready for me."

He nudged her legs further apart and gently touched her core, relishing the shudder that shook her entire body. He stroked her clit and rolled his thumb over the budding tip. At her moan, he slid his finger inside her. Wet from her first orgasm, she was soaking now, so ready for him. He pushed a second finger in, stretching her.

He caressed and pampered her core, plundered her mouth until her breaths hissed and her hips started undulating. Against her lips he murmured, "Finally, together, just the two of us."

Their lips still pulsing, her nod and floating smile registered against his mouth.

"You make me so happy, Wynna." His eyes on her, watching the play of flushed excitement build in the rose of her cheeks, and the breaths rushing through the trembling parting of her lips, as he gently then more urgently palpated her sex.

Until her hips were rising off the mattress to ripple at his hand, and her breathing was tight and rough. Bringing her to the peak, he removed his hand and turned slightly from her.

"Vijay?" her voice a soft whimper.

"Right here, baby." He rolled the condom on and moved between her legs. His mouth covering hers, he thrust his tongue inside her, mirroring what he was about to do. Grasping his swollen, throbbing cock, he put it against her opening.

As slowly as he could, Vijay penetrated her, pressing carefully inside. He pushed gently, stopping every few seconds to let her adapt to him.

She dug her fingers into his chest and turned her face from him. The further he went in, the more she stiffened.

He stopped moving. Cupping her chin, he turned her back to face him. Her face was tense.

271

"All right, Wynna, take a deep breath, let it out and relax your legs. You are rigid and tis making it hard for me to get all the way inside you. Tis making me hurt you."

He kissed her lightly then brushed tendrils of damp hair off the side of her face. His mouth near her ear, he crooned soft words in Romanian. She didn't understand what he was saying, but the deep rumble of his voice relaxed her, made her skin tingle.

It took a few moments, but eventually he felt her legs loosen. He kissed down her face to her neck, seeking her pulse of life. Finding it, he licked it then tugged it with his teeth before sucking her skin, marking her.

She let out a tiny mewl of pleasure and he pushed in some more. Slowly he made his way into her tender channel until he had finally sheathed himself deeply inside her. His sigh blew wisps of her hair while his own long locks brushed against her face.

He asked, "You okay, baby?"

"Mmmm," she murmured, squirming slightly to push him in to the very depth, the very end of her.

Her squirming tightened her sheath on his cock. He growled through his teeth and bit his tongue trying to keep from coming. He slowly drew his length back out of her, feeling her wet silk encase him then pushed smoothly back deep inside her delectable body.

Her humming breath ruffling his face, he started a languid rhythm. Vijay could feel her heart beating against his chest, he could feel it change as it started racing, matching his own racing pulse.

His groin felt electrified, he thrust more quickly, sinking deep, throbbing at her virginal walls. Her hips bucked meeting him thrust for thrust.

Raspy whimpers fell from deep in her throat. Vijay moved to prop himself on his elbows so he could see her.

Her lips were cherry red from their passionate kisses and damp from his mouth. Her lowered lids hid all but a delicious glimmer of blue-green. Her breasts jostled with each thrust, bouncing more as he started driving harder and harder into her.

He reached up to crush a breast in his hand. She whimpered again, but stroked her hands around his waist to scrape up his back. Shifting and kneading her full globe in his fingers, he drove harder, so hard he had to release her breast to brace against the headboard before he inadvertently shoved her into it with his strength.

Angling his body, Vijay searched for her sweet spot, when she gushed an ecstatic cry he knew he'd found it. It was time to lay siege to her.

He grasped her legs, pulling them up to wrap around his lean hips. Feeling her high-heels on his back, he thrust hard, hitting her sweet spot and dragging against her clit on the way out, again and again, until she was writhing under him.

Her fingers plowed furrows up his back to his shoulders where she dug her fingers in so hard he knew he'd have marks later. Scratches on his back blended with the painful pleasure from her nails scraping his shoulders jacked up the intensity of his feelings. *Da*, he would look at them later and get a sexual kick remembering this moment.

Her rapid breathing grew squeaky, her chest ruffled with quills of low cries.

"*Bine, mea dragă*," he rasped. "You are about to go over, look at me. I want to watch you."

Her head rolled back and forth on the mattress, she struggled to raise her heavy lids.

Their eyes connected.

"Wynna, you are so bleeding hot with your red glowing cheeks, lips parted like they are waiting for my tongue to vandalize your tender mouth again and again, and those eyes," his crazed desire growled out in a long coarse sigh.

His words made her pussy hitch against him, her woman's channel clutched his cock in spasms. She smiled at his grating grunts, closed her eyes and licked her lips waiting for his kiss.

"*Nu*, look at me, Wynna."

When she brought her dazed gaze back to his, he rocked his hips into hers. One arm around her shoulder and the other rigid against the headboard, cognizant of her frailty compared to his strength. He thrust sharp and deep, plunging faster until she was gasping, her eyes rolled back then he pounded into her.

Wyn huffed then cried his name as she came, her nipples puckered, her body quivered, she doubled in half up against him.

The hair on his skin stood straight up like from static shock reacting in pleasure at her intense release. He saw her pupils expand as her eyes rolled.

Her head fall back, she kept crying out his name- "*Vijay-Vijay-*" before collapsing back on the bed. With her breathless gasping in his ears, he let himself go.

Wyn peered in dazed disorientation at him. Vijay's face strained, veins on his neck bulged, his thick chest pumped bigger. His burning eyes on her, sweat dampened the hair around his face, his arm so rigid against the headboard his bicep was a giant rock.

Clenching her bottom with his other hand, he lifted her and pounded into her hard, fast, deep with primal grunts until he felt the flash of a struck match surge from his groin through his belly to his heart then his brain.

Her name burst from his lips in a hoarse cry as he came. He continued thrusting until his balls crimped and his engorged penis exploded, shooting his seed.

He pushed deep and held there for a second flinching at the exquisite tremors, then pumped a few more times as his body convulsed. He dropped half on her and half on his side panting as paroxysms shot up and down his body. Sweat dripped on his lashes, his big chest rose and fell like a sail in the rough waters.

Wyn's arms swung right around him, she held him tight, close.

A few minutes passed before he could catch his breath. Vijay nuzzled his face in her hair already wanting to do it again. His panting voice a quiet rumble, he asked, "You okay, Wynna?" His nose stuffed in her hair, he stroked her curly locks with his fingers.

Stretching like a contented cat, her smile clear in her voice, she answered, "I'm perfect, Vijay." A slight giggle, then, "I mean you're perfect." She swiveled to look at him.

He moved to lie on his back.

Wyn said honestly, "I admit I got scared for minute, but," rolling to lie partially on and over him, her breasts lodged like fluffed pillows against the hair on his heavy chest.

Pulling at his lips with hers, she spoke against his mouth, "It was so amazing, like getting blown up with dynamite! I want to do it again." Her hair streamed over him.

A big arm curled over her, hugging her close. With his other hand grasping her bottom, his grin spread ear-to-ear. "Oh *yah*?" He tucked her hair behind her ears and stroked a finger down her face.

"I have waited my whole life to have that mind-blowing sex. It was more, way more than I imagined it to be. I love you, Wynna." He clinched her jaw holding her for a bold lusty kiss.

Tugging his mouth from hers, he said, "There is nothing I would rather do than make love again to you right now. But, I am afraid you are so fresh, and so delicate, you are probably too tender and sore to take my hammering into you. Am I right?" His dark brow rose teasing.

Her lip pulled in then pursed out. "Yes," she admitted reluctantly. "I hate to say it, but I'm kinda burning down…there." Her cheeks pinked shyly. "How long do you think the soreness will last and we can do it again?"

His chest rumbled with his chuckle. "I have never had to worry about it before, baby, I do not know. Rest in my arms where you belong for a while then we will see how you feel."

"Okay." She rubbed her breasts over his chest enjoying the hard slate of it under the soft hair.

"Ah," he nudged her away. "That will not help me wait." He rolled to sit on the edge of the bed. "I have to get rid of the condom, I will be right back." He leaned over and gave her a quick kiss before disappearing into the bathroom.

Wyn heard water running as she started to drift off. But a few minutes later he returned and she felt a warm wet cloth between her legs. "Vijay, what are you doing?"

He dabbed the cloth gently, cleaning her then dried her with a soft towel. Dropping them on the floor, he climbed back into bed and pulled her into his arms.

"Just taking care of *mea* baby. I just want to lie here and savor you." Petting her hair, he said, "I thought when we finally did it that it would take the edge off my extraordinary lust for you, but," one shoulder shrugged, "if anything tis damned worse." He unclasped her high heels and dropped them to the floor.

Drawing a long lock down her back then sifting the curl through his fingers, he said, "Tis like when you avoid that chocolate ice cream, and then give in and tis even ten times better than you expected, and now you have to gobble the whole thing, and look for more."

"You're silly." Smiling, Wyn curled into him, cuddling against his strong body. "I wasn't sure what to expect, Vijay," she said. Sighing, she snuggled closer. "But it was way beyond my imagination, or what the girls have told me. I think they're missing something!" Happy giggles skipped out of her.

Embracing her, Vijay kissed the tip of her nose. His voice gravelly deep, his tone turned serious, he said, "You are mine now, **Wynna Pila,** *mea dragă,* mine. No other man will touch your lips, your luscious tits, your tender pussy," he smiled at her blush. "Or any other part of your delicious body. You are amazing and you are mine."

Giggling, she caressed his face and announced, "Works both ways Mr. Zastrovna."

Hugging her tightly, filled with emotion, his voice husky, Vijay murmured, "Get used to the name, sweetheart, because as soon as I can get you there, you will share the name…as my wife."

Soaking up his body warmth, Wyn purred as he pulled the blankets over them.

Still, she scolded, teasing, "There's that bossiness again. Telling me instead of asking me." Yawning, her hand rested on his chest, she told him, "You better be thinking of a way to *ask* me, Mr. Zastrovna."

Vijay

His voice fell to a low drowsy drone, "*Da*, whatever, *mea dragă*, as long as we marry I will jump through whatever hoops you want me to." He whispered as they both dozed off, "I love you, Wynna."

Vijay had sworn to himself he would leave her alone until at least tomorrow. But, he had been dreaming of Wyn standing there bare-breasted in the harbor's golden light, her hands behind her back undoing her skirt.

Then, lying on the bed with her legs spread in the foxy heels, her arms up in a vulnerable yet 'take me now' position and he woke with a screaming hard-on.

Talk about your wet dream. He kissed her, fondled her breasts, slipped his hand between her legs and caressed her until his hand was wet with her honey then he rolled on a condom.

She never came fully awake, but sighed sweetly and threaded her hands behind his head when he moved between her legs and sank into her.

He rocked against her, gently drawing in and out, whispering Romanian words of love against her ear, until he burst. Keeping in the back of his mind her tenderness, he came as thunderously hard as before, but without pummeling her.

They made love again when the sun rose. She was fully awake this time and participated, giving him thrust for thrust until they both collapsed side-by-side holding hands, panting, chests heaving.

In the shower, he finally allowed her to touch and caress his manhood as much as she wanted.

When she got on her knees to taste him, her lips encircling his shaft, her small hand with the slender fingers cupping his balls, he could only take less than a minute of it before lifting her up and pressing her against the wall and taking her again. Without a condom, he had to pull out just before climaxing.

They dressed and had breakfast on the balcony. Their eyes were on each other instead of the panoramic city.

Finishing his coffee, Vijay reluctantly stood up. "I have to meet with my team. I am picking up Miles then we are going out to prepare a safe house. I do not like this hotel. There are too many possibilities for treachery and danger to get to you."

They walked together to the door. "Call me if you need me, *mea dragă.*" He slid his arms around her, pulling her in close.

"Okay. You watch out for yourself too, Vijay. Especially be careful not to injure this part of you," she pressed her hand over his cock and squeezed gently.

He jerked back. "Good lord, Wynna, I cannot go traipsing down the hall with a hard-on." Admiring the soft as butter skin of her face, he slid his hand around the back of her head to clutch her neck and pulled her face up and kissed her. "We can take care of it when I come back."

Her smile big and leering, she asked, "Promise?"

His gulp caught in his throat. "Uh, how about you wear what you wore last night when I come back?"

"Oo," Wyn licked her lips. "A repeat?" She teased, "How about this time you wear shorts, loose ones and we can go out to dinner so I can do to you what you did to me!"

His wood hardened with every look and word of hers. "*Da,*" he said, fixing his jeans. "I have other ideas we can do sweetheart. Ahh," he sighed around the lump in his throat, "the more I have you, baby, the more I want you."

He leaned in and kissed her, cupping her breasts. Giving in to the urge to do more than grope her, he ignored the hard-on and kissed her more deeply until both were spinning into a blur of tingles and heat.

It was a struggle to release Wyn, and move from her, and open the door. His eyes glowering with adoration and desire, he whispered, "I love you, Wynna."

As he stepped out, he instructed, "Do not open the door to anyone or leave this room unless tis with one of my men."

He gave her a quick hard kiss as she opened her mouth to protest and then closed the door in her face before the magnetic pull of her drew him back in. Another second and he would be unable to leave her at all.

After he left, Wyn exercised then did a bit of yoga. She took a shower then surfed the net for current news while waiting for her hair to dry.

Later, she wandered out to the balcony and watched the city life biding her time until Vijay returned. Every thought of him brought a flood of heat between her legs. She could not wait until he came back.

A knock at the door surprised her. She hurried over with his reminder in her mind to not open to anyone except his team. She peeked through the hole, and frowned.

It was Jack. The guy that had tried to grope her while she was incapacitated earning a vicious punch from Vijay for trying it. That brought a tender smile to her frown. Even that first day Vijay had protected her.

She jumped when there was another, slightly louder knock at the door. Her hand hesitated on the knob; she did not like Jack at all. Nor did she trust him. But, he was part of the team, an obnoxious part, but still… she cautiously opened the door.

Chapter Twenty-Nine

"Hey, Wyn." Jack's surly, thin-lipped smile in his long face held no warmth.

"Hello, Jack. Vijay isn't here." She stood halfway behind the partially opened door.

"I know. He sent me to come and get you, bring you to him."

A crease furrowed her forehead. "Why wouldn't he come himself?"

Jack shrugged narrow shoulders. "He was heavy involved in a meeting. Told me to fetch you. I'm only following orders. So, you ready?" His mop of dark scraggly hair didn't look like he'd even combed it today. He dragged the back of his hand over his long skinny nose.

Hating to be alone with Jack, unsure, Wyn thought about calling Vijay to check with him, but then Jack said he was so busy she hated to disturb him.

"Um, okay. Let me grab a key card." She hurried over to the desk, picked up the card and stuffed in in her jean's pocket then joined him, letting the door close behind her.

Jack headed for the stairwell, Wyn asked, "What's wrong with the elevator?"

"This is faster," he muttered, walking faster.

Wyn hurried down the stairs after him. They had a lot of stairs to go down. When they reached the bottom, Jack practically raced out the side door.

"Jack, wait, slow down." Her legs had to do twice the revolutions as his lean rangy ones.

They strode down the city walk along strips of small shops, moving so quickly Wyn couldn't even see the wares in the windows.

Several blocks away from the hotel, Jack headed towards an old gold Buick. He wrenched the passenger door open and told her to get in.

An uneasiness prickled Wyn's skin. She noticed Jack's round little brown eyes never made contact with hers. He kept his head down, the sharp nose pointing at the ground.

She backed a few steps away from him and stuck her hand in her pocket to get her phone. "I, uh, think I'll just give Vijay a quick call-"

He leaped at Wyn, wrapping his arms around her to hold her arms down. Jack snarled, "Just get in the fucking car, bitch." He lifted her off her feet and carried her to the car.

When he set her down to shove her in, Wyn jabbed her elbow in his eye and kicked back at his knee. He howled and let go of her so abruptly she fell on the ground.

Then- an explosion rocked the city. The earth seemed to shake under Wyn.

Jack was thrown from the blast into the unforgiving side of his car.

Sitting in shock, Wyn could see a flume of smoke and flames shooting to the sky. It looked like it was coming from- she scrambled to her feet, -the hotel. Her hotel. Vijay's hotel-

"Oh my God-" her hand over her mouth, she turned and shoved Jack as he tried to grab her. Off balance, he tumbled hard to the cement walk with a squawk.

Wyn ran. Her heart in her throat- Vijay- the timetable he'd given her that he was following- she just knew he was still inside, she could feel it. She raced back to the hotel.

The entire street had frozen in stunned shock as clouds of ash and chunks of blown building showered them, debris hammering and crashing around the people.

By the time Wyn reached the hotel, the first responders were blazing down the street, sirens blaring, lights whirling.

She ran up to the front of the building but a policeman blocked her.

"I have to get inside!" she cried, frantically punching at him. "I have to get inside!"

The policeman handed her off to a burly officer who held her arms so she couldn't break loose and run into the building. Annoyed at her hysterics he told her, "You can't go in, miss, a fucking bomb went off. Now calm down, don't make me arrest you."

He kept a tight grip on her arm, but Wyn kept fighting him, calling out Vijay's name.

The sirens were deafening, there were so many of them. Firemen rushed inside, those outside hooked up hoses and started spraying the building. Orange flames raged out the broken windows, flumes of black smoke encircled the building.

It seemed forever before the firemen started carrying out survivors.

Anxiously, her heart in her throat, Wyn studied every single body brought out.

People we covered with soot and debris, many were crying, some screaming. Blood covered some like mantles. People arriving that had loved ones in the hotel added to the crescendo of chaos.

Hours seemed to go by. Wyn had tried Vijay's cell again and again but it went to voice mail. She knew he was in there. The policeman told her they were bringing out the survivors first, then later, when the fire was out and it was deemed safe they'd go for the deceased.

A man was carried out on a stretcher. Wyn thought she recognized the long brown hair now singed and sooty. She broke from the officer holding her and rushed over.

Peering at him, she could tell it was Miles. "Miles! Miles!" she cried out to him.

Vijay

His lashes flipped before his dark brown eyes landed on her. He moaned weakly, "Wynna."

She ran alongside the men carrying him shouting, "Miles, Vijay, where is he? Is he inside? Is he all right? Please!"

As they slid the stretcher into an ambulance, Miles croaked through his scorched throat, she could hardly hear him from the bedlam around them, "He's inside…" and the doors were closed, the ambulance took off.

Literally feeling the blood drain from her head, Wyn went numb as she turned and strode back to stand next to the officer who had held her.

The doors to the hotel were completely blocked by fire personnel. Wyn stood helplessly chewing on her knuckles.

Then- another stretcher came out. Long black hair draped over the side.

She ran to him. "Oh my God, Vijay!"

His eyes were closed, face black with soot. A gash down his cheek bled profusely.

"Vijay!" she cried out, striding alongside the men carrying him. "Vijay, talk to me!" Her voice broke with a terrified sob, "Please," she begged. Grasping his arm, she and held onto him as they brought him to the ambulance and shoved him inside. Wyn hopped up and moved in with him.

"Miss, you can't-"

Ignoring him, she sat on a metal box and reached for Vijay's hand.

A paramedic climbed in and perched on his other side and put an oxygen mask over Vijay's mouth and plopped a stethoscope on his chest.

The ambulance fired up and it was a long bumpy ride to the hospital. Vijay didn't gain consciousness even as they hurried inside with him.

Wyn paced the hall, the nurses wouldn't tell her anything. She peeked in the window of the room they had put Vijay in but couldn't see him and they refused her entrance.

She wandered down to Miles' room. There was an older couple in there, she assumed they were his parents and decided not to disturb them.

When she got back to the waiting room, Alex, Roman, Lucian and Gage who had flown in yesterday were there. She had called Alex when she'd gotten to the hospital.

Alex ran to her and gripped her arms. His face white with dread, voice tight with concern, he asked, "Wynna, how is- they won't tell us anything."

She shook her head. "I don't know. They won't tell me either, I'm not family." She thought about Vijay's words telling her to get used to his last name as it would soon be hers and the tears she'd fought to hold back cascaded out and down her face.

His face paled further, Alex hugged her. "He'll be all right. He's tough as fucking nails." He sounded like he was trying to convince himself.

The other men gathered around her. Gage gave her a hug then turned and walked swiftly away from the group. They watched him leave with curiosity.

He returned after about ten minutes striding down the hall to the waiting room. The group sitting in a worried clench stood up.

"Any word?" Alex asked, his voice tight.

Gage replied, "They aren't sure. One of those touch and go things. Time will tell they said."

"How did you get them to talk to you?" Lucian asked dragging his anxious fingers through his slick black hair.

A slight crooked grin, Gabe said, "I'm his brother."

At the arched brows, he smirked, "They didn't bother to ask me for ID. Besides, mixed raced siblings are common now. And you," he said to Wyn, "are his legal Domestic Partner. I told him in our country you can become legal Domestic Partners mostly so one person can receive the health benefits of the other partner, and it also makes you next of kin. He said you and I can go see him."

Her brows disappeared into her blonde hairline. "Really?"

"You fucker, I bet you didn't tell the doctor Vij has five fucking brothers?" Alex scowled at Gage.

Gage took Wyn's arm and twitched a tiny smirk at Alex. "I didn't want to go overboard and make them suspicious. Come on, honey." He led Wyn down the tiled hall.

He didn't stop until they reached a room with the door closed. She started to go in but he caught her and carefully pushed her against the wall. "Honey, you'll freak him out if he sees how upset you are. Take a minute."

"No, Gage I want to see him now." She realized her face was soaked with tears, her eyes were undoubtedly red and she couldn't imagine the look on her face. After hearing the explosion, waiting to see if he was dead or alive and then the long hours upon hours waiting here, she must look a fright. She didn't care, but Gage was right.

"Okay, where's a restroom, Gage, do you know?"

"Right there, in that alcove," he said, pointing down the hall. "I'll wait here for you. Here," he handed her his comb.

The gesture started the tears again. "Thank you." She wanted desperately to just charge into the room and see Vijay, but his needs came first. She hurried to the bathroom.

Looking in the mirror, she saw Gage was right. Her face was not just tear streaked, it was tear ridden like with big wheels. Her eyes were puffy and red, her hair was a mess and her face dirty with ash. Sighing, she washed up and then combed her hair.

After using the facility, she glanced at the mirror again, huh, not gonna win any beauty contests but at least she wouldn't scare Vijay. She hustled out of the bathroom and back to where Gage waited.

He rewarded her with a rare smile as she handed him his comb. "*Da*, much better. Good thing you're a natural beauty. *Bine*, now we're ready," he turned the knob and held the door open for her.

The room was semi-dark, machines blinked and beeped. Vijay was lying on a bed, his feet almost hung off the end he was so tall.

Wyn crept up to him. Her heart broke seeing him so still, his vibrancy dimmed, energy stilled. His beautiful eyes closed. One hand had tubes coming out of it. She reached for the other one and gently clasped it.

She stood holding his hand staring at him trying to fight back the tears. Gage stood beside her.

Then, Vijay's lids raised and the brilliant blue lanced out straight at Wyn.

Her heart pitched. She whispered, "Vijay."

His eyes flit to Gage, back to her then back to Gage. His voice hoarse from breathing in soot he rasped at Gage, "What the fuck is going on?"

A big smile broke across the mountain of a man's face. "*Da*, you'll be okay you son of a bitch."

Puzzled, Vijay frowned at him then turned to Wyn. His gaze softened, tenderly he croaked, "Baby, what tis going on?"

She squeezed his hand gently and caressed his face. Besides the gash on his cheek, he was littered with cuts and bruises.

Quietly, she explained, "There was a bomb, in the hotel, you were…hurt."

He stared intensely at her trying to grasp what she said. Then his gaze bounced around the room, then down to his body with tubes in him and covered with a sheet. The realization struck him that he was in a hospital.

Gage cleared his throat. "I spoke with your doctor. You have a concussion, inhaled a fuckload, pardon me, Wynna, of smoke and the cuts and bruises look worse than they are. You have no broken bones. He says a few days here and you'll be fine."

He sucked in a needed breath and went on, "You gave us quite a fucking, sorry Wynna, scare." He could see Vijay struggling to recall what happened.

Last thing he remembered he was bitching at Miles to get a move on. "Fuck, Miles is he okay?" The alarm in his voice came out with a coughing fit.

"Shit, Vij, calm down, *mea frate*." Gage leaned around Wyn, and patted him on the back. "Miles is in better shape then you. And here I always thought you had the harder head."

He leaned back and laughed at Vijay's raspy grunt. Then he said, "I need to go tell the boys you'll be fine. Alex is pacing a road in the waiting room rug."

"Wait." Vijay looked from him to Wyn. "Are you okay baby? Were you injured?" Now his concern was for her. His forehead hardened at the guilty look on her face. "What, what tis going on?" He glanced at Gage but Gage turned his palms up in an 'I don't know.'

"I, uh," Wyn patted his hand, said with a hint of guilt, "I wasn't in the hotel."

His face darkening with confusion, Vijay said, "I do not understand, where could you be if not there?" Seeing her face blush with guilt he wheezed in then barked, "Answer me!"

"Come on, Vij, calm down," Gage muttered.

"Shut up." Vijay scowled at him and looked back at Wyn's guilty face. Pushing himself up against the pillows he shouted hoarsely, "Fucking answer me, Wynna, where the hell were you?"

She stepped back from the ire in his eyes. "I...well...Jack came by,"

Vijay's eyes narrowed to dark slits. "What the fuck was he doing there?"

"Vij," Gage uttered quietly.

"Shut up," he said again, ignoring Gage's rolling eyes. He pierced Wyn with a hard stare and demanded, "Explain."

She nervously pawed a long lock of hair. "Please calm down, Vijay, you are in rough shape, too rough to be a big bully."

At his reddening face, she said quickly, "Jack said you sent him to get me. That you were busy at a meeting so you sent him to...uh...take me to you." She prepared herself as his face roiled so dark, his eyes barely visible they had narrowed to fierce slits.

Vijay glared at Gage, but he could see Gage staring at Wyn in bewilderment. Gage hadn't known.

At the same time, both men exclaimed, *"What the fuck?"* They looked at each other then at Wyn. Vijay hacked, "Why would he say that?"

Her slender shoulders rose then fell. She combed her fingers through her hair. "I, well I don't know. When we got to his car I started feeling something wasn't right. I told him I was calling you, and when I went to take out my cell he…jumped me. Then, uh, he tried to force me into his car."

Vijay looked thunderous.

Beside her, Gage's face was hardening, his hands rolled into tight fists.

Trying to stay calm, Vijay asked, "What happened? You got away from him?"

Wyn nodded. "He picked me up and was trying to shove me in the car and I elbowed him and then I think I kicked him in the knee. He let go and I fell on the sidewalk. As he started to come after me the explosion happened and knocked him off his feet.

"I forgot about him and ran to the hotel because I knew," her hand started shaking as she drew it down his face. "You were there. I was so scared, Vijay, so scared." She couldn't stop the waterworks. Sobs bubbled up out of her chest and choked out of her.

"Oh baby," Vijay croaked. Sliding his good arm around her, he pulled her down to hold her. Over her head he looked at Gage.

Gage never said a word, he just left.

"C'mere," Vijay squirmed over to make room for her on the bed.

"Oh no." Wyn wiped at her eyes, sniffing back more tears. "I can't, you're hurt."

He pulled her until she had no choice but to lie beside him.

"You are my medicine, *mea dragă*." He cuddled her against him, pressed her head to lay it on his shoulder. They stayed that way until the nurse came in and pitched a fit.

"You! Get out of that bed! If he has burns you can be infecting them, get out!" She practically screeched at Wyn.

Wyn tried to scramble out of the bed but Vijay held her tight.

He said in a cold hoarse voice to the nurse, "You ever yell at her like that again, I am close friends with your chief administrator, John Baker, I will have your ass hauled out of here."

The color flew out of the nurse's face. "But- but she-"

"Get out!" Vijay barked at her.

The nurse fled.

Wyn struggled to sit up, he let her.

"Vijay," she scolded him chuckling, appalled at his audacity speaking to the nurse like that. "She was doing her job."

He set his hand on her thigh. "*Da*, but she was wrong to yell like that. Especially when it was *my* doing, not yours. And no one yells at you, *mea dragă*." He squeezed her thigh then moved his hand up. "You need to be punished for leaving the room against *mea* orders."

"Vijay, stop," she blurted, holding her hand in front of his so he couldn't move it higher. Well, he could if he wanted to, she couldn't stop him. "I did not disobey your orders. You said don't leave without being with one of your team. Jack is one of your team."

Thinking of her in Jack's hands, and then to who else would he have handed her over to? Jack was obviously taking her to someone. What could have happened to her- His hand tightened so hard she squealed. "Sorry." He loosened his grip slightly.

Fury edging his voice, Vijay explained, "He is no longer part of *mea* unit I do not give a fuck who his old man is. Gage is going after him with Lucian. Roman is staying outside my door for tonight."

"Oh. I guess I should go…" she remembered she no longer had a hotel room. "I guess I need to go find another hotel room." She went to stand up but he still held her down.

"*Nu*. Alex is waiting out in the hall for you. He will take you to a safe house. We were trying to set something up. If Miles had not been dicking around we both would have been gone from the hotel before the-" seeing her lips tighten, he said, "Alex will not leave your side until I am with you."

"How do you know all that, about Alex being outside and Gage and Lucian and Roman? You haven't spoken with anyone?" This man never ceased to surprise her.

He stared at her for a moment without answering. Then, coughing some of the soot from his lungs he said, "You are so beautiful, Wynna, inside and out. If you were homely you would still be beautiful because you are such a sweet and kind person, and I would still crave you with my whole heart."

Watching her look uncomfortable at his compliment, he smiled. "Anyway, we have worked as a team for a long time. Gage would know I would want Alex with you, and the second you said what you did about," his lips twisted, "Jack, he would gather the others and go after him."

"How did Jack-" she pressed her knees together as he shifted his hand further up on her thigh.

"Forget about that asshole," he leered at her. "I was kind of getting excited over punishing you again."

Her cheeks brightened. "Vijay, please, someone could hear you!"

"I am thinking, that skirt you wore, I will put you over my lap. The spanking will be easier. I can just push the skirt up and-"

"Vijay!" Mortified that someone could hear him, Wyn again tried to get up but he wouldn't let her.

"I wish you were wearing a dress now, Wynna," he purred and slid his hand up to touch her sex. "I would have my hand under your panties and you would be so wet."

"Please," she half-heartedly pushed him away, but his talk of spanking, and his hand on her sex was rushing heat to her core and was already making her wet.

He moved his hand to clutch her breast and kissed her. "On second thought, stay here tonight with me," he murmured at her lips. "I will clear it with the chief." He slid his hand down then pushed it up under her blouse closing his fingers over the silk covering her breasts. A sound at the door got their attention.

They both looked up, it was just someone passing outside the room with a cart. He gave her a squeeze, pinched her nipple through the silk then rubbed a circle over it with the pad of his finger. "*Zue*, Wynna, I need you right now," his mouth closed over hers again.

She put both hands against his chest and pushed. "Stop it, Vijay, you have been seriously injured, this is not the time and sure as heck is not the place for this. You will have to wait." Giggling, she dodged his attempts to engage her mouth with his.

"Ah," he gave in, "you are right, this time." His hard-on was straining at the sheet, but he released her. "You better go, *dragă*, I want you safe and I do not know if tis safe here. The sooner Alex gets you out of here the better I will feel."

She stood up. "Okay. But what about you? Aren't you in danger here?" She leaned over to kiss him. That was a mistake. He stuck his hand down the front of her blouse to grope her.

"Vijay, now you cut that out!" She kissed him and stood up straight.

He gripped her butt then swatted her. "Go on, before I cannot let you go. Alex will take you back to Chrêshdônia, to our safe house. Once there he will be in contact with me. Give your cell to Alex, he will put it behind lead so it cannot be traced. I do not want anyone to be able access you through me."

Her lips pushed out in a pout. "But, you mean we can't talk, even on the phone? For how long?"

"Until I determine tis safe. Just a few days. I still have other things to attend to, other jobs. I will be out of here tomorrow. Go on now," he swatted her again.

He watched her walk out the door. There, she paused, blew him a kiss and wriggled her fingers in goodbye to him.

He called out, "I love you Wynna."

Chapter Thirty

After they landed at the tiny rural airport, Alex drove over another hour out of town.

They passed miles of woodlands, a few small farms and crop fields until they turned off to a gravel lane.

A mile down the road he pulled into a driveway. A gate and fence enclosed the perimeter of the property.

The driveway curved up to a big house that sat atop a hill and was surrounded by an expanse of lawn. Alex stopped at a gate, plugged in a password and the gate swung open.

As he drove through, he explained, "The grounds are bordered with an electric, barbed-wire fence. If anyone is able to get past it, but don't worry they can't, they would be spotted coming across the grass. There's nothing to hide behind. We have guards coming day after tomorrow that will patrol the entire area 24/7. Additionally we have air alerts for aircraft or even drones approaching."

Wyn asked, "What about Vijay? Is he safe in the hospital?"

Alex nodded. "*Da*, don't worry about him. He has a sixth sense about danger. He told me his neck itched like crazy and he was pressuring Miles to get a move on. They would have missed the bomb if Miles hadn't dawdled. Gage said he was going to leave Roman with Vij.

"When the Gage and Lucian return they will probably stay there too to watch over both Vij and Miles. Miles will come here when he's released and Gage will come here also to help watch over you."

He slanted a confident smile at her. "So, don't worry, *fetita*, everyone is well protected. Besides, the word is there is some political group claiming the bomb attack. There's an assembly of government leaders from a small town in Africa on conference here that apparently this opposing group wants ousted."

He parked in an underground garage and brought her into the house via an elevator. He gave her a tour of the building. It had a comfortable living room, large eat-in kitchen, two wings with five rooms per wing.

Alex told her with a grateful grin, "There are prepared meals in the fridge, we don't have to cook." He took her to the room she would stay in.

"This is nice, Alex." She wandered in. They had to stop at her apartment for her to get another bunch of clothes. Alex set her bag on a table.

The room was white with blue and red accents. A dresser, nightstand, and king-sized bed took up most of the space. The attached bathroom was huge and modern.

They shared a chicken and balsamic rice casserole for dinner then Wyn sat by the big front window with a book while Alex worked at the kitchen table on his computer.

When she grew sleepy, Wyn poked her head in to say goodnight. "Aren't you tired, Alex?" she asked.

He shook his head. "I have a bunch of research I need to get done. I'll have long days and short nights for a while. Pleasant dreams, Wynna. If you're up before me tomorrow, just help yourself to coffee or tea and the stuff in the fridge."

"Okay, thanks. And thank you, Alex for watching out for me."

His abashed expression brought a sweet smile from her grateful lips. She said, "Good night," and left him to finish his work.

The next day Wyn did rise before Alex. She heated up an egg sandwich and made a pot of coffee. Sitting at the table, she saw Alex's computer. Thinking he wouldn't mind, she opened it, it was still on. He hadn't locked it.

She thought she would quickly scan the Net for current news. His email was up. Her gaze flashed at the screen as she went to go to a browser, and was drawn to the last entry.

When she saw Vijay's name she stopped and read the ongoing scroll. It was apparently from the man who was employing them to find her uncle. Her stomach dropped like a rock.

She read:

"Alex, I haven't heard from Zastrovna. Is he making any progress with his planned seduction of the President-elect's niece? What is the status?" It was from a Michael Mann.

Wyn's gasp erupted so loud she slapped her hand over her mouth, her blood ran so cold, her limbs went numb.

Alex had replied:

"No worries. Vij has Wynna Pila under his thumb. It should be no time when she is contacted and then Vij can get her uncle's whereabouts."

The backs of Wyn's eyes stung. She stuffed her knuckles in her mouth and bit down on them so hard she broke the skin.

Mr. Mann responded:

"Fine. Good news. You men have been very lax with your information flow to me. I expect daily reports from now on. I want to speak with Zastrovna. He has been way too vague for too long, he should be well enough to talk now. Tell him to call me this evening."

Vijay

Alex wrote:

"Roger."

The email tail ended, as did Wyn's heart.

She had heard people say when a traumatic event occurred their heart stopped beating, now she knew the feeling. Her heart just…felt like an hourglass with her spirit like sand pouring out, totally dissipating until nothing was left but an empty, brittle vessel.

Her brain a jumble of betrayal and pain, she stood like a block of ice. Vijay had played her. Her heart skipped beats; he had been playing her all along. He must have also lied about Shreva and him, and Wyn just kept buying into his lies.

She rolled her hands into fists and pushed them in her eyes to stop the tears. Her hollow heart started racing, she felt lightheaded, scared, devastated, as if falling from a plane and having no parachute. She couldn't think, she was plunging into a harrowing panic attack.

Her arms wrapped protectively around her body as it shook with the pain of loss. She snapped her head to clear it- she needed to get out of the house, get away- now. Glancing at the clock, she noted it would be an hour before the sun would rise. Alex was sure to sleep until then.

She ran to her room and grabbed her purse. Moving silently past the room Alex was in, it was right next to hers in case she had needed him, she tried to swallow past the lump in her throat but couldn't.

Yeah, she needed him all right; she needed him to give her a gun so she could shoot herself.

Back into the kitchen, she remembered the metal box Alex had put her phone in, she quickly retrieved it and inserted the battery.

Her stomach in knots and blinking back tears, her body trembling all over, Wyn slipped out of the house and ran across the grass to the gate. She'd seen the password Alex had entered when they arrived yesterday.

Her hand was shaking so badly she had to put the password in twice before she got it. The gate swung open and she ran out. And kept running.

Her fuel was adrenalin backed by despair. With only the clothes on her back, jeans, blouse and boots, she ran. Her heart was broken, destroyed.

She vowed as she kept running that she would never love again. What a fool she had been. She had truly loved Vijay with her whole heart, she still loved him.

He betrayed her, used her, made a fool of her, but, sobs broke fighting their way up her throat, she knew she would always love him. Desolation settled over Wyn, binding to her like a cloak knitted of anguish and loss.

She made it to a tiny store outside of town and called information for a taxi service. It took the cab thirty minutes to get to her.

"Where to, Miss?" the driver asked her in a bored voice.

Where to? She didn't know. Thinking, what's the fastest way to get the furthest she could get from there, she told him, "Take me to the bus station."

She rode the bus all the way back to the town her Aunt Odessa and Uncle Sheffield lived in, Voronet. She had another cousin, Clarence Goodwyn who lived in Voronet.

Once she called him to ask if she could stay with him and he agreed, she turned off the phone so Vijay couldn't find her. Just thinking of his name brought violent pangs to her constricted heart, her stomach turned and ached. Her anguish so extreme, she clamped her hand over her mouth to stall the nausea that threatened.

The taxi she took from the bus station dropped her at her cousin's. She'd fled so fast and her mind was such a scramble she hadn't brought her suitcase. She wouldn't have been able to run with it anyway.

As soon as she reached the door to the house it swung open.

It was a four-bedroom home, quite ancient, but then so were most of the houses in the village. It had been her cousin's parents. They had given it to him when they moved to a bigger home.

"Wyn." The young man held his arms out to hug her.

Stumbling into his embrace, Wyn almost lost it, but she managed to keep a grip on the waterworks. Tears trickled down the back of her throat.

"Thank you, Clarence for letting me stay here." The urge to bury her face in his shoulder and never open her eyes again was overwhelming.

His cologne, so different from Vijay's masculine aftershave was like cold water slapping in her face. She pulled from his arms and moved back, her eyes on the ground.

Seeing her abject distress, Clarence stepped aside and said, "Come in, cuz."

Wyn followed him inside.

The furniture was old but comfortable. A few landscapes hung crookedly on the walls that could use a coat of paint. Her cousin had managed to turn the old family home into a bachelor pad. A huge flat screen took up half a wall and take-out boxes and beer cans littered the coffee table.

Clarence adjusted round glasses on his small nose. His brown eyes were small too, but he had a wide smile. He smoothed back fine, light brown hair but it just flopped back over in his eyes. Tall and lanky, his arms and legs were long and thin.

"Come on in, Wyn, I made some tea. Have a seat on the sofa and I'll bring it in."

When he went into the kitchen, Wyn sat on the couch. Her insides felt like drywall. Like there was no blood flowing through her veins. A sparkle caught her eye. She looked down at the bracelet Vijay had given her at the restaurant.

Tears pricked behind her eyes as she numbly fingered it. It was stunning, she remembered that night, their lovemaking- she shook her head and blinked hard. She should rip the damned bracelet off and throw it outside in the sewer.

As her fingers went to unclasp it, Clarence came in carrying a tray with a teapot, cups, lemons, sugar and cream. He set it on the table and sat down next to her.

He glanced at her, saw her distraught face, eyes swollen red and wretched and quickly looked away. Her voice had trembled on the phone. She hadn't told him why she needed a place to stay.

"So, Wyn, is everything okay? I mean, last I heard you were staying at Aunt Odessa's. I mean you're welcome here for as long as you need, but I can see something is terribly wrong. Do you want to tell me about it?" He poured her a cup of tea and handed it to her.

Taking it, she stared at the cup in her hand. "It's…" she gulped down a sob, and closed her mouth.

Clarence waited. When she didn't continue he said, "It's all right, you don't need to tell me if you don't want to. Do you want to call Aunt Odessa and let her know where you are?"

Her head shook adamantly back and forth. "No." She looked wild-eyed at him and begged, "Please, don't call them, don't tell anyone where I am." She set a hand on his arm. "Please Clarence, promise me."

He added cream and sugar to his tea, stirred then took a healthy drink. "Sure, sure, whatever you want."

They sat in silence until the tea was gone.

Wyn mustered the strength to politely ask, "How's the, uh, accounting world?"

He nodded with a wry grin. "Fine, fine, my job isn't the best in the world but it's solid." He glanced at her. Wyn's face was bone white, her eyes bleak. "So, uh, what are you, I mean you came to this country to visit, are you working?"

Not responding, she just held her empty cup and stared blankly at it.

Clarence waited but it was clear she was done conversing. He stood up. "Come on, let me show you where you can sleep. You look like you could do with a rest." He waited patiently while she set her cup on the tray and stood up like her legs were wooden.

She followed him down the hall where he brought her to a small room in tan and white flowered wallpaper with brown curtains and beige rug. It was sparse, only a bed, table beside it and a dresser.

"This is where Shreva and some of my friends stay when they need to get away." He stood still. Wyn just stared blankly at the floor.

"Okay, okay, then, I'll leave you. I showed you the bathroom next door. We can, uh, catch up tomorrow after you've had some rest. If you need anything, don't be afraid to ask. Make yourself at home, okay?" He waited but she said nothing.

As he turned to the door, in a tiny, tear-heavy voice she said miserably, "Thank you, Clarence."

Chapter Thirty-One

Alex woke and could smell the coffee and thanked Wyn out loud, "Great, good girl."

He padded into the bathroom, took a shower, dressed then went to the kitchen. When he passed her door he saw it was closed.

He helped himself to the coffee which had turned off from being on so long the automatic shut off had kicked on. But it was still warm. He heated up an egg sandwich in the microwave and sauntered over to sit down in front of his computer to start work.

Combing his damp hair back with his fingers, he cracked his knuckles then lifted the lid. His stomach clenched.

The screen came on at the bottom of his last email. That wasn't where he'd left it last night. *Oh fuck*, used to being alone or with the team he never bothered to shut it down.

His eyes raced back and forth over the email that was there. His stomach clenched harder and now twisted, he could feel his sandwich trying to climb back up his throat.

Jumping up, he ran down the hall to her room and knocked.

"Wynna?" He knocked harder, waited, then threw the door open. As he thought, the room was empty.

He ran panicked through the entire house but he already knew she was gone. The gate was hooked into the house computer. He raced to it and pulled up the recent history. It showed early this morning it had opened.

Vijay

He slapped his forehead, muttering curses. "Oh *Zue*," he huffed. Fumbling his phone out almost dropping it, he dialed Vijay.

"*What the fuck?*" Vijay roared into his cell when Alex told him what happened. He clenched the phone so hard he could feel it cracking in his hand.

"How could you be so fucking stupid to leave your laptop on?" He dragged his agitated fingers like claws hard through his hair digging them into his scalp. He didn't wait for a response from him, Alex already knew he'd screwed up.

Vijay hammered questions at him, "How long? When did she leave? Where could she have gone?" He was staying in a hotel still in Monaco until he knew for sure why the other hotel had been bombed and if it had anything to do with them.

Alex told him when she'd left. It was hours ago. Stating the obvious, he said, "She could be anywhere. I will call the taxi companies, there's no other way to get from way out here to anywhere else." He took a deep breath, said quietly, "I'm so sorry, Vij."

"Call me right back when you know." Vijay clicked him off then immediately dialed Wyn's number.

Ten times it went to voice mail. He ran over to his laptop and turned it on. He kept dragging his hands over his hair as he waited for it to come on. When it did, he went to the program where he had all of his teams' and Wyn's GPS.

He pulled hers up and started the track. It led to the village where the safe house was near. A mile and it disappeared. He called Alex. "I have the address where she shut her phone off."

Alex said with an exhale, "I know. She went to the bus station. I hacked the terminal's records. She took a bus to the town where she was living before, Voronet, where Gage went and got her." He took a pained breath before continuing.

"I will call the taxi and car-share services to see where she went next. Unfortunately it's Sunday and there is little activity in this tiny town, and many services are closed."

Vijay squeezed the space between his eyes; he couldn't believe they'd chased her right back to that fucking place. "I will charter a plane and fly straight there. Call and rent a car for me."

"*Bine*, what do you want us to-" Alex was speaking to a dead phone.

****

Of course Wyn didn't sleep a wink. His face was right in front of her every time she closed her eyes. And when they were open. Still, she lay on her back until late morning. She didn't have the energy to get up.

Clarence lightly knocked on her door once, when she didn't answer he quietly walked away.

She finally got up in the afternoon and strode wearily to the kitchen. Clarence heard her and came in.

"Gee, Wyn, I was really starting to get worried. You need to eat." He came in and leaned his narrow hips against the counter. He wore a brown sweater over brown corduroys and loafers. His nose twitched as he unconsciously shrugged his glasses up his nose.

"I'm not hungry, thanks." She'll never eat again.

"Uh, how about some coffee then? I'll make some, okay?" He moved to the coffee maker and picked up a filter.

Her shoulders barely rose in a shrug. She didn't really care. About anything.

"All right." He rattled awkwardly, "Why don't you go sit in the living room and I'll bring it to you." He watched her walk away; shoulders slumped dragging her feet, her head down. He let out a big held breath and grabbed up the can of coffee.

Wyn flopped on the sofa and let her head drop back over the back of it. Her throat burned from trying to keep from crying all night. What to do next? She should call her parents and ask for a plane ticket home.

She wouldn't use the credit card Vijay had given her, and he had given her a lot of cash but it wouldn't be enough for the entire flight. She needed to call her folks, but she just felt like not moving. Maybe she could just sit here and…die.

Clarence brought the coffee, clearing his throat when he came into the room. Wyn didn't move.

He set the tray down and pushed a mug into her hands. "You need to have liquids, Wyn, please. If you don't do something I'm afraid I'll have to call Aunt-"

She sat up hard with a dark frown. "You can't call, you promised you wouldn't."

His nose twitched. "Yeah, yeah but, if I'm worried about your health, I have to-"

"All right." Her beleaguered sigh was long and irritated. She took a sip and saw Clarence's face relax. Wow, she didn't know he cared so much.

They hadn't gotten along too well when their families visited when they were younger. He had been a whiner and a tattletale. Maybe he'd grown up, she sighed, like they all had. She felt she'd lived a hundred years since yesterday. It seemed to make him happy so Wyn drank most of her coffee.

Clarence didn't drink any. His mug sat there getting cold. He chattered though, on and on about nothing. Their other cousins, his job, his last girlfriend and how she dumped him and he was angry and then… Wyn only heard blah, blah, blah. Her brain was frozen and her head hurt.

She yawned. She suddenly felt so sleepy. No sleep last night must be catching up with her.

Soon, she was embarrassed but couldn't stop herself from falling over on the couch. On her back, one leg and arm were dangling off the edge, she felt…paralyzed. Then all went black.

Chapter Thirty-Two

Her head felt fuzzy, like stuffed with cotton, her eyes so heavy she couldn't lift her lids no matter how hard she tried.

Wyn went to move her arm to wipe her eyes, and she couldn't. Her arms were over her head. She tried again, her wrists only moved a few inches then stopped.

Licking her dry lips, Wyn heard voices. Male voices. They moved closer.

"Ah, there you go, little fucking *scorpie*, bitch," the sound of a nasty sneer accompanied the voice.

Her heart that she thought was dead and stone cold started pounding. She recognized the voice. Panic pushed at her lids, they opened a crack. Wincing at the pain in her head she could just barely make out two blurry figures.

Around them was a lot of green. She could smell rich earth, and spring grass, and fresh air, a breeze ruffled over her, she was outside.

Struggling to clear her vision, she tried again to move her arm, then her other arm, then her legs. Every part of her felt numb, even her back, she couldn't tell what she was lying on.

She tried harder to move her limbs. Dread crawled through her body, shriveling her skin with burgeoning terror. *Oh my God*, she realized, her arms and legs were tied down.

"Come on, wake up, *scorpie*, this is no fun if you aren't aware of it," the nasty voice taunted her.

A hand gripped her jaw lifting it up. "Open your fucking eyes," he commanded, the familiar voice grating and irate. He said to the other blurry figure, "She's still fucking dopey, how much of that shit did that asshole give her?"

The other blur mumbled, then his voice grew clearer as he moved closer. "She's small, he probably dosed her enough for a man."

"Stupid fuck," he spat and shook Wyn's jaw. It made the pain in her head wrack with stabs of agony.

"Jack," she whispered through her dry throat and pinched jaw.

"Ahh," sadistic joy infiltrated the nasty voice. "You are waking, my little princess. You are so clever to recognize my voice. Now, open your fucking eyes and look at me." When she didn't, he shook her jaw harder then slapped her.

"Hey," the other guy complained, "she has to be in good condition for the sacrifice to be accepted. You can't hit her."

"Fuck off, Erik. I'm going to do a lot more than hit the bitch."

Through the crack under her lids, Wyn could barely make out the second man.

She saw a fuzzy male around thirty, raggedy looking in a hippyish kind of way. His hair straggled long and messy down his narrow back. He had a heavy nose, and lips that spiked in the corners. He was talking, "You can't fuck her, Jack; she has to be fresh for the sacrifice. She hasn't been with a man for at least 48 hours, my man confirmed that."

Wyn's thick lids felt like they weighed a ton, they lowered, closing out the sight of the two malevolent males.

Still holding her jaw in a hard grip, Jack said, "So what? I'll fuck her all night and then you wait another 48 hours. What's the difference?"

Jack leaned over Wyn demanding, "You open your fucking eyes right now or I'll pop you again, harder." His fingers dug hard enough into her jaw to draw tears.

It took all her strength to get her lids up; they felt like they had anchors on them. The last person she would have wanted to see, well, one of the last, she was starting to get a list of people she never wanted to cross paths with again, was glaring down at her.

His thin lips turned up in a wide leering grin that made his long skinny nose longer. "Ah, there ya go, *scorpie*." Jack released his grip but then caressed her face then her neck, her collarbone down to the top of her blouse when the other man barked.

"Goddammit, Jack, you can't have her. I need to make the sacrifice now. The Olde Fandarie book says it has to be done weeks before the election to guarantee the President-elect will die at the full moon. I don't have time to wait," his voice ended in a paint-peeling whine.

Jack groused, "Oh get fucked you and your stupid witchcraft, fucking spells and sacrifices. I only came in with you because her fucking cousin contacted you that she was at his place. You needed help in moving her, and I wanted her. So, we both get what we want, you just have to wait a little longer, but I get what I want right now."

He shoved his hand down the top of Wyn's blouse to grab her breast. "Ahh, nice little *scorpie*, so nice." He knew he hurt her with his rough squeeze. She couldn't stop the wince that flickered over her face.

Becoming more aware, Wyn looked around the best she could. She was lying on a type of iron table. Her wrists and ankles were tied, she was spread eagle. Thank God she still had her clothes on. But the lascivious leer in Jack's eyes indicated it would not be for long.

She was outside as she'd thought. They were in a small clearing surrounded by trees; they must be in the forest. Her body tingled with stark terror, she was tied down on an iron table in the woods and the other freak kept talking about a sacrifice.

Jack squeezed her breast harder to get her attention back on him. "Ya got it figured out yet, *fetita*? Yeah, I picked up some of their Romanian shit."

Kneading her breast roughly, he nodded at the other man who frowned back at him. "This crazy loon read in some antique book on witchcraft that if he made this sacrifice of a young female relative of the man he wanted dead, it would happen. He wants your Uncle David dead, so, here you are. Unlucky for you, your stupid cousin and this freak are psycho buds and you dropped yourself right on his porch. Like a lamb on a silver platter."

He glanced at the freak. "How's that for fate, hmm?"

Eric said, "Jack, man, it is the fates that brought her to me, now quit-"

Jack shrugged one shoulder while deliberately crushing Wyn's breast. Squeezing fiercely and chuckling at the pain he elicited scrunching over Wyn's delicate face he gloated, "That pretty much covers it. But, I'll bet you wonder why we just didn't grab your other cousin, Shreva?"

At the freak's snort. Jack told Wyn, "Well, the picture in his book closely resembled you, and it said pure. But you've been with that fuck Vijay." Just thinking about that struck Jack with black rage, he pulled his hand out of her blouse and slapped her hard.

Wyn bit her tongue to not cry out at her stinging face.

Jack grabbed her jaw again. "You ain't pure no more, but you are sure a hell of a lot more pure than that hag, Shreva. Course, by time I'm done with you, you will be a lot less pure."

He shoved her face then squeezed both breasts over her blouse. Dragging a hand down her body to cup her sex, he rubbed his erection over his pants. "And, I'm starting right now. We have such unfinished business you and me."

Wyn wasn't going to give him the satisfaction of crying or begging him. She did not want to look into his eyes and let him see her terror, and revulsion. She was woefully helpless but she'd be damned if she showed him her fear and desperation. The creep fed on it.

Grasping her jaw again, Jack leaned over her bringing his face close to hers, so close she could smell the beer and cigarettes he'd had while waiting for her to awaken.

"All I wanted from you, at first anyway, was a little fucking feel of your fine tits. But instead, fucking Vij smashed my goddamned nose in. Well," he sneered fiercely, crushing her breasts again in his hands, "now I'm gonna get the whole enchilada, baby, and that bastard is nowhere around to stop me.

"I don't know what he did to make you run from him, but, fuck him," he stroked his hands back down between her legs, gripping her sex. "You're mine now to do whatever the fuck I want."

He leaned closer, stuck his long tongue out and licked her lips. "Baby, I can think of a lot of things I want to do to you."

Turning her head with a grimace, Wyn struggled at her restraints, tugging for all her worth but she was secured. She twisted her body to avoid Jack's ruthless hands but she had nowhere to go. He reached for her blouse.

"Shall I just rip it, you won't need be needing it anymore, or should I prolong my lust with anticipation, unbuttoning it slowly and watching you squirm as you get more and more naked growing more and more afraid?"

He pondered, "Hmm, what the hell, I have as long as I want, I might as well enjoy every bit of it. I owe you so much for getting me hit by that fuck Vijay." He opened one button, she squirmed, he laughed, and opened the next and the next until he spread her blouse apart exposing her lacey black bra.

Wyn struggled to not panic, keep her chest breathing low and shallow to not draw more attention to her breasts, but her heart was banging out of her chest. She jerked so hard at her restraints tears stung her eyes.

"Oh, fucking yeah," Jack drooled and reached down and unbuttoned her pants. "Oh shit, I'm gonna have to cut them off you, and your bra."

His sneering grin dripped lewd malice. "I like you tied like this, no fighting me, I can just slide right in. The other stuff I'll have to untie you for, but for now- *oomph-*"

Erik shoved Jack aside and started to untie one of Wyn's wrists.

Jack stumbled back several feet before gaining his balance. "What the fuck!" he barked.

"I told you to wait, that you can screw her when she's dead. But, no," Erik kept pulling at Wyn's restraints getting one hand free. "So now I'm taking her someplace else where you can't get your filthy hands on her. I need her pure before she dies."

Jack came at Erik with a roared growl and punched him.

Erik fell backwards landing on his butt.

"Asshole," Jack sneered. "Now I'm gonna keep her longer just 'cause you're an asshole. You're not taking her anywhere."

He grabbed Wyn's arm as she was leaning over trying to untie her other hand and slammed her back down on her back. Then he gripped her head and bashed it on the metal table, the slam hard enough to partially knock her out.

Erik got to his feet waving a curved machete at Jack that he planned to use to stab Wyn with during the sacrifice. He demanded, "Get away from her, Jack, she's mine." He turned and raised the machete over Wyn pronouncing, "I'm killing her now!"

Wyn saw stars, she tried to clear her head but it was spinning. Cracking her lids, the men were blurry moving blobs again. She lifted her free arm, twisted and struggled to move to untie her other hand, but she was too dizzy and couldn't reach her wrist anyway with her legs so tightly bound. Falling on her back again she almost passed out.

Suddenly, a fierce enraged voice broke through the clearing- was she dreaming?

"How about I fucking kill the both of you instead of you touching a hair on her head?" His face dark with rabid wrath, Vijay cursed a violent streak, stomping towards them.

Wyn forced her eyes open, it *was* Vijay. What was he, how the heck did he get here? Her head just spun and spun like a top. She watched Vijay go straight to Erik.

Erik held his machete over his head swinging it to cut off Vijay's head.

A breathy squeal squeezed out of Wyn- but Vijay, in a flash caught Erik's arm and he brought it down and snapped it over his knee.

Erik screamed and dropped the knife. Vijay punched him square in the face. When he landed flat on the ground, Vijay stomped on his face with his big boots then his neck until he was dead.

Wyn gave a hoarse squeaked warning- "Jack has a gun!"

Vijay swung around with his leg in the air kicking the gun out of Jack's hand. At that split second, the look on Jack's face reflected he knew he was a dead man.

He turned to run, but Vijay caught his collar, dragged him over and slammed his head into a stalwart tree again and again while barking curses until Jack no longer drew a breath.

Vijay dropped him and hurried over to Wyn.

Leaning over her, he cried, "Baby, Wynna, are you all right?" Piercing distress crunched his face and bled in his eyes.

She couldn't answer him, she was passing out again.

"Baby," she heard his voice faint, way in the back of her mind. She felt his big hands at her wrist then her feet, untying her. Once freed of her restraints, she felt her body lifted up in his strong arms, braced against his thick chest.

As he strode through the forest with her, Wyn passed out completely.

She woke hours later. Without moving, she peeped through low pained lids. She was in the backseat of Vijay's car. She could see the back of his head, the tattoo spiraling up his neck, as he drove.

Her head hurt, her heart ached, he came for her only because he still needs to get to her uncle to get paid. Swallowing the sobs of his heartbreaking betrayal, she pretended to still be unconscious.

It felt another hour passed before he stopped the car. Wyn heard the car door open then close. Gingerly, she sat up holding her head and peered out the side window.

They were parked in front of a hotel in the center of the town she recognized as being near her aunt's. He must be inside getting a room so he could continue his seduction of her.

Vijay

He rescued her, but Wyn couldn't bear to look at him. See him lie to her face, touch her body when he had no true desire for her, he only wanted her uncle which equaled money to the mercenary.

She pushed the door open and slid out. The rest she'd had helped clear her head. Glancing around, she saw rows and rows of shops. Staggering at first, she wobbly ran to them. There were so many buildings she could easily hide, he'd never find her. Her heart broke all over again as she ducked into the biggest one.

Wyn waited two hours before going to a clerk and begging to use their phone. Her purse was likely still back at Clarence's.

Her own cousin had betrayed her too. He had drugged her then threw her to a deranged psychopathic killer, and a violent sociopathic rapist. *I wonder how much I cost?*

She had no choice, there was nowhere else to go, she had to go back to Aunt Odessa's.

Alisha answered the door. "Miss Wyn! Oh my gosh! What are you doing here?"

"Can I just come in, please," the words barely tumbled from her weary lips. Wyn knew she looked like hell, really, who wouldn't after narrowly escaping being sacrificed in the woods by two maniacs?

"Can you get someone to pay the taxi?"

"Of- of course, Miss." Alisha stood aside so Wyn could enter the mansion.

Once she cleared the threshold, Alisha closed the door and regarded Wyn with concern. "Miss-"

"Listen Alisha," Wyn cut her off, "please, no questions. I just want to go to my room. Please do me a big favor and tell Aunt Odessa I'm here, but tell her," she thought a moment. "Tell her I'm very sick, contagious maybe, and they need to stay away. Can you do that for me?"

Alisha stared at her aghast, uncertain, worried. She nodded her affirmation. "Of course. Come on, let me take you up and get you settled. Thank goodness they had your door fixed."

She bit back a twisted smile and said, "You don't have to worry about Jazer, he's out of the hospital and recovering at his home. The rumor is no one wants to talk about what happened. Not Jazer or your aunt and uncle. They are all too afraid of the…" She grinned with admiration before saying, "That behemoth that rescued you. Mr. Zastrovna and your man have them terrified into silence."

Wyn's mouth quivered into a weak, sad smile and the two trudged up the stairs fortunately without running into anyone.

In her room, so tired her bones ached, Wyn said, "Please, Alisha, I don't want to see anyone but you. That means anyone from outside the family too."

Her brows arched. "Oh! But surely Mr. Zastro-"

"No!" Wyn snarled. "Especially not him." She lowered her voice to a sorrowful hush insisting, "Please, no one."

Alisha covered her mouth with her hand to hide her astonished look at the pain creasing Wyn's beauty, and the dismal clouds in her eyes. "Um, of course. I will bring you something to eat."

"No, thank you," Wyn said half-hearted. "I want nothing. Just to be left alone." She closed the door to Alisha's confused expression. Trudging to her bed, she fell face-down on it and wept bitter, grievous tears.

Chapter Thirty-Three

No one bothered her too much. At first they were reluctant to have her stay there, they were afraid of Vijay's wrath.

Wyn allowed her aunt a very brief conversation in which Wyn refused to tell Odessa anything that had occurred. She advised that Vijay would not be coming for her.

Odessa had said with a haughty 'I told you so', "I said he was an outlaw ruffian. No good, is what I told you. But, no, you had to learn on your own. Now, about your future-"

Sighing with beleaguered depression, Wyn told her, "I just ask that I may stay in my room until I can arrange for travel back to the States. Also, please ask Uncle Sheffield to return my money so I can pay for passage back home."

Odessa said she would do as Wyn asked to gain time. She gave Wyn some space and then. Since it was apparently over between her and that thug, as soon as he was on his feet she would ensure Jazer press his suit on her again. Sure he was seriously injured and afraid, but money can cure so many evils.

That was three weeks ago.

Wyn had hardly left her room, seldom ate or slept. Sometimes she went out on the lawns and drifted aimlessly around.

The good news was she was finally able to connect with a close friend of her uncle's to tell him what had transpired, and who the people were who were looking for him.

Then the election was held and her uncle won by a landslide. He could finally come out of hiding. And Wyn was safe now, no one would be coming after her. Especially not Vijay.

Even though she would refuse to speak to him, she was dismayed and further depressed that Vijay hadn't tried to contact her or come to the mansion and demand to see her. She had been right all along, all he wanted from her was contact with her uncle.

One tiny part of her brain had held out hope that he really did care about her. But, she sighed morosely, now she finally had the final conviction that he had never been interested in Wyn, everything he had said was all lies.

There was a big party tonight. Everyone was all atwitter. It was in honor of her uncle's election to premier of Chrêshdônia.

Wyn had no desire to move very far from the doors of the mansion, much less attend a party. But everyone said if she didn't show that it would be a slap in the face to her uncle after all he'd been through.

Her limbs felt filled with lead, her moves lethargic, cotton balls of despair stuffed her brain and her heart. Wyn struggled to do as she was asked.

She had borrowed yet another dress from Shreva. It had taken all her effort to shower and climb into the dress.

Alisha murmured words of soft encouragement as she flittered around her doing her hair and makeup, helping her with the dress.

Slipping on her heels, Wyn thought about the last time she'd worn one of Shreva's dresses. An ach deep in the pit of her gut still pinched when she thought of Vijay. She just couldn't fully delete at the back of her mind, the thread of hope he'd come for her. But, the election was over, he no longer needed her.

Of course she'd kept her phone turned off. Yet, the lingered hope of him standing on the mansion's doorstep begging for her to forgive him still- *agh*, she shook her head.

"Stop it," she scolded herself, "you need to forget him." She looked in the mirror.

Vijay

Her cheeks were still round but the rest of her face was wan and thin, waifish. Her black pupils engulfed much of the blue-green sadness. If he were there he would be calling her *fetita*, little girl again. *Damn, would he never get out of her head?*

Her gaze drifted down her reflection. Sighing, she'd obviously lost weight, but her breasts still molded with plump swells over the low décolletage. Of course, did Shreva own anything not low cut or skin tight?

The dress was red. Eew. Last thing she needed was to be wearing the color of…love. Her throat tightened and her eyes stung. Dabbing a tissue under her eyes to preserve her makeup, Wyn smoothed the skirt running her palms down the silky material.

The dress fit snug from the bodice down her slender, thinly curved waist, clinging to her hips then swirled above her knees. She slipped on the red pumps and was ready to go.

The chauffeur drove the family to the country club where the festivities were in full swing.

Shreva gabbled the entire way there. "Oh, this is so exciting! There will be loads and loads of stinking rich men. This dress will be a man killer, huh Wyn?" Nodding at her figure, she crossed her legs, the micro-short skirt of the lemon yellow, chiffon bandage style slid way up her thighs.

Her big breasts bounced. Every so often she had to tuck a nipple back in ignoring Sheffield's horrified look, and Shreva's mother's and Aunt Odessa's shocked gasps. Thank goodness her father and brother were sitting up front of the limo with the driver.

"So," Shreva blathered on, "we can be each other's wing women if need be."

Wyn blinked wordlessly. Shreva didn't care, she kept blathering on.

Her red glossy lips lifting in a big shiny bow, she told Wyn, "Of course I shouldn't need any help bagging a good one, but you probably will. With all that skin and bones and sorrowful stuff going on. For Pete's sake, Wyn, you look like a starving model with fake tits."

315

She reached over and cupped one of Wyn's breasts, squeezing it before Wyn could react. An ironic smile twisted Shreva's glossed lips. "But yeah, they are real aren't they? Big and soft and supple as shit, no wonder Zastrovna-"

"Shreva! Please!" her mother squawked appalled.

"Oh get over it, Mother. It's the 21st Century, women don't have to talk like ladies any more, haven't you heard? And promiscuity is no longer déclassé; women can sleep with as many men as men do with women and not be called a whore. The word slut is so outdated. Anyway," she crossed her legs again revealing she had nothing on under the dress and blathered on.

Shreva's voice yammered like a dusty mist in and out of Wyn's ears.

Catching an eyeful of Shreva's 'commando', a flash of Vijay asking her to leave her panties off when they had gone out to dinner struck her, and what he'd done under the table in the restaurant- damn. Wyn closed her eyes to dispel the vision. But it didn't stop the heat from radiating between her legs.

Shreva was still yammering, "I can't help the way my cousin looks," she said to her mother curling a sad eye at Wyn. "As thin as she is, she still has those outrageous curves. Sticks like her only look like they have fake boobs because they're so skinny. She's just all big haunted eyes and tits, huh. And the bitch still keeps that perfect onion shaped ass," she sniffed, steeping in jealousy.

"That – is- e- nough- Shreva!" Vivid spots streaked across her mother's face.

A tiny smirk curved Shreva's thickly varnished lips, she loved to push buttons. "Eh, we're here anyway. Let's go have fun, I need a damned drink."

Not waiting for the driver to come and open the doors, she slid out inelegantly with her dress up past her thighs. She barely smoothed it down before tripping up the drive in her sky-high heels leaving the rest of them behind.

Wyn sat unmoving as everyone piled out.

Sheffield poked his head back in. "Come on Wyn, you promised. You mustn't make David look bad." Holding a hand to her, he spoke quietly, carefully.

He had treated her quite judiciously since the episode with Gage, the man Vijay had sent to retrieve Wyn.

Sheffield shuddered as he recalled that event. For heaven's sake, the enormous tattooed, shaved-head, earring wearing Black behemoth like some fearsome, bloodletting warrior from ages past, had actually snapped the damned shotgun in two over his knee, with a shit-eating grin no less, daring them to retaliate! Who the hell does that? Who knows what else those men would do if he was so much as rude to his niece?

Sighing the weight of the world on her shoulders, Wyn slowly slid out and walked lethargically but with her head high, holding her uncle's arm as they followed the others already up the path to the club.

Inside were millions of lights. Dozens of chandeliers hung like diamond umbrellas, and strings of crystal lights draped the walls.

The huge room was white with gold-flecked walls, and huge floral arrangements, vibrant sprays of color set upon white tablecloths.

It was packed. People in formal dress moved around talking and laughing, and it was loud with some guests calling across the room to each other.

Sheffield took Wyn to greet her Uncle David.

David's brilliant smile indicated how pleased he was to see her. He greeted with deep fondness, "My darling Wyn."

David and Wyn had met earlier in the week where he had professed how proud he was of her bravery and loyalty, and anguish at the devastating assaults and experiences she had suffered on his behalf.

Although Wyn had downplayed much of what had happened, David was astute enough to guess the gist of it and he was horrified and enraged at how she had been brutalized because she was his niece. And how stalwart she had been through it all.

Sheffield had indicated a confusing bit about the man who had rescued Wyn from the kidnapping felon Kreis Warwick, and had apparently broken her heart.

When things slow down somewhat, David planned on looking further into this man. He wanted to thank him for saving Wyn, but then take him to task for hurting her. However, he'd do nothing until he had the full information.

David and Wyn shared solemn pleasantries. David could clearly see Wyn's despair.

Her face lovely as always now had a lucent sheerness. Grief draining the color until her skin was pure alabaster with only a hint of roses on her cheeks, and that was from added blush. The blue-green eyes misted with a sheen of unshed tears, the plump lips a firm steady line. She was still grace and elegance, but so waifish now, and even more delicate than before.

David feared she looked so fragile if he hugged her she would shatter in his hands.

He left her with a gentle kiss on her pale cheek and a promise of a longer visit later.

Sheffield ushered her to their table where they feasted on prawns and filet of beef, stuffed artichokes, and pearl onion soup, buttered toasted rolls and sautéed greens and roasted potatoes.

Wyn pushed her food around on her plate while the buzz of excited conversation whisked around her.

After dessert and coffee, the lights were lowered, after-dinner cocktails were served as people gathered on the dance floor and the bang swung into song.

Wyn's gaze wandered the room with no interest. It was loud and colorful and cheerful. Bursts of joyful, and drunken laughter bounded around the room. Then, Jazer was standing in front of her.

He stood politely with his hands folded behind his back, his spine straight, head bowed slightly. The chestnut hair tidy and shining, his jaw was smooth, and the chocolate eyes were slightly withdrawn but a gleam of carnal interest still wallowed in the depths. The trace of a scar left from Gage was faintly visible on the side of his chin.

He said coolly, "Wyn, I would request the honor of a dance."

Her scowl so black he nearly took a step back, she said in a low, hard voice, "You are lucky, Jazer Edrei, that you are neither in a jail cell or dead. How dare you even speak to me?"

His tongue slid quickly around his lips. Rolling his shoulders, he straightened his sleeves then tugged down the hem of his tux.

With a small cough, he started, "My," he paused, then said, "parents know nothing of what…uh… happened. They only know that you broke my heart."

He continued on, ignoring the indignant rise of her brows, "But they ask me every fucking day if we're getting back together."

Her lips compressed, brows down straight over her eyes, which would normally be furious, but she was so despondent she could barely dredge up any feeling at all, she said nothing.

Watching her, studying her expression for some indication of how hard he'd have to work to convince her of his remorse, Jazer veered to an unexpected tact.

His tone softened, "You know my mother is very ill." His arrogant eyes turned bleak for a second. "She is begging to see me married and have a baby on the way before she dies. Please, Wyn," the timber in his voice lowered to a scratchy plea.

"Please, for my mother. Let her…die…happy. All I need is for her to see us dance. Father will video it on his phone." He stopped there, didn't want to lay it on too deep. He waited for her response.

Wyn couldn't believe the king-sized nerve of- something caught her eye- *oh my gosh*- her mouth dropped. Her heart if it could fall further- plummeted, but it also puttered to a slight whir, like helicopter propellers started to turn.

On the dance floor, it couldn't be, but, there was no one that tall, with shoulders that broad. His black hair was neatly tied back.

He held a young woman very close and had his lips near her ear. She was smiling and snuggling against him.

Wyn felt like she was dying. Right in her chair. Everything inside her sank, her gut cringed. What was he doing here? It must have something to do with the job he was paid to do regarding her uncle.

Fierce stabs of jealousy sliced and diced into her at the woman embraced in his huge arms. Wyn's lids just kept fluttering and fluttering, in the back of her mind she heard Jazer still saying 'please.'

She stood up with a cold smile. "Sure. Why not."

Jazer looked so shocked she almost broke out in a horrible laugh.

He took her hand and brought her to the dance floor. His gaze went straight down the front of her dress. He said with crude ignominy, "You have such amazing damned tits, Wyn, we-"

She snapped, "One more word like that and we stop dancing and I march right over to your father and tell him what you did to me." Her words struck him like a slap.

Brows down hard, his mouth a pressed line. He muttered crossly, "Fine. Whatever." But his eyes kept dipping low.

Every few steps, he pulled her closer watching her breasts swell up even more as they pressed harder and harder against his chest. He watched them like if he crushed her hard enough they would pop out of the dress.

"Okay, that's enough, Jazer. I've had it, I'm done." Wyn pulled her hands off him and started to go back to the table but he caught her upper arms and jerked her back so hard she banged into his chest.

"You aren't going anywhere, Wyn." With a crass growl mean with command he said, "Until we hash this shit out." He wound his arms around her holding her like barbed wire so she couldn't move her arms. He astutely kept his hips turned slightly so she couldn't knee him.

They were already near the outside balcony, he moved them closer, trying to get her out the French doors.

Vijay

"Jazer, dammit, let go of me or I'll scream."

"Oh come on, we both know you're not going to make a scene at your uncle's celebration party. You will come outside with me peacefully, we need to talk."

Wyn opened her mouth but he kept her trapped in his arms as he hustled her outside.

The balcony overlooked the harbor. The lights of ships on the water shimmered in wavering streams. Once out on the deck, Jazer literally pushed her to the stairs.

Uttering, "No," Wyn grabbed the railing. "Stop, I swear I'll scream, let go of me!"

Jazer grasped her arms pushing them behind her back, and held them with one hand while gripping her jaw with the other. He was growing angry and impatient. He dug each finger into her skin holding her taut.

His voice steeped with irritation, he snarled, "You will listen to me. There has been enough of you running around and doing whatever the hell you want. In this country single women do as their family, or their husbands tell them to do. Except of course your slut of a cousin Shreva. Her parents have legal holds over her but they choose not to utilize them."

His smile turned smug and nasty. "But I will. I have your aunt and uncle's permission to do to you as I see fit. I can take you in the morning to the island off the coast to the east of here and marry you without a license like they do in Vegas. I can drug the shit out of you so that you can't fight it. Enough dough in a bribe and any official will ordain the ceremony, honey."

Her back was pressed against the railing. He mangled her wrists in his hand. Pushing her until her spine bent against the rail, he clutched her jaw like his fingers were nails.

Wyn tried to shake her head, but he held her immobile. Through her taut jaw she murmured, "My parents will stop you."

A short harsh laugh barked out and he released her jaw. But, he clinched his broad hand around her neck holding her secure.

Short of making a humiliating and scandalous scene, Wyn was for the moment under Jazer's control.

321

"Honey, you signed all sorts of governmental documents when you agreed to come into this country. Here, children under 25 are still considered under the legal consent of their guardians, in this case, that would be your aunt and uncle.

"You signed legally binding agreements that you would submit and adhere to any and all wishes of your legal guardians. Failure to abide by them can and, believe me, sweetheart," his lip a cunning curl, "will result in incarceration."

He took a breath, "Lengthy incarceration. Actually, you would be in custody until you either turned 25 the age of legal consent, which is a few years off, or you submit to your guardians' will."

"Don't be ridiculous, Jazer, I am an adult. Regardless, my Uncle David will-"

He held a hand up to stop her. "Ah, let it go, hon, this is all legal in this country, neither you nor your parents have any rights here. You signed fully legal documents agreeing to this country's terms, laws, and policies. Your uncle David will not be able to help you because even as of now he has a cocoon of security closing in on him, no one will be able to get near to him, not even you."

"Now," he said, wrapping his fingers around her neck, his other hand gripped her forearm. "I can, but I would prefer not to have to knock you out to take you out of here. I could easily tell people you are drunk and I have to carry you. So, if you would rather avoid all that embarrassment, you will just do as I say, and come along peacefully."

Chapter Thirty-Four

"No, Jazer, stop!" Wyn jerked her arm, it was futile because he held it and his hand around her neck tightened in annoyance.

She threaded her fingers around his trying to pull them away.

"Come on, Wyn, after a few weeks of wedded bliss and after you learn some obedience to me, and trust me, I am not averse to disciplining my spouse, you will calm down and accept things."

He let go of her neck and gripped her jaw again, "You-"

"The only man Wynna will be marrying is me," Vijay's deep accented voice came out of the dark.

Jazer froze. He still held Wyn so tightly she couldn't even look away from him. His shoulders stiffened and rose. He inadvertently squeezed Wyn's face harder in the sudden tense tightening of his body.

"You," he spat, turning his head slightly in Vijay's direction. "I am tired of you getting involved between me and my girl." He sucked in a rush of air and threatened, "Unless you get the fuck out of here right now, Zastrovna, I will call Security, they will throw you out on your gangster ass."

Vijay didn't say a word. He just came up to Jazer and put one hand around the back of his neck and squeezed.

It only took a few seconds before Jazer released Wyn, and just one more before he silently sank to his knees, his neck so compressed he couldn't let out a whimper. His handsome face twisted in an agonized grimace.

Avoiding blood gushing the balcony, instead of pummeling him, Vijay crouched with him as he went down, another second and Jazer was out cold on the floor.

Vijay shoved Jazer until he rolled over the edge of the patio. They could hear him crash onto thick bushes before he splatted to the pavement.

Wyn stood stock still with her hands covering her mouth.

Vijay murmured, "Baby, *mea* Wynna," he moved closer then frowned when she recoiled from him.

She stepped back, her hands reached blindly behind her to grasp the railing to steady herself. She didn't dare look up at the large, strong, fearless man who cast such a broad, protective, and possessive shadow over her.

One look at him and she would lose it. Lose all the work she'd done to keep her sorrow and loss at bay.

He didn't move closer to her, she was clearly already strung tight.

Their eyes collided, hers were filled with such stringent anguish over Vijay's betrayal, and now what she'd had to endure Jazer's threats.

Vijay's eyes that used to be as chillingly blank and vicious as a shark's, were now shaded with grief too, but also overflowing with the love he felt for Wyn that he didn't hold back.

He waited patiently for her to speak. She was never getting out of his sight again so he'd wait for her forever.

A desolate shudder wriggled through her body. Shaking her head, she looked over to where Jazer had disappeared. She didn't raise her eyes back to Vijay.

Growling, "Baby," he reached for her hands. She pulled them away, still staring at the floor.

His tone deep, confident but with a huge hole where his contentment had been, he said, "Wynna, the emails you saw, they were-"

Now she did look at him and he almost buckled at the pain in her eyes.

"Wynna, I told you I was no longer actively working for the man who hired me to find your uncle. But we, *mea* team, we did not know what was really going on, with the bombs, and people kidnapping you, we had decided to tell Mann that I was, uh, seducing you to keep him off our backs. We were just trying to keep things status quo until we had a handle on what the hell was really going on."

Wincing at her frail state and still staring away, he continued quickly, "The problem was," his grim grin was slightly lop-sided. "Mann expected regular reports on our progress. So we just kept saying what he wanted to hear. *Mea* feelings for you, Wynna, they are real, they always have been.

"There was never a planned seduction, that was for *mea* employer only to shut him up and stay out of our way until we had things figured out." He closed his mouth and watched her.

The huge, hurt blue-green eyes lifted morosely to him. She wanted to believe him, he could see her struggle, but she'd been wounded so badly.

"Wynna, I am so sorry I hurt you. It kills me that you suffered like you have. I…" his voice broke, "when you ran from me, *Zue,* Wynna," he untied the band from his hair and forked his fingers through the locks. "Baby, I cannot go through that again. Not ever."

His gaze swept and flooded every inch of her like a thirsty man looking at a spring of fresh water in a desert.

Wyn kept her mouth shut and her eyes back to the floor.

"Mea dragă, I told you to never doubt me again." He spared a contemptuous glance at where Jazer had fallen over. "What you put me through, baby, then I come here and that, *pula,*" he jerked his head regarding Jazer, "has his hands all over you, again. I-"

"Why are you here?" The strain in her voice made it come out creaky. Her heart cried out to run into his arms but her brain screamed 'betrayal!'

He smiled. "For you, of course. I came for you, Wynna. I knew I could not get near you at the mansion and you were not leaving it. Your phone was off and your family refused to call you to the phone or forward my messages. But I knew, or hoped, prayed actually, that you would be here tonight."

The blue eyes glowing fiercely kept moving from her head to her toes and back again like he couldn't get enough of looking at her. His fingers twitched with the strain of holding them back from grabbing her and pulling her close into the shelter of his embrace.

"Huh," she snorted, "you came because," she broke off at a loss as to why he would be here.

Nodding, he said, "*Da*, your uncle is safe, the election is over. There is only one reason in the world for me to be here."

Her gaze hovered around his face, her brows dragged down. "If you came for me why didn't you come and talk to me?"

"You were surrounded by your aunt and uncle. There would only be a scene. I was waiting. Then I saw you actually agree to dance with that fuck-" his face hardened, eyes narrowed. "Why the hell would you-"

"He pretty much forced me to. He threatened to, well, never mind. You still didn't come near me; you were too busy hugging up that- that woman you came with. I saw you with her. You don't want me, you just want to be able to screw any woman you want any time you-" She snapped her head to the side letting her hair cover her face so he couldn't see the tears.

"Ah, *mea dragă, mea Zue*, I love this jealousy and would love to enjoy it for a moment, alas I cannot stand to see your pain."

"I am not jealous!" she stormed, crossing her arms. "I don't care. I have put you out of my mind. I need to go," but her feet didn't move.

He dropped his head back and barked a laugh, then looked at her with joy scrawled all over his rugged face. "You are jealous, *mea* beautiful Wynna. And you still care, you are wearing the bracelet I gave you," he motioned to the bangle twinkling on her wrist.

Her eyes wide and pained, she lied, "I- I, I couldn't get if off, the clasp is stuck."

"Give it up, *mea fetita.*" He curled his hands behind her back and drew her to his chest.

"You are not the strongest person I know, but even you could have broken it off it you had wanted to. Now, c'mere and let me show you how much I have literally ached with real pain without you in my arms, under *mea* body, against *mea* lips." He could feel her start to melt, then she stiffened putting her hands up to stop him.

"That woman, I won't share you, you can't possibly care for me as much as you say and hold her the way you did," she pushed at him.

He chuckled and told her, "Then I need to re-evaluate my actions, because that woman that was in *mea* arms was *mea* sister, Bethanne. She is going to get a kick out of that!"

Stifling his humor, he said, "Sweetheart," and pulled her close. "*Mea* sister and one of *mea,* ah, my brothers came in the other day. Unfortunately, I am terrible at keeping in touch with my family and my mother sent them out here to torture me for my lack of contact."

His sister? The election is over and he is here, telling her he wants her? The tight pain around her heart started unkinking bit by bit, hope spiraled through her senses. Could it be true? Had she misjudged him?

Curling into his embrace, Wyn toyed with a button on his shirt. He wore a tuxedo, as did all the men attending the celebration party. This man was made for a tux. Handsome, debonair and dangerous all rolled into one hunky male.

She asked, "How did you find me, that day out in the woods with…well, how did you?"

Vijay caressed her cheek, her shoulder, petted her hair, he kept touching her as if to convince himself she wasn't a mirage, a figment of his devastated imagination. The past weeks had tortured him with heart-stopping fear of never seeing her again. Pictures of her being harmed, or…killed had plundered his dreams and every waking moment. The weeks of them apart had been killing him. But she had questions and he wanted to indulge anything her in anything she desired.

He explained, "Alex and I traced your taxi to the bus then to the taxi that had brought you to your cousin. Then I had a chat with *Clarence*," the word sounded acidic on his lips.

Vijay didn't describe how the man had crumpled with fear the second he and Alex stood on his doorstep. He'd tried to close the door on them, but Alex stuck his foot in it and Vijay had easily shoved it open, knocking Clarence to the floor.

"He told us he had…sorry baby, that he had sold you to that freak that wanted to sacrifice you. He gave up pretty quickly where you were in the woods." He didn't tell her the vicious pounding Vijay had given Clarence for doing that to her. She'd no doubt hear about it soon enough.

Wyn mused, considering how pole thin Clarence was and as big and brutal as Vijay looked, he probably spilled his guts the second Vijay raised his fist. "Where is your family staying?"

A grin tipping the side of his mouth, he replied, "At the hotel near here."

"Uh huh. Are you staying there?"

He slid a hand under chin and raised it. "*Nu.*"

She blinked. "What? Where are you staying?" Disappointment brought her lips down. "Are you leaving?" Of course, his mission was over, he'd be returning to his own country.

Chapter Thirty-Five

$\mathcal{A}$ small chuckle stirred her hair as Vijay lowered his head. "I would let you worry about it because you are so damned cute when you are jealous or caring about me, but," he caught her lips and they both moaned as he closed his mouth over hers.

One hand spread across her back feeling her soft warmth, the other strode up the back of her neck to hold her steady for his room-spinning kiss.

She pulled back. Her lips parted, eyes hazy and wobbling, voice harsh with pain, she said, "No, no Vijay, if you're leaving, I can't, I won't, it'll make it too hard to see you go."

"Oh baby, tis already hard, it was the second I laid eyes on you tonight." To prove it, he lowered both hands to cup her butt bringing her in to press against his raging erection.

"Vijay, no." Wyn couldn't let herself be drawn to him to spend a single night and then he would leave her, she looked about to cry.

It hurt his heart to see her suffering. Keeping his hands on her back holding her close, he told her firmly, "Wynna, I am not going anywhere without you. Never, ever, again."

He set two fingertips under her chin lifting her mouth so he could capture it. Showing her with his lips, his tongue, his hands how much he missed her, he kissed her until they were both breathless and their heads spinning with desire. Then he moved back slightly.

"Now come, *mea mici* sweetheart, let me show you where I am staying." He took her hand and led her down the steps to the lawn.

Breathless and misty-eyed, she tripped along with him stating, "But, Vijay, I don't understand, where are we going? There's nothing out here except the boathouse."

He didn't answer her, just pulled her along over the grass and to the path to the boathouse, occasionally glancing over to watch her breasts jiggling in the low cut dress.

Her entire body rocked with her trippy steps in the heels. He pulled her in tightly as he guided her so she wouldn't stumble.

When they reached the boathouse, Vijay pushed her up against a wall and assaulted her mouth with his, plundering the very depths of her being until both were panting, and their hearts pounding.

Her rushing breaths heavy, Wyn's eyes clouding with arousal, blurred with the sensations he could always elicit in her. She cried softly, bewildered, "Vijay, please what are you doing?"

He caught her chin between his finger and thumb to hold her. "I missed looking at you so much, Wynna, I will never get enough of it. We will never be able to make up for the loss of time we had while apart. You are done running from me."

Glancing away, he said, "I am just waiting for," he craned his head looking beyond the back of the boathouse. "Just a few minutes more." Back to her, his gaze dropped to the top of the dress.

Her cheeks pinked seeing his pupils flare with lust. "Vijay, you, uh…"

"I believe you promised me you would never wear a dress like that again if you were not with me. I can imagine what all the other men you flaunted your assets at were thinking. I know it made me want to bend you over the dining room table, lift that flirty little skirt, rip another pair your panties and take you, baby, fast, hard, with your tits in my hands."

Pushing aside the flash of heat that sprang between her legs, Wyn's forehead knit revealing again the pain she'd felt at his betrayal. "We were through, Vijay, I didn't care what I wore."

"Ah, that is where you are wrong, *mea dragă,* because we were not, and we will never be through. Instead of trusting me, again you let your mind believe the worst and you ran with it." He drew a finger down the side of her face.

"But that is the last time. You will damn well trust me from now on. You will come directly to me if there is any question or doubt you have about me, or us."

He kissed her gently. "Now," his smile greedy and urgent, "I cannot decide whether to thrust *mea* hands down that bodacious fucking top and grab those beautiful tits, or push up that skirt and feel that tender moist skin I know tis getting wet as I speak."

"Vij-"

"The top wins for now," he announced and laid his palm on the swell of her breasts. "I have missed these, honey, so goddamned bad," and he nestled his hand down the front and grasped one of her breasts.

"Tis not enough," he sighed and pulled the top down exposing both breasts, soft ivory in the moonlight. "*Zue,* Wynna," he crowed, covered them both with his big hands and caressed them growling a husky moan.

She tried to scold him, the words were right there, but all Wyn could do was revel in his ravenous kneading of her flesh until he lowered his head and sucked a nipple into his mouth.

A shiver raced through her. The fresh balmy air was so soft and breezy it felt wonderful and oh so decadent on her bare skin, along with his rough yet tender hands, then she remembered where they were. "Vijay, stop, we're outside, please," she pushed at him.

He cupped each breast, licked one nipple then the other, then he kissed them and pulled her top up, fixing it so it was secure.

"That is for running out on me when I took you from the woods and put you in *mea* car."

He suddenly grabbed her arms hard. "Dammit Wynna, after what I had just gone through knowing you were in that fucker

331

Jack's hands, *mea* heart was in *mea* throat the entire time it took to track you down. If I had not been able to trace you to your cousin's house-" He broke off, the horrifying thought didn't need to permeate his still terrified brain.

He sucked in an agonized breath. "Then seeing you there tied to that table about to be fucking sacrificed or raped or both. I was so scared I could not draw a breath, Wynna, *mea* fucking knees buckled. Then after getting you the fuck out of there and to safety, I come back to *mea* car and you were- gone."

The rest of his air whooshed out, sad and scared, filled with disbelief that she would run again from him. His eyes rolled to hers. His voice brimming with torment, he whispered, "The panic, the dread, the fear, baby."

Wyn touched the side of his face with her palm. He leaned into it for a second. Took a breath and shook his head, pushed back his long hair.

"I was out of *mea* mind with terror, baby, *mea Zue*, there were maniacs out there after you, and you were injured. *Zue*, baby, I," tears sparkled in the twilight, he swallowed a rough breath. "And to know it was all because you thought I had betrayed you. Baby, I..." he couldn't go on.

"Vijay, I'm so sorry, I thought you were taking me to your employer. I was afraid he was going to- to kill me, because I would never help anyone harm my uncle." She put both palms on his face and kissed him gently.

"*Zue*," Vijay groaned and clasped her against his chest. "I know honey, I am sorry." He leaned back and smiled lewdly at her. One hand around her back he slid the other up to cradle a breast. "You know, you ran from me twice. That deserves punishment. A lot of punishment." He squeezed her breast with a suggestive grin.

Wyn smiled. "Well, if that's how you are going to punish me, I wouldn't be complaining. It's certainly better than spanking me." She stroked his chin.

One brow rose in a leer. "Oh yeah? I think you liked the spanking. We will give it another go and see. These dresses, you must wear them every time I need to punish you, it will make it so much easier to get *mea* palm quickly on your bare butt, and other strategic places."

He grinned at her telling blush. "So, Wynna, no more running from me, no more dancing with other men. You will marry me, right?"

A grin spread over her soft face. "Finally, someone *asking* me instead of telling me." She stroked her fingers over his cheek, down his neck to his chest were she grazed his nipple. A giggle erupted when his hand covered hers with a quiver.

"*Bine, basta* baby, enough of that. We have to wait until," he craned his neck, "ah, there it tis."

"What? Where what is?" She tried to follow his gaze, but there was nothing there except a yacht being tethered to the dock.

"Come on." He grasped her hand and brought her down the dock to the boat.

"Well?" He stood grinning broadly at her.

"Uh, well what? I don't understand." The breeze lifted her curls tossing them gently around her shoulders and back.

He gripped her hand tightly. "You said you wanted to travel the world by sea. This is ours, baby."

Her eyes flew from the boat to him. "What? But how?"

He drew her hand up and tenderly kissed her knuckles. "I told you I was at least as much if not wealthier than your relatives. I bought this for you." The blue eyes beamed his pure love to her.

"But, we can't, I mean, for me? I mean, I can't," she blathered on as he led her down to the boat.

"*Da*, tis for you, for us. We will live any way, anywhere, anyhow you want, *mea dragă*. I do not care where or how, as long as tis with you."

Her wide eyes scanned the beautiful sleek boat with awe. "But, we can't just…" painted across the side of the hull in bold script was: **Mea Dragă, Wynna**.

"*Da, yah* we can. You do not owe anyone anything. Your Uncle David will be too busy to think of you much for the time being, and who cares about your shit-ass aunt and uncle, and that ridiculous tramp cousin of yours, Shreva. All we need to do is step aboard. I have a crew, small enough to keep out of our way, and a smaller boat aboard so we can go explore and have even more privacy. Just think, Wynna, you and me, naked on a deserted island?"

"We can't just…"

"And I can fatten you up." He frowned with concern as he glared at her body.

"You have lost weight, baby, and tis *mea* fault. So you have to allow me to take care of you, pamper you. I got a computer set up and a study for you ready for whenever you want to start your schooling."

At her wide eyes bouncing from him to the boat and back, he said, "We can get married out there, anywhere, the sooner the better. You can send your folks a post card. Or if you want to wait and have them present, I can fly them out anywhere you want them to meet us."

Taking a breath, he sighed. "But then we would have to include *mea* family and *mea* team," he rolled his eyes and shook his head.

"*Da*, Alex, Gage, Lucian and Roman, Miles too, and a bunch of others, would never forgive me if I left them out. They would be furious they were not there to tease me the entire time that I finally lost *mea* head over a woman."

He squeezed both her hands, his voice dropped somberly as he said, "And what a woman. Will you marry me? Say yes, Wynna. I love you with *mea* whole being. I cannot live without you." His eyes glued to hers, he waited for her to answer him.

She faced him, slid her hands up his shoulders to cradle his head, and said, "Yes, Vijay, my love, I can't wait to marry you," and deluged him with her own deep kiss.

They enjoyed their happy, blissful, grateful, moment.

Then Vijay took her hand. "Come on, *mea dragă*, let us get aboard our new home. For as long, or as short as you want it to be." He winked with another leer, adding, "We can get started on our children."

They held hands walking up the gangplank.

As soon as they were aboard, Vijay nodded at a person in a dark uniform, and the man nodded back.

Within minutes the boat started pulling away from the dock.

Vijay brought Wyn up to the top deck.

Holding hands, they leaned over the railing watching Monaco shrink as the boat headed out over the deep sapphire blue of the Mediterranean Sea under a black shell of twinkling stars.

Then he took her face in his hands and captured her mouth, and she strung her hands around his neck as they sailed off to…wherever.

The End

Dear Reader, thank you for purchasing Vijay! *I know you could have picked any number of books to read, but you picked this book and for that I am extremely grateful.*

I hope you enjoyed this novel, and if you did, <u>please leave a review where you purchased it</u>, *and look for other exciting titles in my name!*

About the Author

Louise Furley loves writing romance with a huge helping of suspense. She finds it exciting to study new lands and learn everything she can about the area and the natives that call it home.

Her idea of fun is researching ideas, studying enigmatic modes of science, archeology, and different ways to kill someone.

Her Significant Other finds the last to be particularly notable. He remains wary yet gives Louise his full support with her writing adventures.

Sunny Florida is home where Louise is a graduate of St. Thomas University with a master's degree in Mental Health. This degree is essential for exploring the deviant soul, and

Louise Furley

understanding the mind of a killer, while finding it exhilarating, frightening and sad all at the same time.

With artistic license, Louise can be judge, jury, and sometimes executioner!

Louise is the author of numerous published novels. When not researching or writing, she is dreaming of unique plots, and discovering fresh ventures she hasn't yet experienced in the world.

Ride along with her as she travels new and thrilling journeys!